PERDITION

D1426998

ALSO BY R. JEAN REID

Roots of Murder

PERDITION

A Novel of Suspense

R. JEAN REID

MIDNIGHT INK
WOODBURY, MINNESOTA

Perdition © 2017 by R. Jean Reid. All rights reserved. No part of this book may be used or reproduced in any manner whatsoever, including Internet usage, without written permission from Midnight Ink, except in the case of brief quotations embodied in critical articles and reviews.

FIRST EDITION
First Printing, 2017

Book format by Cassie Kanzenbach
Cover design by Lisa Novak

Midnight Ink, an imprint of Llewellyn Worldwide Ltd.

This is a work of fiction. Names, characters, places, and incidents are either the product of the author's imagination or are used fictitiously, and any resemblance to actual persons living or dead, business establishments, events, or locales is entirely coincidental.

Library of Congress Cataloging-in-Publication Data

Names: Reid, R. Jean, author.
Title: Perdition / R. Jean Reid.
Description: First edition. | Woodbury, Minnesota : Midnight Ink, [2017] | Series: A Nell McGraw investigation ; #2
Identifiers: LCCN 2017001153 (print) | LCCN 2017006032 (ebook) | ISBN 9780738750651 | ISBN 9780738751795
Subjects: | GSAFD: Mystery fiction.
Classification: LCC PS3568.E3617 P47 2017 (print) | LCC PS3568.E3617 (ebook) | DDC 813/.54—dc23
LC record available at https://lccn.loc.gov/2017001153

Midnight Ink
Llewellyn Worldwide Ltd.
2143 Wooddale Drive
Woodbury, MN 55125-2989
www.midnightinkbooks.com

Printed in the United States of America

To GMR

For the Sazeracs

PROLOGUE

THEY SAY THAT POWER corrupts, but power didn't corrupt him. It seduced him. He found that the most seductive power of all was life and death.

He had learned that when he was young. Teddy kept following him, the idiot little brother he couldn't shake. He hated Teddy with his drool, his labored, clumsy speech, the thick glasses that made his face always look like a Halloween mask, and especially the way the other kids laughed at them both. Teddy just laughed along, too stupid to know he was the butt of the joke. But he knew, knew how they made fun of him and his retard brother. He had to take Teddy with him after school, the time between when his father woke up and went off to his shift. Dad didn't like Teddy much either and was liable to slap Teddy around, or him, too, for not keeping Teddy's spit-dripped face out of sight.

One day Teddy had come into his room when he wanted to be alone, just listening to music. He had his hand in his pants and Teddy wouldn't stop asking him what he was doing, Teddy knew he had caught him touching some place he shouldn't. At first he tried not to answer Teddy, until he realized that he could use his stupid and slow brother. He asked Teddy to play a game. Teddy was always happy when his brother included him. He told Teddy to suck on it like a lollipop. He closed his eyes and imagined Betty Dawson, one of the high school cheerleaders, doing it. That the only contact they had ever had was her calling him a "freshman freak" made the image of her kneeling before him even better.

They played this game a couple of times a week. When Teddy coughed or choked, he told Teddy that the point was to learn to take things like a man.

He always played music, to cover up the sounds that Teddy made, to make it easier to imagine Betty there.

But the music covered up his father's footsteps; he had come home without warning. He was jerked out of his fantasy by the sound of his door being throw open and Teddy's whimper.

"What the hell are you doing?" his father roared. But it was all too obvious what they were doing. He glared at them for several seconds, the explosion building. "You want to be a cocksucker, you stupid retard?! Suck a real cock."

His father strode over to where they were and unzipped his pants. He was a big man and he dwarfed his son's undeveloped body.

"Suck this," he said as he shoved into Teddy's mouth. Teddy whimpered and tried to twist away. "Hold him, dammit," his father yelled at him.

He did as he was told, holding Teddy by the upper arms, so he couldn't grab or twist away. His father was rough. "Get your fucking teeth away," he growled, cuffing Teddy on the side of the head. Finally, he finished, leaving Teddy gagging and retching on the floor.

He went to the bathroom, but came back right after the toilet flushed.

"Your turn, boy," his father told him. He yanked Teddy off the floor and held him expectantly.

He had never dared to disobey his father. He looked once at Teddy's face, covered with the slime of spit and tears, then he closed his eyes and thought of Betty Dawson. When he finished, they again let Teddy fall to the floor.

It became their punishment, although only Teddy really was punished. Sometimes he couldn't imagine the girls, and saw his little brother's face with the scrunched-up look that he knew meant that Teddy was trying to be good but didn't like what was happening, like eating lima beans. Several times a week, his father would find something they had done wrong and made them go upstairs to his room. But it wasn't that bad for Teddy, he told himself, maybe just like the lima beans. At least their dad was paying attention to Teddy; sometimes before, weeks could go by and he didn't even notice that he had two sons. After their mom had run off, their dad had taken to drinking more and he'd had to watch out for Teddy, fixing him peanut butter and jelly sandwiches so Teddy wouldn't try to do it himself and make a big mess.

After the second week, his father broke the silence, barking at him, "What are you thinking right now? You got boys on your mind or girls?"

His father seemed to approve when he gasped out Betty Dawson's name. "Oh, yeah, she's a hot little one. What's she doing to you, boy?" That became part of it, him telling his father what he was imagining. He started to tell the stories his father seemed to favor, like having whatever girl they used being pulled over for a ticket and what she would do to get out of it.

But one day Teddy fought back, screeching out, "No, I don't play no more." Then, with his jaw clenched, he whipped his body back and forth whenever they tried to grab him. He would only unclench his jaw enough to yell, "No, no, no, hurts, hurts me," as loud as he could. His father threatened him, but Teddy was locked in his own little world and nothing seemed to touch him. Even when his father took his belt off, Teddy still wouldn't stop yelling and twisting.

"I'm going to teach you a lesson you'll never forget," his father said. Then he roughly grabbed Teddy, threw him face down on the bed, and ripped his pants down to his ankles. The belt cracked against Teddy's naked flesh, over and over again. Teddy finally stopped yelling, subsiding into a whimpering cry. "I'm going to teach you to never disobey me again," his father said. Then he got on top of Teddy, pushing his groin against the beaten flesh. Teddy let out one piercing shriek before his father shoved his head into the mattress, and Teddy again subsided into his whimpering cry.

This was different. He had hit both of them before, but only when he was drunk and then only once or twice to get them out of his way. He watched his father hurt Teddy. For a wild moment, he thought about grabbing his father and pulling him off . . . and then doing what? He just stood and watched. Maybe it wasn't hurting Teddy that much. Teddy didn't understand things, maybe he didn't hurt as much as other people either. He was stupid and slow and maybe just felt things like a deer being shot or a fish being hooked.

When his father finished, he said, "Your turn." He didn't want to, but he knew that if he didn't do it, their dad would probably just beat both of them. As he listened to Teddy sobbing under him, the pillow wet with his snot and tears, he thought he wouldn't be a crybaby like that. Whatever their dad had done to him, he hadn't cried.

He had been belted the way Teddy was and he hadn't sobbed, not even once.

After he was finished, he realized that something had changed. His father needed him and they were in it together. It used to be him and Teddy, now it was him and his father.

He hated that he still had to look out for Teddy when his father was out patrolling. It didn't feel fair that he should be babysitting his crybaby brother. Sometimes his dad would let him come along, and he could ride up front, his hand almost resting on the shotgun that was holstered between the seats, and listen to the sound of voices on the radio as they talked back and forth. That was where he should be, instead of still stuck with Teddy.

When it happened, he'd only wanted to get away from Teddy, just for a few minutes, the time it took the train to pass. He'd sprinted ahead at the sound of the whistle, just making it in front of the engine, the engineer hitting a heavy blast on the horn as an admonition at his daring. Teddy had whimpered on the other side of the tracks, his moon face blinking in and out as the wheels rushed by.

"How you get ...?" Teddy had cried from the far side of the clacking train.

"It's the timing," he had yelled back. "If you time it right, you can roll between the wheels." He just wanted to tease Teddy, to remind Teddy that he was older and stronger. He hadn't even bothered to wonder if Teddy would believe him. Or that Teddy might try it. "I did it up at the engine where it's really hard. It's easy now, just box cars," he taunted.

Teddy had tried, tried to roll his stupid body between the cars. It ended like that, no more Teddy following him around.

That was when he first felt it, a hot surge of power, when he stood there beside the tracks, looking at what was left of Teddy. He had done this and it had been so easy, so quick. He knew he should have felt sick or upset at seeing the bloodied, mauled body, one of the arms a good twenty yards away. But he didn't.

The power felt good. He hadn't even intended to kill Teddy and it felt this good. What would it feel like if he did plan it, if he could enjoy thinking about what he was going to do? A giddy laugh escaped him.

Then he set himself to the task at hand, to act as the upset older brother, running to try and save his kid brother who had gotten away from him and fallen under the train.

He was very good at his act; he didn't smile once at the funeral. No one, not even his father, knew what had really happened.

A month after the funeral, his father came into his room and told him that he needed to be punished.

"But Teddy's not here," he had protested.

"No, Teddy's not here, so you'll have to do," his father told him, then grabbed him off the bed and shoved him down to his knees. He made him take the place of Teddy. When he fought, his father did the same thing that he'd done to Teddy. Even then, he hadn't cried. His father made him keep telling the stories, but now demanded, "Tell me, girl, tell me how you like what I'm doing to you right now."

When he was seventeen, his father was murdered. Someone broke into their home after they were asleep and battered his head in with an ax. While he was dying, the murderer had rolled him over and forced a broom handle up his rectum.

His father had angered a number of people over the years, "When it's my red light flashing in your window, you do it my way," he would say and make them squirm. He'd make sober judges walk a line if they had made him wait in court or let a defense attorney ask him too many questions. He hadn't sent any murderers to prison, but he had made more arrests than anyone else. He had also had more of those arrests thrown out. Betty Dawson's father was claiming that he'd forced her to fellate him to get out of a ticket. Mr. Dawson's ax was missing and was found the day after the murder in a drainage ditch, covered in blood. But nothing could be proven, and his father's killer was never arrested.

The town set up a fund for the remaining son, the one who was woken from his sleep by the sound of his father being killed, who had rushed in to try and save him, then, covered in his blood, run down the street to the corner phone to call for help. When asked why he hadn't called from home, he said that he just had to get out of that house, that he was scared the killer was still there. Ironically, the phone was half a block from where the ax was discovered.

He had been right. It was so much better when he planned it, when he knew the power that he had and could savor it.

ONE

A STORM WAS COMING, the rising wind a harbinger of the tempest.

Nell reached down to grab at the stray sheet of newspaper as it scuttled across the parking lot in front of her. The light newsprint and the gusty wind conspired against her, but no one else was around to watch her awkward lunge. Spring was here with a vengeance, no lambs only lions, this brooding storm one of several in the past few weeks.

She finally nabbed the paper when the eddying wind blew it back against her calf. With it safely in hand, she headed for the trash can located outside the rear door of the city hall complex.

Nell paused at the garbage can. How easily I throw away my name, she thought. The wayward sheet was the editorial page, her name at the top of the masthead: Naomi Nelligan McGraw, Editor-in-Chief. It had taken her months to notice the change. "Who did this?" she'd asked Dolan Ferguson, the business manager. "You do the job, you get the title," was his laconic reply. He hadn't answered her question and Nell knew he wouldn't.

The Editor-in-Chief is dead—long live his widow, the new Editor-in-Chief. The bitter thought caught Nell off guard. It's been almost six months, she admonished herself, I should be over it. But she admitted she didn't know how to lose the anger and grief that still blindsided her. How do you get over it? Or do you just learn to accept that you never will? One drunken driver, and the man she'd planned to share her life with was gone. Here she was, living his dream to run the paper that his great-grandfather had founded. Raising their two children alone.

What memories the wind brings, Nell thought as she again looked at the crumpled paper in her hand. She threw it in the trash can and entered the building.

She had intended to go right, along the covered walkway that led from the city hall building to the library, but a glance down the hall to her left, in the direction of the mayor's office, changed her mind.

A group of men were coming in her direction. She waited.

"Hi, Buddy," she said as they got nearer. "Going to indict anyone I should know about?"

Buddy Guy, the county DA, was an astute-enough politician to know that Nell's seemingly bantering question was really a reporter's query.

"Howdy, Nell," he drawled. "Always a pleasure to run into you." He extended his hand in the perfect politician's handshake.

Buddy Guy—she always wanted to ask him if that was his real name or if a focus group had chosen it for him—had been coming down the hall with Douglas Shaun, the chief of police, Clureman Hickson, the sheriff, and Harold Reed, Buddy's top prosecutor. Seeing the police chief and the sheriff together was enough to raise Nell's reporter's suspicion.

Sheriff Hickson was so close to the archetypal good ole boy that Nell had to constantly remind herself he had to be more than just a walking stereotype. He had a beer belly, some of it gained while on duty; the sheriff saw nothing wrong with tossing one back with the boys. He'd been sheriff for over twenty years, so ensconced that no one had run against him for at least the last ten. His balding head and slicked-back gray hair was usually hidden under a battered cowboy hat. He had never gone beyond high school and believed in "old fashioned law enforcement," whatever that was. Nell suspected it was more a way of covering his mistrust of new techniques and the upheaval of change.

He and Nell were always polite to each other, but it was apparent he didn't think that women should be working at all. To have one as editor-in-chief of his hometown newspaper was a change he'd clearly hoped to avoid in his lifetime.

Douglas Shaun, the police chief, was in many ways his opposite. He was new in Pelican Bay, only four months on the job, and was younger, in shape, and taller than the tall sheriff, indeed taller than most men. His hair was a curly, sandy brown and he had a chiseled chin that wouldn't look out of place on a movie star. His face had just enough lines and his hair enough gray to add maturity to the strong masculine handsomeness that many women found appealing. Nell didn't consider herself one of them. Thom had had a boyish bookishness about him, and that was what she found attractive.

Chief Shaun's shirt and pants were always crisp and clean and his belt was loaded down with everything: gun, handcuffs, night stick. He didn't treat her like a problem he hoped would go away, as Sheriff Hickson did. Shaun was an educated man and quite aware that having a good relationship with the editor of the paper could be very useful. He cultivated Nell, dropping by the office to brief her on things, even escorting her home one rainy night.

Nell was neither fooled nor flattered by it, but the police chief's openness was a welcome change from the sheriff's patronizing obtuseness.

There was an intense and ongoing rivalry between the two men, which made their appearance together unusual. The sheriff patrolled Tchula County and managed the county jail. In theory, he ceded jurisdiction to the town police at the city line. But there seemed to be a good deal of misunderstanding about exactly where the town boundaries were, and who ruled what.

The latest scuffle was the recent drunk driving arrests made by Sheriff Hickson. Of course, he'd consulted no one about setting up the roadblocks in town. "I got a right to clamp down on drunken driving wherever and whenever," he had given as his statement the next day. "'Specially if no one else is doing it."

Chief Shaun couldn't publicly go after the sheriff—he couldn't risk being seen as soft of drunk driving. His official quote was, "We're always glad for the help of our fellow law enforcement officers, especially when we're busy with crimes against property and persons. It's good to have the lesser problems like drinking taken care of." Behind the scenes, a number of people, the chief included, made grumbling noises about a set-up to embarrass the Pelican Bay Yacht Club and the people who went there.

Nell knew the sheriff well enough to know that he had his own standards—he'd placed his deputies the same distance away from both the yacht club and Ray's Bar. He'd stopped all the cars and treated everyone the same. It wasn't his fault that the drive to and from the yacht club followed a leafy, curving roadway, making it impossible for anyone to know the patrol cars were there. Ray's Bar didn't have any posh foliage blocking the patrons' view, which gave them more warning than the denizens of the yacht club had.

More to the point, the police chief never turned down an invitation to one of the yacht club parties, whereas a goodly portion of the sheriff's corpulent stomach had probably come directly from the taps at Ray's Bar.

Nell had to admit that although she couldn't disagree with the chief's assessment about the sheriff wanting to embarrass the yacht club as much as catch drunk drivers, her sympathies in this case leaned toward the sheriff. A drunk driver was a drunk driver—it didn't matter how he got there, cheap beer or single malt Scotch.

Admittedly, some of her lack of sympathy for the yacht club's embarrassment was caused by its commodore's clumsy attempt to cajole her to his view point.

"What's the big deal?" Philip Yorst, the commodore, had said, having made a special trip to the newspaper office so Nell could get his side directly from him. "Some of our members are really sacrificing to pay those fines. We party and have a good time. A few drinks isn't going to hurt anyone. You know that."

Nell stared at him. She'd never much liked him but was always careful to not show it. She considered Yorst a social climber. He was known for having devised a uniform for the commodore to wear, something "befitting the position," as he said. If he was going to pull the trigger on the starting pistol for the yacht club regattas, he obviously had to be properly attired to handle a weapon.

"No, I don't know that. But I do know," Nell had replied, her voice giving way to a steely anger she rarely showed, "that I'm a widow, Mr. Yorst, because someone had a few drinks." She'd walked past him and out of her office, forcing him to foolishly stand there.

Nell tried to be a neutral reporter when caught between rivalries, but her editorial on the "sacrifices" of the ticketed drivers had been scathing.

Yet more often than not, Nell found herself leaning towards, for lack of a better description, Chief Shaun's/the yacht club's side of things. She had more in common with them than she had with the sheriff and the rough shrimpers who frequented Ray's Bar. She'd been a journalist long enough to know that perfect objectivity was a myth. She tried to be honest and fair and keep her sympathies well hidden. It usually meant that the liberals thought her a right-wing dupe and the conservatives found her to be a godless Commie. Thom used to say, "Balance is pissing everybody off."

She suspected she was going to come fairly close to that desired objective today. She doubted the men were rehashing the drunk driving skirmish, so she pressed them on the one other problem that might bring them together: "This conclave wouldn't have anything to do with the girl's body that was washed ashore by the harbor?" she asked.

"This ain't a press conference," Sheriff Hickson said.

"So, you've made no progress?" Nell queried.

"Well, I wouldn't say that," Buddy, the politician, interjected.

"Was it murder?" Nell asked.

Buddy looked at his compatriots, as if not wanting to give an answer that might hurt his next election. Harold wouldn't answer for his boss. Sheriff Hickson wasn't going to answer a blunt question like that from a woman.

That left Chief Shaun. "We're not sure. The body is badly decomposed, so there's no clear indication. It's possible the child drowned."

13

"The fishes didn't leave us much to go on," Sheriff Hickson said. "You're welcome to hop over to the morgue and take a look for yourself."

"I'm very well aware of what seawater can do to human flesh." Every sexist editor Nell had ever worked for thought it was fun to send the new girl reporter off to look at bodies. "So, are you investigating this as a murder or not?"

"Soon as we got evidence it's a murder, we'll treat it like a murder," the sheriff retorted. "But unless someone confesses, that's not likely to happen anytime soon."

"It's a question of resources," Chief Shaun said, giving the educated, slick version of the sheriff's answer. "The local medical examiner can't find anything to indicate it was a homicide. Most likely a tragic drowning. Can we afford to spend the kind of money it would take to chase this down?"

"Those people don't seem to much care, why should we?" Sheriff Hickson added.

Buddy Guy rolled his eyes at the sheriff's remark but didn't directly contradict him. Harold Reed's face remained impassive.

"Would the lack of resources apply if this were the child of a white middle-class family instead of a poor black one?" Nell pushed. She'd been a better reporter than Thom. Sometimes she forgot the ways she balanced him out. She would ask the hard questions, push and probe until she got past the polite facade or carefully spun news releases.

"Hell," Sheriff Hickson spat out, "the dad's got a dozen check kiting arrests and dear lovin' mom spent some time on the streets. You arguin' to spend the taxpayers money on those kinds of people? I'm not a racist, lot of fine, upstanding black folk in this community, but these ain't them."

"Is the arrest report public record or can I quote you?" Nell asked him.

The sheriff didn't answer, and to make clear that that was all he had to say, he turned on his heel and left the building.

"It's a tough call, Nell," Buddy said, trying to undo the damage. "Oh, hell, Harold, you explain it, I got a meeting to get to." Buddy did a much more decorous exit than the sheriff. He clearly was avoiding the possibility that a quote from him about not doing an investigation would end up in the paper. Harold was on his own. If he said something that reflected badly on his boss, Buddy could deny it.

"We investigate all cases thoroughly," Chief Shaun said. "It comes down to the evidence, not the class or color of the person." Clearly a quote designed for attribution. With that, he slapped his braided cap on his head and also left the building.

All those familiar with the inner workings of the Tchula County Courthouse knew that Buddy Guy was a very good politician and a not-very-good lawyer. His enviable record was the result of the man standing before Nell. She knew Harold only in a professional role. As always, he was impeccably dressed, in a conservative charcoal-gray suit with a sedate burgundy tie.

Camouflage or armor, Nell wondered. Or both?

"Don't worry," she said. "I won't quote you on anything that will have Buddy worried about losing a few votes."

Harold gave her a slight smile. "I wish we could go after justice, no matter what it takes. I wish we weren't bound by rules and money and always weighing, what will it cost? Can we prove it? But, I'm sure you've covered enough cases to know how fragile the search for justice can be."

"I know, we settle for the rules of law and hope that they come close."

"We investigate and what do we find? An imperfect family, but nothing to indicate that either the mother or father are the kind of monsters who would kill their own daughter. As Sheriff Hickson so bluntly pointed out, we've got a suspicious body, but no evidence proving murder or abuse. We could make some phone calls, ship her to New Orleans or maybe even Atlanta and get a second opinion. And probably end up exactly where we are now. A girl dead and we don't know how or why. Some deaths you have to let God take care of," he finished with a sad smile.

"How do you stand it?" Nell suddenly asked, a question that pushed past the polite professional roles they'd always presented to each other. "Hickson's 'I'm not a racist' racism? That a slick good ole boy like Buddy gets elected, but ..."

"But I never will?" he finished for her. "Not while Tchula County is sixty-four percent white? Twenty years ago Buddy would never have hired me, no matter how many cases I won. It's progress."

"Is it enough?"

"No," Harold answered quickly, a hint of carefully controlled anger seeping out. "No, of course it's not enough. It probably won't be enough in our lifetimes. I teach my children what the word nigger means. They'll probably teach their children."

Nell suddenly felt the hot flash of a parent, at not just having to explain to your child that the world is an unfair place, but at knowing your child will inevitably run into a brutal wall of hatred. "What a horrid thing for a child to understand!"

"But they will run into it," he said softly. "We have to prepare them."

Nell thought of all the things she worried about and scrambled to keep her children safe from—from something resembling good nutrition to whether she should be talking to Lizzie about condoms and HIV. Maybe even Josh. It was such a balancing act. What would it be like to add the burden of racial hatred to the life of a young child? "How do you teach them to stand it?" she asked.

For a moment, Harold was silent. Nell wondered if he was weighing his words, looking for the careful ones that wouldn't sound too angry or strident to a white person.

"I tell them it's possible that every day of their life, they will run into injustice, some slight, some moment when they'll wonder, would I be treated this way if I weren't black? They can fight every single battle and be angry every single day. And live an angry life. Or they can learn to pick the few important ones and let the rest go."

"A hard lesson to learn. Thank you for answering my impertinent question," Nell said.

"Most white people don't thank black folks for being up front," he said with a wry smile.

"You were honest. I'm a journalist. I like getting at least one honest answer a day." Nell returned his wry smile. Then she became a reporter again and said, "I'd like to follow up on the girl's death."

"Why? Will it do any good?" Harold Reed asked, but it was an honest question, not a challenge.

"If she was murdered, it might remind the killer that murder has no statute of limitations. At least give him a few more sleepless nights. Maybe a story in the paper will jog someone's memory. And if it was a senseless drowning, it might remind a few parents to watch over their children."

"And maybe the killer will be so overcome with remorse at seeing it in the paper, he'll confess," Harold said with a small, sad smile.

"But you're right, we shouldn't forget our dead so easily. Best person to talk to is her grandmother. She was more or less raising Tasha. Ella Jackson, on Rail Street. Should be in the phone book."

"Thanks, Harold," Nell said. There were rules—often overlooked—about giving out information. Letting her look up the phone number kept them just barely inside the lines. But Nell knew Harold Reed wouldn't have given her the tip if he didn't think she'd do the right kind of story. She took it as a compliment.

"Time to get back to the piled-high desk."

"Please call me if there are any further developments," Nell said.

"Of course. I'll even call you and let you know if nothing can be done. Just don't quote me on it."

Nell gave him a nod to indicate she'd honor his request. He did have to work for Buddy Guy, after all.

As soon as Harold had disappeared through the outer door, Nell pulled a small notebook from her purse and jotted down the gist of the encounter. She wouldn't take a story directly from this hallway meeting, although it was tempting to splash some of Sheriff Hickson's quotes across the front page. But the notes could be useful.

She was glad that she'd been able to get at least a little bit beyond Harold's careful mask. On a personal level, she knew he was a very intelligent man and his honesty was a compliment to her. On a professional level, she'd formed a connection with a man who could give her better information and stories than anyone else in the DA's office. Nell had a feeling that they could use each other, in the good sense of the word. Harold would have information she wanted, and she had the power to get out stories that would otherwise be shuffled away.

Nell put the notebook back in her purse. Not a bad twenty minutes, she thought. She headed out along the walkway toward the library.

As she stepped through the door, she heard someone behind her say, "Rayburn, look out for that lady."

But Rayburn, newly six, wasn't looking for a woman standing on the far side of the door he was slingshotting around. He caromed into Nell, then spun away with aplomb, as if running into the legs of strange women was an everyday occurrence.

"Rayburn, you slow down now," his mother called after him as he sped into the library.

His mother apologized to Nell. "Sorry, 'bout that. He's just got so much energy," she said in a way that told Nell she was proud of her energetic boy.

Velma Gautier. Nell knew her name—the births and deaths of Pelican Bay were with her every day. Velma had had Rayburn when she was forty-two, the last of eight children and five years younger than the previous sibling. Velma's voice held a touch of pride that an old lady like her could produce such a robust young son. Six of her other children were girls and the only other son had very bad asthma.

"It's okay," Nell said as she diverted her thoughts from the tragedy of a young girl whose death had only questions and no answers. "He's certainly an active young man."

"Oh, yes, that he is. Keeps me hoppin'," Velma answered.

Nell found herself wondering how she would write Velma's story. It was something she often did with people, made them into newspaper stories. Sometimes she wondered if it was a way to control and encapsulate people, or if it was just habit and the way her brain worked and not something she should worry about.

Wind and water had aged Velma and roughened her; she looked more like Rayburn's grandmother than his mother. She worked at the seafood store located at the mouth of the harbor, sorting and peeling the shrimp and crabs that the boats brought to the docks. Her husband, Ray—was it shortened to "Ray" or had his son been named for him?—used to be a shrimper until an accident had taken off most of his left arm. Then he'd rented the unused cement block building on the harbor's edge and turned it into Ray's Bar, the name in hot pink neon, with beer signs in all four windows.

Ray and his bar had occasionally demanded Nell's attention because at least once a year, the yacht club would try to get Ray's Bar zoned out of existence. The club had come so close to getting the unused building torn down that they felt cheated when Ray had revived it and turned it into a bar. Located on the other side of the harbor, the yacht club didn't want its sea-front vista to contain pink neon bar signs and advertisements for Miller, Dixie, and Bud.

Last month, Philip Yorst had written a letter to the editor complaining about drunk drivers in the harbor vicinity, which had been the match that lit the drunk driver fire. Sheriff Clureman Hickson had set up his spot checks for the following Saturday night. His men (and one woman—things were progressing a bit) arrested one drunk driver on Ray's side of the harbor and ten coming out of a yacht club party.

The town alderman (no women there, yet) had mouthed the usual platitudes and, as usual, when the votes were taken, no one wanted to go on record for rezoning Ray's Bar, with its one-armed father of eight, out of existence while allowing the yacht club to continue its well-lubricated events.

Velma often worked in the bar after her day in the seafood place (it had a name, but everyone referred to it as the seafood place and that was how Nell thought of it). The older kids were left to take care of the younger ones.

It was a life that had produced the woman in front of Nell— Velma's face etched in lines, her hair course and gray, the body lumpy and sagging.

"How's Miz Thomas doing? Haven't seen her in the shop of late," Velma asked Nell now. Miz Thomas was Mrs. Thomas Upton McGraw, Sr., Thom's mother.

"She's fine," Nell replied. "I talked to her just yesterday."

"Good to hear. Sometimes you just wonder when you don't see people around. Well, let me go find Rayburn 'fore he runs all over."

Nell held the door for Velma to enter the library, then stopped at the water fountain to avoid tagging silently behind the slower woman.

Thom would have been bantering with Velma Gautier, offering to carry her stack of books, asking about her other kids and Ray and what had just gotten off the boat, was the red snapper or the speckled trout good today? He had been the charmer, the one who could move from the yacht club to Ray's Bar with a patter of small talk and jokes that opened people up. He'd sometimes referred to himself as the beauty and Nell the brains of the operation.

Nell could be genial—she'd learned a lot from Thom during their marriage—but never with the ease that he had. Like now. She had thought of the things to say to Velma, but only when it was too late, with Velma already at the library counter checking her books back in.

Nell joined her, putting her books down just as a crack of thunder boomed overhead.

Marion, the librarian, flashed a quick smile at her as she checked in Velma's books.

"Wow! Dinosaurs," came Rayburn's voice from the children's corner.

"Rayburn, you be quiet," his mother shushed him.

"It's okay, let him enjoy his dinosaurs," Marion said. "Just us in the library right now."

21

Nell glanced at the stack of books Velma was returning. Several children's books clearly for Rayburn, quite a few romances—Nell wondered if Velma was a romance reader, then remembered the romances in her own to-be-returned pile. She had just one teenage daughter and Velma had several.

Someone looking at her stack of books might have had a few questions about the reading taste of Naomi Nelligan McGraw, Editor-in-Chief of the *Pelican Bay Crier*. At least Marion the librarian knew the truth. She knew the romances and makeup books Lizzie had picked out, the animal stories and bicycling books for Josh, and which books Nell chose.

Nell had always liked Marion, sensed that they might become friends some day. So far their meetings had been only during Nell's weekly library trips and a few social events here and there. And Thom's funeral. Marion had been there.

Nell watched her as she checked in Velma's books. Marion was an attractive woman and Nell wondered why, at thirty-four, she'd never married. Attractive in a bookish way, she had to admit. Marion's dark hair was cut in a short, practical style, her glasses a rounded tortoise shell, the kind that branded her as a serious book reader. She was tall. Nell, at five-seven, had to look up to her.

She wondered if Marion remained in Pelican Bay to care for her mother. Thom's mother and Marion's mother were close friends, and Nell had occasionally heard them discussing and comparing their children. Peyton Nash, Marion's father, had died a while ago and Nell knew that Erma, her mother, was in frail health. Her two brothers had moved on, one in the military and the other working in computers out in California. Marion, the single daughter, had returned.

Nell had gathered all this information from Mrs. Thomas, Sr., not from Marion herself, and the information suffered from Mrs. Thomas's way of looking at the world.

"C'mon, Rayburn, get your favorite books 'fore the rain starts," Velma called to him.

He spun up to the desk with a handful of books, one of them hanging open showing a picture of "our friend, the policeman." Running seemed to be his preferred method of locomotion.

Nell left her returned books on the countertop and wandered over to the New Books shelf. Nothing really caught her interest, but she hadn't been planning on taking out any books; today's errand was really just to avoid missing the return deadline. She'd bring Josh and Lizzie to get new books. She'd have leisure then to look for herself while Josh searched for books about whales or bicycling, his two current obsessions. Lizzie could spend ten minutes looking at one book, measuring it in ways that Nell couldn't fathom, before deciding whether it was worthy to be carried home or not.

The purpose of her dawdling, Nell admitted, wasn't the books, but to take the first tentative steps past acquaintanceship to friendship. The immobility of her grief at Thom's death was lifting and loneliness was seeping in. She decided that when Velma and the boisterous Rayburn left and there was a quiet moment, she would ask Marion to go for coffee sometime.

Nell had had one of those nights last night, lonely and discontented, far enough past the numbness to know how empty the bed was. The sleepless night had firmed up her resolve to cut away some of the loneliness.

For Thom, it would have been easy. He'd just plop the books on the counter and say, "How about coffee? I'd love to talk about books with you."

But Nell was too deliberate, too cautious just to brazen into friendship. Sometimes she wondered if she was mythologizing Thom, erasing his faults, giving him a perfection that real life would never challenge.

With a shake of her head, Nell decided, I don't need to do that, his mother does it well enough for both of us. Her relationship with Thom's mother had never been easy, but now there was a subtle, unspoken war between them over … over what? Thom's memory? What he might have done, might have said? His soul?

"Do you think Thom would really agree with that editorial?" his mother would politely ask. Or, "Thom's father never would have done that. I suppose it's something he learned in journalism school." Nell heard the unspoken "in journalism school and from you, because he certainly didn't learn it from us."

Clearly I need someone to talk to, Nell thought as she turned from the book shelves.

"Any new books you'd recommend?" she asked Marion.

"Plenty I'd recommend. But you'll have to go to a bookstore for them. The first thing to go in the city budget is the library."

"If you've got Dickens and Shakespeare, what more do you need, right?"

"As if our city councilmen know who Dickens and Master Will are. No, they like the latest bestsellers, so that's the direction my meager funds go. Do I buy the most interesting books or the books that more people will read?"

"It's a book-eat-book world," Nell replied, getting a smile from Marion. "How about going out for coffee sometime? Lizzie and Josh have at least a decade to go before we can talk about the same books."

"Coffee?" Marion repeated slowly, possibly with hesitation but Nell wasn't sure. *Maybe I'm seeing more here than there really is,* Nell suddenly thought, but then Marion continued, "That would be nice—if we can work it into our hectic schedules."

"Mine's kids and the paper. How about Friday? That's best for me. The paper's out and I'd just as soon not be near a phone to hear about things like misspelled names or our editorial page being run by leftists to the left of Marxist-atheistic Communists."

"Friday, let me think…" Marion again replied slowly.

"Or you can get back to me, if you like," Nell added, still sensing hesitation on Marion's part. She didn't know the woman well enough to be able to judge whether this was just the way she did things or if she had some reservations about seeing Nell outside of their limited library meetings.

"Friday doesn't work. How about sometime this weekend? I was just trying to remember Mama's schedule," Marion said. "I'll call and let you know what works."

"Sounds good to me," Nell said, giving Marion her cell phone number. The work one. She'd eschewed having to juggle two cell phones, so her official Crier one, an ancient flip phone, did double duty.

Just then a gaggle of school children rushed in. They surrounded Marion at the main desk and bombarded her with questions about the settling of this part of the Gulf Coast. It had the unmistakable earmarks of research paper due tomorrow.

Nell couldn't see herself being heard above their cacophony. She gave Marion a smile and a wave and headed out the library door.

As she opened the door of the city hall building to leave, the rain came down, windy sheets that made an umbrella useless.

The storm had come.

TWO

It would be the last time, he thought, waiting in the woods. The wet leaves glistened as the final rays of the sun returned from the clouds.

Rayburn Gautier watched his mother get in the car to go to work at Dad's place. Dolly, the sister charged with watching him, had gotten on the phone the second his mother stepped through the door.

Rayburn felt it was her duty to watch him. If she didn't, it wasn't really his fault if he slipped away. From past experience, he knew she'd not notice him gone much before dinnertime. He just had to reappear as she was dumping a can of spaghetti into a sauce pan. He could ask, of course, and she'd probably say yes, but it was more fun to slip away. Sometimes she said no, or worse, wanted to go with him.

He wasn't supposed to cross the street, but it wasn't a busy street, not like near the school or the library. Still, Rayburn carefully looked both ways, then ran quickly across to give any car less of a chance at him. Rayburn felt that the less time he took in a transgression, the less of a transgression it was.

The sun had come back out after the heavy rain. Rayburn skipped around the puddles the storm had left. Wet shoes might be hard to explain.

He headed quickly up the street to the turn onto the dead end road. It was a rarely used street. Only by Old Man Young—all the kids liked to call him that because it sounded so funny, Old Man Young, Young Old Man. He was old and he lived alone in the only house on the road. It was an old oyster shell track, not kept up because of its limited use. Only Old Man Young's beat-up truck used it.

Rayburn crept quietly by his house. Old Man Young had once been out on his porch and, on seeing Rayburn, had asked him where he was going. Not even waiting for an answer, he'd told Rayburn that he should be heading back to his home. The woods behind the harbor wasn't a good place for kids to be playing. Rayburn didn't want to be caught again.

He had promised that he would be there.

The road ended at a grand old oak tree, its black, heavy limbs spreading out like a giant spider. One Halloween, some of the older kids in the neighborhood had decorated its branches with grinning skulls and severed limbs, using flashlights covered with green plastic to light the gristly props.

Rayburn considered getting past the oak tree to be his greatest challenge. He thought of it as the monster tree and was always ready for another bloody hand to suddenly be reaching out for him.

He scurried under the low-hanging limbs, slipping once on the rain-slicked leaves and getting his left knee dirty and wet. But he was safely beyond the threat of grasping fingers.

The harbor, a natural one, was a small L-shaped inlet, petering out to a shallow swampy stream. The town had slowly developed around it, especially at the beach end. It was a natural beach, unlike many on the coast, man-made with dredged sand. But this tail end of the harbor had never been developed. It was too low and marshy originally to do anything with, so the houses had been built around it. Nowadays, too many well-to-do property owners liked having their backyards end in woods to let any developer in. They argued that it was flood control, this low-lying wooded area not far from the center of town.

Past the oak tree, the ground slanted down. Rayburn carefully picked his way across the slippery oak leaves. It wouldn't do to get too muddy or dirty. One knee could happen in the backyard, but both knees and his behind would be suspicious.

At the center of the woods was the ruin of a long-abandoned house—the hermit's place, the kids in the neighborhood called it. One crumbling wooden wall still stood, held in place only by the tree it was leaning against and the vines that encased it. Half a chimney remained, only barely taller than Rayburn. The bricks were soft and crumbling, every bit of wind and rain creating another pile of dust and ashes. A less densely overgrown patch between the wall and the chimney was the only other indication that some long-ago time, a person had lived there.

Parents warned children to stay away from the old house, afraid that the wall might escape its vine shroud, or that someone would step into the well that was now hidden in the underbrush behind the chimney and crumbling into the same dust. All manner of things were said to be at the bottom of the well. A doorway to China, or a treasure chest, or a dead body.

Rayburn had occasionally dared to peek down the well, but he'd only seen leaves and slime that thickened into a dense blackness. He usually stayed away from the skeleton house, preferring the fiddler crabs and salamanders to be found at the stream's edge.

Once there had been a big and very dead gar floating there. Rayburn had come back three days in a row, watching how quickly the crabs chewed away pieces of the dead flesh. Rain had kept him away for two days, and when he'd come again, there was no sign, nothing to indicate that a dead fish had been there. Rayburn had been hoping to at least get the skull and add it to his collection. One of his father's friends had given him the jaws of a shark.

But today he turned into the woods instead of heading down to the stream.

———

It would be the last time, he thought, as he heard the whoosh of leaves that let him know someone was coming. It was getting too dangerous. It felt too easy, and for him that was always a danger sign. It was the initial approach and seduction, the feint and parry, that kept him sharp and always watching. When everything was at risk, he was at his best, senses flashing and alert, ready to jump at the slightest shift of wind. He liked being unsure, testing himself.

Now he expected the soft shush of footsteps through the woods. Knew there would be only one set of feet gliding along the leaves.

It had become too easy. It was time for it to end.

THREE

Nell glanced out her window, surprised to see that the sun had returned. It had been a downpour when she'd sat down.

Well, the story was edited. Carrie wasn't a bad reporter, but it was obvious that she'd been an English major, not a journalism major—voice superseded "just the facts." She'd probably done her thesis on *Wuthering Heights* and was now trying to write Wuthering Harbor, one article at a time.

Josh wouldn't be upset if she was a little late; he loved hanging out at the bike shop. But Nell didn't know if Kate Ryan, the new owner, would like to be both shopkeeper and babysitter.

She sat a moment longer, trying to decide whether to come back to the office after getting Josh and dropping him at home, or just going home with him.

Leaving Lizzie and Josh together could always be volatile. At twelve, or almost thirteen as he constantly pointed out, Josh didn't much like being reminded that he still needed to be babysat—a word that Nell avoided at all costs. Lizzie, at fourteen, was in the early stages of adolescent rebellion, and her reaction to being given the last-minute assignment of watching her younger brother could range from an "Ah, Mom, I've got things I need to do" to wheedling for compensatory allowance to an outburst of "This isn't fair! Why do I get stuck with him? I didn't make you have another kid!" Every once in a while she'd say "Okay, no problem," just to keep the mix in constant flux.

Most of the items left on Nell's to-do list were phone calls. Better to make those the next morning, she decided. She did want to contact Ella Jackson about her granddaughter—she'd looked up the number in the phone book and called twice already, but there was no answer and Ella Jackson either couldn't afford an answering machine or didn't believe in them. Despite her brave words to Harold Reed, Nell also questioned whether it was better to probe publicly into someone's grief or just let them suffer the loss without the prying of a newspaper reporter, no matter how altruistic her motives. And if she really wanted to talk to Ella Jackson, she should probably visit her in the evening when she was likely to be home from work. Nell just didn't know if she wanted to.

On the more mundane level, she'd mostly dried off from her hurried dash in the rain earlier, but her shoes and socks were still soggy. Happy children and dry feet were enough incentive to go home.

Leaving the edited story on Carrie's desk—another chore postponed until the morning was placating Carrie's stricken look at the number of red marks on her prose—Nell crossed the newsroom. Her wet feet squashed in a less than dignified manner.

Jacko looked up as she walked by his desk. He and Carrie were the cub reporters. A paper the size of the *Pelican Bay Crier* didn't have too many bear reporters. Nell had accepted it as one of her duties: to mentor the young, then watch them move on. The Crier was a start-out-at paper, not an end-up-at paper, unless you ended up owning it. It had its rewards and challenges, and at this particular time Jacko was the reward and Carrie the challenge.

He didn't call himself Jacko, but his blond, earnest good looks and youthful enthusiasm had demanded a diminutive of Jack.

"What are you working on?" she asked, hoping it came across as a friendly question and not the inquiry of the editor.

"The fast-paced, exciting city council meeting," he answered.

"Drainage ditches and trash pick-up?"

"Oh, no, this one had sex in it."

"Sex? Enlighten me."

"Cat mating. Very serious problem. Cats yowling through the night. The city council, in a very bold move, voted to allot the funds to purchase two cat traps—humane ones, of course. Concerned citizens can check out the traps kept at either the police station or the sheriff's department, to be decided by who's better at ducking out of being know as the Pussy Trapper of Pelican Bay."

Jacko suddenly blushed, clearly just realizing not only what he'd said, but that he'd said it to the older woman who was his boss.

What do they think, that I'm forty-one and some tight-assed prude? Nell wondered. Having two children had considerably cleaned up the language of her younger days, but she still knew what the words meant. Or, she wondered, because I'm a widow, do they think I'm asexual?

"Maybe we should solve the problem for them and offer to keep the cages here," Nell said. "We could even start a Pussy Trapper column. Who brought in the most. Best places to find … cats."

Jacko half-smiled, as if he was pretty sure she was joking. He was still blushing slightly.

I wonder if he thinks I'm flirting with him, Nell suddenly thought.

"Don't work too late. I'm off to get the kids. You're allowed to leave five minutes after the boss with no penalty." She headed out the door, lest any lingering give him the wrong signals. Jacko was cute, but Nell could more easily see him dating Lizzie in five or six years than as an older woman-younger man fling for herself.

She missed Thom terribly, sometimes for the hard passion that had always flared between them, but more for the daily touches, an embrace while cooking dinner, the neck rubs they traded off, sitting next to each other while reading or watching TV, their thighs leaning against each other with the ease of long intimacy. At night, in bed, she could look at his empty side and know he would never return. But sometimes in the kitchen or in the office they used to share, she still expected to feel the warmth of his hands.

Sex without love, or at least the possibility of love, seemed cold and barren to Nell. Masturbation with a body temperature prop. She couldn't imagine ever falling in love with Jacko, so she found the idea of sex ludicrous. Passion is such an odd, elusive thing, she thought.

It was too painful to think about holding Thom, so she'd conjured up the perfect stranger when she wanted to imagine herself in someone's arms. The tall, dark, handsome man, a moonlit island, all a safe, unattainable fantasy. It hurt too much to remember Thom, and it hurt too much to wonder if she would ever find love again.

Nell unlocked her car and dismissed the thoughts. It was time to find her son.

Beck's Bike and Camping Store had been a fixture in Pelican Bay since before Nell had even met Thom. Tobias Beck, the owner, could always be counted on to sponsor Little League teams and

Scout Troops both Boy and Girl, or to fix up old bicycles for free to give to needy children at Christmas. He had never married; Nell had heard a few whispered rumors of an injury when he'd served in Vietnam.

A few years ago, he'd gone to New Orleans, seen some doctors there, and come back with the announcement that he had cancer.

His niece, Kate, had come to town to take care of him, and after he died, she took over the bike shop. Nell had always wondered what the arrangement was, whether it had been an up-front trade or whether he'd always been her favorite uncle and her care had been a gift for which he'd given in return the only thing he could—his business. Kate had taken good care of him; Nell knew this not only from seeing it during the times she'd visited Toby, but also from hearing others talk about it. Small towns have no secrets.

She wondered if she might ever know Kate well enough to ask that question—not in crass terms, but to discover what had caused her to choose a life in Pelican Bay, where the only person she knew was her uncle.

Nell doubted that she'd ever ask Kate the other question she had. Toby Beck's death certificate had not listed cancer as the cause of death, but liver failure, caused by hepatitis C and HIV infection. Maybe she was wrong; maybe small towns did have secrets, ones that were fiercely guarded, as their residents were without the shield of anonymity that larger cities could offer.

Nell had always liked Toby, and the idea that he'd had a secret life was disturbing. She and Thom had had him over for dinner; he had taken them out fishing in his boat.

Surely Kate would know if her uncle was a gay man and the death wasn't the cancer he claimed. But it was not a question Nell could see asking her.

Sometimes she wondered if that was one of the things that attracted her to journalism: the desire to know secrets, to have an excuse to probe and inquire. She always felt like she'd slipped up when a secret completely eluded her. But Toby had taken his secrets to the grave, and Nell could come up with no good reason to disturb his rest.

She parked her car and entered the bike shop, feeling a bit chagrined when she noticed that Josh was the only remaining child from the Bike Care and Maintenance class. Her son was happily leafing through one of the bicycling magazines; Kate was behind the counter, sorting some odd nut-and-bolt type things. She was a handsome woman, though not conventionally pretty, with a very strong chin and a slight hook in her nose. Although in her early thirties, her blue eyes showed the lines made by sun and wind, and laughter. She was tall for a woman, with more clearly defined muscles than most women would care to display. Her hair was a straw blond, with shades from chestnut brown to glints of red.

Nell admired Kate's easy manner with the kids who swarmed the shop. Via Josh, she'd learned that Kate used to be a forest ranger out in the Pacific Northwest, and that she'd been to Alaska and even Australia.

"Hey, Mom," Josh called out, catching sight of her.

Kate looked up from her counting.

Her hello was stepped on by Josh's excited "Guess what? I changed a tire faster than anyone else, even Bryan." Bryan was the oldest and biggest boy in the class.

"Keep it up and I may have to hire you," Kate said.

"Wow! Really?" Josh exclaimed.

Kate gave Nell a quick look, as if to say oops, got to be careful bantering around kids. "As soon as child labor laws permit," she said.

"Sorry I'm a bit late," Nell apologized.

"It's okay, Mom," Josh answered. "I was straightening up the books and magazines."

"Looks like I'm already violating those child labor laws," Kate said to Nell.

"I saw reading, not hard labor, when I came in," Nell replied.

"Then my automatic mother-warning system works."

Nell suddenly had an urge to say, "Let's do lunch some time, I want to hear about Alaska and Australia," but Josh cut in.

"I *was* working. I brought the box from the back and now it's empty. Everything's on the shelf just like Kate asked."

If it's not a crush yet, Nell thought, it will be in a year or two. She felt just the tiniest stab of jealousy at the woman who'd taken her son's affections. When Nell asked Josh to help with the groceries or clean up his room, she usually got an "Ah, Mom ..." or "Just a sec," which always stretched into much more than a second. But the jealousy was quickly quelled by a streak of pride; Josh had picked an intelligent, independent woman. Nell took it as a compliment that she was raising a feminist son.

"Since you've gone to the trouble of carting and stacking them, I guess you should take one home and read it," Nell said.

"Thanks, Mom," Josh said, clearly relieved that he had gotten the magazine without having to directly ask for it.

Kate started to wave away the money Nell was taking out of her purse, but Nell said, "The stacking is in exchange for my being late, but I owe you for the magazine." After paying, she and Josh left the bike shop.

When they got home, the door to the den was shut, with the telephone missing from its charger. Lizzie was home and on the phone, more usual than not. Also as usual, she hadn't done the dishes left from breakfast, as Nell had asked her to do.

Forty-one-year-olds, not teenagers, are supposed to have this kind of memory problem, Nell thought. Three cereal bowls and spoons wasn't a major transgression, but Nell was tempted to breach the sanctuary of the closed door. However, she already knew Lizzie's excuses: "I was just going to do it, you're home early"; "The phone rang, so I had to answer it"; "I forgot, let me finish talking to …" Lizzie would then talk for at least another half hour.

Nell decided that cereal bowls weren't worth the battle of wills that would ensue. Battles with rebellious teenagers had to be judiciously picked. But she might still be able to use Lizzie's dereliction to her advantage. Nell glanced at her watch. Josh on the computer and Lizzie on the phone should keep them content long enough for her to ask a grandmother a few questions about a granddaughter.

Nell breached the barricade of the closed door to inform Lizzie, "I've gone ahead and done the breakfast dishes, but I need to run out for about an hour. Josh's here, so the two of you watch out for each other."

Lizzie had stopped mid-sentence, clearly discussing things mothers must never hear from their daughters' lips, and listened. With a head nod, she agreed, adding a sigh to indicate that she realized she hadn't gotten out of any chores, just exchanged one for another at her mother's exchange rate.

Nell closed the door and wondered what lesson she was giving her daughter—not to shirk responsibility, or that those in power set the terms.

"I'll be back in about an hour," she told Josh, who echoed his sister with a nod of acknowledgment as he stared at the computer screen.

They'll be fine, Nell told herself as she closed the door behind her. The worst that could happen was for Lizzie to decide she needed the computer and Nell could come home to two quarreling kids.

She caught herself and remembered that she was going to visit a grandmother whose granddaughter had died young. But the moment of worry was replaced with the thought that what had happened to Tasha Jackson couldn't happen to her children. Tasha had been killed either in a random accident or through the intent of someone close to her.

Rail Street was a prosaic name for the street closest to the railroad track. Several of the houses on the block had been recently painted; one was clearly derelict, with a badly overgrown yard and a listing porch, while the rest fit somewhere in between. But even the painted houses made it clear that the paychecks of those who lived here did little more than keep them tottering on the edge of poverty.

As Nell scanned the houses for Ella Jackson's address, she wondered if it was that hard cycle of work, overtime at the factory, and night work as a waitress that had created the gap for Tasha to slip away in, unnoticed.

Further down the block, a car stopped and let out an older woman. As Nell got closer, she realized that the woman was climbing the steps at the address she had for Ella Jackson. She was moving slowly, as if tired from a long day and with no place to hurry to.

Nell quickly parked and caught up with her as she was putting the key in her door. "Ella Jackson?" she asked.

The women turned to look, her eyes flicking over Nell, clearly noting how out of place she was in this neighborhood. She paused for another moment before finally replying, "I'm Ella Jackson."

"Nell McGraw. I'm with the *Pelican Bay Crier*." That did little to change the wary look on Ella Jackson's face, so Nell continued. "I'm here to talk to you about your granddaughter, Tasha. I know that this is a hard time for you and you may not want to answer questions—if so, I understand. But I'd like to do a follow-up story on her."

"Why?" Ella Jackson cut in. "To make public that my son isn't the best father? That he messed up some years ago, and make it seem like that's why his daughter got killed? Or that now I'm taking care of her while he and his wife work over at the casinos and I have a beer when I get home from work because it makes my knees hurt less? And make it like that beer killed her?" Ella Jackson's voice didn't get louder, but it gained in intensity as her anger came through.

"The police and the sheriff have been asking a lot of rough questions, haven't they?" Nell said, conscious of keeping her tone of voice quiet and polite. "I guess that's their job, to catch the criminals, and it makes them see the world that way. But I'm not here to find blame, Mrs. Jackson. Something happened to Tasha that shouldn't happen to any child anywhere, but particularly in a small, supposedly safe town like Pelican Bay. Maybe I'm really here because I have two children and what happened to her could happen to them."

Ella Jackson looked at her for a moment, then said, "How old?"

"A girl, fourteen, and a boy, twelve."

She paused again, turned back to finish opening her door, and then said, "I suppose that you'd better come in."

Nell followed her into a living room, the furniture a mixture that suggested some had been bought, some found, at different times and places. But it was tidy and clean, the stack of morning newspapers and the coffee mug left out indicating that this was the way Ella Jackson lived, not just made neat for some company expected later.

Mrs. Jackson offered Nell something to drink, including the beer she'd mentioned earlier. Nell declined automatically, then wondered if she shouldn't just join her in a beer. It wasn't like Josh and Lizzie were going to check her breath when she came back. And it might have proved to Ella Jackson that Nell didn't think having one beer after work led to children being killed.

The woman glanced at Nell warily as she put away her coat and purse and took a moment in the kitchen to grab a sip of water. She didn't get a beer after all, and Nell wondered if she'd decided not to drink in front of her.

Ella Jackson joined her back in the living room, sitting at the other end of the couch Nell had chosen. She watched Nell expectantly. Nell quickly glanced down at the notepad she'd taken out, searching for a question that would start the interview off right.

But it was Ella Jackson who spoke first. "It was your husband who was killed last fall, wasn't it?"

Nell kept her eyes on the blank paper, now searching for an answer instead of a question. "Yes, it was," she finally said.

"That must be hard for you," Mrs. Jackson said.

This time Nell looked up at her. Ella Jackson's eyes were clear and direct. She knew what hard was. Nell realized that she had no perfect question—that there were no perfect questions and maybe all she needed to do was talk to this woman. "It isn't easy," she softly replied.

"With two children." Ella Jackson made it a statement.

"That's the hardest part. No matter how I try, I can't make up for ..." Nell trailed off.

"A father gone." Again, it was a simple statement, but it held acknowledgment that many people shied away from. As if not mentioning Thom's death could let Nell escape feeling the loss.

"What do you think happened to Tasha?" Nell asked her question.

"What usually happens to little black girls. Some man thought his needs were greater than her life."

Nell nodded. It was what she thought, too. But she still had to ask. "Could she have just wandered away?"

Lizzie wouldn't just wander away, but some man could take her as Tasha had been taken. I don't want to think about that, Nell admitted to herself.

Ella Jackson looked straight at her. "Tasha did not 'just wander' away. She wasn't like that. I know that child. Twelve years I've known that child. Wander away, no. Something happened to her."

A child that still lived in present tense, Nell noted. She also understood that Ella Jackson had rendered her verdict and no question would get another answer.

"What would you like the police to do?"

"Justice, that's all I want." Ella Jackson quietly added, "That's all we ever wanted."

Nell left the question unasked: how rarely black women her age got justice from the still-too-white police and sheriff departments.

Instead, she asked about Tasha, wanting to make the girl real and her death matter.

Tasha had been a good student, mostly A's and B's, liked animals, and was going to be able to get a dog on her next birthday. "She was the kind of girl who'd take good care of it," Ella Jackson said. Tasha had last been seen walking home from school.

"I'll let you look at the story before I run it," Nell offered as she got up to leave. That was something she very rarely did, but she didn't want to add to Ella Jackson's pain.

"You don't need to do that. Just ask for justice. Ask that they find the man who hurt my little girl." Her eyes clouded for a moment, then she turned away to open the door for Nell. "Tasha was a good girl. She didn't just wander away."

Tasha was now past tense. With tears brimming in her eyes, Ella Jackson gently closed the door.

Nell walked slowly to her car. Why do we need evil to explain the tragedies in life? Ella Jackson's certainty of foul play wasn't hers. While it could have been the stranger that all girl children are warned of, it could also have been something as banal as Tasha's first stirrings of adolescent rebellion, a forbidden swim turned to tragedy by a cramp and a current. Or stumbling off the dock and hitting her head. Was it even possible that Pelican Bay held the kind of monster that Ella Jackson thought had killed her granddaughter?

Nell got in her car. For a moment, she desperately wished she could fulfill the woman's request for justice. But she knew the most likely outcome was a newspaper story that reminded people that a young girl had died, but the moment would pass and they would turn the page.

She started the car and drove home.

Lizzie emerged from her phone cocoon just in time to eat.

After supper, she and Nell had a discussion about the supper dishes, with Lizzie promising she'd get to it before she went to bed.

It was a quiet evening, Josh reading his bicycling magazine cover to cover, including all the ads. Nell only had to remind Lizzie once about the dishes.

FOUR

THE PHONE WOKE NELL. One shrill ring, then a second pierced the darkness. She hastily grabbed for the receiver next to the bed.

"Hello?" she said, the harsh ring having fully woken her. Phones in the night sent a jolt of fear through her. There had been a time when the ring meant a breaking story, news so important it couldn't wait until morning. Until the night she'd taken the call that told her her father had died, a sudden heart attack. The quiet man who'd rarely argued with her strident mother except to insist Nell go to college, go live a life far from the Indiana farms her siblings had settled for. After that, every late phone call carried the threat that it could shatter her life.

"Hello?" she repeated to the silence on the line.

"Nell McGraw?" a voice asked, though it wasn't much of a question, more to show that the caller had access to her name.

"Who is this?" she demanded. She didn't recognize the voice. It sounded muffled and distorted.

"Nell McGraw. The story is in the woods. You'd do well to look there."

"Who is this?" she demanded again, trying to keep the edge of fear out of her voice. This anonymous voice, breaking into her night, had no benign intent.

"The woods, Nell. You'd do well to look there," the caller repeated, then hung up.

Nell stared at the receiver for a moment, then jumped out of bed. The caller had meant to disturb her, and he—she was reasonably sure it was a man's voice—had succeeded.

It wasn't even a conscious decision, but Nell found herself in the hallway at Josh's door. As quietly as she could, she opened it. Caught in a faint beam of moonlight, her son was sprawled across the bed. Safe and asleep.

Lizzie was curled around the big stuffed black panther she still slept with.

Nell quietly made her way back to her bedroom. The call had tainted her night. The fear from the ringing phone, and the disturbing message, had taken sleep from her.

Nell picked up the receiver and dialed the police station.

After five rings, a voice drawled, "Jenkins here."

Damn, Nell thought. Officer Boyce Jenkins was a swaggering bully. She had rarely seen him without his hands hooked provocatively into his belt, one index finger just barely touching above the tight bulge in his pants.

"This is Nell McGraw," she said, then wished she'd just hung up.

"Miz McGraw. Always a pleasure to hear from you," Jenkins said.

"This isn't a pleasure call," Nell retorted, more sharply than she'd intended.

"Sorry, ma'am," Jenkins replied, using his annoyingly slow drawl. "But I do get lots of late night calls from lonely women."

Getting her angry or flustered was what he wanted. Keeping her tone neutral, Nell said, "Is there a police officer on duty? I need to speak to someone about a criminal matter."

"I'm on duty. What can I do for you?" His question still had the lazy insinuation of sex in it.

Take me seriously and get your hand out of your pants, Nell almost snapped at him. "I need to report a disturbing phone call."

"Obscene?" he cut in, too quickly.

"No," Nell said firmly. "Someone I don't know asked for me by name, then said, 'the story is in the woods.' Then he said—"

"In the woods, huh?" Jenkins interrupted her. "You want you and me to take a nice moonlit walk in the woods?"

There's no way to get through to him, Nell decided. "I'll call back in the morning," she said, allowing herself to slam the receiver with enough force to tell Jenkins he'd been dismissed.

She sat for a moment, the disturbing phone call further disturbed by Jenkins's insolence. What could she really report him on? Tone of voice? Attitude? Just the facts, ma'am—and a woman's feelings weren't facts.

Even that phone call—what did it give her? "The story is in the woods." "Woods" wasn't a very specific location. Five minutes in any direction, except south to the Gulf, would take one to a wooded area. What story could be worth covering that expanse of forest for?

"You'd do well to look there.'" He had repeated that. Well to look there.

Suddenly Nell was hit with one of those disparate connections that Thom swore she pulled out of the air. It was another of the things that had made her a better reporter than he was.

Only one woods had a well in it, the small patch that still remained at the swampy upper end of the harbor.

Nell recalled how, only a few months prior, she'd taken Jacko and Carrie into the woods to do a feature story on the bits and pieces humans had left: the rotting remains of a dock that no longer touched water, a few boards nailed to a tree that no longer had a tree house. The overgrown clearing of the hermit's lost cabin and the well he'd dug there.

Nell again picked up the phone. This time she called the sheriff's office. She expected only a marginally better response than from Jenkins. At least she was on polite terms with Jenkins's boss, not something she could say about Sheriff Hickson.

A voice she didn't recognize answered, "Sheriff."

Nell simply repeated the content of the phone call and her guess about the well. The deputy took it all down and ended with a non-committal "We'll look into it."

I've done what I can do, Nell thought as she put the phone down. Short of grabbing a flashlight and plunging through the woods to the well—which she had no intention of doing.

She wasn't satisfied. The adrenaline of fear wasn't appeased by the noncommittal phone call and sitting waiting.

I should try to get back to sleep, Nell told herself, but she couldn't. She felt as if she had to be vigilant, to guard her home and children against the shrill assaults of the darkness.

The phone rang again.

Nell snatched it up, as if stopping the jar of the bell could limit the damage.

"Mrs. McGraw?"

This time Nell recognized the voice. It was Sheriff Hickson.

"Speaking," Nell answered. "I'm sorry, Sheriff, I didn't mean to wake you ..." She was surprised that he'd called her at this hour.

He cut her off. "I was awake."

Nell braced herself for the "foolish woman wasting my time" speech. It didn't come. He continued, "Little Rayburn Gautier didn't come home for his supper. We been looking for him since sundown. Guess we better look in the well."

Nell felt the jolt of connection again, this time with an icy chill surrounding it.

"I want you to remember as much as you can 'bout that voice, Mrs. McGraw," he gruffly ordered her. "You remember and you write it down."

"I'll do that, but I don't think it will be much help. The voice was muffled and distorted. A deliberate disguise, I would guess."

"Huh," the sheriff grunted. "We got a missing boy, someone calls the Editor-in-Chief to go look for a story in the woods. And he hides his voice."

He let the facts hang in the air.

Nell simply said, "Call me … when you know something."

"I'll call. You stay out of the woods. No place for you on a night like tonight," he admonished her.

"I'm staying home, Sheriff. I'm staying here with my children."

He grunted a goodbye.

Nell stared for a moment at the dim shadowed moonlight outsider her window. Then she got up and again checked on Josh and Lizzie. Still sleeping. Still safe.

It could always be worse, Thom used to say. The phone call in the night could be to tell you that your child had died.

Dawn was still a long way away when the phone rang again.

The body of Rayburn Gautier had been discovered at the bottom of the well.

FIVE

INSTEAD OF LETTING JOSH and Lizzie catch the bus to school, Nell had decided to take them. Maybe next week she'd let them go back to the bus—they were probably just as safe with thirty other children and the bus driver as with her. But for now she didn't just want them safe, but to know that they were safe, to see for herself as they entered the brick school building.

Can I ever protect them enough? she wondered as she watched them split off in their separate directions, Josh to the middle school and Lizzie across the courtyard to the high school.

The front page of the Crier only had a small story on it that Friday: *"Boy's body found. Authorities are investigating."* It was all Nell could do before the deadline. She'd considered going back to sleep, but knew sleep would not come, so she'd hastily written the article and called the printing press, reworking the front page over the phone with them to get the story in.

Sheriff Hickson had been blunt in his comment. "Call it an accident. We don't know anything more than that." He hadn't told her not to mention the phone call. Nell assumed that he figured she'd be a typical reporter and use whatever she could for the story. Or maybe he thought that telling a woman to do something would be the way to guarantee that she would do the opposite. But the location of Rayburn's body was something that only a killer would know. Nell was already thinking of the caller as the killer, although it was possible that some sick person had stumbled across the child's body and decided to play a depraved joke. Nell wasn't keeping the phone call out of the paper in order to later prove the sheriff wrong, but to, in some small way, thwart the murderer. He'd called her to get noticed, to have his deeds splashed across the front page. She resented him turning her into a chess piece in his obscene game.

Nell pulled Jacko off his usual stories and sent him to the sheriff's office with orders to put most of his time and energy into the story of Rayburn Gautier's ... death. Nell held herself back from saying "murder," even to her staff. It would come. That word would invade their lives soon enough.

Even though she thought that Jacko was a better reporter than Carrie, she'd always treated them with a rough equality, assigning both of them scut work as well as feature stories. However, this decision had stripped away that veneer of equality. Pelican Bay was a medium-size town with a medium-size number of murders—a few that could be front page anywhere, but mostly just the occasional drunken brawl that got out of hand. A dead child was clearly a major story.

"Are you sending him because he's a man?" Carrie demanded, standing in the doorway to Nell's office. She obviously resented having Jacko's sewage and water board meetings dumped on her.

Nell was both tired and wired from the jolt of fear, then the worry that had torn apart her night. She quelled her desire to snap, "It's not his penis, but his brain." Instead she merely said, "No, I'm not."

"Are you sure?" Carrie shot back. "Women of your generation often have some latent sexism still lingering in them."

"If you want equality with Jacko," Nell retorted, still holding her tongue but not as tightly, "you have to earn it. Of course I'm going to give a major story to the reporter who stays late instead of the one watching the clock; the one who digs further instead of me having to give explicit instructions on every step; the one who does unassigned stories on his own time. And I'm from the generation that had to earn our equality instead of assuming it would be handed to us. Be aware of your own assumptions."

Carrie flushed, high color in both her cheeks, whether in anger or embarrassment Nell couldn't tell. Nor could she care. The young woman spun on her heel and, without another word, disappeared.

Nell briefly wondered if the sewer and water board would get any coverage at all this month. Skipping it might be a service to the readers, she thought as she closed the door to her office. She rarely closed it; only when she really needed to work on something and didn't want to be disturbed. Or when a surge of grief hit her and she didn't want to display it.

Nell wrote down everything she could remember about the phone call. The time—a little before one in the morning. The description of the voice—low, with an electronic buzz running through it, as if the person was speaking into something instead of directly into the phone. She noted that it could be one of those synthesizers that change voices, made a man sound like a woman or vice versa. The syntax had been simple—no big words, but no grammatical mistakes either.

When she was done, she looked at that single sheet of paper. It seemed so insubstantial, an ineffectual weapon against the kind of monster that killed children and then called to gloat about it.

Nell left one thing off the sheet—the harsh knowledge she'd gleaned from the call that caused her hands to shake as she typed.

The silent, awkward deputy, searching for words. His silence had told her that Thom was dead, slammed her into the brutal unfairness of life. How quickly the ones we love can be taken from us, bare seconds between life and death. Nell had hated the drunk driver who'd veered out of his lane, had cursed him and wished him dead and called him evil.

But last night she'd learned what evil really was. A willful malice had entered her life.

Whatever the sins of the drunk that had taken Thom from her—and he had many—he had not set out with the intention to kill a man.

Her hands still shaking, Nell removed the fragile sheet of paper from the printer. Something evil was out there and it wanted her to pay attention to it. She had found Ella Jackson's monster. Now she could only hope for justice.

SIX

NELL WOKE WITH A start, the early morning light too faint to be her usual waking time. She immediately sat up and swung her legs out of bed. She was halfway to the door to check on Josh and Lizzie before she remembered that neither of them had spent the night at home. Josh was off at a camp-out with his Boy Scout troop and Lizzie was at a slumber party. She'd spent yesterday in a frenzy getting them ready—how could a sleeping bag get so lost in their not-large house—before nodding off in front of the TV and dragging herself to bed.

Holding still, Nell searched the room with her eyes, listening intently for any sound, any sign, of what had jolted her from sleep. The yowling wail of a cat in heat sounded outside her window. She spun toward the sound, half angry and half relieved.

"You may have to do what comes naturally, but you don't have to do it under my window," she said in a loud voice as she pushed aside the curtains and opened the window. Part of her loudness was for the cats' sake—to let them know that their amorous tryst had a less-than-happy witness, but also to help banish the lingering fear in the room.

No cats were visible in the early gray light, but Nell had heard a satisfying rustle through the bushes at the sound of the opening window.

Will I ever get a good night's sleep? she wondered. Her nights had been uneasy, broken by Josh's cough, Lizzie turning over and pushing her stuffed panther off the bed. Small, innocuous noises that shouldn't have disturbed her slumber. The phone call—and the grisly reality that followed—had shaken Nell, pushed her into a hyper-vigilant state.

The cats yowled again, but from a safer distance. Nell glanced at her bed with a sigh. Sleep seemed unlikely. Both the howling cats and the silence of the house were unsettling.

Usually a night with both Josh and Lizzie gone would have given her a voluptuous solitude, but instead their absence only made Nell feel more alone and vulnerable. Even when the realistic part of her brain pointed out that a twelve-year-old boy and fourteen-year-old girl weren't much protection, and that if she was going to be attacked, better her children be as far away as possible, didn't quell the empty feeling.

The sheriff still wasn't calling the death a murder, at least not officially. It was possible that little Rayburn had tripped and fallen into the well, making it an accident. Then some sicko had stumbled across the body and decided to have a few jollies at the Editor-in-Chief's expense—*to put those feminists back into their place*, Sheriff Hickson hadn't added. He'd only mumbled, after Nell's third follow-up call, "Wish Thom were still here. Make it all easier."

Nell hadn't replied to that, although she too fervently wished that Thom were here. She doubted that her reasons and the sheriff's were the same.

Hickson obviously felt that Thom wouldn't have gotten that kind of call, that Nell had been targeted because she was a woman and alone. And therefore more of a burden to him and his deputies. They felt they had to replace the protection a husband would have given her. "We'll drive by your house ev'ry so often, and you might get a gun," he had mumbled at her, although clearly skeptical that a gun would be much use wielded by a middle-aged woman.

Nell wanted Thom, her partner, her equal, back. She wanted him around to run decisions by, such as her decision to print nothing about the phone call in Friday's paper. Was it a greater good to warn the public, let them know what was going on? Or was it better to keep knowledge of the call to only a few people, the better to trap the killer? Would splashing it in banner headlines only egg him on for more attention, more killings? Or would her seeming to ignore him do it?

She'd also wanted someone to help her write the obituary for Rayburn Gautier. It had been a short one; a short life. As short as the obituary she'd written for Tasha Jackson—another life too short. As Nell wrote it, she couldn't help but think that this could have been Josh or Lizzie. She desperately wanted Thom there to share her fears. There were two children dead now. That shouldn't happen here.

But the bed was empty, only her side rumpled and slept in. Suddenly Nell felt the sharp stab of pain. So much of the routine of her life had been empty of Thom for the last few months that the daily moments had lost their sharp edges. But these new places she felt herself entering, this sudden yawning fear and threat, created a glaring emptiness where Thom should have been.

Nell fought the tightening in her throat, marching to the bathroom to splash cold water on her face.

"Oh, Thom, I need you," she said softly to her reflection in the mirror. Then quietly added, "But you'll never be here again, will you?" She stared at her face, pale skin smudged by dark circles under her eyes. Eyes that were called blue on her driver's license, but could vary from a deep blue-green to a chilly gray, were rimmed in red from the threatening tears, their color now a cloudy blue-gray. Her hair was long around her shoulders, still mussed from sleep, more strands of gray visible in the chestnut brown. She usually wore it up in a bun or chignon, something only possible because her hair was very cooperative in the matter.

Nell watched herself in the mirror for a moment longer, watched the grief spread over her features, before she turned away, burying her face in a towel to catch the tears, holding the cloth for the scant comfort it could give.

She let herself cry for several minutes, the emotions a swirl: grief for Thom, anger and fear at the invasion into her life of the phone call; even, she had to admit, self-pity at being alone.

Finally the tears slowed, then stopped. Nell again washed her face, slowly and gently, letting the water run warm.

When she again glanced at herself, the warm washing seemed to have helped. It didn't take away the sleepless smudges, but made them less harsh.

"Okay, you've had your cry, time to get on with life," she told the reflection. And to get out of the house, she decided, away from ringing phones and empty beds.

She took a brief shower, savoring the heat, a luxury she usually didn't allow herself lest one child or the other complain about luke-warm leftovers. Then she hurriedly dressed: jeans, an old sweatshirt of Thom's that she'd always worn more than he had. Thom had referred to it as "your sweatshirt that used to be mine."

The shimmer of sunrise was now on the far horizon as Nell stepped out the door, replacing the diffuse gray. She paused for a moment, deciding where to go. And, she realized, checking out her surroundings, the fear and alertness not letting go.

"Even maniac killers have to sleep sometime," she muttered, again using the sound of her voice to chase the fear. She rejected a walk to the beach in favor of riding her bike to the state park.

Josh had been trying to get her to go on some of the bike trips that Kate organized. He had gone on some of the shorter ones himself, and Nell had been caught in the parental guilt trap of not wanting him to go by himself on the longer overnight trips but not having the time—or the bicycling stamina—to go with him.

Early morning with no one, especially her energetic son, to see her would make for a good time to check out what shape her legs were in.

Not too bad, she thought as she cycled up to the entrance of the park. She had taken the back route around the harbor, with the state park another mile past it. Admittedly, she'd puffed a bit going up the hills, but it might only take a little work to get in respectable shape for a bike trip with Josh.

Nell rode into the park, past the oaks draped in Spanish moss and the deserted picnic area, to the trail that led to the marsh. She pulled her bike off the road, onto the path. Of course, there was no place to lock a bike save to the trees. Not willing to drag a chain around some young sapling, Nell left her bike leaning against the sturdiest tree in range. Pelican Bay wasn't the kind of town that had bike thieves skulking about early in the morning.

Just murderers. Even if the sheriff didn't want to believe that Rayburn Gautier had been deliberately killed, didn't want to face the possibility that this kind of violence had invaded his town, Nell had few doubts. She'd heard the voice on the phone.

The trail led to a wooden observation deck hidden in the trees just at the edge of the marsh. Plank steps spiraled up the outside of the platform. It was about ten feet high, making Nell feel, as she climbed, like she was in the trees and not just some earthbound observer. Looking in one direction, she had a view of the marsh as it led to the waters of the bay. Straight in front of her was a perfect view of the sun rising over the trees on the far side of the morass. To her left, she had a view of the road as it continued on past the trail.

She tried to concentrate on the light, finding the far corners of the marsh as the sun rose in the sky, tried to enjoy the cool in the air. It would be temperate, even warm when the sun was fully up. A few of the trees were showing spring colors, the muted greens that stayed all winter overlaid with the light green of new leaves.

She couldn't help glancing at the road every so often and occasionally turning around to check the trail behind her. But no one seemed about on this early and still-chilly Sunday morning.

For about ten minutes, she had the world to herself, then the quiet morning brought the sound of footsteps on the road.

Nell found herself listening carefully. I can't let it go, can I, she thought as her relief at what seemed like the purposeful stride of an early morning walker was broken by the thought that the killer might feel no need for stealth if he knew only Nell would hear him.

But the footsteps didn't turn onto the trail, and a minute later, Nell caught sight of Marion taking a morning walk.

"Good Lord, I've been spooked by Marion the librarian," Nell muttered softly.

Another figure emerged from the opposite direction, but this time Nell easily recognized the person as Kate Ryan, with her distinctive purple helmet and metallic gray bike.

As she watched them approach, Nell wondered if Kate and Marion knew each other. She'd never seen them together, never seen Marion on a bike or Kate in the library, but this was a small town. She found herself slipping into the role of observer, observing the two women. She also realized that their presence made the morning safer for her.

Kate slowed her bike, then stopped, just as she reached Marion.

Nell couldn't hear what they were saying, but she could read the body language—Marion resting her hand in a friendly way on Kate's handlebars, Kate swinging off the bike, then taking her helmet off.

Clearly they were friends. Nell felt a brief stab of envy. No, not really envy, more a longing for a friend that she could meet up with in the morning after a lonely night.

She watched as Marion threw back her head in laughter, then pulled Kate into an embrace that turned into the kiss of a lover.

There was too much ease and intimacy—and passion—for it to be the first time they had kissed.

Nell backed away from the edge of the platform. She didn't think they could see her, but she wanted to be sure they didn't. She could still glimpse the women through the tree branches; turning her back now wouldn't change what she knew. Nell was curious to learn what they did next, and practical enough to want to make sure that "next" wasn't heading for the privacy of the observation deck.

She wondered at her surprise, trying to gauge whether it was shock that these two women she wanted to be friends with were involved, or if it was the fact that she'd again completely missed one of Pelican Bay's secrets.

Kate and Marion broke their kiss, but they remained in each other's arms for a few moments longer.

This time Nell felt a deeper stab of longing, seeing the easy intimacy of their touching, their quietly talking to each other. She suddenly was lonely and cold, hidden on the platform, staring again into the empty place in her life where there used to be love and a person to hold.

Kate and Marion slipped out of their embrace. Kate joined Marion on her walk, one arm still around her, the other guiding her bike. They stopped briefly for Kate to secure her helmet to the bike's rack, then continued on, arm in arm.

Nell watched them until they disappeared around the far turn in the road. She knew Kate and Marion wouldn't have been so free and open with each other if they suspected they were being observed, but Nell felt no guilt about it. She would tell no one of their secret, as clearly they intended to be discreet. Given the number of times that Nell went to both the library and the bike shop, she would have seen them together at least a few times unless they were deliberately staying apart.

The reasons were obvious. Beyond the prying eyes and gossip of a small town, Nell had seen Mrs. Nash, Marion's mother, at enough social gatherings to know she was a very conservative, even rigid, woman. That alone would keep Marion silent; throw in Mrs. Nash's heart condition and "nerves" and it seemed impossible that Marion could ever tell her mother who she was and who she loved. Her mother had been vocal in her disapproval of the changing laws.

How sad, Nell thought, to find love—and even in their brief pantomime, she had little doubt that there was real intimacy and affection between Kate and Marion—and have to hide it so deeply away. The liberal ways of New York, or even New Orleans, had barely touched this small Mississippi town.

As she climbed down from the deck, she probed at her reactions. Part of her felt stupid and unobservant. I've been living in this small town so long, I'm starting to see the world through small town eyes, she thought. Two intelligent women, in their thirties, unmarried, and it had never occurred to her that they might be lesbian. Like no one gay is any closer than New Orleans. She was relieved to note that she didn't feel any qualms about leaving her son with Kate. Or even Lizzie, for that matter.

No, her surprise was either that Kate and Marion hide their secret so well, played their roles so perfectly, that even she, the woman who liked to know secrets, hadn't come close to guessing it. Or, more likely, that the clues were there, and she should have had enough of an inkling to not have been so caught out by it.

Nell got back on her bike and pedaled out of the park.

From hidden love affairs to murders, Pelican Bay was changing—from what seemed to be a straightforward small town to a labyrinth of lies and secrets, love as well as hate hidden under layers of deception.

SEVEN

HOME WAS STILL QUIET, bereft of children. Neither of them would be back until the afternoon, so after a quick shower and a change into still-comfortable but more professional clothes, Nell headed to the office.

There was always stuff to do at the paper. She usually had about five or so letters on her desk from people listing the reasons that they should take over as the film reviewer. One of the current ones offered to cover the art films in New Orleans and Atlanta. All he needed was his expenses—hotel, food, transportation, and ticket prices—covered.

One of the benefits to Stanley, the present film reviewer, was that he did it on his own time and with his own money. He was also, as he said, "just a guy that likes movies," and his reviews paid attention to the things that Pelican Bay readers were interested in: was it a good time and could you bring the kids?

Four of the five would get the polite rejection letter, including Mr. All Expenses Paid. One had possibilities; it was from a retired film professor. She and her husband had just moved to the area, and she was offering to do a few pieces on films for "the fame of seeing my name in print." She enclosed several clippings, and they indicated that she might be a good counterpart to Stanley. She had a subtly feminist viewpoint, something Nell was always trying to sneak in, and a breezy, unpretentious writing style, something Nell was beginning to think was rarer than … pelican's teeth. The professor wouldn't get the form letter, which meant that Nell had to write an un-form letter.

Then she had to edit Ina Claire's cooking column.

Ina managed the classified section, with a style that was a cross between a fifth grade teacher and a pit bull. Sometimes Nell suspected that people took out ads because Ina tapped into that primal fear that they would flunk geography if they didn't. Ina wasn't above suggesting classifieds. "Now, Miz Adams, I hear you're moving to Hawaii, and a garage sale in the classifieds always does a brisk business." Ina also never met a Past Due that she wouldn't call again, often to sell another ad as well as to collect payment. "Now if you use that language with me, young man, I will have to pray for your immortal soul this Sunday" was as flustered as she ever got.

The trade-off for having a little old lady Machiavelli keeping the classified profits up was the cooking column.

Ina Claire could cook, but she couldn't write. Fortunately, she either never noticed how extensively Nell rewrote her or was savvy enough to know that her "Soup is a liquid food that can be cooked even when it's hot or cold out" was improved when Nell changed it to "Soup is a versatile dish, as appropriate in the summer as in the winter."

The real problem with Ina's columns was that she belonged to the "a dash," "a smidgen," "just enough" school of cooking. So Nell's Herculean task was to transform those into useful measurements.

Nell had become fairly fluent in Ina-speak, but she still had to gather the sets of measuring spoons and cups she kept in a desk drawer and make a trek to Ina's desk before she actually ran the column. "Now is this"—showing the ½ teaspoon—"or this"—the ⅓—"what you mean by a dollop?" was part of the editing process.

Nell had finished rewriting the text and was in the midst of roughing in the measurements when she heard footsteps in the outer office.

Both she and Thom, and Thom's father before him, had always left the office open when someone was there. "Sometimes it's a bother, but sometimes a story walks in," Thom had quoted his father.

Nell was suddenly aware that she was alone in the building and that there was little traffic in this secular part of town on a weekend morning.

"Jacko?" she called out loudly, trying to keep the mounting fear from her voice. She stood up as if ready to run.

Suddenly Police Chief Shaun stood in her doorway.

Without even thinking, Nell grabbed a letter opener, as if it could be a weapon against this tall man and his gun.

"Nell? Did I scare you?" the chief asked.

Nell glanced from him to the useless letter opener. She quickly dropped it, feeling silly at her overreaction. "I'm sorry," she fumbled. "I guess I wasn't expecting anyone…"

"I didn't mean to frighten you. I saw your car in the parking lot and that the door was open."

"I know. It's usually not a problem. It's just … that phone call in the middle of the night … and finding Rayburn's body … has me on edge."

"I can understand. That's actually what I came to talk to you about. May I come in?"

He was, Nell realized, still standing in the doorway, and she was barricaded behind the desk, ready to run one way or the other.

"Yes, please, have a seat," she said, letting herself relax into hers. She made a point of putting the letter opener into a drawer. She couldn't be much safer than with the chief of police and his big gun between her and the door.

"What can I do for you?" she continued as he sat down. Ask the first question, control the interview. Nell was amused at how quickly her reporter's instincts replaced the fear.

"I'm just curious about why you called the sheriff's office instead of the police station about that phone call. I thought that you and I had a better relationship than you and Sheriff Hickson."

"I called the police station first," Nell replied.

"You did?" He seemed both surprised at her answer and relieved that his rival hadn't been her first choice. "There was no record of that call in the evening's log."

"I'm not surprised. The officer that I spoke to didn't take it very seriously."

"He still should have logged it."

"And leave proof that I did call and that he took down no information and didn't ask a single question?"

A hard and distant look came into Chief Shaun's eyes, as if reconciling himself to the idea that his men would not only disobey him and flaunt the rules, but be nefarious enough to deliberately cover their tracks. "Who took the call?"

"Boyce Jenkins." From the look in Chief Shaun's eyes, Nell knew that Jenkins was going to pay for pawning her off to the sheriff.

"How did he handle it? Can you give me details?"

"Offhandedly, like it couldn't be important." Nell stopped at that, wondering if it would do any good to bring up the sexual angle.

She didn't know the chief well enough to know whether he would give it a "boys will be boys" shrug or not.

"So, he sort of blew it off and hung up on you?"

"Does it really matter?"

"Yes, it does. That phone call was important, and we let it slip away. I don't ever want that to happen again. You're a strong, intelligent woman and you know your way around and it mattered enough to you that you went ahead and called the sheriff's office." He fixed her with an intent, earnest look and Nell began to understand why so many women found him attractive.

Flattery is a useful interview technique, she reminded herself, but she didn't like him less because he'd called her strong and intelligent. "He seemed more interested in flirting than getting any information about the call."

"Flirting? How?"

"Tone. A lazy drawl. Nothing really damning I can quote him on. He did make a comment about lots of lonely women calling him in the middle of the night. When I mentioned that the caller had said 'in the woods,' he cut in and suggested we take a 'moonlit walk in the woods.'"

"And then what did he say?"

"That's when I gave up and said I'd call back in the morning."

"So, to sum up, Jenkins didn't think there was any substance to your complaint, used it as an excuse to play macho hunk, and so alienated you that you felt you had to end the call?"

"That sums it up from my end, Chief Shaun." More than his earlier compliments, Nell appreciated that he seemed to be taking the matter with the seriousness that she felt it deserved.

"Hey, that chief stuff is just when I want to impress people. Why don't you call me Doug?"

"Okay, Doug. Thanks for looking into this."

"I wish you'd come to me about it. I take it seriously when my men don't do their jobs."

"I was afraid that you'd dismiss it as 'boys will be boys' and any complaints as some feminist reaction."

"Naw, that's Sheriff Hickson. In my town, the boys better be police officers first. They forget that, then maybe they need to be working at the casinos in Biloxi."

"Is the sheriff cooperating with you on the case?" Nell had her problem solved; now it was time to get in a few moments of reporting.

"I suppose he is. By the time his deputies finished tromping around in the woods, anything resembling forensic evidence was gone. He doesn't like the idea that young boys can be murdered in his part of the world, so he's still touting his theory that maybe Rayburn tripped and fell into the well and that phone call to you was just a bizarre coincidence—that's his theory, not mine," he said in response to the clear look of disbelief on Nell's face. "Or that some sicko chanced on the body and made the phone call to get his jollies off."

"The first would be a hell of a coincidence. The second, highly unlikely, although I guess we can't rule it out entirely."

"Or that maybe you just made up the phone call as a female attention-getting device—"

"And somehow knew about the body," Nell interjected angrily.

"Pretty soon, he'll claim you planted the body there just to be able to sell a few papers."

"That's beyond ridiculous."

"I know. I'll do my best to find the real murderer before the sheriff arrests you," he said with a boyish grin.

"That would be most kind of you."

Doug Shaun took a pen off her desk, then pulled a business card out of his chest pocket. As he wrote, he said, "Home, cell phone, direct work line. If anything else happens, call me. Call me first, if you want to."

Nell took the card. "Thanks. I hope I never have to use it."

The chief stood up to go. "Me, too. Unless it's something like the speckled trout are biting right now." With that, he was gone.

He can move very quietly for a big man, Nell noted. Then she turned her attention to Ina's measurements, his card on her desk as protection.

EIGHT

INA WAS AS REWRITTEN as she was going to get and the rejection letters to the erstwhile film critics were signed, sealed, and awaiting delivery. The stack of press releases on her desk had been read through and put into their usual three piles: newsworthy or charitable enough to get in; barely disguised advertisement from people who regularly advertised in the Crier; and barely disguised advertisements from those who did not. Like his father, Thom had subscribed to the notion that those who regularly paid to advertise were more likely to get the free ones than those who didn't. Nell saw nothing to argue with, and given that there had to be some system of yea or nay, this was as good as any.

She glanced at her watch. Time to turn from editor princess (sans glass slippers and waiting prince, she had to admit) into mother pumpkin.

Nell tidied her desk—set the example for the cub reporters, she told herself, but in reality, arriving in the morning to a desk strewn with expectant papers wasn't how she liked to start her day. Also, the process of neatening forced her to set priorities, put the most important at the top of the pile. She never knew where her day would end, but she knew where it would start. Having her first five minutes decided was better than none. With the desk as neat as she cared to make it, Nell closed the office as usual, fumbling with the heavy key for the outer door.

As she was walking to her car, she was surprised to hear an angry male voice from across the square call out "Goddamn bitch!"

Nell turned toward the sound. She was even more surprised to realize that it was directed at her.

"You goddamn bitch, you happy now?" Boyce Jenkins's face was a mottled, angry red, all the lazy insolence in his eyes replaced by a hardened fury.

The offices of the Crier were catty-corner on the town square from the complex that contained the city hall and police station, and directly across from the library. The square was an impressive green space—sometimes an annoying amount of space, if Nell had to repeatedly cross it several times a day.

Boyce's angry stride was rapidly covering the distance.

Thom had actually been punched once, when he'd asked the wrong person the wrong question. He wasn't a weak man or one given to much complaining, but he'd been hurt then, and he wasn't afraid to admit it.

Nell quickly dismissed trying to run away. Boyce would easily catch her before she got to her car, and there was nowhere else that offered any shelter. Some visceral part of her didn't want to turn her back on him, even to attempt escape. And he wanted her fear, wanted to see her afraid. That was the one thing Nell was determined not to give him.

"You fucking bitch! You got me fired!"

Nell made no reply. His actions had caused his firing, but pointing that out was hardly a way to defuse the situation.

"Hey, Boyce, cool it," another voice called out.

"Shut the fuck up, you asshole," Boyce yelled back.

He was now close enough for Nell to see the spittle emphasizing the anger of his words.

He's beyond control, Nell realized, tensing for the blows she was now felt sure would come—unless some part of the now ex-cop could understand, in the next twenty yards, that an assault and battery arrest was going to inflict much more damage to his life than being fired ever could.

Stay calm, Nell told herself. Not reacting—at least visibly—as he expected, with fear, might jar him into rethinking. Or at least thinking.

Stay calm and kick hard.

After he had been attacked, Thom had taken self-defense classes. He'd insisted that Nell learn at least a few of the basics. The eyes, the nose, the solar plexus, the groin, and the knees, Nell silently recited. Those were the vulnerable parts. She curled her hands into fists, silently cursing her untrimmed nails as they dug into the flesh of her palms. She knew it was a slim hope that she could strike a blow that would stop him.

I can't just let him pummel me, she thought as she felt the bile of fear roil in her stomach. Her fists, weakened by her nails gouging her palms, seemed like such puny weapons against this raging man. I can't just stand here and let him batter me, she repeated to herself.

"I'm a widow with two children," she said aloud, in what she hoped was a steady and calming voice.

"Shoulda thought of that before you fucked with me," he spat back, his stride not slowing.

At that, Nell felt a surge of anger override her fear. Boyce Jenkins was a bully without a scrap of decency in his soul, strong enough to beat up women when he though no one was looking. Nell tightened her fists, taking more anger from the cut of her nails.

Suddenly the jarring crack of a gunshot cut into their violent dance.

Then another.

"One more step and you're a dead man, Boyce," the voice of Chief Shaun boomed across the square.

Boyce was too defiant not to take a step, but it was a faltering one, and then he stopped. "Fucking go ahead and shoot me, you asshole," he shouted, but he didn't turn from Nell—still staring at her, willing his hatred to cover the remaining few feet between them, daring Doug Shaun to shoot him in the back. "Cunt," he hissed softly at Nell, quiet enough that only she heard.

A bully and a coward, Nell flashed mentally. She had enough control not to say or do anything that would goad him to cross the last few feet to her. The chief would stop him, but even one punch— or a stray bullet—might do damage beyond repair.

Her attention was so focused on Boyce that she only saw Chief Shaun when he ran directly into her line of sight.

"What the hell do you think you're pulling, Boyce?" he demanded, his gun still in his hand.

"Man's gotta protect himself," Boyce retorted, his voice regaining some of its practiced insolence.

"By beating up women?" the chief spat at him.

"Yeah, you're real tough with that gun in your hand."

"You think you're man enough to take me? You're just a little boy." Chief Shaun clicked on the gun's safety, then tossed it into the grass behind him.

"You're goin' to find out how fuckin' old you are," Boyce Jenkins snarled, finally turning from Nell to face Chief Shaun.

The grass was the same green, the familiar shapes of the town square still held, but Nell suddenly felt like she was in a foreign land. They wanted the fight, wanted the violence. She could do nothing but stand and watch as these two men willingly chose something that she would have done anything to avoid.

For a tense minute they circled, slowly shifting their positions, but keeping the distance between them.

Doug Shaun broke the silence first. "Come on, little boy. Not quite as tough when you get down to it, huh?"

"I don't see you rushin' in, old man," Boyce threw back.

"Fools rush in, thought I'd leave that to you."

It was easy to see what Chief Shaun was doing, Nell thought—provoke Jenkins into losing control. The young man had already proven that he had little of it.

"Fuck you, asshole," was all Boyce could sputter in reply.

Suddenly he lunged at the chief. Just as suddenly, a blur of leg and Boyce's gasp as he rocked back with his hands covering his crotch told Nell that he'd been kicked close to the groin.

She was reminded of a cat toying with its prey. Part of her was disgusted with the spectacle, but another primal part wanted Boyce beaten and defeated.

Boyce took a deep breath and stood up straight. "You got lucky, old man. Your luck's runnin' out." But he didn't lunge, instead took up the earlier slow shifting of positions.

As they continued circling, Nell couldn't help but think, "Not with a bang but a whimper." She could almost see them locked in this circling, neither willing to back down but both wanting to avoid real hurt and pain.

Yet Boyce had been kicked, and he wasn't going to leave until he had kicked back.

He feinted to the left, then quickly pivoted back to the right. He was young and he had a young man's speed and reflexes. He didn't have the chief's experience, but he did know how to fight; his moves were those of someone who'd trained in boxing and karate.

Chief Shaun spun away and was able to keep Boyce's foot from landing in his groin, but he still took a solid kick to the muscle of his thigh. Nell saw the hardening of anger and pain in the chief's eyes.

Boyce kicked again, landing a second blow in the same place.

It's not like the movies, Nell thought as she watched them. The real pounding of flesh on flesh was a sickening hollow thud, not the painless and practiced slap of stunt men.

She backed away from the raw violence of it. That, and the fear that if Chief Shaun lost, Boyce would come for her.

The chief staggered as Boyce landed a third kick. Taking advantage, Boyce moved in for a punch, but he was overconfident and threw a sloppy blow that Chief Shaun blocked. The chief held Boyce's wrist and there was a thud as the chief's elbow connected with Boyce's jaw.

Then the two men were flailing at each other, in close range. In the blurred barrage of fists and arms, Nell heard rather than saw the pounding of flesh that told her some of the blows were hitting their mark. Then there was a sharp crack and blood blossomed on Boyce Jenkins's face.

This time, the chief gave Boyce no space for recovery. He hammered Boyce's chest, going for the solar plexus.

The younger man staggered back as one of the punches found its target.

The chief hit him again.

"Stop it!" Nell suddenly found herself yelling, her voice—and decency—unleashed now that she knew that Boyce was no longer a threat to her. She'd wanted Doug Shaun to win, to make Boyce pay for what he'd done. Frontier justice, Nell admitted; but with the outcome no longer in doubt, her unease at the savagery of the fight took over. "Enough! Stop!"

Her voice seemed to unleash a cacophony in the square. But the reality was that Sheriff Hickson and his men had just arrived.

Although it had seemed to Nell when she'd entered this foreign land of violence that the outside world had stopped, of course, it hadn't. Someone had called the sheriff, since it didn't appear that calling the police was an option.

"What in thunderation is going on here?" Sheriff Hickson bellowed.

Boyce staggered and fell to his knees, the blood from his battered nose soaking his chest.

Chief Shaun rubbed his repeatedly kicked thigh but didn't turn to face the sheriff. He instead watched Boyce, as if savoring his victory.

"A fistfight on the town square," the sheriff continued. "What in hell is going on?" he demanded again.

But Chief Shaun had no interest in answering Sheriff Hickson's questions.

"Someone take this boy to his doctor," the chief said. "To his pediatrician. If you're good, maybe they'll give you a lollipop."

Boyce tried to reply, but the dripping blood choked him, the red liquid bubbling on his strangled words.

The sheriff came face to face with Doug Shaun. "I think I need an explanation."

"This isn't your jurisdiction," the chief answered, then continued. "Boyce Jenkins was threatening Nell. I had to stop him."

Hickson turned to Nell. "Threatening you? What the hell for?"

"I made a complaint and he was fired," Nell answered.

"A complaint about Boyce?" the sheriff asked.

Several men were lifting Boyce to his feet, leading him away, although whether they were his friends or doing it in response to the chief's order was hard to tell.

"He was being...sexually harassing," Nell answered reluctantly.

"Sexually harassing?" the sheriff echoed. "To you?"

The sheriff's obvious incredulity that a young man like Boyce could have any sexual interest in a middle-aged woman like her rankled Nell, but before she could reply, the sheriff continued. "You fired him 'cause he asked you out on a date?"

"She didn't fire him, I did," Chief Shaun cut in. "It had nothing to do with dating, but behaving in an entirely inappropriate manner while on duty. Slacking off, not responding appropriately in police matters."

"So why'd he have to get the crap beat out of him for that?" the sheriff demanded.

Nell suspected that Hickson's questions arose as much from a desire to needle Chief Shaun as from any desire to know what had really happened.

"Boyce had just been told to clear out of the police station and he evidently stalked out the door, saw Nell, and went after her," the chief explained, not too patiently.

"So how'd he get the bloody nose?"

"I had no choice but to physically restrain him."

"That true?" the sheriff demanded of Nell.

"Boyce Jenkins did threaten me and I feel that if Chief Shaun hadn't intervened, Boyce would have physically assaulted me," Nell said carefully. Doug Shaun had had a choice, she knew, but she wasn't going to directly contradict him in front of the sheriff. Whatever unease she might feel, the end result was that she wasn't the one with the blood running down her face.

"Intervened, huh? With a fistfight in the town square?" The sheriff snorted. "I guess all your newfangled police training didn't teach you how to stop a fight without turning it into a Clint Eastwood movie."

"I did what I had to do," Chief Shaun said shortly.

"This gonna be front-page news?" the sheriff demanded of Nell.

"I wasn't here as a reporter," she rejoined coldly. Sheriff Hickson's harsh questioning was just an older man's version of the macho posturing she'd already had enough of for one day.

"Fine example for the folks of Pelican Bay," the sheriff muttered under his breath. Then, a little more distinctly, "Well, guess I'll go tell Wendell that his boy's kind of bruised up and needs to be taken home."

"That's not necessary," Chief Shaun said. "As soon as he's done at the doctor's he's going to jail."

"To jail? What on earth for?" Hickson bellowed.

"Nell's pressing charges," Shaun calmly said.

"You are? What in hell for? Pardon my language, Miz McGraw, but the boy's been fired today, beaten up, and you want to arrest him on top of that?"

Nell stared at the sheriff for a moment, without replying, as she made the connections. Boyce Jenkins was the son of Wendell Jenkins. Wendell owned a series of car dealerships in the area. He was a friend of and frequent campaign contributor to Sheriff Hickson. As much as she didn't like Chief Shaun's easy assumption that she would follow his lead, she had no tolerance for the sheriff's "good ole boy" brand of justice.

"I thought that assault and attempted battery were crimes. Or are you suggesting that I set the 'fine example' of leniency for the sons of campaign contributors?"

The sheriff glared at her, then said, "There's justice and there's vengeance, little lady. You might want to learn the difference." He spun about and walked away.

"Save your lecture on vengeance for those who truly need it," Nell yelled after him, suddenly tired of being controlled and polite when it seemed like no one else was.

"He's a jerk, don't worry about him," the chief said.

"I'm not your patsy," Nell snapped at him. "I went along with you only because I happen to agree that Boyce Jenkins shouldn't escape the consequences of his actions. While I appreciate being saved from a beating, the fight between the two of you had nothing to do with that."

"Hey, calm down, I'm on your side. That fight was about respect. Jenkins made quite a few comments about my competence as the police chief, and as a man, on his way out the door. I told him to stay away from you. So, first thing he does is directly disobey me. I can't be the chief of police if my men can disobey me. Sometimes I've got to teach them that lesson in the only way they'll understand."

Nell looked at Doug Shaun for a moment, wondering if what he said made sense or if it was just his rationalization for what he'd done. The blaze of anger gone, she felt enervated and unable to think about more than going home. Getting the kids and going home, she reminded herself.

At the thought of her children, a deeper fury flashed through her. A child had been murdered, perhaps two, and these men were concerned about their macho posturing. But that anger, too, disappeared into her enveloping weariness.

"I can't argue with the outcome," she admitted, chagrined to notice that her words were slightly slurred, she was so tired and addled. "I've got to get my kids."

With that as her farewell, she turned from Doug Shaun and continued the trek to her car. It wasn't far, only a block to the lot hidden away from the pristine lines of the green square, but now it seemed like such a distance. It should, Nell thought; I've traveled to so many emotional places since I left the office of the Crier. She fumbled for her car keys.

"Nell, are you okay?"

She felt a hand on her shoulder and turned to see Marion beside her. They had arranged to meet for coffee today—Nell had lost that in the tumult of what had just happened. A tumble of emotions washed through her—fear that she hadn't noticed Marion approaching, then anger at the fear and how necessary it had become, and finally relief that it was Marion, a friend, with her hand on Nell's shoulder.

"I didn't get beaten up," was all she replied.

"No, but you came awfully close."

"I was scared," Nell softly admitted. It was only now that she could comprehend the scope of her fear. Boyce Jenkins had come close to hurting her, even killing her. She felt her eyes tear up. I'm not going to cry, Nell willed herself. One tear still escaped. She hurriedly bushed it away.

"It's okay to cry," Marion said, her hand still on Nell's arm.

"Not when you're a mother and the editor-in-chief," Nell said, wiping away another tear.

"No kids or newspaper staff around."

Nell wiped away a few more tears. "Thanks, Marion. It's good to be with someone who doesn't think that just because I didn't get the crap beaten out of me everything is okay."

"Let me drive you home," Marion offered as Nell opened her car door.

"I'm okay."

"You just said that you're not," Marion replied matter-of-factly. "Let me drive."

"How will you get your car?" Nell asked as she fished the car keys out of her purse.

"My brother Rob is in town. I can call him to come get me."

Or Kate could do it, Nell thought but didn't say. She wasn't supposed to know that, and now didn't seem like the time to blurt it out. She handed her keys to Marion. "Thanks."

Marion took the keys and took over. She opened the passenger door for Nell.

As the librarian slid into the driver's seat, Nell said, "My kids. Where are my kids?" She was thinking aloud. "Lizzie's at a slumber party and went there with her best friend Leslie, who will bring her home. Josh's on a camping trip and he'll call if he needs to be picked up ... I hope he hasn't called yet." She glanced at her watch. Only fifteen minutes had passed since she'd walked out of the Crier's office. Can so much really happen in fifteen minutes? she wondered. She answered her question, an answer she now knew too well—it had taken only a few seconds for Thom to die.

Other than mentioning directions, they talked little on the way home. Nell let some of the pent-up tears out and Marion was sensible enough to just let her cry.

No children were home, and there was no blinking light on the answering machine indicating that Nell had been a neglectful mother.

"What works for you?" Marion asked. "Coffee, tea, something stronger?"

"I have a decent bottle of pinot noir."

"Sit, let me do this," Marion told her. She took the wine bottle Nell had just taken out of a cabinet, then pointed at a chair at the kitchen table. "Just tell me where your corkscrew and glasses are."

Nell felt a surge of relief at being taken care of. In the past few months she'd had so many burdens of care—Josh, Lizzie, Thom's mother, the staff of the Crier—that even these minor moments of being cared for had been denied her. She and Thom had traded care of each other, and he was gone.

Marion sat a glass of wine in front of Nell, then joined her at the table.

Nell raised her glass and said, "To … friendship."

"Cheers," Marion replied, touching her glass to Nell's.

They didn't talk about what had happened. Nell didn't feel able to yet, it was still too raw and emotional for her. She tried not to think aloud; she preferred to have time for reflection and to know that she'd examined not just the immediate emotions and ideas, but also the underlying ones, the consequences beyond the consequences. She knew that she would, at some point, like to talk things over with Marion, who'd lived in Pelican Bay all her life, to see if the librarian's reaction was similar to her own at Chief Shaun's rational for the fight.

Instead they talked of books and covered the ground that new friends cover.

Josh and Lizzie both came home after a while and seemed to find nothing odd about Marion visiting. It was just grown-up stuff and couldn't compete with Lizzie wanting to get on the computer to email the girls she'd just spent the night with or Josh wanting to compare the plant specimens he'd gathered with the books in his room. Nell gave his handful of leaves a quick glance to assure that her budding scientist wasn't going to learn how to identify poison ivy the hard way. She was somewhat relieved that neither of her children sensed that anything more than Mom and a friend having a chat in the kitchen was going on. Even the wine bottle didn't give them away.

Marion even ended up staying for dinner, helping in the kitchen and allowing Lizzie to escape dreaded dish duty.

As she watched Marion scrape plates, Nell wondered if she was stealing her away from an evening with Kate, but it wasn't a question she could ask yet.

She resolved to make a point in the near future to get together with Marion at a time and place where they could talk—she could ask to reschedule the coffee date and do it then. Nell wanted Marion to know that she didn't have to hide her true relationship with Kate from her. She suspected that the hidden life was responsible for some of Marion's earlier reluctance in accepting the coffee date.

Her new friend left a little after nine. Nell was strict about the ten o'clock bedtime, telling Josh and Lizzie that it was a school night. But her real reason was that, with Marion gone, the tiredness of the day hit her and she needed to go to bed, even if her children didn't. As she lay down, she heard rustlings and murmurs from the living room, clues enough to tell her that Lizzie had sneaked back to the computer. Nell was too tired to get up and again send her daughter to bed, but decided that Lizzie would get no snooze button mercy in the morning.

NINE

MONDAY MORNING AT THE office usually started with a story conference. Since the Crier was a weekly paper, published on Fridays, at times Nell missed the adrenaline and "do or die, write now" pace of a daily. But this wasn't one of those times. The last thing she wanted to do was try to write—or edit—a story about yesterday's events on the town square. She had a myriad of choices and none was satisfactory. She could just ignore it, but her journalistic standards quelled that; a just-fired police officer threatening the editor of the paper and then having a fistfight with the chief of police, was, by Pelican Bay standards, a major story. Even in a major city it would be a big story—a fistfight between two police officers in Jackson Square would certainly make the front page of the New Orleans paper, she thought. Nell didn't want to write it herself, though, partly because she didn't want to relive it enough to write about it. Also, as a participant, however unwillingly, she knew she had no journalistic objectivity.

If Jacko weren't already covering the murder of Rayburn Gautier, she could give the story to him and have done with it. But to give him two big stories in a row might be such a blatant act of favoritism that Carrie would retreat permanently into her passive-aggressive persona. In their discussion right now, she was going into great detail about the burden that covering the city council meeting and the school board meeting would cause her.

"I just don't know the names of the councilmen like Jacko does…" she was complaining.

"I can give you a seating chart. They always take the same seats," Jacko offered.

"They'd probably switch just to mess me up."

If she wanted to attempt to be fair and equal, Nell knew, she should give the fistfight story to Carrie, but she could not bring herself to play witness to the young woman's fumbling interview questions. Nor did she trust herself not to get revenge when editing.

"You know how chauvinistic those councilmen are," Carrie continued. "They accept you and cooperate with you, Jacko, because you're a man, but with me it's hey, little lady, come sit on my lap…"

Nell sighed quietly. What Carrie was saying was true—the city council weren't men who could manage even fifth place in the most tepid feminist award—but Nell could find little sisterly solidarity with Carrie using their sexism as a way to avoid an assignment that she didn't want.

Dolan, who as business manager got to skip these meetings, stuck his head in her office door and broke into Carrie's monologue. "Nell, there's someone here to see you. Says he can't wait."

Carrie pursed her lips, miffed at being cut off. When she first started working at the paper, Dolan had been polite; however, now he, like everyone else, had learned that waiting for a natural break in one of Carrie's "the world is unfair to me" diatribes could take a long time.

Nell recognized the man coming up behind Dolan. She'd never met him before, but had watched him more than enough times on his TV commercials: "Deals on Wheels! Feel like some red-hot deals on some red-hot wheels? Jenkins Automotive Superstore for real deals on the best wheels, an army of salesmen at your command"—with the camera showing a long line of not-so-Army-trained salesmen in uniform. "I order my men to give you the best deals," ended the ad, with a close-up of Wendell in a supremely braided and ribboned general's outfit. Why does my brain remember this crap, Nell wondered, annoyed at both knowing the jingle and seeing the man in her doorway.

Wendell Jenkins, Boyce Jenkins's father, wanted to see her.

"We'll continue this meeting later," she said.

"But—" Carrie started.

"Later," Nell instructed.

Jacko had already taken the hint and was out the door. Carrie followed him at her wounded pace.

"Won't you sit down, Mr. Jenkins?" Nell asked.

He expressed no surprise that she knew who he was. Nell was somewhat relieved to notice that Jacko and Dolan were hanging out only as far away as politeness dictated, clearly visible to both her and Jenkins through the glass in her office door.

Wendell Jenkins sat down heavily, a big man like his son, bigger with the weight of good living and his years.

"Mr. Jenkins," Nell said, "you didn't have to come to apologize for your son. He's an adult and he makes his own choices." She had no illusions that Wendell Jenkins had any thought of apologizing for his son—she expected he was there to attempt to browbeat her into dropping the charges. Nell had no intention of making it easy for him.

Jenkins just stared at her for a moment. He obviously had a prepared speech and Nell had just forced him to abandon it.

"Well, Mrs. McGraw, you're right, he does make his choices." The frenetic sales pitch voice of the TV was replaced by the drawl of a man accustomed to being listened to. "But he's a young boy. Seems a shame to ruin his life over one stupid, hot-headed moment."

"That 'hot-headed' moment nearly ended with me being physically assaulted, Mr. Jenkins," she replied. "The only reason your son didn't batter me was because someone bigger and stronger intervened."

"But nothing happened. He didn't hit you. Seems to me the outcome is what should count."

"Your son didn't choose that outcome."

"He wouldn't have really hurt you. He was just angry and wanted to scare you."

"Congratulate him, because he succeeded. He convinced me that I was about to be beaten and end up in the hospital. Or the morgue. I was scared that my children would be left motherless because of your son's hot-headed moment."

"Look, all that boy ever wanted to be was a policeman. He's lost that. Isn't that punishment enough?"

"Clearly, if his reaction to stress is to turn into a renegade bully, then he has no business in law enforcement."

"What do you want, Nell? A car? I'll give you one for exactly what it cost me. Not a penny in dealer markup."

Nell wasn't surprised that Wendell Jenkins wasn't really responding to what she was saying. But he was oblivious to the anger behind her words. He'd completely misread her stubbornness, thinking it a veiled request for a bribe.

"I don't need a car, Mr. Jenkins. Mine is in perfect working order and I can't see replacing it anytime soon."

"You want me to just give you a car for free?" He still thought he could bribe her, just at a higher cost than he wanted to pay.

"I want you to stop preventing your son from ever feeling the consequences of his actions. If he gets away with it this time, next time he may do more than just 'scare' someone. It's past time he learn that Daddy can't always cover for him."

This time, Jenkins understood what she meant. His face took on an angry purple-red hue. "You'll regret this, Nell McGraw."

"How? Are you threatening me the way your son did?"

"You're a hard-assed Yankee bitch, aren't you?" he hissed, the polite drawl gone.

"Good day, Mr. Jenkins."

"My son goes to jail, you'll wish you'd found it in your heart to be a little forgiving."

Nell motioned to Dolan and Jacko. Might as well give them a chance to be heroes, she thought. And, she had to admit, signal to Jenkins that she had some protection of her own.

He glanced over his shoulder at the two men now just outside the doorway. He stood and angrily pushed his chair back, then thrust his way past Jacko and Dolan, who did nothing to block his exit and needed no pushing to let him leave.

For a moment the three of them watched Jenkins's retreating back. Then Dolan said, "Guess when I buy the wife a new car, I'm going to need to head over to Biloxi to do it."

"Can we get him for bribery?" Jacko asked.

"I'm not a public official, I don't count," Nell replied.

"It's a tradition for *Pelican Bay Crier* editors," Dolan said. "They can't be bought and they drive old cars."

Jacko glanced from Dolan to Nell, still young enough not to be sure whether Dolan was just spinning a yarn.

These are my friends, Nell suddenly thought. No, not deep-unburden-your-soul friends, but good, kind dependable men. She'd been so lost in grief in recent month that they were just Dolan and Jacko, fixtures in the office she said hello and goodbye to. She'd walked through their small moments of kindness, the times when one or the other of them stayed late only because she did, talked to Josh or Lizzie while she was busy, left tuna salad sandwiches on her desk when she was working through lunch—they didn't ask, they just did it.

"Speaking of buying," Nell said, "why don't we head across the street to Sara's and let me buy you a cup of coffee? We can listen to Dolan create more stories about Crier editors."

"Great! I could use some coffee," Jacko said. Clearly breakfast wasn't an important part of his day.

Dolan smiled and nodded in agreement. Also, Nell felt, in approval. When Thom was alive, they'd often gone across the street for coffee, or out for the special Friday catfish dinner at TJ's or other "jaunts into the real world," as Thom had called them. Some of it was to discuss business, but most of the time it was just to be together. Since his death, Nell had come to the office, taken care of business, and gone home to her children. The unscheduled moments had been too threatening, and listening to jokes and banter, relaxing over coffee, had been beyond her.

So they hadn't gone out, and had gotten into the habit of not going out. This was the first time since Thom's death that Nell had suggested one of their "real world" ventures.

Dolan had been with the paper for almost twenty years, Nell reminded herself. He'd been hired by Thom's father. It was more a part of his life than of hers, and he'd patiently waited for her to do something as simple as suggest coffee.

She linked her arms in theirs. She and Dolan knew how big a change this was.

They were a happy trio in the coffee shop. Dolan told stories of times gone by, of holding flashlights on the typewriter Thom's father was pounding a story out on, a hurricane having taken away the power but, by golly, they had a paper to get out. Or the alligator in the town square, with Mr. McGraw determined to get a good picture of it and Mrs. McGraw trailing behind, just as determined that her husband wasn't going to get close enough to risk having a hand or foot nipped off.

For the moment, Nell could ignore all the threats in her life, from late-night phone calls to used car dealers.

TEN

At three thirty, Nell found herself at the school, listening to Lizzie explain that she was going over to Jennifer's house to practice flute together so Nell shouldn't have come by for her. Josh had gone with Joey to the Boy Scout meeting.

"I guess I just forgot about your practice with Jennifer today," Nell told her daughter, giving Lizzie an out in front of her friends but fooling neither of them that Nell's "forgetfulness" was the issue.

"I thought I told you..." Lizzie trailed off.

"No matter. When will you be home?"

"Well, they're having tacos tonight and I usually help cut things up..."

With a glance at Jennifer's mother to make sure that it really was okay for Lizzie to stay for dinner, Nell got to the point. "Okay, but if you're not walking through the door at nine, I want a phone call and you'd better be on your way home."

"Okay, Mom. Thanks." With that, Lizzie and Jennifer bounded off toward the car. Jennifer's mother gave Nell a wave and followed at a more adult pace.

Nell felt a sudden pang. She wanted to hold her daughter in this moment, when the worst that could happen was Mom saying no to dinner at Jennifer's, and a yes called forth a bounding exuberance.

As Nell headed back to her own car—not so old, she thought, remembering Dolan's comment. Yet given the number of miles she put on it, her opinion about years of use might be optimistic.

A sheriff's car was cruising through the school parking lot. Nell noticed it in passing—an occasional display of law enforcement was routine near the adjacent middle and high schools—but then the car stopped next to her.

Sheriff Hickson himself got out. "Miz McGraw," he said, as she somehow expected he would. "Can I talk to you for a bit?" He didn't wait for her assent, but continued. "I was just having a chat with my friend Wendell Jenkins. I got to tell you, Wendell's not a man to be crossed lightly."

"He does little advertising in the Crier, so he can't hurt me there. What else are you suggesting that he might do, Sheriff Hickson? I can't think of any legal way he can do anything to me," Nell retorted, only a thin patina of politeness in her tone.

"Miz McGraw, I just felt I needed to warn you that Wendell's buzzing worse than a hornet's nest a snake slithered into. He put a lot of his future into Boyce—he won't let it go easy."

"Are you threatening me, Sheriff?" Nell asked bluntly. "What kind of deal does Wendell give you on his cars to get you to be his bully boy?"

After the words were out of her mouth, she wondered at her temerity. This was a man with a gun and only the football team, on a far away practice field, was in sight.

But a look of surprise, not anger or calculation, came across the sheriff's face.

"Oh, no, ma'am, no, ma'am, you got this all wrong. Wendell didn't tell me to talk to you … and if he did, I'd tell him where to shove his car deals. Beggin' your pardon, Miz McGraw."

"So why are you here?" Nell demanded.

"Just to give you a warning. Let you know the score, so to speak."

"Sheriff, I didn't think that Wendell Jenkins left my office as a happy man this morning. Being a woman doesn't make me stupid or naïve."

"Miz McGraw, I'm not saying you're stupid." He didn't mention naïve, Nell noticed. "And Wendell and I may be friends, but he's got to obey the law just like anyone else."

"A friend who discounts cars to the sheriff's office."

"He don't give us straight wholesale. I figure, he makes a little money, we save a little money, and that's it."

"And that has nothing to do with why Wendell's good friend Clureman Hickson is trying to get me to drop charges against his son Boyce?"

The sheriff let out a sigh. "You and I might not quite agree, but I figure it's my job to keep the peace, make things run smooth. I just don't see how putting Boyce in jail is gonna do that."

"Letting a man who tried to assault me go free doesn't do much for keeping my peace."

"Now, Miz McGraw, I can see your point, but I know both Wendell and Boyce, and Wendell may be a hot-head, and Boyce a hotter head, but when they're cool, they're not a worry."

"So why are you warning me about Wendell Jenkins? Or does he take a few years to cool down?" Even if the sheriff believed he was talking to her purely on his own initiative, Nell suspected he might not be such a proactive mediator on behalf of someone who didn't have discount cars to sell.

"No, he'll cool down right quick unless his son goes to jail. You see, Boyce already got a small drug rap, so this is gonna hurt him more than just the first-time thing. And that marijuana thing was a while back, but still it'll hurt him. Wendell and I started out in the state troopers together, way long time back. Wendell got in a motorcycle wreck and bummed his leg, so he washed out. He always wanted a son to succeed where he didn't. Now that just won't happen, but it's one thing not to have your son make it as an officer of the law, a whole other thing for him to go to jail."

"So, he should get away with attempting assault?"

"I'm not saying get away with, I'm just saying not go to jail."

"Daddy gives him a talking to, cuts his allowance for a few weeks, is that what you're saying? And six months later he shows up as a deputy sheriff and you can get your cars at straight wholesale."

"No, ma'am, it won't work that way. I wouldn't have Boyce in my department. The deal I'm offering is—"

But Nell cut in to ask, "You wouldn't hire Boyce?"

The sheriff looked down at the ground, as if weighing how disloyal he wanted to be and if it would help appease Nell. "Wendell asked me a while back to take on Boyce. Had to tell him no. Too hot-headed. Bad judgment in smoking dope—did it at his high school prom, but he was over eighteen by then. Just should of known better. I gotta admit that he's used to having his daddy take care of things and that don't work when you're out patrolling."

Nell was surprised at this admission, admitting to herself that she'd labeled Sheriff Hickson as someone who would never put professionalism before patronage.

"Wendell got hot-headed about it, and I have to tell you I didn't get a campaign contribution that year," the sheriff continued. "But in the end, even he had to admit that his boy just wasn't ready. And, after this stunt, I'd think he knows there's no way Boyce's ever gonna be ready for a lawman's responsibility."

"What's going to happen to Boyce?"

"Time for him to move on out of Pelican Bay. If you agree to drop the charges, I'll have a little talk with the boy. It might do him some good to be somewhere where he isn't Wendell Jenkins's son, but just another guy."

"And if he doesn't want to leave? You can't force him to move."

"Well, I can't pack up his suitcase and drag him to the bus, but Wendell might only set him up somewhere else, and cut the purse strings if he hangs around here. Don't you think that would be better for everyone? Boyce stays out of jail and gets a chance to straighten himself up. You don't have to worry about him being here with nothing better to do than harass you, and you don't have to go through being grilled by his defense attorneys and the mess of a trial. All you gotta do is drop the charges."

"I'll think about it," was all the reply Nell gave. With that, she turned and walked away. Even if she did agree to the sheriff's proposal, she wasn't going to do it immediately. She was angry at being caught in a web of connections and favors and the good ole boy way of doing things. While she wasn't going to make it hard on herself, she wasn't going to make it easy on them, either.

A trial would be a difficult ordeal to put herself through. She had no doubts that Wendell Jenkins would buy the best lawyers for his son and they would do everything they could to discredit her and to make it look like she'd "asked for" what she got. But she found it hard to just hand Boyce over to the back-room school of justice—a slap on the wrist and a bit of daddy waving money to make him behave.

She would have to think long and hard about it.

ELEVEN

Tuesday morning brought back the interrupted story meeting.

"I'll write the story about Saturday's incident," Nell said. At least that decision was made.

"And what do I get, the dog catchers' meeting?" Carrie muttered, just loud enough to make sure she was heard.

"If you want to," Nell answered calmly, knowing it was time to throw Carrie a bone, a doggie bone in this case. "Why don't you do a story about the animal pound? Something more in-depth than our usual pet of the month story. Perhaps a day-in-the-life thing, like a day-in-the-life of an animal at the pound, or one of the workers. Or you could do a more hard-news angle, something about how unwanted strays affect a community—birds eaten by cats, the possibility of disease spread." Nell knew that she had to give Carrie concrete ideas but also let her have enough choices to find something she liked. With Jacko, she could just say, "Do a feature about the pound," and he would come up with something interesting. "If you get some good pictures, we can make it front page," she added to further mollify Carrie. Then she turned to Jacko. "What have you got on the killings of Rayburn Gautier and Tasha Jackson so far?"

"The usual behind-the-scenes backstabbing. The sheriff is claiming that the Gautier case is his, sort of 'finders keepers,' and Chief Shaun is arguing that his office should handle it. At the moment, the sheriff is taking things in—the evidence from the scene, interviewing the family—then handing it over to the chief. As you can imagine, neither of them is very happy. The sheriff is still holding to his theory that it could be some bizarre accident, with no relation between the two deaths."

"What does the chief think?"

"That it's murder and the sheriff is dragging his feet and possibly letting a murderer get away. Although he won't say that on the record. And maybe the two cases are related."

"Not surprising. Keep digging. We're going to be low-key about this story. Probably no more than a small blurb along the lines of 'still investigating a suspicious death.' I want to keep it small until something major breaks. But when it does, I want us to have the inside story."

"I'll do my best," Jacko said, his earnestness mixed with a bravado he could only have picked up from the movies. Nell knew this had to the first murder investigation he'd covered.

She intended to follow the story closely. It was one thing to send reporters to the pound and give them free rein—if that didn't work, you simply spiked the story. But Rayburn Gautier's death had to be covered, and she wanted it done right. She didn't want to leave Jacko out on his own, for the paper's sake as well as his sake, but make sure he was heading in the right direction, asking the questions that needed to be asked, walking the line between not involving the family at all and invading their privacy.

Also, Nell had to admit, the phone call in the night had made it personal. How she covered the murder was her only way to fight back. She didn't intend to give the killer the glory of seeing his deed splashed across the front page until there was something more to report than a dead boy and a dead girl but no leads in either case. He'd called her because he *wanted* that kind of coverage. She had no intention of giving it to him.

———

The paper lay by the door, as if waiting to be read, still folded neatly. It was last week's paper. As if he'd intended to read it but was just too busy. The small blurb happened to be facing up, so he could see it every time he entered or left.

It wasn't the mechanical act of killing that gave him pleasure; the hands around the throat, the quick blow to the head were only means to an end to him. It was the power reflected in the eyes of the victims when they realized that their life or death was his to choose. Not all of them understood that—too stupid, too young. From them he derived other satisfactions.

The next issue of the paper would have bold headlines heralding his act. Parents would lock their children up, the town council would meet, the police would step up patrols. Like a stone rippling along water, his act would have many repercussions. The killing was easy, but now he wanted death that would reach out and disrupt as many lives as possible. Kill the right person, and he could walk down the street and see the fear he inspired in the eyes of the passersby.

That was his challenge now—to not just kill, but to find a killing that would cause as many aftershocks as possible. He wanted more than just a death that people read about in the paper, but a murder that crept into their lives.

The first had been a mistake—no, not a mistake. It had gone as he planned, except for how long it had taken them to find the girl's body. He knew where it was, but it would have been a slip-up to have been the one to discover her body. He didn't make those kinds of mistakes.

Her death hadn't had the effect that he'd hoped for. The boy was another matter—a brutal murder in a small town that didn't even know what a barroom brawl was, let alone the deliberate killing of a child.

That kind of death would send out many ripples. He prided himself on not going the easy route, killing the most favored child of the most prominent citizen. Of course attention would be paid to that. No, he preferred to find that border line between the obscure and the easily noticeable. Which people seemed to be merely background, unimportant, until they were killed? In some ways, he was doing his victims a favor, making them more important in death than they ever had been in life. He did it well, giving them news and TV coverage that most people would never have in a lifetime.

He scored himself. The little blurb on the untouched paper was worth only one point. He routinely made the front page with banner headlines, which was worth fifty points. Extra things like the editorial page or special columns on how to protect yourself, or your child, got bonus points. He expected to easily score over a thousand points this time. It was very important to him that each murder have a higher score than the one before. He was a logical, scientific man and the numbers were his way of judging himself.

He wanted to be in next week's paper. Between the passing mention on the TV stations and the small story already in the paper, he had barely ten points. That was way too low. Two murders and only ten points. Not good enough, not good enough by far.

TWELVE

"Nell, can I talk to you for a moment?" Chief Shaun called to Nell as she was leaving the Crier building.

"Of course," she answered. "But it has to truly be a moment, otherwise my kids will be left standing on the street." A week ago, that would have been just banter, Nell realized, but now it was important her children not be left waiting with no one she trusted to watch over them.

"The sheriff and I had a chat, and we both agreed that holding Boyce wouldn't be the best thing. So we decided to let him go, with the deal that he would get out of town. I hope you understand."

Nell stared at him, reining in her fury. "I understand that you have let someone who attempted to assault me go and didn't bother to let me have any say on the matter."

"I know you're upset," he said with what she suspected was a supercilious calm.

"Don't patronize me," Nell snapped back. "Are you going to escort him out of town? And guarantee he doesn't come back? What's he doing right now? Packing? Or torching my house? Would you even know?"

Chief Shaun seemed taken aback by her vehemence. Maybe he's not much better than Sheriff Hickson, Nell thought, expecting the little woman to be glad that the men were taking care of things. And I have to get my kids and I don't want to stand here arguing with him.

"Don't worry, we'll make sure nothing happens."

"Fine," she said. "When he comes in the middle of the night, I'll dodge him until you can manage to get there to beat the crap out of him again." She turned away from the chief and strode toward her car.

"Nell, be realistic," he said, following her. "If you press charges, Wendell won't let it go, and it's going to be one of the bloodiest legal battles this town has seen in a long time."

"Yes, it might bring up the fact that the chief of police engaged in a needless fistfight, a bit of bloody macho posturing. Not a legal battle *you* want to fight, I'd guess."

"I explained to you why I had to do that."

"Rationalized, you mean. You didn't need that fight, you chose it."

"Wendell Jenkins isn't a man to take on lightly."

"I expected that kind of talk out of Sheriff Hickson. I didn't think you were so bought. Tell me, what kind of discount does he give the police on new cars?"

"Not fair. Remember, I'm appointed, not elected. And we don't get our cars from Jenkins. It's a bidding process done through the city comptroller. I'm trying to do you a favor, even protect you, although you seem not to want that. We'd get along much better if you weren't so suspicious of my motives."

"We'll also get along better if you don't make my decisions for me, Chief Shaun. I really do have to get my children. I presume there will be a police car outside my house until Boyce Jenkins is very far out of town."

"We do our best to serve, ma'am," he said with a mock salute.

Nell didn't reply, just unlocked her car and got in. There wasn't much to say. The boys had made their deal and she would have to live with it. I should have seen this coming, she chastised herself. If she pressed charges against Boyce, it was guaranteed that Boyce would press charges against Chief Shaun. No lawyer would let that one go. And of course Chief Shaun wasn't going to let his beating of Boyce Jenkins be paraded in front of a court room.

When Nell got to the school, Lizzie was where she was supposed to be, but Josh wasn't.

"Oh, he offered to ride Joey's bike to the shop to do some maintenance on it," Lizzie explained.

"You let him go off by himself?" Nell demanded.

"You didn't tell me to tie him down," Lizzie mumbled.

"I told you to wait with Josh and meet me here."

"What was I supposed to do? Throw myself in front of the bike?" Lizzie retorted.

"Did you remind him that I told him to wait here?" Nell could feel herself sliding into one of those irrational mother moments. She was angry at Shaun and Hickson and their deals, and now scared about Boyce Jenkins as well as the voice behind her late-night call. All these weights were turning what should have been a minor transgression by her child into a major problem. "Get in the car. Let's go find him," she snapped at Lizzie.

"You go. I'll just walk behind. I'm sure you'd like to leave me here anyway," Lizzie grumbled, picking the wrong time to turn into her truculent teenage self.

"Get in the car now! I haven't time for this."

"You never have time for anything," Lizzie flung back at her. But she got in the car, albeit the back seat, making her point while still complying with Nell.

I have to find Josh, Nell thought. Once I know he's okay, then I can deal with Lizzie. How do these things fall apart so quickly? she wondered. Is there any way I can be such a perfect mother to never provoke Lizzie? Little Nell Sunshine, all light and compassion and understanding, never angry or upset. Or worried about my son, who should have been waiting at school but wasn't. Nell glanced in her rearview mirror, looking for traffic, but also caught a glimpse of her daughter. Lizzie had retreated behind headphones, her eyes closed as if shutting out the world and particularly her mean mother.

Nell drove slowly down the streets she guessed were Josh's most likely route to the bike shop. Twice she saw a cyclist ahead of her, but her relief was quickly quashed when she realized that they were either too old or too female.

Could he have already made it to the shop? she thought as she passed the second non-Josh cyclist. Maybe he was taking a different route. Or he'd stopped at a friend's house along the way. She tried not to think of the other possibility, though it loomed with every empty block.

Finally, she was at the bike shop. Still no sign of her son.

"Wait here," Nell instructed Lizzie. Lizzie looked like she had no intention of doing anything else; still immersed in her music, she didn't respond.

Nell got out, scanning the street for any signs of Josh. Entering the bike shop, she first looked for her son. He wasn't there. Only then did she notice that Marion was standing at the counter talking to Kate.

"And I thought a bike might make sense for getting around town," Marion said, as if she were a customer talking to a sales person.

"Have you seen Josh?" Nell asked. She considered adding that she knew, they didn't need to pretend, but now was not the time.

"Josh?" Kate asked. "No, not this afternoon."

"He and Lizzie were supposed to meet me at school, but Lizzie said that Josh rode a friend's bike over here to have it looked at," Nell blurted out. "I didn't see him along the way and he should be here by now…"

"Maybe he went a different way," Marion said.

"Or he might have ended up walking the bike if it has problems," Kate added.

Nell found a small relief at finding another reasonable possibility for Josh's not being there yet.

"Maybe I should keep looking for him," she said. She had the feeling she was interrupting a private conversation and forcing Marion and Kate to put on their company act. Marion had moved away from the counter where she'd been when Nell first entered.

"Do you want us to help?" Kate asked.

"No, someone needs to be here in case Josh shows up. To tie him up if need be," Nell answered.

"I should be heading back to the library. I can look for him along the way," Marion said. "I'll think about a bike," she added to Kate, but Nell suspected it was for her benefit.

The door of the shop opened. Lizzie held it for Josh as he wheeled in the broken bike.

Lizzie said, "I told him you're not happy he took off without permission."

"I just rode Joey's bike straight here from school. He has only three speeds. I told you about it," he said, countering Lizzie's suggestion that he was in trouble.

Nell was more relieved than angry, but she knew the only reason Lizzie was standing holding the door was to see if her anger at Josh's leaving school was going to be appropriately expressed.

"You were supposed to meet me at school," Nell told her son, hoping she was putting enough sternness into her voice to placate Lizzie.

"I told Lizzie where I was going. I came right here. I'm okay. What's the big deal?" Josh asked.

"Not a big deal," Nell said, but she wondered, how do I explain to them why I'm so worried about Josh doing one of his usual bicycle stunts? How do I scare them just the right amount without adding terror to their lives? "Just please don't haul off when I expect you to be somewhere" was what she said.

"But I promised Joey that I'd get his bike taken care of," Josh protested.

"Fine, but it wouldn't have hurt you or Joey's bike to have waited for me. Then I could have followed you to the store instead of wondering where you were or if you were stuck somewhere with a broken bike."

"It's just a shifting problem. Nothing to stop me from riding it."

"Josh." It was time to use the no-arguments-mother voice. "The point isn't the bike. The point is don't needlessly worry me or place your sister in the position of explaining why you're doing something you shouldn't be doing. Understand?"

"Yes, ma'am." He looked down at the floor, not meeting Nell's eyes.

Now I've done it, Nell realized. Lectured him in front of Kate, his idol. Her mother karma was getting major negative points today.

It didn't help that no one said anything after the lecture until Marion broke the silence by saying goodbye and heading back to the library. She'd probably hoped for a few minutes with Kate, taking advantage of the afternoon lull to slip out of the library to a bike shop with no customers.

"So, what's the problem with the bike?" Kate asked.

Josh wheeled the bike past Nell, still not looking at her. "It's the derailleur. It's not shifting right. I think Joey hasn't been doing a good job of taking care of it."

Kate examined the bike. Lizzie had abandoned her door post, clamping her headphones back on and retreating to the car. Good thing children can't divorce their parents, Nell thought as Kate and Josh talked in incomprehensible bike jargon. She knew that Kate was defusing Josh's humiliation and she was both grateful and annoyed. Grateful that someone was undoing the damage she'd done, but feeling like she was being judged and found wanting.

They finally decided that Josh would leave the bike overnight, and tomorrow they would work on it during the bike maintenance class.

That settled, Kate had to attend to other customers, and Nell reclaimed her son.

Josh still didn't say anything as they went back to the car. Nell wasn't sure how to apologize without diluting her message. It was important that he not just take off—not with things the way they were—Boyce loose and possibly aiming to get in one last piece of revenge before leaving town, and the voice that had destroyed her night. That person had already killed one young boy.

The drive home was silent save for the escaped chings and hisses of Lizzie's headphones.

Take those off, don't destroy your hearing. Don't talk back. Don't not be where you're supposed to be. Don't talk to strangers. Tell an adult if you see anything that doesn't feel right. Nell ran over the litany in her head. How do I get them to hold in all these don'ts, keep them safe from the things that they don't know enough to be scared of?

Nell made one last attempt at patching things as best she could. She led the way into the house and before they could disperse to their rooms, said, "I know I haven't been in the best mood today and I'm sorry if I haven't communicated my concerns well." She could see their eyes glazing over—Mom was in formal mode, using big words. What would Thom have said? "I'm sorry I've been a bear, but I was worried." But she wasn't Thom and she couldn't make up for his absence. "I shouldn't have been so upset, but I was worried, okay? Don't worry me and I won't get so upset. Deal?"

Josh and Lizzie both nodded. Nell wasn't sure if they really had a deal or if agreement was just the quickest way out of the kitchen, to the phone for Lizzie and the computer for Josh.

She let them order pizza for supper, and even dispensed with her usual hints that the veggie pizza might be a healthier choice than the pepperoni and sausage one.

THIRTEEN

THE NEXT MORNING, JOSH and Lizzie were safely dropped off at school before Nell headed to the office.

She'd been surprised to see a police car cruise by the house several times during the night. She'd doubted Chief Shaun took her fears seriously enough to do that. No, of course he doesn't take my fears seriously—he's placating me, she thought. When she arrived at the office, Nell told Dolan what was happening. His office was right next to the front door of the Crier, so consequently he was usually the first person to see anyone coming in. And the first person to have to deal with whatever came in.

So far, the day was a usual quiet day, with the most unpleasant task Nell faced that of prodding Carrie about her stories. Not that she was writing anything that had to be in this week's edition, but Nell was roughing out the layout and having a story or not having a story made a difference. At the moment she was regretting her decision to proffer a possible front-page place to Carrie. Having to hold space on the front page for a possible no-show story and its pictures wasn't the key to easing the tension she felt. If Carrie's story wasn't going to make it, then she needed to have something else lined up. Yesterday, Carrie had said that she was "working on it," but Nell knew that when Carrie was really working on it, everyone in the office usually heard about it. So far, all was quiet on the Carrie front, and that didn't make Nell sanguine about the appearance of the pound story.

"Hi, Nell," Jacko said, poking his head into her office. "How much of a story do you want from me about the murder of the Gautier boy?"

"How much of a story do you have? Any breaks in the case?"

"Well, I'm not sure. The sheriff says we need more proof to even be sure that it's a murder, but the chief is hinting that he's got some solid leads."

"Solid evidence? What did he say?"

"Just something about the murderer is going to be convicted and on death row by the time Sheriff Hickson notices the boy was killed."

"That's probably just bragging. Perhaps you've noticed a slight rivalry between them."

"Slight, right. Open warfare, more like. But the chief said the heavy-footed stomping of the sheriff's men didn't destroy all the evidence after all." Then Jacko quickly added, "I asked what he found, but he won't tell me. Just said, 'You'll see.'"

"Evidence hinted at isn't anything I'm going to put in the paper. Let's stick with the small piece—you can drop the possibility of it being homicide but don't play it up—and hope nothing major breaks the second we go to press."

"One small story it is, then." Jacko went back to his desk.

As Jacko exited, Alessandra Charles came into Nell's office.

"Have you seen this?" she asked, tossing a flyer onto Nell's desk.

Alessandra was the advertising manager for the Crier. It had taken Nell a while to admit that Alessandra was actually good at her job, mainly because she considered the woman to be everything that she was not. She'd always wondered how much Alessandra's blond good looks and ample bosom had influenced Thom's decision to hire her. She was the kind of women who could wear a navy blue suit in the middle of July and not show a drop of sweat. She didn't have bad hair days, only perfectly coifed days and days of a wind-swept look that usually required a high-priced stylist to achieve.

Nell had argued with Thom about the hiring. "Give the job to someone who really needs it," she'd said, a reference to Alessandra's reputed generous divorce settlement from the much older man she'd married when she was twenty-one. He had divorced her when she reached thirty-one, and given his success in building casinos, could easily afford his generosity.

Alessandra seemed to want the job more as something to do than because she needed the money. That had been Nell's argument. But Thom had countered by saying the point of the job wasn't to give someone a paycheck but for that person to procure ads for the paper.

That, Alessandra did very well. She came across as the poised cheerleader you always wanted to like you in high school. People who bought ads enjoyed the favor of her charm.

But she and Nell had never been close—the bookworm and the cheerleader—even though Alessandra had a son, Rafe, just about Josh's age and they occasionally played together.

Nell glanced at the flyer on her desk.

"*Pelican Bay Lier*" was boldly printed across the top.

Nell glanced up. "They could use a better editor. Where did you find this?"

"Too many places. At the community bulletin board at the grocery store, on just about every phone pole in the city, stacked anywhere people might pick it up."

Nell glanced at the rest of the flyer. *"Don't believe what you read in the paper. Too many lies get told every week. Don't trust the people that advertise in the Lier. Buy from them and you support lying."*

She tossed the paper back on her desk. "Wendell Jenkins's first shot."

"You know it's Wendell?" Alessandra asked. "That's what I'm hearing, but why?"

"Because I threatened to press charges against his son for almost assaulting me."

"Nothing like being the last to know," Alessandra said. "Nell, it would be helpful if you shared things like that with me—things that might affect our ad accounts."

"I didn't think he'd do anything. Particularly this … petty," Nell said with exasperation.

"Believe it or not, you and I are on the same side. I want to sell ads and make money for the paper. It helps me if I have some warning when something like this is in the air."

"Okay, well, the boys in blue and tan decided it would be better for all concerned to not try to put Boyce in jail, but instead let him leave town. So, he might be packing to go or he might be planning an assault on the offices. But the real reason Boyce was let off was that Chief Shaun got his jollies out of beating him up instead of arresting him. Also, someone murdered Rayburn Gautier and yesterday Josh wasn't waiting for me at school like he was supposed to, so I panicked and fell into the bad-mother-yelling-at-her-kids trap. Now you can worry about Rafe, too. Sheriff Hickson and Chief Shaun are doing their usual arguing about jurisdiction and how to handle the investigation. Maybe we can sell space to alarm companies and gun stores."

"Guard dogs, too. There are a couple of kennels out of town that could use the exposure."

"You are joking, aren't you?" Nell felt stupid for asking, but she never could tell with Alessandra. She had such a perfect, perky exterior.

"Nell, of course I am. Good grief, you make this town sound like a soap opera."

"But with real people and real lives and no scriptwriter to make it all come out okay in the end. Or at least be the fault of the evil twin."

"What do you want me to do about this?" Alessandra asked, pointing to the flyer on the desk.

"I guess we ignore it. Why give them the attention?"

"It's all over town, I don't know if you can ignore it."

Nell looked at the flyer for a moment, with its misspellings and grammatical errors. "I have an idea. We'll put it on the front page and edit it."

"Edit a flyer?"

"Make fun of it. The spelling, the grammar. Instead of doing a serious rebuttal, we'll show their version, then an edited version with all the mistakes removed and the text rewritten to make it better."

"It might be dangerous to mock a man like Wendell Jenkins."

"Not you, too. That's all I hear these days—'Don't take on Wendell Jenkins.' Why doesn't anyone say, 'Don't take on Nell McGraw'?"

Alessandra let out a laugh.

"It's not that funny," Nell said, only half kidding.

"No, I'm not laughing at you. But that's a great idea. 'Don't take on Nell McGraw—who knows what's hidden in the archives of the Crier?' That should get their attention. And you're right—we can't ignore this flyer, but we can't take it seriously either. Nothing like reducing it to the level of a junior high paper. Okay, Nell, you edit and I'll sell."

"You really think it's the best way to handle it?"

"Look, if the boys are going to be pricks, we have to make fun of them. It's good to see you with your fighting spirit back."

"Okay, then. I edit, you sell." Nell smiled at Alessandra.

Alessandra returned the smile as she left to do battle with the pricks of the world, stopping on her way out to flirt with both Jacko and Dolan.

Nell pondered her last comment. "With your fighting spirit back"—had she been so detached that even Alessandra had noticed it? She thought she'd carried her grief and shock well—taking care of her children, taking care of business, keeping her sorrow to herself during working hours.

Fighting spirit, Nell thought, then picked up the phone. Thom claimed that a moment like this was when he fell in love with her—when, in response to his "You just can't call someone up on the phone and ask them that," she'd picked up the phone and asked them that. As she'd told Thom afterward, "Of course, they won't answer the question, but what they do say can be very interesting."

"May I speak to Mr. Jenkins, please?" she asked. Then, not even waiting for the reply, "This is Nell McGraw, the editor of the Crier."

As she expected, she was on hold for quite a few minutes.

Finally, he drawled, "Wendell Jenkins here."

"You need a better editor for you flyers, Mr. Jenkins," Nell said.

"My flyers? What flyers are you talking about?" His voice had the same lazy insolence his son's had.

"The flyers that are all around town, you know the ones," Nell said, hoping that her voice conveyed an easy assurance that he was responsible for the flyers and they both knew it.

111

"I'm sorry, I have no idea what you're going on about. I can't imagine you'd think I'd do anything improper."

"It was the sloppy editing that gave it away. At the bottom of the flyer, in 4-point type, is something obviously meant to be a document marker. WJenkins.doc. It just looks like a smudge unless you're paying attention."

The silence at the other end of the line was satisfying.

"I guess you didn't notice it when you read things over," Nell added.

"Goddamn it!" Jenkins finally let out. "I can't believe that son of a . . ." Then he remembered who he was speaking with. "Nice talking to you, Miz McGraw," he said in a tone that told her it wasn't. He slammed down the phone.

Don't mess with Nell McGraw, Nell thought as she gently replaced the receiver.

After several hours of wading through the less exciting tasks of running a newspaper, Nell finally decided she needed to stretch her legs. The two overdue library books she'd discovered in Josh's room last night gave her an excuse and a destination.

She found herself walking hurriedly across the square, a tension in her shoulders. She realized she was bracing for the attack that had happened the last time she'd crossed it. Boyce must be gone by now, she told herself. Or at least not foolish enough to risk both going to jail and losing Daddy's money. All that confronted her was a perfect spring day, bright sunshine, and a gentle breeze that brought the smell of the gulf.

She left behind the sunshine for the cool fluorescent of the library. Clearly she wasn't the only one with overdue books, as there were several people at the counter. The woman at the front of the line, well dressed with a piece of jewelry in every place that jewelry could be tastefully placed, was explaining why she didn't think she really owed the six dollars and fifty cents in fines she had incurred. "My husband was out of town, and these are his books, and he put them in the trunk for me to return them, then he forgot to remind me they were in the trunk."

Be sure you make him pay you back in the divorce settlement, Nell thought to herself as the woman continued her sad story of life with a husband who couldn't be bothered to remind her of books to return to the library. Finally realizing that standing there arguing could make her late for her hair appointment, she asked, "Do you take credit cards?"

She seemed shocked when Marion told her that no, they couldn't take a credit card for a fine of six dollars and fifty cents. A little more wrangling produced a check, and the woman who believed that she should be exempt from library fines left. Finally, the two older women behind her were able to rest their books on the counter. They were friends who'd come to the library together.

A teenage girl joined the line behind Nell. She had a stack of books, and on the top Nell recognized the picture book she'd seen Rayburn Gautier check out. Realizing she must be one of Rayburn's sisters, Nell stole another glance at her. Her face was pale, with sleepless smudges under the eyes. Her eyes had a confused, almost glassy look, as if the world had become too brutal to comprehend. She seemed both afraid of and defiant toward the eyes she knew would stare at her.

It was Nell's turn, but she stepped aside to let the girl go in front. Rayburn's sister gave her a bare nod as she placed the books on the counter.

"I'm returning these," she mumbled.

"Oh, Dolly," one of the older women said. "How's your mama?"

"She's okay," Dolly mumbled in the same monotone.

"We were so sorry to hear about Rayburn. He was such a lively boy," the other woman said.

But the girl's grief was too barely held in check to be able to withstand even these slight condolences. Tears started streaming down her face as she stood, returning the books that her brother would never read.

"Oh, honey, we're sorry," the first old woman said, patting Dolly's arm, unsure how to comfort the girl.

Nell watched for a moment more, the tears falling and the wordless anguish of a teenage girl facing a sorrow that would haunt her for the rest of her life. Placing her books on the counter to free her arms, she pulled the girl to her, letting her cry on her shoulder. Nell didn't even attempt words, just held Dolly and let her cry.

It was a long time before the girl finally lifted her head, then murmured, "I'm sorry."

"It's okay, you needed to cry," Nell said, keeping one arm around Dolly as she fumbled in her purse for a tissue.

Dolly took it, wiping first her eyes, then her nose. "I was supposed to be looking after Rayburn. I just turned my back for a minute..."

Haunted by guilt and sorrow, Nell thought. What a burden for a child to bear. It should have been minor—a young boy sneaking out to play in the woods where generations of other boys had played with no worse consequences than scraped knees.

At her confession, the tears threatened Dolly again, but she angrily wiped them away with the soggy tissue as if she didn't deserve to cry. "Thank you, Mrs. McGraw," she said trying to live in a grown-up world and play the part.

"It's okay, honey," Nell said. "Yesterday, my son Josh was supposed to wait for me at school, but he decided to take off and ride a friend's bike to the bike shop. He disobeyed me and I didn't know where he was or what he was doing. He made it to the shop okay. But none of us are perfect enough to watch them every moment of every day."

The look of relief on her face was palpable. "I think they blame it on me," Dolly said very softly. "Like I wanted him to get killed."

"Of course you didn't. And they do know it's not your fault, but grief and loss also carry anger within them. Sometimes in the initial shock, anger comes out in ways it shouldn't."

Dolly nodded, then gave Nell a wan smile.

At least I can be a good parent to children not my own, Nell thought.

"I think some of these are late," Dolly said, attending to the business at hand. "And I think that ... that some of them might have crayon marks in them."

"Don't worry about it," Marion reassured her, taking the books. "I appreciate your returning these. I know you and your family are going through a hard time."

Dolly again gave a bare nod in acknowledgment.

It's too new and it's too hard for her, Nell thought. It still blots out the rest of the world.

"I gotta go," the girl said. "Mama's not expecting me to take too long." She turned and hurried away, briefly turning back to say, "Sorry. Hope I didn't mess up your blouse." Then she was out the door.

"And finally, my overdue books," Nell said. Her fine was a dollar and a quarter, but she gave Marion a five dollar bill and told her to keep the change. It would help to pay to replace the crayon-marked books. They started to chat, but more overdue books demanded Marion's attention. Nell managed to ask to schedule coffee and they left it at they'd text each other.

No shouted curses met her on her walk back across the square, although she still found herself paying attention in a way she had hoped she would not have to in the town of Pelican Bay. Can we ever be safe here again? Nell wondered as she reached the sanctity of the Crier building.

Alessandra was in her office waiting for her.

"Okay, what did you do?" was how she greeted Nell.

"Do?"

"Do, do, do," Alessandra sang. "What might possess Wendell Jenkins to send his sales boys, still in their shiny new sales uniforms, scurrying around town grabbing up every flyer they can find? I asked one of them and he only mumbled something about civic duty and making the town clean. Which I find hard to believe."

"I seem to have misread a smudge on the bottom of the flyer. I thought it said, in a very small font, WJenkins.doc."

"And you called Wendell and told him."

"I merely suggested that he needed a more competent editor."

"Girl, you have balls to take on the son of a bitch." Then Alessandra let out a hoot and added, "I bet he doubles his blood pressure medication for the next month."

"Just as long as he doesn't drop dead and let little sonny boy Boyce come back to claim his inheritance."

"Those are two slimewads. That prick certainly didn't fall far from his porcupine papa. Mr. Boyce spent too much time flirting with the junior high girls."

"I thought he would flirt with anything female," Nell said.

"He'd try, but most women over eighteen are too mature to fall for his little boy macho stuff. Rumor is that he got a fourteen-year-old pregnant last year."

"Rumor? Good one or shaky?"

"The girl's aunt. She and I have our nails done on the same day."

"What happened?"

"The girl went to New Orleans and got un-pregnant. Daddy Wendell gave away a few new cars."

"What about the girl? Is she okay?"

"Okay? She flunked ninth grade and is repeating it. Was a B student before then."

"What a bastard," Nell said.

"Suppose he learned it somewhere. Some other rumors—shaky —about Daddy Wendell and the girls he likes to take to the casinos over in Biloxi."

"Almost makes me wish we could do a tabloid edition of the Crier. It'd be fun to run a good 'gotcha' picture of Wendell on the front page."

"Oh, wouldn't that be lovely? Mr. Wendell with a blond young enough to be his daughter on his arm, her Jungle Red lipstick on his cheek?"

"We'd never buy a car in this town again," Nell replied, laughing. She didn't think she and Alessandra would ever be close friends, but at least they could be allies in certain matters.

"Hey, you really ought to consider that idea. Might boost circulation." With that, Alessandra gave a wave and headed off to sell a few more ads and flirt with anyone she'd missed before.

Nell wasn't sure if Alessandra was kidding or serious. She decided not to ask.

FOURTEEN

THE KIDS HAD BEEN picked up, Lizzie deposited to practice flute with her friend Janet (and to practice her rudimentary flirting skills with Janet's older brother, Nell suspected), and Josh was at bike maintenance class. Nell returned to the Crier offices to finish up a few things.

Sheriff Hickson caught her just as she was entering the door.

"Miz McGraw, can I have a word with you?"

Nell wondered what he would do if she said no, he couldn't have a word with her.

But he didn't wait for any kind of answer from her. "Can you tell me what your boyfriend is up to?"

"My ... what?"

"Chief Shaun. Your knight in shining armor."

"None of the above. I have no idea what you're talking about."

"He's making noises about making an arrest very soon. Thought for sure a publicity hog like him would make sure the newspaper cameras were at his heels."

"Perhaps television cameras, but he's told us nothing. Nor am I privy to his plans in the way you're insinuating."

"Well, he's sure not sharing things with the sheriff's department. Don't suppose that you'd want to do an editorial about cooperation between law enforcement agencies."

It wasn't a question, but Nell answered anyway. "Now that's a thought. I could drag out that quote of yours from when Doug Shaun took over as police chief. Didn't you say something like 'he's young and he's pretty, but he's got to prove his worth'? And then there's that roadblock you put up at the yacht club, without any noticeable cooperation on your part. Plus that time—"

Sheriff Hickson interrupted her. "This is murder, little lady. A whole different ball park than that minor stuff. Shaun's still new enough 'round here he ought to step a little more lightly."

Nell straightened her back, standing as tall as she could; she wanted to make sure the sheriff knew the "little lady" he was talking to was tall enough to see his bald spot. "I don't have much respect for lack of cooperation among law enforcement, but if you want to get cooperation, it helps if you give a little. You want a truce with Chief Shaun? You have to be a big enough boy to ask for it."

"Glad to know you have the citizens of Pelican Bay at the front of your thoughts, Miz McGraw," the sheriff answered.

"But I do, Sheriff Hickson," Nell retorted as he was turning his back to her. "That's why I think you and the chief should find a front-door way to work together instead of prowling around looking for a back door. Which I'm not, by the way."

"Not what?" the sheriff demanded.

"Not your back door to communicating with Chief Shaun. He tells me what he chooses to tell me, just as he does you. He just finds me more useful than you do."

"You get any more late-night phone calls, you call me first, you hear?" And with that, the sheriff spun on his heels and walked away. Unlike Chief Shaun, he didn't give her any additional phone numbers.

Nell resisted staring at his back as he stalked away and instead entered the Crier offices. She had work to do, a paper to get out. This was crunch time, gathering all the stories, the editing, getting the paper ready to go to press tomorrow.

On her desk was a note from Carrie. "Almost done with the story, have some more fact-checking to do. Will have it by tomorrow." Nell snatched up the note, tore it into pieces, and threw it into the trash. I'm not going to hold the front page until the last minute, she fumed.

She knew she was blending angers here, but she didn't really care. There was no one around to see her pique and its expression in tiny pieces of torn paper. And she was aware that the end result—a decision to run a different story—would be the same. It was too much stress and worry to have to wait until the last minute for something that wasn't breaking news. There were other things she could run on the front page.

Nell ran through the pile on her desk. She had already roughed out space for the timely ones, the stories that had, as Thom had said, "a sell-by date" on them—upcoming events, coverage of this week's football game, news that people were following such as last week's update on shellfish safety, which had been occasioned by several people becoming ill from eating tainted oysters.

Then there were the other stories, like Carrie's tardy animal pound story. Those could be bumped to next week if something came up, or used to fill a skinny paper. Jacko had done a good story on how the casinos on the beach in Biloxi were affecting the seafood industry, which used to be located on that waterfront property. She started to pull that one out of the stack, then stopped. Carrie wasn't going to like losing the front page slot, and she was going to hate losing it to Jacko. Was it worth the storm that it would create? Nell put Jacko's piece back. Instead she took out a story that she, with Josh's help, had done, about places to bike around Pelican Bay. If she ran that story, it would avoid the Carrie blow-up—or at least attenuate it—and it would help her make up with Josh for berating him in front of Kate.

If only the people who accused her of all sorts of agendas in running stories knew her real reasons for choosing one over the other, Nell thought wryly. To placate an irritable reporter and make up with her son.

She decided to give Josh a byline, which he deserved, as he'd done most of the leg work—pedal work?—for the story. There were also some good pictures, one of his bike class in front of Kate's shop and another of a biker riding along a sun-dappled trail. Josh had suggested that place to take the shot.

So, that was settled. This week's *Pelican Bay Crier* would have on its front page the mayor's latest drone about education and needing more money from the state, and why reading scores weren't as high as they should be but the football team was doing real well; a story about a rabid dog that was captured outside of town; the bike story; and the small follow-up story from Jacko about Rayburn Gautier's death.

The next day was the rush of the final set-up of the paper, the last minute ads and stories—an alligator seen in the harbor. Nell held off on the front page until the last minute. In the end she deliberately left Tasha Jackson's death out of the small story about Rayburn. If they weren't connected, that was the right thing to do. If they were, it might tip the killer off to what they were thinking. Or give him the attention he was so clearly seeking. She wanted to do neither of those.

FIFTEEN

Not everyone was as happy with Nell's front page choices as Josh had been.

"Wow, Mom! You put it on the front page! With my name!" was how he greeted the paper when he saw it at breakfast. "Oh, wow, and the picture of the bike group, too. Hey, Lizzie, I got my name and my picture in the paper!"

Lizzie, with typical teenage insouciance, replied, "Your mother is the editor. Makes it easy to get your picture in the paper."

Josh was too thrilled to let even Lizzie's older sister condescension dispel his happiness. "You're jealous because you're not in the paper. Maybe you could talk Mom into letting you report the stupid makeup that you and your friends wear. 'Lizzie's Made-up Makeup Tips.'"

When Nell got to the office, she walked in on Sheriff Hickson rumbling at Jacko about using the word "murder" in his story on Rayburn Gautier.

"Since when are you a police officer, son?" the sheriff was saying as Nell entered. "Murder is kind of a yellow journalism word to be throwing around, don't you think?"

"What's going on here?" Nell cut into his tirade.

"You may not think that Wendell is a good editor"—the sheriff turned to her—"but y'all got some gaps in that department, too. No solid proof that poor boy was murdered and now it's on the front page of the paper, so of course everyone's going to believe it. How many scared parents you got running around here?"

"Better scared parents than complacent parents if there's a killer around," Nell replied. She quickly continued, not wanting Sheriff Hickson to get rolling again. "And what word would you have me use for the suspicious death of a young boy? We have to include the possibility of murder. In fact, I just got off the phone with the coroner. According to her, there were indications of his being strangled. I've never heard of an accidental fall into a well accomplishing that."

"That's right, give away everything we got to the general public."

"There's no mention in the story of *how* Rayburn was probably killed, Sheriff Hickson," Jacko said. "We didn't even have that information."

"Can't you at least run these sorts of stories by me before they come out?" the sheriff demanded.

"No," Nell said bluntly.

He stared at her for a moment before finally saying, "No? You don't want accurate stories."

Nell flared, "I run accurate stories! I don't want censored stories. If I let you read the articles before they come out, then I'm going to have to let Chief Shaun read them, and if the mayor wants in on it, then I can't very well deny him. And we might as well have a paper run by the aldermen of the town."

"Well, I got to disagree with you here. Murder is a hard word to hear in this town and I think you need to be real careful about where you say it."

"I will be careful. I will also tell the truth. We didn't pull the word murder out of thin air. Chief Shaun has labeled it murder. The evidence from the coroner's office clearly indicates murder."

"I just think it's a little early to be saying that in public."

"I run a newspaper, Sheriff. It's my job to say things in public."

"Well, you want cooperation with my office"—and he gave a pointed look at Jacko—"I like to get a little cooperation in return."

"I'll gladly provide cooperation, Sheriff. I just won't allow censorship," Nell said, as politically as she could.

He stared to her, weighing how much he could use good press coverage versus how heavy a hand he could play—just as Nell was doing. She didn't want to totally alienate him and lose all access to what was going on at the sheriff's department, but nor was she willing to be the nice little southern girl who kowtowed to the powerful men.

After a moment more of consideration, he said, "Okay, Miz McGraw, you win this one. I have to admit I didn't mind your coverage of those drunken yacht club drivers. And I guess a better paper doesn't take any one side all the time. And if I don't cooperate with you, then only Chief Shaun's side gets in, and you and I both know I wouldn't be pleased by that."

It was probably as close as the sheriff would ever get to perestroika with her. "I won't make promises to please everyone, or even anyone, but I will try to make the stories as fair and accurate as possible," Nell said.

"I s'pose that'll do, Miz McGraw." He tipped his hat and left.

Nell waited until the door was firmly closed behind him before turning to Jacko and saying, "And on the eighth day, God turned the sheriff into a reasonable man."

"I guess he doesn't like the idea of young boys being murdered here," Jacko said. "Can't come around to saying the word."

"Maybe," Nell replied. "But don't make assumptions. It's always a good idea to look into the stories behind the story. Why are the police chief and the sheriff so reluctant to cooperate? Is it just stupid macho rivalry? Or is there something else going on? And why is the sheriff so set against calling this murder? A murder investigation could expose a number of things that an accidental death wouldn't."

"So you think that there's something suspicious about how the sheriff is acting?" Jacko asked quickly.

The soul of a reporter, Nell thought as she saw that glint of excitement in his eyes. Jacko enjoyed the hunt, the searching, the knowing. As she did. And as Thom had. She remembered the times she and Thom had tossed around possibilities, pondering everything, from what were the essential questions to far-fetched "what ifs." That was one of the things she liked about Jacko—he was energized by her pushing him, by making him look at things differently. Carrie would just sigh and see it as more work.

"My best guess is that Sheriff Hickson sees this as out of his league and something that Chief Shaun can handle much better—which he has to find galling—and also doesn't want to say the word murder, because saying it makes it true in his mind. Probably nothing more than that. But it can't hurt to dig a little."

"Have shovel, will report," Jacko answered with a mock salute. He started to turn away, but stopped. "It doesn't feel right to have this much fun over ... over some poor kid being killed."

Nell had faced the same dilemma, feeling her adrenaline run when word of another disaster struck. And she'd finally come to her answer: "We're just telling the story, not causing the tragedy."

Jacko nodded and went back to his desk.

SIXTEEN

HE HAD BARELY GLANCED at the *Pelican Bay Crier* when he was at work. It wouldn't do for him to be seen poring over the local paper. But now he was home, and he could stare at the front page. He read the story, barely three paragraphs long, about Rayburn Gautier's murder. "Possible murder." He read it again, then gently set the paper down on the table. He noticed his hands shaking and that made him even angrier.

It was almost as if she knew how to enrage him, was throwing a gauntlet in his face. No headline, below the fold, the same size typeface as the hokey story about some old lady spotting a log and deciding it was an alligator. Only three paragraphs, "possible murder" according to the Chief of Police. No murders in this town for close to three years, and the ones before that had mostly been drunken brawls where the men killed were the kind only missed by drinking buddies, and even then it only took a few beers for the memory to fade to a worn story: "Guy that used to sit at that stool got killed in a fight, can't remember his name."

Rayburn Gautier was different, very different. He wanted it noticed.

He suddenly snatched up the paper and savagely ripped it in half. Then threw the torn pieces to the floor and walked over them, as if his feet were striking back at the sin of ignoring him.

"What does it take to get your attention, Nell McGraw?" he demanded out loud as he crossed again over the newsprint. "Next paper I want the top of the front page."

What would be impossible for her to ignore? He stopped his pacing and retrieved the paper from the floor. His anger was passing and the untidiness of it bothered him. Holding the two pieces together, he again glanced at the front page, skimming over the other stories.

And then he knew how he would get her attention.

SEVENTEEN

I T SEEMED SO QUIET and peaceful here, Nell thought. Perhaps it's just the illusion of not having children home. This Saturday had taken Lizzie off to the mall with several of her friends. She would stay there for hours and come home with nothing more than a pair of socks. Nell knew it all had to do with teenage bonding, although she wished her daughter was involved in something like biking or science fairs, as Josh was. Admit it, Nell told herself: Lizzie should choose something her mom could see a point to, instead of aimlessly wandering around a shopping mall. Although she supposed it was probably better for Lizzie to be indoctrinated by crass commercialism than drugs and alcohol.

Josh was engaged in a more mother-approved activity. His article about places to ride had inspired the bicycle maintenance class to take their well-oiled bikes out on a trail featured in the story.

Nell was using her quiet time to putter around the house, catch up on some letter-writing, actually clean the kitchen, and think about cooking and what to eat in place of the weekday hastily thrown-together meals. She was standing at the sink, washing grapes, watching sunshine in the green leaves of the oak tree next door.

Boyce Jenkins seemed to indeed have cleared out of town. And if he hadn't, he was avoiding her. There had been no phone calls in the night, no phone calls where no one talked; none of those things that would make her wonder if there was a threat behind it. Were they connected? Jenkins's leaving and the absence of calls? Although no one had been arrested for the murder of Rayburn Gautier, no one else had been harmed either. Jacko was doggedly following up with Chief Shaun, to get more details on his claims that they had a suspect. When Jacko had last talked to him late yesterday afternoon, he'd said, "We had some solid leads and we're working on them." Nell hoped that meant an arrest was soon coming and this terror could permanently go away.

The phone rang, but it was a bright afternoon and she had no fear in picking it up.

"Nell? This is Marion Nash."

"Marion, hi, how are you?" Nell was pleasantly surprised to hear her voice. They'd managed to squeeze in their coffee date yesterday after work. The coffee shop had been crowded with high school kids, so their talk ranged from books to women in the south to town politics. They hadn't discussed their private lives, so Nell wasn't able to bring up the topic of Kate, but she felt like they'd had a connected conversation, one that flowed easily and showed promise of going into deeper things.

"I'm good, but my mother isn't," Marion replied. "I'm going to have to spend all weekend with her."

"I'm sorry to hear that," Nell said. "That must be hard on you."

"Southern daughters, remember? We do our duty. Your mother-in-law came over this morning and sat with her while I went and got groceries."

"I hope you didn't have to hear too much about what a horrible job I'm doing of raising Thom's kids."

"There was a comment about Lizzie wearing makeup, but it was restrained and moderate."

"Well, she and I can actually agree on that. I wish Lizzie wouldn't wear makeup either. But I want to save the 'no' battles for something more toxic than Hot Tropic Peach lip gloss."

"At least it's peach and not lime green or black."

"That's probably next week's battle." Nell sighed.

"However, I didn't call to discuss teenage shades of lipstick, but something a bit more serious."

"Yes?"

"One of the books that Dolly, Rayburn's sister, turned in had some … drawings in them."

"What kind of drawings?"

"Something that shouldn't be in a kid's book. I can't really explain right now, not with Mama in the next room."

"Is it something you should take to the police?"

"Well … I'm not sure," Marion said slowly. "That's why I'm involving you. I need another pair of eyes to tell me if what I'm seeing is … is what I'm seeing."

"Okay, when can we get together? Monday after work?"

"No, can't do it then. I have to take Monday afternoon off to drive Mama to her doctor in Biloxi. Tuesday?"

"Tuesday … Tuesday I promised Lizzie we'd hit the sale at her favorite shoe shop. Can it wait until later in the week? I'm afraid if I don't let her get the shoes she wants it'll be black lipstick for a month."

"Nothing will bring Rayburn back," Marion said softly. "I'll call you next week and we can set something up."

"Fine," Nell agreed. She wanted to ask more questions but knew it would have to wait. As she replaced the receiver, she realized she hadn't even asked if Marion knew for sure that Rayburn had done the drawings. Nell assumed it was the case, but hadn't she just been warning Jacko about making assumptions?

The phone rang again. Hoping it was Marion with an alternative time to meet, she quickly picked it up.

"Hello, Nell, I'm glad to catch you at home. I know Lizzie is growing into a young woman, but I don't think she realizes how garish all that makeup looks on her," said Mrs. Thomas McGraw, Sr.

Nell held silent for a moment, her thoughts running from just how like Mrs. Thomas it was to barge into a conversation with a criticism, to thinking how to defend Lizzie for doing something that she didn't agree with either.

"Actually, I think Lizzie does realize how garish it looks. It's called teenage rebellion and finding new ways to annoy the adults in her life."

"I suppose. I don't remember Thom ever rebelling like that."

"I suppose that boys in his generation weren't likely to use garish makeup to rebel in any case."

The silence at the other end told Nell that Mrs. Thomas was not amused. Finally, her mother-in-law replied, "I meant that he didn't act out, like you're accusing Lizzie of doing."

"Really? I seem to recall him mentioning things like being arrested and hauled before the judge for leading a toilet-paper rolling of the high school stadium."

Again there was the censorious pause. "That was one-time high jinks and he was seventeen when he did that, not fourteen like Lizzie is."

Nell briefly considered rattling off a list of "one-time high jinks" that Thom had admitted to, but by now she knew that a battle over

Thom's memory would only waste her time. Plus, his mother might not have been aware of most of them. There could be a time to tell her, after the freezing over of hell, but this was not it.

"I want to take Lizzie with me to New Orleans next weekend," Mrs. Thomas continued. "I thought that if she's going to wear makeup, she should do it right. One of my usual stores, Saks, I think, is offering makeovers and I think Lizzie could use one."

"I'll tell Lizzie to call you when she gets back," Nell said.

"You'll tell her you think it's a good idea, won't you?" Mrs. Thomas asked, her tone clearly indicating that girls Lizzie's age shouldn't have free will about things like attending needed makeup classes.

"I'd be more than happy to see my daughter in something more becoming than what she presently chooses to wear, but she may have some band things next weekend, so I'll have to see." Nell was reasonably sure that Lizzie had no band practice then, but she wanted to give her an out that didn't require directly saying no to her grandmother.

After a few more questions about when Lizzie would be home and what was Josh doing, Mrs. Thomas hung up.

So much for a perfectly peaceful Saturday afternoon, Nell thought.

The phone rang again. And this one stole the peace in a way that the others hadn't been able to.

"Nell? This is Kate. We're going to be late getting back from the bike trip. Joey, one of the boys, hasn't come back yet, so we're going to stay in the park and look for him."

"Is Josh there?" Nell immediately asked. Then just as immediately chastised herself—that's right, only worry about your own son.

"He's right here. Do you want to talk to him?"

"No," Nell said, deciding to spare Josh the embarrassment of having Mom so visibly worry over him. "But ... keep everyone together. Don't let him play macho little boy and go off looking for his friend."

"We're all sticking together. Any searching will be done by adults," Kate responded. More softly, she added, "I'm going to give him another fifteen minutes to straggle back and then call the sheriff. It's probably nothing. A wrong turn on the trail and he's heading east when he should be heading west."

"I hope you're right," Nell answered. "Is there anything I can do? I'll come out and join you to ..." *make sure that Josh is safe*, she didn't add.

"Not at this point." Kate answered her first question. And then her second: "It might help to have you out here. Aaron and Frank, the dads who came with us, are down the trail looking for him, so I'm the only grown-up with the kids."

"I'm on my way."

"Okay. Let me get on to calling the other parents."

Nell returned to the kitchen, the sun still shining brightly through the trees, a golden afternoon that would soon slide into evening. It can't be, she thought. Not on a perfect day like today. This kind of horror can't just walk in on such a perfect day.

Nell shook herself. Kate's probably right; Joey just took the wrong fork and will show up any minute now. She again looked out the window. Bright sunshine produced such dark shadows.

She locked the kitchen door, usually left open for children to wander in, as if wanting to make sure that any of the horrors out there couldn't invade her home.

Josh's okay, and Joey will be okay, she told herself as she drove to the park. He'll have returned by the time I get there. The worst it can be is that he fell off his bike and broke a leg.

She found herself sliding through stop signs. This is stupid, Nell thought. Speeding won't help anyone. She took a deep breath and deliberately slowed to a more reasonable speed. Joey will already be back when I arrive.

But he wasn't.

When Nell pulled in, Kate was still on the phone and the children from the bike class where all sitting at one of the picnic tables near the entrance of the park.

Kate nodded at Nell as she approached, finishing up what appeared to be another conversation with a parent.

"Hi, Nell," she said. "Thanks for coming."

"No sign yet?"

"No, not yet. Aaron just called me. They've gotten as far as our turn-around place." Kate, her back to the kids, allowed a worried look to cross her face.

"What do we do now?"

"I'll call the sheriff and his men. Best to make use of the daylight while we have it."

Nell glanced at her watch; it was just after four o'clock. Only a few hours of light left.

Kate took a few steps further away from the children to make the call.

As an added distraction, Nell joined them at the picnic table. If Joey was okay, they didn't need to see the worry—and if he wasn't, they'd know soon enough. She wondered, what is it that makes us so protective of our children? Makes us want to keep them from pain and fear, as if we can really keep these cares out of their lives? Maybe it's to delay the blow for as long as possible, to give them time to grow and mature and be ready for the inevitable pain. As if it's ever possible to be ready, she thought.

"Hi, kids," she greeted them.

"Are you here as my mom or a reporter?" Josh asked.

"A bit of both," she answered, considering it the best way to mollify him. That way he would feel that he was worried about, but not too publicly worried about. "Who saw Joey last?" she asked.

"I did," Josh replied. "He couldn't have gone too far. He was just a little in front of me. There was a dead snake and I stopped to look at it. Then I sped up to catch up with him, but he wasn't waiting for me."

"About where was this on the ride?"

"Well, we were going to meet at the uprooted oak tree and wait for everyone else to catch up ... but Joey wasn't there, so I went a little further," Josh admitted.

"I was already at the tree," Bryan, the oldest boy in the class, said. "I was back in the trees, swigging water when you guys came riding by."

"I didn't see you," Josh said.

"Yeah, well, I saw you," Bryan countered.

"What did you see, Bryan?" Nell asked.

"Well, just Josh and Joey riding by."

"Together?"

"Uh ... no, I guess not. I saw Josh, and Joey's usually with him."

"Did you see Joey separately from Josh?"

"Uh ... I think so." But his hesitancy made Nell suspect he wasn't sure.

"How long were you there before Josh arrived?"

"Uh ... I think about ten or fifteen minutes."

"Seconds, more like," Josh interjected.

"Hey, I can't help it if you're slow."

"How long after Josh went by before the others arrived?" Nell wanted to keep the conversation on what had happened.

"Uh ... maybe another ten minutes or so."

She guessed his estimated times were on the high side. Two minutes can seem like ten for a young boy just sitting. Still, it told her that there'd been a noticeable gap of time between when Josh passed him and the others got there.

"What happened then?" Nell asked. "When did anyone notice that Joey was missing?"

"I was the one," Josh said. "I couldn't seem to catch up with him. I kept going, but when I hit half a mile, I stopped and started wondering if he'd pulled one over on me. So I doubled back to the meeting point."

Nell knew that Josh had some kind of meter thing on his bike, so the half-mile distance would be fairly accurate.

"But at this point you weren't sure whether he was lost or fooling with you?"

"Well, he didn't come back to join us," Bryan said, grabbing Nell's attention away from Josh. "I watched you buzz by and only you came back."

"About how long were you all waiting before Josh returned?" Nell asked.

"Ugh … I guess, maybe another ten minutes," Bryan answered.

"So Joey was gone for a total of about twenty minutes from when he first passed by you?"

"Uh … twenty minutes?"

"You guessed about ten minutes between when Josh passed and the rest of the group arrived, and then another ten minutes before Josh returned," Nell explained.

"Ten and ten makes twenty," Josh added.

"I can count," Bryan said. "Yeah, I'd say twenty minutes is about right."

"Josh, about how long were you past the tree before you realized Joey wasn't ahead of you?"

"I was just past it; I only meant to go up the road for a little. Maybe an eighth of a mile, tops. So, that would mean I went about three eighths of a mile past the turn-around point before giving up and coming back."

Nell would ask later, without Bryan around to contradict things, how long it would take to ride that distance. She wasn't sure what she wanted to learn from these questions, but experience told her it was possible to know too little but not to know too much.

"Did anyone notice anything unusual? Any people not from the group? Any tracks, like from bike or car tires?" Nell noticed that Kate, her phone call made, had joined them and was standing behind Josh, listening to her questions.

"I did," said one of the two girls. Susan, Nell thought her name was. "I heard a gunshot."

All the children turned to look at her.

"You did not, "Bryan said.

"You didn't. I did," Susan said firmly.

"When did you hear it?" Nell asked.

"Just before Josh came back. Everyone else was there. I heard the shot and then Josh appeared. It was real faint, I barely heard it."

"How do you know it was a gun?" Bryan demanded. "Could have been a firecracker or something."

"No, I know what guns sound like. My mom's in the Air Force and she teaches people how to shoot."

That stopped Bryan's questioning.

"So you barely heard the shot?" Nell asked, wanting to see if she could tease any more details out of Susan.

"Yeah, like it was far away."

"Maybe a hunter," Nell suggested.

"Maybe. But it sounded more like a pistol that a rifle," Susan said. "But people do target shooting sometimes."

"It's not terribly unusual to hear gunshots out here," Kate said. "No one should be hunting—or target shooting—in the park, but it happens."

"Was it just one shot?" Nell asked.

"I only heard one. But I only heard it 'cause there was a quiet moment. Then Josh arrived and people started talking and stuff."

"Did anyone hear anything else?" Nell asked.

There was silence, heads either turning to look to see who might speak or staring down at the table as if trying to remember.

Finally, it was Susan who said, "I heard a motor."

"You heard everything, didn't you?" Bryan said. "Next it'll be an airplane. Or aliens landing."

Susan gave Bryan a look that Nell suspected she'd watched her mother use with new Air Force recruits, then continued. "I did. I heard a motor. It was when we were getting ready to ride back here. Kate had called us all together, and we got quiet to listen to her."

"Did it sound close or far away?" Nell asked.

"Different from the gun. Not close, but a different direction. Maybe from the water. I just thought it was a boat motor, but I don't know why I thought that."

In an eerie echo of her words, the sound of several cars reached them. No one said anything as they listened to their approach.

It was the sheriff and several of his deputies. The children looked first at each other, then at Kate, as if seeking either an explanation or some reassurance that this wasn't as serious as it appeared to be.

"I called Sheriff Hickson," Kate said. "It's possible that Joey had a wreck and twisted his ankle or something."

"Or he was kidnapped by the mysterious monster of the woods," Bryan offered.

"That's not funny," Josh shot back. The worried look on his face told Nell he was scared something really had happened to his friend.

"Joey's probably okay," Nell said. "But he could be lost and frightened or even, as Kate suggested, he could have had a wreck and possibly hurt himself."

"He was wearing a helmet," Josh said. "He shouldn't be hurt too bad."

"No," Kate replied. "But if his bike's wrecked, he may have to walk out to here, and that can take time. We're worried he may even have a broken arm or leg. He'll be okay—but we do need to find him."

Nell was impressed with Kate's explanations. It was both reassuring and honest. She hadn't been sure how to talk about it without overly worrying the children.

Sheriff Hickson got out of his car and approached Kate. Nell noticed there were two cars of deputies, along with a truck containing a dog on a leash and his handler. The sheriff gave Nell a pointed look, and she put her hand on Josh's shoulder so Hickson would know she was here as a mother, not as a reporter. Or at least, not officially as a reporter.

He didn't address her, just turned to Kate. "So what's going on, Miz Ryan?"

Kate gave him a quick rundown of what had happened, including the fact that the two fathers riding with the group were still out searching for Joey.

"When do you expect them back? No need for us to miss each other and hunt up and down the woods when the boy's been home for hours."

"Aaron has a cell phone and we've been keeping in touch that way," Kate answered.

It was only then that the sheriff noticed the phone she was holding in her hand. He was probably so used to his radio that he forgot civilians had advanced communication these days.

"Can you call them up and let me speak to them?"

Kate did as he requested, and after a brief hello she handed the phone to Sheriff Hickson. He gingerly took it, the small thing looking out of place in his meaty hand.

"You found the boy yet?" Then there was a long pause, punctuated only by a few grunts from the sheriff. Then he said, "Now, don't go messing nothin' up. You find anything like clothes or bloodstains, you leave them be."

Nell had to restrain herself from shouting at him not to say those things right where the children could hear them. She felt the muscles in Josh's shoulder tense under her hand at the sheriff's words.

His conversation finished, Hickson handed the phone back to Kate. "You got something of the boy's?" he asked her, with a nod at the dog.

"I do," Josh said. "He gave me a pair of his old cycling shorts, the kind with real chamois in it." He sprang up and ran to his bike. A moment of rummaging through his handlebar bag produced the black shorts. He ran back to the sheriff, proffering the limp cloth as if it were a prize.

Sheriff Hickson didn't reach down to take them, just asked, "They been washed? No good if they're washed."

"No, not yet. Joey got a new pair the other day and he took these off and gave them to me," Josh said, his embarrassment at having the dirty shorts overcome by their newfound usefulness.

Still not taking the proven dirty shorts, Sheriff Hickson nodded to the deputy with the dog.

As the dog was doing his business of sniffing, another car arrived. Nell recognized the woman getting out as Joey's mother. Although Joey and Josh were good friends, his mother and Nell knew each other only as the "dropping off/picking up" mother. It took her a moment to remember the woman's name; she was so used to thinking of her as Joey's mother. Aline, that was it.

Aline hastily searched the area with her eyes. Once, twice, quickly; then the third time slowly, as if not wanting to believe her son wasn't here yet.

"Mrs. Sayton," Kate said. "I'm sorry, Joey hasn't returned yet. Bryan's dad and Susan's step-dad are out looking for him. I called Sheriff Hickson to help because I wanted to make sure that Joey was found before it got dark."

The sheriff took over. "Don't you worry, Aline, it'll take about ten minutes with Mitch and Sixer to find your boy. He probably took the wrong turn and couldn't find the right turn to get back."

Aline Sayton just nodded, her eyes again looking round the picnic area, seeing all the children there except for hers. "It's not like Joey to get lost," she said very softly.

"Now, ma'am, boys will be boys," the sheriff said. "Just seems when they get a certain age, they pull stunts. Hell, he might be sitting in the woods right now watching us and enjoying the commotion."

Aline nodded slowly, not so much in agreement, it seemed, but because it was something she wanted to believe.

"Mrs. Sayton," Kate said gently, "do you think that Joey might do something like that? Play this sort of a joke?"

"He never has before ..." she said slowly.

"He might have ducked out on me to play a joke," Josh interjected. "But he wouldn't stay away like this. Joey's not a...he doesn't have the patience to hide like this."

"Well, sometimes you just don't know," Sheriff Hickson said. "Let's go find the boy and get this over with 'fore it gets any darker." With that, he nodded at Mitch and his dog. All the men conferred, looking at a rough map of the area that someone had drawn. They decided to use an old logging road to get close to the place where Joey was last seen. Then the sheriff, Mitch and Sixer, and one of the other deputies got in the truck and drove off. The other two deputies started walking in along the trail, in case Joey was on his way back.

And then there was nothing to do but wait. Conversation seemed impossible. Every fifteen minutes or so, Kate would get a call from Frank and Aaron, but the calls were always the same—nothing to report, and they would keep on looking. The only variation was when they finally met up with the sheriff and his men. But still no Joey.

Several of the parents came and took their children home. Nell knew that Josh wouldn't want to leave, so she didn't suggest it, even when the numbers had dwindled down to him, Kate, Aline, and herself still there.

When the sun was slanting low in the sky, a rich golden color that seemed mockingly out of place, Kate spent several minutes on the phone with the sheriff. Nell over heard enough of the conversation to know they hadn't found him yet and the sheriff wanted to intensify the search.

As darkness approached, another, larger search team arrived. Nell recognized a number of them; most of the fire department was there, as well as a number of volunteer firefighters from the smaller towns in the area. They brought lamps and more dogs and several different types of off-road vehicles, from scruffy Motocross bikes to fancy four-wheeled things.

For about half an hour, the picnic clearing was ablaze with lights and voices. For another half an hour, they listened as the lights and voices receded into the forest. Several women, wives and mothers and sisters, remained behind, setting up one of the picnic tables with sandwiches, a big pot of coffee, and an ice chest full of water and soft drinks.

Somewhere along the way, Nell had turned into a reporter, taking a notebook from her car and scribbling down notes for a story—one she desperately wanted a happy ending for.

Kate had gone into the woods with the second wave.

Aline's husband had come and insisted she come wait at home. He'd been kind about it, as if he wanted to protect her from what might emerge from the woods. If Joey was okay, he would be okay—if not, then he didn't want her to witness it. He finally won her over by pointing out that the searchers might not come back to this place and they'd be much closer to other meeting points, like the hospital or the sheriff's office, from their house.

Nell finally used the same argument with Josh. They couldn't help Joey by sitting in the dark, and Kate would certainly call them when he was found. She also wondered if she, too, was protecting her son from what might come out of the woods. She knew something had happened to Joey—he was five hours overdue, and she doubted that a boy his age would continue a practical joke through hours of darkness in the woods.

"This just isn't like Joey," Josh said as they got in the car. "He might fool around, but not worry everyone like this. Do you think he's going to be in a lot of trouble with his parents?"

Nell could see that Josh was still holding to the belief that nothing could happen to his friend, his world still so young and new that it wasn't familiar with those sharp turns that can change an ordinary moment into a haunted one.

"Hard to tell. It might depend on why he's been gone. I doubt they'll be upset with him if he couldn't get back because he broke his leg," Nell answered.

"But if he broke his leg, why can't they find him?" Josh asked the question that had been haunting her for the last few hours. "He couldn't have gone that far from where I last saw him."

"Do you think maybe he, say, broke the bike and hurt himself and tried to get out another way? He might have gone one direction while everyone else was going another," Nell offered. It was the most reasonable explanation she could come up with.

"The quickest way back was the way we came," Josh said. "Unless he crossed the water."

"You were close to the water?"

"Yeah, there's a bayou that runs into the park. It's pretty near where we were. You think they're checking the bayou?"

"Where does it go? The bayou?"

"Straight out to the sound. It's about a few hundred yards from the mouth of the harbor."

Nell decided not to ask Josh how he was so familiar with the meandering of the bayou. She suspected it was from an unauthorized exploration, because she knew she'd never given her son permission to go boating—or worse, swimming—in the myriad inlets and bayous that dotted this part of the coast.

"That's what must have happened," Josh said, his voice animated with relief. "Joey messed up his bike and decided not to walk the long way out, but take the water way."

"Swimming?" Nell asked. It was late enough that few other cars were out. She turned on the high beams, wanting to light the shadows that loomed on the sides of the road. "Or was there a boat there?"

Josh hesitated for a moment, as if realizing he was going to have to admit he'd been doing something he shouldn't. "Well, sometimes there are some rowboats or canoes back there. I guess he might have borrowed one. But it's really not that far of a swim from there to the mouth of the harbor.

"Have you done it?" Nell asked.

Josh again hesitated.

Time to be a mother, Nell thought. "Josh, if you've done it, you've done it. We both know you aren't supposed to be exploring the bayous around here by yourself or with friends your own age. But this time, there will be no lecture, no scolding, okay? All I ask is that you tell me what you know. And that you don't do it again."

"Okay. Sorry, Mom," Josh said.

Nell was glad he didn't try to deny his misbehavior. Lizzie had taken to denying even the glaringly obvious—such as claiming innocence that she'd anything to do with Nell's good perfume ending up in her room. I hope Josh doesn't become like that when he hits his teenage years, Nell thought.

"We borrowed a rowboat once from behind the yacht club," Josh started.

"Borrowed?" Nell couldn't stop herself from interjecting.

"Mostly," he answered. "It was me, Joey, and Dylan Yorst, and he said it was okay to take. That the adults did it all the time."

"Dylan Yorst, Philip Yorst's son?" Nell asked.

"Yeah."

"I didn't know you were friends with him."

"Well, not really, but we sometimes let him hang out with us. He's kind of weird. But we ran into him at the beach and he had a key to the gate around the yacht club boats."

So the boat really was "borrowed," Nell thought—as in, the son of the yacht club commodore wouldn't get in trouble for taking one of the generic boats they kept there.

"Anyway, we rowed around for a while, really just planning to go along the beach from the yacht club, but that got boring so we decided to see how far we could get down that bayou. We only went until we saw the interstate and then turned around."

Nell squelched the mother noise she wanted to make—the interstate was about ten miles or so inland. That seemed a long journey. It also meant they'd crossed the harbor channel—not something she wanted to think about, a small boat of inexperienced young boys chancing a run-in with commercial shrimping boats. They'd presumably kept close enough to the beach at first to be reasonably safe, but when they crossed the harbor channel—the other side a brief spit of land before the marsh took over—and went from there to the bayou, there would have been no safe place to land a small dingy.

But that conversation would have to wait. Josh was okay and she'd have to be content with that until Joey was home safe. Then she and Josh could talk about how risky the adventure had been.

"How did you know the bayou comes so close to where you were in the park?" she asked.

"I recognized that oak tree—the one we met at on our bikes. You can see it from the water. We pulled the boat ashore there, since we were getting tired. There's a path from the bayou to the trail. Not official, but you can see it's been tramped down. Kate told me it's probably how poachers get in and out of the park. They can't drive by the ranger station, so they go by water."

Nell noted that Josh had shared his water adventures with Kate. She wondered if she should have a discussion with Kate about letting her in on some of her son's escapades or if that was one of those places it was just wiser not to go.

"So the tree you met at today was close enough to the bayou to be seen from it?" Nell asked.

"Yeah, but the trail is hidden. You only know it's there if you come from the water. We need to call the sheriff and let him know about it. They might not find it otherwise."

"But Kate knows about it," Nell said.

"Well, I told her about it, but she's never seen it," Josh said.

"We'll call when we get home," Nell assured him. They were coming back into town, the lights from houses now doing the job of fighting the shadows. Nell turned off the high beams, not wanting to rake them through anyone's window.

"What if Joey's hurt or something?" Josh pleaded. "Can't we at least go to the harbor and see if we can see anything?"

"Like what?"

"Maybe he's just getting to shore, swimming, hurt and tired and needing someone to help. Or I can recognize one of the old canoes we saw along the bayou. One was purple. You can stop and call Kate from there."

The mother in Nell wanted to get Josh home and safe, but she also knew that he needed to feel like he was doing something. A quick drive around the harbor wasn't too far out of the way. And, she reminded herself, there should be enough patrons at Ray's Bar on the far side to make it safe enough.

She took the turn that would take them to the harbor instead of straight home.

There were few cars around as she drove to the parking area near the mouth of the harbor. The chilly night would keep people from hanging around boats and water past sundown. Nell parked at the foot of the fishing pier that stretched about fifty yards into the Gulf.

Josh barely let the car stop before jumping out and running onto the pier. Nell followed more slowly, understanding his need to feel motion and action. And understanding how little could be done. She had a moment's panic at the unbidden image of a body caught in the pilings of the dock. What if that was what was waiting for them? She had, indeed, seen a few bodies pulled from the water or after weeks in the woods, and knew the full horror of such a sight. Those were nameless, faceless people, only touching her life in the brief story she wrote for the next day's edition.

Her pace quickened to catch up with Josh, now at the far end of the pier. She noticed that their car was the only one at this end of the harbor. The night was quiet, as if waiting for something. She realized the sounds she'd expected were absent and glanced across the harbor to Ray's Bar. It was dark—none of the familiar neon lights blinking on and off. It was closed. Of course, Nell thought. They're still in mourning.

It should have been a quiet, peaceful night, but the palpable reminder of Rayburn's murder and the mounting apprehension about Joey's absence created fear and tension in every shadow.

"Do you see anything?" Nell called to Josh, wanting to leave and get to the safety of their home.

"Can't really tell," he replied. "Wish I had my binoculars. Might be a skiff out by the bayou."

"Can you be sure?" Nell asked as she joined him.

"No," Josh said in exasperation. "Too dark, too far. I need one of those big lights and my binoculars," he repeated.

Nell strained to see what he was seeing, but she could only make out vague, darkened shapes that could be anything she wanted them to be.

"I'm going to call the sheriff." She started to head back to get her phone, which she'd securely stuck in her purse.

"You left the phone in the car?" Josh sighed at her breaking his strained concentration.

As she walked back along the pier, Nell noticed a car coming around from the beach road. It slowed as it came to the bend at the harbor's mouth. As it turned through the bend, though, it didn't pick up speed but slowed even more. The car came to a stop. Then it slowly nosed in beside Nell's car.

Damn, she cursed herself. My cell phone will be attached to my hip from now on.

She veered to the ancient pay phone in a sheltered area, hoping it had at least been updated to link to the emergency system.

Someone got out of the car, but the street lights were behind whomever it was, making the figure nothing more than an outlined shadow.

Nell picked up the phone, trying to make a hurried decision between calling 911 or dialing Chief Shaun, as he'd asked. Trying to keep fear at bay, she reminded herself that the harbor fishing pier was a public place, easily visible by anyone driving by. Any late-night drinkers at the yacht club, plus anyone in the houses on this side of the harbor, could easily hear … a scream? Don't let it come to that, Nell told herself. Fumbling the card out of her pocket, she made her decision to call the police chief.

A scrape of shoe on wood told her the person was now on the pier.

As she punched in the numbers, Nell found herself thinking, I'm between Josh and this stranger. If need be, I can hold him off long enough for Josh to jump in and swim across the harbor. And escape a bullet?

He was close enough for Nell to be reasonably sure it was a man, a tall man at that.

Ring, damn it, she cursed the phone as it slowly clicked its way into connecting with the world. Maybe I should have called 911, she second-guessed herself. At least they were guaranteed to answer. Doug Shaun might not have his cell phone with him, or turned on.

The man was now halfway to the sheltered area.

Finally, she heard the first buzz of a ringing phone.

The expectant night gave its first distinct sound: a ringing phone.

The second ring was cut short with, "Douglas Shaun."

"Damn it, Chief, you might give a little warning," Nell called out, her fear turning into anger.

"Nell?" he asked. "Where are you?"

"About twenty feet from where you are," she replied, hearing his voice in both the phone and her free ear.

"Here on the dock?" he asked.

"No, swimming under the water. Of course I'm here on the dock. At the pay phone in the shelter." She hung up, feeling ridiculous at talking on the phone to a man standing only a few feet away. "You scared me," she said, stating the obvious as the police chief approached.

"Sorry. I swear I didn't see you," he answered as he tucked his cell phone back into a holster on his belt. "I'm not in the habit of frightening people who write editorials."

He was now close enough for her to see the wry smile on his face. He continued, "I just saw the car parked there and thought I'd

150

check it out. Maybe catch some hardened criminal illegally stealing from crab traps."

"You know that Joey Sayton is missing, don't you?" Nell said.

"Joey Sayton?" he repeated, but Nell's tone had erased the banter in his voice.

"Aline and Mike's son," Nell answered, then gave a quick rundown of the ill-fated bike trip, ending with why she and Josh were at the harbor.

"Damn," Chief Shaun softly swore. "Sheriff Hickson didn't see fit to place a call to the police station. This is the first I've heard someone's missing."

In a very soft voice, Nell asked, "Could they be related? Joey and Rayburn Gautier?" She didn't want Josh to hear her worries.

"Time will tell. I hope not, but ... he's been gone a long time." He paused for a moment, the silence letting the fears in, then continued. "So Josh says there's a waterway from the park out to the Gulf?"

"Seems he, Joey, and Dylan Yorst borrowed a dingy from the yacht club and went exploring," Nell admitted.

"Didn't know you were a member of the yacht club. I've never seen you there."

"We're not. But Dylan's family certainly is, which is how they got into the grounds."

Chief Shaun nodded, content to leave the boat in the "borrowed" category. "Hey, Josh," he called out as he headed in the boy's direction. "Did you swim the bayou or just row the distance?"

Nell followed the chief to the end of the dock.

Josh looked from her to the police chief. "You told him about us being there?" He directed the question to Nell.

The chief answered. "It might be important. Don't worry, I'm not going to arrest you for boat borrowing. Did you try to swim or just row?"

"We thought about swimming, but then Joey was worried about snakes, so we didn't. But we figured we could have."

"You think that Joey might have tried to play a joke and swim back here?"

Josh thought for a moment, then answered, "Maybe, but he would have told me about it."

"Not if he wanted to fool everyone and meet them back here," Chief Shaun said.

"Maybe, but I still think he would have at least hinted." Josh clearly didn't like the idea of being left out of his friend's prank. "Besides, he would have made it here by now."

"He could have gotten tired. Or lost. Swimming at water level can make things look a lot different than rowing up in a boat."

The chief took his cell phone out and, without explanation, dialed a number. "I need some men and a boat," he said into it. "At the mouth of the harbor. We're going to explore the bayous looking for a lost boy." There was a brief pause, and then he said, "The sooner the better" and ended the call.

"Are you going to call the sheriff?" Nell asked. "They might be already searching the bayou."

"I don't hear any boats out there. Besides, he doesn't tell me what he's doing, why should I tell him?"

"Because it would be the professional, competent thing to do," Nell answered, trying to hide her exasperation at these men and their games. "Not to mention, it's always better to let men with guns know that you're in the area."

"I'll leave word at the station to forward a message," he tersely replied.

"Can I go?" Josh asked. "I know the way."

"No, absolutely not," Nell answered quickly.

"Chief?" Josh appealed.

"Well, not if your mother doesn't approve."

"But it's okay with you?" Josh said, seeing an opening.

"No," Nell said. "It's too dark and late for you to be out on the water."

"I'll be with the chief of police, Mom. I'll be okay."

Nell shot Shaun a look. She didn't want to come out and say she wasn't about to risk Josh being one of the first to find Joey's body. Or whatever else might be out there in the water.

But Shaun had other ideas of how to make boys into men. "He'll be okay. There'll be five or six of us. Since Josh's been there before, he'll be helpful in showing us where Joey might have gone."

Nell looked from her son, the eager pleading look on his face, to Chief Shaun. He looked sober and reasonable. Maybe he had a point—maybe Josh would be a useful guide. Or maybe he understood how much Josh needed to help. *Am I being overly protective?* Nell suddenly wondered. *Has losing Thom made me afraid to let them go, even to places they need to go? And how do I best protect my son—by keeping him safe and in the house while a close friend of his might be hurt and needing help, or by letting him know that he did all he could?*

"Okay," she relented. "But you should call the sheriff now. Or I'll do it for you. I don't want there to be any confusion if they run into people they don't expect to be out there."

"Yes ma'am," Chief Shaun said, giving her a mock salute. "Your son's as safe with me as if he were my own."

"Thanks, Mom," Josh chimed in.

Nell hoped to get a chance for a few private words with the chief to let him know she didn't want her son exposed to the body of his friend, if that should be the grisly end of their search. But she didn't get a chance amid the bustle of the boat launching and the gruff banter of the five police officers who had joined them.

She had to settle for a quick hug that Josh squirmed out of—and his embarrassment when one of the men flirted, "Hey, I could use a hug from a pretty lady, too." But the man said it with a friendly smile and Nell took no offense.

She stood at the end of the dock until she could no longer even hear the motors of the two skiffs.

It's cold and there's nothing more I can do here, she told herself as she turned to go. And she did intend to call Sheriff Hickson to be doubly sure he wouldn't think the skiffs contained some deranged killers.

As she drove away from the harbor, Nell realized how tired she was. Sometimes waiting is the most exhausting thing there is. Maybe she should have volunteered to go with Josh and the chief, she thought. It might have been better than the yawning wait that was before her. She knew that sleep would be impossible. Or, she wryly admitted, if not impossible then unthinkable, at least until Josh returned.

The house was dark. Where is Lizzie? Nell suddenly wondered. Was she already asleep? Somehow she couldn't imagine her daughter not taking advantage of a parental absence to be up all night on the phone or playing on the computer. Maybe she'd gone over to one of her friends' houses. With no mother around to say no, she got an automatic yes.

As Nell pulled into the driveway, her headlights caught the movement of someone by the porch. She clicked on the high beams to catch whoever it was. The bright lights caught Lizzie flinging her arm across her eyes to protect them.

Nell immediately switched the lights back and finished pulling into the driveway.

She got out of the car and asked, "What are you doing out here?"

"The door's locked!" Lizzie answered in an angry wail. As she got closer, Nell could see the red blotches of recent crying.

She felt a wave of dismay come over her. How long have I left my daughter out here by herself? she thought. When she'd left to help Kate search, she was sure she'd be back before Lizzie got home. And then, in the press of events, she'd completely forgotten that she'd locked the door.

"Oh, honey, I'm sorry," Nell said, instinctively reaching out to hug her daughter.

Lizzie spun away. "Or maybe you meant to leave me out here!" she spat. "Where the hell were you?"

Nell let the obscenity pass. Given her transgression, it didn't seem the time to chide Lizzie about curse words. And in her child's place, she doubted she'd have confined herself to just "hell." "Please, Lizzie, I'm so sorry. This has been a crazy night."

"Easy for you to say. You haven't been stuck out here in the cold. Why did you lock the door?"

"Let's go inside and talk." Nell noticed that Lizzie was shivering. "I am so sorry, honey."

"I've been stuck out here for over two hours. And that weird cop came by, told me I'd better be careful, that bad things could happen to girls alone at night. That really gave me the creeps," Lizzie said as Nell opened the door.

"Weird cop?" Nell asked, turning to face her daughter.

Lizzie walked past her, clicking on the kitchen lights as she did and going straight to the refrigerator. "Yeah, the same one."

"Was it Boyce Jenkins?" Nell asked.

"I don't know his name, just that he didn't seem really friendly." Lizzie took advantage of her wounded status to drink out of the milk carton. She'd been reading about building strong bones and was on a milk-drinking kick.

"How did you know he was a cop?"

"Had on a cop uniform."

Nell considered calling Chief Shaun out in the swamp to tell him his little scheme to get rid of Boyce wasn't exactly going as he'd promised. Apparently Boyce was not only still around, but still wearing his uniform and pretending to be a policeman.

"Did he do anything else, say anything else?"

"No, just that. I told him I was waiting for some of the guys on the wrestling team, to help them sew their uniforms. I just don't like him. He was hanging around school a couple of weeks ago when he thought no one was watching him."

"Why didn't you mention this at the time?"

Lizzie shrugged as if this was a stupid question. "It was just one weird moment. There are a lot of them. I don't tell you them all. It was seeing him again that creeped me out."

"How did you see him?" Nell handed her daughter a glass, her hint that even under duress, drinking out of the milk carton was not okay. "The wrestling team and sewing was a nice touch," she added. Lizzie's idea of sewing was an iron-on patch.

"I was staying late practicing with this new jazz group some of us put together, and some of the guys were arguing about which piece to do next, so I wandered over to the window and there he was, watching the school."

"Does Ms. Daniels know about this group?"

"Of course she does," Lizzie returned. "Can't exactly hang out in the band hall without the band director's permission. And don't worry, she's usually somewhere around doing paperwork, so we're properly chaperoned."

"What did the guy do besides watch?"

"He just watched. Not the usual look-around-and-check-things-out. He stood in the same place for a while, looking off in the same direction—I think the place where the buses drop the kids off. Then he left like he was in a real hurry."

"Anything else?"

"No, that's it," Lizzie answered before taking a long drink of milk, now out of a glass. "And I wouldn't have been outside if you hadn't locked the door on me."

Nell's questioning clearly wasn't going to cause her daughter to forget what had happened. Nor should it, Nell thought. She hadn't bothered to worry about Lizzie the entire time she was with Josh. She'd made a stupid mistake and her daughter had suffered.

"Lizzie, there have been some things that have me worried," she began slowly. How would Thom handle this? she wondered. Then she thought, it doesn't matter what Thom would have done. He's not here and won't be here and I have to learn to cope. How will *I* handle this is the question I have to ask myself. "A young boy was murdered recently."

Lizzie paused in mid-gulp. "Murdered? Here? How? Was he bored to death?"

Nell saw her flip remark for what it really was: the reflex of protection against horrors that could escape the movie theater and enter real life. "He was strangled," she replied slowly, wondering how much to tell her daughter. "He was sexually assaulted and murdered." Jacko had seen the autopsy report. "Sexual assault" was as nice a term as she could use for what had happened to Rayburn Gautier before he died. His internal injuries alone would have killed him.

Lizzie was now looking directly at Nell, the milk and building-strong-bones forgotten. "That's sick!"

"Yes, it is. It's very sick and very scary. Today a boy from Josh's bike trip is missing. That's where I was, waiting to see if they found him."

"Who was it?"

"Joey Sayton."

"Joey? Little Joey? Josh's friend?" Lizzie's face crumpled into tears as she realized that the horror might be closer to her than she'd ever thought possible.

This time she didn't pull away as Nell hugged her. "They're still looking for him. It's possible Joey decided to play a joke and hide, maybe got lost. Or he might have hurt himself, broken a leg and couldn't get back. There's a big search going on right now. Josh is with the police, helping them search the bayous where he and Joey explored."

"Will Josh be okay?" Lizzie sniffed into Nell's shoulder.

"Josh's fine. He's with a bunch of policemen. He's probably ... as safe as we are." Nell almost said "safer than we are," which might well have been true, but Lizzie didn't need to be made aware of that.

Her daughter gave a final sniff and pulled away. "Well, locking me out is a good way to keep me away from mad killers. Maybe you should get me an extra cell phone charger and backup battery."

"Maybe I should," Nell admitted, not pointing out that Lizzie should be better about making sure her phone was charged. Cell phone use was an ongoing issue. Nell, of course, used the one that officially belonged to the Crier. She'd relented and gotten both

Lizzie and Josh the most basic phones: text, email, and actual voice connections only. Her mother-in-law had done an end-around her at Christmas and bought the latest smartphones for Josh and Lizzie, enrolling the three of them in a family plan. Lizzie hadn't done a good job of adjusting to how quickly the battery drained on hers and was hinting she needed a charger pack. Nell, piqued at Mrs. Thomas for giving her children something she wasn't sure they were ready for (not to mention leaving her in the tech dust), had been reluctant to add anything to her mother-in-law's gift.

"Really?" Lizzie asked, almost surprised that her ploy had worked.

"Maybe, really," Nell said. "We can talk about it tomorrow. It's past midnight now and way past your bedtime."

"Okay," Lizzie said, managing to put the milk back and her glass in the sink without being prompted. "But what about Josh? Are you going to wait up for him?"

"I'm not going to bed until he gets back," Nell assured her.

Lizzie yawned in response. "Okay. Do you want me to stay up with you?"

"One of us should get some sleep," Nell said, but she was touched by Lizzie's offer. At times her daughter seemed lost in the self-absorbed world of a teenage girl, but every once in a while something hopeful peeked through. Nell knew that her request for the cell phone extras had more than an edge of self interest in it, but it could have made a difference tonight.

"Oh, and Mom?" Lizzie said as she started down the hallway to her room. "Can I have a house key?"

"Yes, honey," Nell told her tired daughter. "First thing tomorrow, I'll go to the locksmith and have some made. Now get some sleep."

Lizzie nodded and headed off to bed.

Nell sat down to read, in the chair facing the street.

She was chagrined to realize she'd been nodding out when she heard the sound of an engine, then a car door slam, which she hoped heralded Josh's return. She hurriedly went to the door, both out of anxiousness and to shake the sleep out of her features.

It was in fact Josh, brought home by one of the policemen. His dejected walk from the car to the house didn't auger well for them finding Joey alive and healthy.

Nell waved a goodbye to the policeman. Josh noticed her wave and hastily added one of his own, his manners overcoming his dejection.

"Welcome home," Nell said as he slipped into the house. "What happened?" She closed and locked the door behind him.

"Nothing. Couldn't find him."

In the light, Nell could see the tiredness in his face, the dark circles under his eyes. She was slightly relieved to hear that his despondency wasn't from finding Joey and having to accompany him to the morgue.

"Maybe the sheriff already found him," Nell said, then wondered why we so desperately want to hold on to hope.

"Yeah, maybe," Josh tiredly replied. "But if this is some joke of his, I'm going to kill him." Exhausted as he was, his frustration and worry burbled into anger.

"Do you want anything to eat, or do you want to just head straight to bed?" Nell asked.

"Bed, I guess. We had sandwiches on the boat. Night, Mom." With that, Josh headed for his room.

Nell considered calling the sheriff's office to see if there was any definite word, but chose to leave it to the morning that would soon be here. If they hadn't found Joey yet, at least Josh would have some sleep before having that to worry about.

She puttered in the kitchen as she listened to Josh finish in the bathroom and then go back to his room. Somehow it seemed important that she be awake and vigilant until her children were safely asleep. Once the light under his door went out, Nell allowed herself to find her way to bed. Tomorrow, she was afraid, would be one of those long, waiting days, with nothing to fill the hours except both hoping and dreading that the phone would ring.

EIGHTEEN

Nell was wrong. She didn't have to wait long for the phone to ring. Her sleep was so deep that at first she fumbled with the clock, thinking the alarm had truncated her rest. But it was still night outside, and the clock told her only an hour had passed since her head hit the pillow.

This time she chased the shrill ring to its source—the phone—and quickly picked up the handset to silence it.

"Hello?" she mumbled.

Silence answered, until she again said, "Hello?"

"Nell McGraw." It was the same voice, she was sure of it. "Do I have your attention now, Nell?"

"Who is this?" she said, although she knew her question wouldn't be answered.

"I'd help you sell papers, Nell, if you'd let me." The voice had a friendly, almost cajoling tone to it.

"What do you want?" Nell demanded, a cold fury rising inside her.

"I like you, Nell. You've got spunk. I like that in a gal."

He was baiting her. Part of Nell just wanted to slam the phone down as hard as she could, but she clenched her hand tightly around it, willing herself to keep it to her ear. What he said, and the more he said, might help stop his madness.

"Where's Joey?" she said, with a tired certainty that he would know the answer.

"Spunk and to the point. Promise me you'll sell a few papers with this one, Nell."

She didn't reply to that, nor did she repeat her question; instead just left a silence for him to fill.

He did. "In plain sight. That's where Joey is. Just hanging around in plain sight. If you go back to the beginning, you'll find the end."

"Can't you just tell me?" Nell demanded.

"You're a smart girl and full of spunk. I know you like a puzzle."

"You don't know a damn thing about me," Nell retorted.

"But I do, Nell. I know a lot of things about you. And I'm learning more every day." He paused to let his words sink in, then said, "Good night, Nell. Sleep well."

"Why?" Nell almost shouted into the phone, to keep him talking. "Why kill ... children?" she demanded, again expecting no answer.

"Why? Because I can." The line went dead.

She sat in bed, staring at the phone in her hand as if it were some strange, unknown thing.

"Mom?"

She glanced up to see Josh standing in the doorway. "Yes, honey, what is it?" she said almost automatically.

"I heard the phone ring. I just wondered ..." He trailed off.

Nell knew it was beyond her to explain to Josh the phone call that had just taken place—the implicit threat to her and the stark reality that Joey was dead. "It was a wrong number. Some drunk who couldn't seem to understand he'd punched in the wrong digits. I know you're worried, but try to get some sleep."

"Okay, Mom." Josh said, apparently satisfied with what seemed to Nell to be a glaring lie that shouldn't have fooled a five-year-old.

He softly closed her bedroom door, and a moment later Nell heard an answering click from his door.

She got out of bed and went to the window, edging the curtain back so she could see out. The night was quiet, the usual scene one would expect in the deep of night in a small town. A few porch lights on, the street light at the corner the main illumination. There were no cars on the street, the houses mostly dark and shuttered. She wanted to be sure that Josh was asleep before she made the phone call she would have to make.

The approaching headlights of a car swept around the corner, illuminating the window for a second. Nell shrank back, as if they could see her through the crack in the curtains. As if they were even looking, she chided herself. But the car drove by slowly, taking its time passing her house. Nell felt the fear start to return until she realized it was a police car. Maybe Chief Shaun was doing something about Boyce and his threats. Or maybe they were still patrolling because of the call she'd received.

It was time to call the chief. She listened for a moment more to see if she heard the sounds of restless kids, then picked up the phone.

"Doug Shaun," he answered on the first ring. He didn't sound like he'd even attempted sleep yet.

"Doug, this is Nell McGraw. He called again."

"The killer?" he asked quickly.

"The same voice. Taunting me this time about selling papers. And ... hinting where to look for Joey ... Joey's body."

"What did he say?"

Nell repeated the words the caller had left her with.

"Hanging around? Ends where it begins?" Chief Shaun repeated slowly after her, as if puzzling it out. "Any thoughts?"

Nell had thoughts, thoughts that she hoped were wrong. "Yes, 'hanging' could be just that, up in a tree. 'Where it began'—probably at the picnic tables in the park, where both the bike trip and the search began." She wanted to be wrong, not to be left with the possibility that Joey had been hanging above their heads all that time.

"Huh," Chief Shaun let out, as if thinking about her guess. "That'll really piss the sheriff off, if that's true. Them looking all that time and not finding him right under their noses. Right over their noses, I should say."

"I would hope the sheriff gets pissed off that Joey was murdered, not about a contest over who found him," Nell replied.

"Did you call him?"

"Call who?"

"Sheriff Hickson."

"No, I didn't. I'll let you do that. Tell the sheriff I was too tired to have more than one phone call tonight." Then she added, "But I will talk to him tomorrow. Even if the two of you can't cooperate, I intend to cooperate with both of you."

"If you want to waste your time with him . . ." The chief trailed off, then said, "But he doesn't have a clue how to operate a real murder investigation."

He sounded far too awake for her, almost as if he was hoping she'd ask a follow-up question so he could rattle off all the things he'd do that the sheriff wouldn't ever think of doing. Nell had no patience for this rivalry tonight. "I'm tired, Doug. I'm going to check on my children one more time, then try to get at least a little sleep. I'll talk to you tomorrow." She didn't even give him a chance to reply before gently putting down the handset, hanging up on him as politely as she could.

Her mind was debating just falling back into bed, but her body was already standing up, on some primal instinct to do what she could to ensure safety for her children. She first looked in on them, relieved they both seemed asleep, young enough to think that nightmares could be easily woken from. Then she checked the locks on both the front door and the kitchen door. Should I get extra locks for the doors? she wondered. Would a heavier bolt keep the nightmares safely outside? She shrugged, settling for the practicality that they couldn't hurt.

Nell trudged slowly back to bed, wondering if there was anything else she needed to do tonight, anything that might make her feel safer. Tomorrow, she told herself as she lay down. Cell phone backups and locks tomorrow.

But even as tired as she was, Nell still didn't find sleep until the first light of dawn, as if the rising sun offered some safety.

NINETEEN

THE SUN HAD NOT been up long when the jangling of the alarm clock woke Nell. Groggily she fumbled for the phone before realizing it wasn't the culprit this time. For a brief moment, she was a sleepy woman in a room filled with bright sunshine, then as she awoke further, she recalled the events of the previous day.

Another jarring ring interrupted her thoughts, and this time it was the phone.

Warily, she picked it up.

"Nell, why in tarnation didn't you call me?" the sheriff asked without any preamble. "You knew that was my jurisdiction. I was already working on it. Now I've got Doug Shaun all over the place, puffed up and trying to call the shots."

"Good morning to you, too, Sheriff," Nell couldn't help responding. Not wanting to give him much of an opening, she quickly continued. "Chief Shaun gave me a card with every single phone number he has so I could reach him at any time. I didn't think it best to pass the message on to an underling deputy, and I had no

167

way to reach you directly." There, she thought as the excuse came out of her mouth. Make it his fault.

"Sorry, I don't waste the taxpayers' money on things like cell phones."

"It was Chief Shaun's personal phone," Nell countered, even though she had no idea if that was true.

"My men always know how to contact me. Wouldn't of taken but about five minutes or so for me to get back to you."

"It was the middle of the night, Sheriff. I didn't need ringing phones waking my children," Nell replied tersely.

"You know that Shaun ain't gonna call me," the sheriff huffed back at her. "Did he promise you an exclusive if he got to be the one to cut the body down?"

"The body?" she found herself stupidly repeating.

"You didn't think we'd find that poor boy alive hanging up in that tree, did you?"

"I didn't know … I didn't know," Nell repeated as the shock hit her. "I didn't know what … to think," she stumbled. "I guess I hoped that … the caller was … lying."

"Sorry," Sheriff Hickson said, no hint of apology in his voice. "I'd of thought by now Chief Shaun would've told you everything you needed to know. That poor boy was swinging in a tree, a rope around his neck."

"Which tree?" Nell asked, then quickly said, "Don't answer that. I don't want to know."

"That oak tree nearest the picnic table you were sitting at when I first got there," he answered.

Nell refused to ask him the question screaming in her head— had Joey been there the whole time?

The sheriff continued. "I got to see the sight of him being low-ered down by Chief Shaun and his men. Arrived back at our staging area at the site. Thank you, Miz McGraw. Chief had the morgue van and everything there. Just told me to stay out of his way. Nothing like being told to stay out of the way in my own jurisdiction."

"Just like you called the chief and cooperated with him when you found the body of Rayburn Gautier in his jurisdiction," Nell reminded him.

"So that's your game, huh? Make it all my fault?" the sheriff re-torted angrily.

"No, I'm just pointing out that if you'd set an example of coop-eration, maybe you'd be getting some in return. I wish both of you would act like grown-ups—"

But the sheriff overrode her. "I suppose if I want to know what's really going on, I'm gonna have to read about it in the paper, now you and your boyfriend got it wrapped up."

"He's not my boyfriend," Nell retorted into the line that was al-ready dead.

Angry at the harsh start to her day, she slammed down the phone. Only then did she become aware that Josh was standing in the doorway of her bedroom.

"Joey's dead, isn't he?" her son asked very softly, letting her know he'd overheard enough of the conversation to figure that out.

Nell couldn't delay the inevitable blow any longer. "Yes, honey, I'm sorry."

Josh's face crumpled into anguished tears. Nell swung out of bed and went to him, wrapping her arms around him, letting him sob in her embrace. A minute or two later, Lizzie joined them.

She asked the same anguished question. "Is Joey dead?"

Nell merely nodded, then reached out with one arm to pull Lizzie into their embrace. She found herself crying with her children.

The three of them remained holding each other for what seemed to be a long time. Lizzie was the first to break away, mumbling, "I can't breathe. Got to blow my nose."

Josh slowly disengaged, saying "I can't either." He headed for the bathroom Lizzie wasn't using. Nell, with no bathroom available, settled for pragmatically wiping her face and nose on the sheets, telling herself they needed to be washed anyway.

Lizzie was the first to free up a bathroom, so Nell had her turn at a proper face washing. When she got out, she heard noises in the kitchen and found Lizzie fixing pancakes. She was pleasantly astonished to see her daughter cooking without being coerced into it.

"Josh likes pancakes," was Lizzie's only comment when she saw Nell.

They spent the day like that, the three of them, giving small comforts and mercies that they could. Lizzie even told a friend who called she couldn't talk and came back into the living room to watch a movie with them. They made a brief trip, all three of them, to get extra spare keys made and extra phone chargers for both Lizzie and Josh, although Josh, not being the talker that Lizzie was, didn't have battery problems. But Nell wanted to be fair and give them both something.

She'd slipped away after breakfast back to her room, ostensibly to get dressed, but she also phoned Jacko. It was going to be a working day for him.

It was only late in the evening, when she and Lizzie were finishing up the supper dishes, that the question Nell had dreaded all day came up. Josh had already completed his chore of clearing the table and taking out the garbage and had gone to his room to read.

"Mom, how did he die?" Lizzie asked.

"They're not really sure yet," Nell said. She didn't want to lie, but to be gentle with the truth. "It may not have been … natural causes."

"You mean someone killed him?"

"It's possible. There will be an investigation."

"Murdered him?" Lizzie repeated. "That's sick! Why would anyone … that's just sick."

"It has me worried," Nell admitted. "I want you and Josh to watch out for each other."

"But so far only boys have been killed," Lizzie said.

Nell was surprised at her observation. She hadn't thought her brief mention of Rayburn Gautier's death had caught more than a glancing moment of Lizzie's attention. "Maybe. But there was a young girl found a few weeks ago. They assumed she drowned and didn't really investigate. But with what's going on, you need to be as careful as Josh does."

"Thanks for the cell phone stuff. I didn't think you'd give in so easily."

"I'm not always a mean mom," Nell said.

"I promise not to talk forever. Only 'hello, I'm on my way, good-bye' or 'help, I've been kidnapped, drop the ransom off on the park bench.'"

Nell understood that Lizzie's bantering was to fight the fear. "If you do get kidnapped, remind them your mother is a newspaper editor, not a banker. Suggest a year of free quarter-page ads instead of actual money."

With that the dishes were done, and Lizzie finally felt free to have a truncated evening of phone chatter.

But that night, when she and Josh went to bed, they both left their doors open, as did Nell.

TWENTY

THE MONDAY MORNING STORY meeting found Carrie in a major snit.

"When am I ever going to get a break?" was how she greeted Nell. "You call Jacko and give him the best stories!"

Jacko was doing his best to ignore her outburst, scribbling some notes on his pad. Nell was tempted to glance at what he was writing, because she suspected it had little to do with the story and more to do with avoiding Carrie.

"Jacko was already covering the story and I felt it was better to drag him out of bed on a Sunday morning."

"So he gets the big stories and I get the sewage and water board?" Carrie fumed.

"I needed someone following developments yesterday, okay? That doesn't mean that Jacko gets the exclusive. With two murders, we're going to have to give this major coverage. There are going to be a lot of stories to write. You'll get your chance."

"So, what do you want me to do?" Carrie asked.

"This is the murder of a child. What kind of coverage should we be giving it?" Nell tossed the question back at her. You want to be a reporter, learn to look for stories, not expect them to be handed to you, she thought to herself as she watched the puzzled frown on Carrie's face.

"What do you mean, 'what kind of coverage'?" the young woman asked.

We'll be here all day asking the same question, Nell thought. She tried not to let what she was thinking show on her face. "Of course, there's the straight news angle. But what else should we be doing? Where else do we dig? What feature stories should we consider?"

There was an awkward silence. Carrie glanced at Jacko, hoping he would give the answers Nell clearly wasn't going to offer. Jacko gave Nell a quick glance, then looked down again at his doodles, pretending to search for answers there. Nell suspected he had ideas but was trying to avoid the "brown-nosing" accusation that Carrie would be likely to sling at him if he voiced them.

Nell gave them another beat, then decided she had a paper to run. "What do people want to know? Other than what we can't know at the moment—who the killer is. How about a story on what the experts recommend doing to protect your children? Or looking at crime in the area? Is there any other story that this might tie to? One of those 'back in 1940 a similar murder occurred' type of things?"

Carrie's face was blank at these suggestions; she'd apparently decided that neither of these stories was the route to the Pulitzer and therefore they were beneath her.

"What about a look at how a typical murder investigation proceeds—something like real live vs. TV life?" Jacko offered.

"That's an idea," Nell said, then pointedly added, "Do any of these stories appeal to you, Carrie?"

"I get to do the fluff and he gets to do the actual investigation of the murder? I mean, I can talk to Chief Shaun and Sheriff Hickson just as well as Jacko can."

We got trouble right here in Pelican Bay, Nell sighed internally. "Okay, Carrie, why don't you follow Sheriff Hickson, and Jacko, you take on Chief Shaun. I want you to work together on this, keep each other up to date. Don't play Watergate, but one of the stories here might be the rivalry between the two men and the way it affects the investigation."

"Why do I get the sheriff?" Carrie asked. It wasn't quite a whine, but it was close, as if assuming she was automatically given the lesser of the choices.

"Because the sheriff fancies himself a true Southern gentleman and a little flirtation will go a long way with him. Get him showing off for you and he may spill a lot."

"You're suggesting I flirt with Sheriff Hickson?" Carrie asked, her opinion of the sexual attractiveness of the portly sheriff clear in her tone.

"No, nothing so blatant, but a 'gee, you must have a lot of responsibility, and you carry it so well and people must trust you a lot to keep electing you' approach might be useful." Nell inwardly sighed again, wondering if she was going to have to teach Carrie some of the most basic things about how to be a woman in a man's business. A reporter used whatever tools he or she could, and sometimes for a woman it went back to that old sexual thing.

"I don't know—Jacko's got prettier eyelashes than I do. He might do a better job of flirting with the sheriff," Carrie said, but her tone lacked that whine that would have told Nell she still wasn't satisfied. "But then again, he might do a better job of flirting with Chief Shaun than I would, too," she added.

Jacko didn't look up from his pad, ignoring what seemed to be a dig at him. Nell wondered if she should have a talk with Carrie, tell her that impugning Jacko's sexuality in front of her wasn't accomplishing anything she might have thought it would accomplish. It didn't make Nell think that Jacko was gay, only that Carrie was a petulant brat. She decided to let it pass this time. They were adults, after all, and they could figure it out. Besides, a lecture from her would probably fall on the same deaf ears that her lectures to her children fell on. And given that she was feeding, housing, and clothing her children, they had more incentive to listen to her than the cub reporters.

"What about the features? Do you want to do any of them, Jacko?"

"You know me, I love the musty old library. Can I see what other nefarious crimes have taken place here?"

"Okay, go to it. Carrie, why don't you do the 'how to safeguard the kids' one? That has to be a big concern for everybody now, and that should get front page play along with the murder story." Front page should keep her happy.

"This week's edition?" Carrie asked.

"If I get the copy in time," Nell said.

"Well, I'll try my best … but flirting with Sheriff Hickson might take a lot of time and effort …" Carrie trailed off, clearly not about to promise to meet Nell's deadline.

Nell chose not to respond to her hedge. Instead she waved them off with her usual "Go forth and report." She did notice that Carrie followed Jacko to his desk, quizzing him on where he thought she might find what she needed to know. His answer seemed to be the library, as a few minutes later they both left, walking across the green in that direction.

Nell spent the rest of the morning doing her most hated task: balancing the newspaper bank accounts and going over financial statements. When Thom was alive, they'd traded off, first trying every other month, but then realizing that a little more continuity was useful, so each got half a year. "And you still had three months to go," Nell muttered as she re-added a column.

Jacko appeared in the early afternoon, but Carrie wasn't with him.

"So, have fun at the library?" Nell asked. She'd done her financial duty and was on her way to her reward, a turkey and avocado sandwich from the deli down the street.

"Do you know what this town was originally called?" Jacko asked.

Nell thought about pretending she didn't, to let Jacko have his moment. But her vanity got the better of her—she wasn't going to have her cub reporter tell her something she should know. "Perdition Point," she answered.

"And do you know why it was named that?"

"Because the explorers that landed here found bones on the beach."

"Skulls, do you think?"

"Most likely animal bones, from fishing and hunting," Nell answered. "Still, they didn't take it as a good omen and only lingered long enough to name the place."

"According to the old newspapers, Perdition Point has had its share of troubles. In 1947 a shrimp boat was stolen with the owner's lad still asleep below deck. Lad, boat, and thieves were caught in the big hurricane that year and the only clue to their fate was a battered board with the boat's name on it."

"I presume it came ashore in the same place the D'Iberville brothers saw their bones?" Nell joshed.

"Same beach, close enough. And in 1951 there was an interesting fight between two gentlemen. Seems they were both interested in the same woman at the same time and they managed to shoot each other at the same time, so they died at the same time. The woman spent six months in jail for 'fomenting murder' and being the kind of hussy that would drive men to such depths."

"Any murders of children?" Nell asked.

"Only one. In 1964 the sheriff's office investigated a family living on the far outskirts of town. The complaint was cruelty to animals. They had several skinny dogs chained in the back yard. Turns out that the kids were chained, too. They were left in their own excrement and severely malnourished. One of the kids was dead when they got there—had been dead for almost a week, still chained with the other kids." Jacko ended the story there.

"That doesn't sound like a good story to rehash," Nell said.

"No, it doesn't. Particularly with the whispers about negligent parents."

"What are the whispers?"

"What were the boys doing in the woods by themselves?" Jacko answered. "Neither of Rayburn's parents were even home when he went to the woods; he was left in the care of his thirteen-year-old sister. Then on the bike trip, why wasn't at least one of the adults in the lead? Why'd they let those boys ride on ahead?"

"People desperately want to blame, don't they?" Nell said softly, aware she was one of those parents who had let her son ride into the woods.

"Yes, they do. Like we should always know where the monsters are," Jacko quietly agreed.

"We won't run that 'past crimes' story. At least not now. Maybe later, in a few months, when …" Nell left the sentence unfinished.

"I don't think we should even mention the bones on the beach."

Nell gave him a wan smile and turned to go. Let sleeping bones lie. It was time for lunch.

TWENTY-ONE

"THE TOWN USED TO be called Perdition Point," the TV newsman intoned. "With two children murdered, it seems to be reverting to its old name." The camera pulled back to reveal a handsome, windswept man walking along the beach. "The French explorers who first landed on this shore were astonished to find the beach littered with bleached bones. Clearly, murder and mayhem are deeply imbedded in the soul of this sleepy Gulf Coast town. Today it lives up to its name, with the gristly murders of two young boys…"

He turned the sound down. The VCR would capture it for later. He found TV to be blaring and simple, and this was one of his least-favorite reporters. Instead he turned to the paper, this time in satisfaction. He'd taken the entire front page. The lead story, of course was the murder of Joseph Sayton. There were quotes from everybody that had anything to do with it: the sheriff, the police chief, the district attorney, each given equal weight; local prominent citizens; several quotes from the searchers; some from the kids on the bike tour, although he did notice that Nell McGraw didn't include her son. He savored his own quote, how concerned he seemed. The story byline was Jack Evens but he was sure the editor had had something to do with it. Then there was a brief story on the punishment for this kind of crime: premeditated murder was a death penalty in this state. It seemed that the good people of Pelican Bay wanted a foretaste of justice. That story, too, was bylined Jack Evens. The final story was one on how to protect children. Give them secret words that only the family knows, to keep a stranger from enticing them away with promises of rewards, or lies that a mother was sick and wanted the child to go with that stranger. He was familiar with all the rules listed there. They might work—but only with a stranger.

He actually liked Nell's old fashioned reticence. The TV played up the sexual angle, harping on the ways the boys had been abused before they died. "Repeatedly sodomized…" The TV droned into his thoughts. But Nell seemed to understand what it was really about. It wasn't sex, it was power. Sexually, he was normal. He liked women. Sometimes he could play a little rough, but only when they wanted it. Or deserved it. But even that only left a few bruises and reddened buttocks.

The murders are brutal. Evil isn't too strong a word, he read in Nell's editorial. *They don't just kill a child; they shatter the trust and innocence of the entire community. Our sons and daughters now live with our fears…*

That was why he had sex with the children. The more ways he violated them, the more fear he created. He couldn't claim he didn't enjoy it, but it was for the power, watching them struggle and fight and finally understand there was nothing they could do. Everything was his choice. If they tried to scream, he tightened the gag. If they tried to kick and scratch, he would bind them. And enjoy it when he told them how much more it would hurt with their legs firmly bound together. He toyed with them, told them if they were quiet for a few minutes, he'd let them go. Of course he made it hard for them to be silent, thrusting longer and harder, enjoying the smell of blood and fear.

The TV reporter was labeling him a sexual psychopath, but he wasn't. He was a man who enjoyed power and had the courage and wit to take more than the rest dared. Most people would do what he did if they thought they could get away with it. But they were cowards and he wasn't. And he had the brains to not get caught at it.

He looked at the phone and thought about calling Nell again and telling her how much he approved of the coverage the paper was giving his daring. But he was too smart to be trapped by his petty temptations. It wasn't a good idea to use his home phone. He would call later. He liked the sound of her voice. She liked power, too; he knew that. It was in her voice and in the way she ran the paper. She could have sold it after her husband died, but she liked the power too much to let go. It was particularly gratifying when he could hear fear in her voice. He very much liked to hear terror in powerful voices.

He smiled at the memory, and then at the reaction that the memory produced. Power wasn't about sex, but it could be sexual. Very sexual. He folded the paper and put it down.

TWENTY-TWO

NELL WAS FIELDING THE more than usual barrage of calls that awaited her on Monday. Why had the paper devoted so much coverage to a mad killer? Why didn't the paper do a better job of covering the murders—the whole paper should be devoted to the matter! The paper really needed to investigate our next door neighbor, he was very strange and probably the killer.

"And what evidence do you have?" Nell patiently asked.

"Well, he's trying to sell his house, so he leaves his garbage in front of our house. And he's not very friendly, you know. We might have been okay about the garbage if he'd asked, but he didn't. Everything from cut-up banana trees to pizza boxes."

Nell agreed that this was not a polite and neighborly thing to do, but didn't concede that wayward pizza boxes were the sure sign of a brutal killer. She civilly told her caller that she had a long-distance call and had to go. Someday I'm going to have to keep track of the lies I tell callers so I don't keep telling the same caller the same lie, she thought.

"Hey, Nell," Dolan called to her. "Chief Shaun is holding on line two. Says he needs to talk to you."

"Nell," he said as she picked up the line. "I don't want a media circus, but I thought you might like to snap a few pictures."

"Pictures?"

"I'm going to make an arrest."

"An arrest for what?" Nell asked, but the triumph in his voice made her question only a formality.

"Murder. You don't think I'd call up if I was arresting someone for littering?"

"Where are you?"

"I'm at the station. Meet me here in about ten minutes or we leave without you." He put the phone down without waiting for a reply.

Nell hurriedly jumped up and grabbed a camera. "Chief Shaun's about to make an arrest," she announced to the main room as she came out of her office. "Jacko, I want you to come with me. Carrie, head over to the sheriff's office. Be there to catch his reaction."

"You're sticking me with the sheriff again?" Carrie grumbled.

"Look, it makes more sense to stick with the same people you're already covering," Nell said.

"Yeah, once again, take the man to the real stuff. I get stuck watching the beer-drinking Sheriff burp."

"Oh, I'll bet he'll do more than burp when he hears that the chief has made an arrest right under his nose," Jacko said.

"If you think it's going to be so interesting, why don't you baby-sit the sheriff?" Carrie shot back at him.

"Fine by me," Jacko said, with a glance at Nell and a small shrug, as if to say there were other stories.

"Fine. Let's go then," Nell said curtly, doing a less-than-perfect job of hiding her irritation.

Carrie was digging in her desk, presumably for her purse, forcing Nell to stand and wait.

"Okay, do I ask the sheriff his reaction to the chief's making an arrest?" Jacko asked. "Or should I just hang around until something happens?"

"Ask away. Get him going and maybe he'll forget to take it off the record," Nell answered as she decided that Carrie had five more seconds before she headed out the door.

Carrie took the full five seconds, only jumping up when Nell's hand was actually on the door handle.

"I've never seen anyone arrested before, have you?" Carrie babbled as they crossed the town green to the police station.

"Yes, numerous times."

"You think there'll be shooting or anything like that?" Carrie asked.

Nell considered telling her it would be very dangerous, maybe even adding that she was wearing a bulletproof vest. Carrie seemed happy she'd gotten her way and was oblivious enough to think that if she was happy, everyone else should be.

"I'm sure if there's danger involved, Chief Shaun wouldn't invite us along." Nell chose as her reply one she assumed was truthful.

She was spared from further conversation as Chief Shaun came out of the building with several of his officers.

"Nell, right on time," he greeted her, then gave Carrie a questioning glance.

"Hi, Chief. This is Carrie Brody, one of my cub reporters. She wanted to come along and see her first arrest." Petty, Nell, petty, she chastised herself as the words came out, but her guilt was minimal.

"Keeping the pretty ones hidden from me, Nell?" Chief Shaun said flirtatiously. "Jacko's nice, but he's not this nice." He radiated an excited energy, almost exuberant.

"It never crossed my mind to assign reporters by gender," Nell blandly replied. Carrie, she noted, was blushing and giving the chief that kind of look that signaled the beginning of an infatuation. "How did you discover who did it?" she continued, more interested in getting the scoop she knew this was than watching the chief and Carrie flirt.

"I'll tell you on the way. Nell, why don't you ride with me. Gar, take the pretty young lady with you." He was already walking to his car.

Nell followed, motioning Carrie to go with the other cop. There were two other cars idling as well. Clearly this was a major arrest.

"Any danger?" Nell asked as she slid into the car. Chief Shaun was already turning the ignition.

"I doubt it. He doesn't know we're coming."

Nell barely managed to get her seat belt fastened before the chief sped out of the parking lot.

"How did you find him?" Nell asked again. The chief wanted attention; she would give it to him.

"Someone spotted a suspicious car near one of the locations. We ran a check on it and discovered that the owner had been arrested for sex crimes. So we got a warrant and searched his home about an hour ago." He was silent, waiting for her next question. Almost a game of questions.

"What sex crime was he arrested for?" Nell guessed the chief would expect her to ask what he'd found in the search, and she wasn't going to be so compliant with his question game to ask the ones that he expected.

"Does it matter?"

"Both prostitution and child molesting are sex crimes. I'm interested in what specific sex crime this person committed, and why it was potent enough for you to get a warrant based on it."

185

"It was an arrest and not a conviction, so I'm not at liberty to say."

"Off the record?" Nell asked, curious as to why Chief Shaun seemed reluctant to divulge the information. She suspected he'd cut a few corners to get here, corners he might not want a noisy reporter poking into.

"Don't you want to know what I found in the search?"

"Yes, but I'm still not clear on why you felt you had enough probable cause to go after a search warrant."

"How about because kids are being killed and I felt I needed to move on this?"

That was probably as close as she was going to get to him admitting that everything wasn't by the book. But it was something to do some research on later. "Tell me about the search."

"He kept trophies."

"Such as?"

"Underwear. A lock of hair. And pictures. Sick bastard."

"He took pictures of the murders?"

"Of the bodies afterward. Like some hunter with his kill."

"You're right," Nell said. "A sick bastard." She started to add, I know you skipped a few steps here—and I don't care. Just get this brute off the streets so that my kids and I can sleep tonight. But she decided the chief could earn that.

Nell assumed they would be heading to some secluded place on the outskirts of town—that was her image of the killer—so she was surprised when they turned onto the main street. And even more surprised when the chief stopped the car in front of Ron's Flower Shoppe.

She vaguely knew Ronald Hebert. Mrs. Thomas, Sr. was an avid gardener, so choosing purchased flowers over her mother-in-law's homegrown ones wasn't something that Nell did often. Ronald occasionally advertised in the Crier, at times like Mother's Day or Valentine's Day. The mild-mannered florist she recalled from his few visits to the paper seemed very far from someone who would be the murderer of children.

But isn't that often the case? Nell thought. Evil was banal and sold flowers on Washington Avenue. Still, the three police cars with their lights flashing seemed a bit much next to the pastel colors of the flower store.

"Make sure you get my good side," Chief Shaun said as he got out.

Nell also got out, staying on her side of the car. Just in case, she was keeping something between herself and the flower shop. She propped her elbows on the roof and aimed the camera at the door, catching a few pictures of the chief and his officers entering.

"What do you think will happen?" Carrie asked as she joined Nell.

"I'm going to take pictures, you're going to write a story," Nell told her, annoyed at the distraction. Her reporter had the soul of a gossip columnist.

"What do you want me to do?"

"Carrie, if you make me miss this shot, you're fired." Nell put enough bite into her voice to let the young woman know she was close to meaning it. "Jot down notes, describe the scene, the people. Catch reactions, pretend you're a reporter." Nice didn't seem to work with Carrie; maybe not-so-nice would.

Carrie at least understood something. She ambled away from Nell and even pulled out a notebook and started scribbling something down. Probably *I hate my boss, I hate my boss*, Nell thought.

The three police cars and their flashing lights quickly attracted the curious and the bored. Nell glanced at the growing crowd. For a sleepy small town, Pelican Bay could quickly produce a lot of people, giving a hint about how many people were behind the closed doors. She noticed Wendell Jenkins at the far end of the crowd, talking into a cell phone, his gesturing hands indicating his agitation. Nell would bet money that Wendell was on the phone with his good friend Sheriff Hickson. She just hoped Jacko was in the vicinity also. He would be taking notes.

Just then the door to the flower shop burst open, its usual gentle bell a harsh jangle from the force with which the door was thrown back. Two of the cops pushed through, with Ronald handcuffed between them.

Nell snapped the picture and kept her camera focused as they led him to one of the police cars. "Pathetic" was the only word she could think of to describe the florist. His eyes were red-rimmed, as if he was on the verge of tears. He looked small and powerless wedged between the two large police men, his handcuffed arms stiffly held out in front. Looking at him, Nell found it hard to picture him as the man who'd called her in the night. *I just want a better opponent*, she told herself. *Not this banal, scared man.*

The chief came out of the flower shop then, followed by two more policemen. They didn't bother closing the door.

The first two cops kept Ronald next to the police car. Nell heard the chief read him his rights, wanting to make the arrest a public display. Ronald just shook his head in bewilderment, as if he didn't understand what was going on.

A camera crew from one of the television stations appeared. Maybe that was who Wendell Jenkins was calling.

Nell edged around the car to get a better picture of Ronald and the circle surrounding him. With four cops, the chief, and a television camera, the florist seemed even smaller, incongruous even. Nell couldn't shake the sense that this was almost ludicrous—all this show of force to capture one abject man amid his flowers, as if the roses would rise to protect him.

But Nell was reporter enough to step in front of the TV camera to get the shot of them putting the florist into the back seat of the police car. She was close enough to hear him say "This is wrong" before the door was shut.

As she waited for Chief Shaun to finish talking to the inquiring TV reporter, Nell took one last picture of the open door of the flower shop. She wondered what would happen to it, to the daisies and irises still there. Who wouldn't get roses tonight?

Nell turned the *Open* sign around so that it said *Closed*, then shut the door. Neither the shop nor the flowers were guilty.

She joined the chief at his car. He still exuded exuberance. The mighty hunter, Nell thought. And I'm glad of it, she reminded herself. If her intellectual side didn't exactly approve of Chief Shaun cutting corners, the much greater part of her, that of a mother, was incredibly relieved there would be no more late-night phone calls and no more murdered children.

"What happens now?" she asked as Chief Shaun held the door for her. "Do you want me to try to get a picture of Sheriff Hickson's face as you drop your suspect off at his jail?"

The chief just smiled, clearly liking the thought. He didn't answer until he got into the driver's seat. "I'm sure the sheriff will be glad to have a vicious murderer off the street."

"Okay, that's the quote I'll print," Nell told him. "But you've got to get some satisfaction out of capturing this killer. And you and I both know that Sheriff Hickson wasn't really up to the task."

Doug Shaun smiled at her again, and Nell noticed how much the smile transformed the stern uniformed police chief into a handsome man. "You and I both know that. But I see no point in rubbing his face in it. Tempting as it is." He started the car.

"How forgiving of you, Chief Shaun. I didn't know you had it in you."

"Doug. Really, call me Doug. How about dinner tonight to celebrate?"

Nell almost said yes. She suddenly realized she longed for companionship, the frisson of going out with a man. She would enjoy sharing this moment with him. The killer had invaded her days; she deserved a chance to celebrate his capture.

"Two kids," she answered instead, with a rueful smile. "It makes it hard to just go out for dinner on the spur of the moment. Although this is certainly something to revel in."

"Ah, well, maybe the next murderer I capture," he said with a shrug.

Nell wondered if she should suggest another time or if she wanted him to. Damn, this is all so complicated, she thought. "How about lunch tomorrow?" she offered. It was a hedge; lunchtime could be work instead of romantic.

"I may be jawing with the DA, all the paperwork. But if I can get away, we can manage lunch."

That was where they left it. If he called her sometime in the late morning, then they'd arrange something. No call and she could assume he was tied up with the arrest of Ronald Hebert, Jr.

Chief Shaun dropped her off in front of the police station; he was off to the courthouse to talk to Buddy Guy, leaving his men the joy of delivering the prisoner to Sheriff Hickson.

Nell wasn't spared Carrie's company any longer. Gar had been right behind the chief and deposited his passenger beside her.

"Wasn't that exciting?" Carrie gushed. "Nothing like beefy men in uniform and lots of guns."

"Glad it made your day," Nell said dryly.

"C'mon, Nell, even you have to admit that Doug Shaun is a hunk."

Nell decided she didn't have to admit that. She also ignored the implicit insult in Carrie's "even you," as if she were some dried-up, sexless shell. She even forwent the petty revenge of casually mentioning that he had asked her out.

"Now, I'd like to do a feature story on him," Carrie continued. "Get to sit down and ask him some personal questions."

A feature story on Chief Shaun might not be a bad idea, Nell admitted, although only to herself. He had only been police chief for about six months—in Pelican Bay terms that was still brand new. She wasn't sure she wanted to assign it to Carrie; although that, too, might be interesting, seeing how she'd perform on a subject she was interested in.

But some response was clearly expected. "Get the story around today's arrest first," Nell said. "I want you to find out everything you can about Ronald Hebert. If you do a good enough story on him, I might consider letting you tackle Doug Shaun."

"Who should I talk to? I mean, I can't exactly go interview the florist," Carrie said.

"Start with the businesses next to his," Nell instructed. "Find out if there were any other employees at the shop and talk to them. You might be able to get the names of family members, or at least an outline of who he was. Happily married or the weird loner? At least get some quotes from them."

"Should I go back there or can I do it on the phone?"

Nell opened the door to the Crier building and stifled the sigh that wanted to escape at the young woman's question. "You have to go there. You won't get the same response over the phone, nor will you get the people next door coming over to talk to you. Do the entire block, both sides. "

Carrie didn't stifle her sigh. "That's a lot of work."

"Most good stories are."

Nell headed for her office. She noticed that Jacko wasn't there. He, at least, seemed not to need to be told how to cover a story. After going through about ten phone messages, including three from Lizzie involving asking to be picked up, then not needing a ride, then asking if she could spend the night with Janet, Nell noticed that Carrie was still in the office. She glanced at her watch; it was almost four o'clock. I have children at home, Nell thought. I don't need them at work.

She got up and stood in her office doorway. "A lot of those shops will close at five," she said, loud enough to get Carrie's attention.

"It's only four now," the young woman said defensively.

"You're going to interview ten to fifteen businesses in an hour?"

Carrie grabbed her bag and got up. "Okay, I'm on my way now." With that she headed out the door.

Nell settled back in her office, enjoying the peace of being alone. She started writing the straight news story of Ronald Hebert's arrest. If Carrie actually came up with something, she might run it as a separate story of the actual capture. If not, then Carrie could kiss good-bye any chance in hell of interviewing Douglas Shaun.

Dolan arrived a little while later, returning from an errand at the bank, but neither Carrie nor Jacko came back to the office before Nell left. She took the route home that led through town. The *Closed* sign was still in the door of Ron's Flower Shoppe. She didn't see Carrie's car anywhere around.

Home also was peaceably quiet. Lizzie took not getting a response from Nell as a yes to her overnight with Janet, and Josh was at the bike shop according to his hastily scribbled note. Nell started to pick up the phone to call the respective places where her children allegedly were, to check up on them and make sure that they were okay. But she put the receiver down.

It's over, she reminded herself. The monster is in the county jail and my children are safe.

Josh came in just at the outer limits of suppertime. Another half an hour and he would have been eating leftovers, and not just any leftovers but leftovers from Nell's cooking when she wasn't cooking for the kids. They compromised on meatloaf, although Nell insisted on a salad. Josh drowned his in dressing, but at least he ate it. Lizzie usually just pushed hers around on her plate, rearranging the greens, as if the point was to touch it with a fork, not actually eat it.

Josh watched TV and Nell read and the evening passed that way. There was no more than the usual minor dawdling at bedtime. Nell planned on getting a decent night's sleep for once.

The phone rang in the middle of the night. Nell grabbed it up, fear brought on by the jarring bell, racing her heart.

"Hello?" she said.

But there was only silence on the other side.

"Hello, who's calling?" Nell demanded.

She heard what she thought was a soft breath, then the click of a phone being hung up.

He's in jail, she told herself as she slowly put the phone back down. Her heart still raced. It was just a stupid wrong number at a stupid time. It took her a long time to fall back to sleep.

TWENTY-THREE

THE MORNING WAS A perfect spring morning: clear, bright, enough coolness to make the brilliant sunshine more than welcome. Josh didn't even linger with breakfast, hurrying so he could ride his bike the long route to school.

When Nell got to the paper, she unlocked the door, always proof that she was the first one there. Dolan came in a little while later, Ina Claire right behind him. She put her latest recipe in Nell's box. But with the exception of offering a good morning, both of them left Nell alone. Of course, they both had heard about the arrest and seemed to know that the news this week would once again be something very different from high school football scores.

Nell used the time to continue working on the story. She doubted that Carrie was going to come through with anything save a few desultory interviews with the neighboring shop owners, and she wanted a good article. She'd already put calls in to Buddy Guy (that would be the official political statement); Harold Reed (for the true story); Sheriff Hickson (for his official statement, with the hope that Jacko had gotten something more interesting and on the record); and Chief Shaun (for follow-up). Nell intended to find out which corners he'd cut, not so much for the story itself but because she wanted to know what had really happened. Plus, she wanted to have a better idea who Doug Shaun was. Especially if she was going out to a meal with him.

However, the only one of her phone calls that was returned was Doug Shaun's, saying he couldn't meet her today. They agreed on lunch tomorrow.

She held off on doing much research into Ronald Hebert, as that was what Carrie was supposed to be doing, but her frustration built as she didn't hear from or see Carrie all morning. It would have been helpful to know what Carrie had come up with so she could decide how to divide their stories. Nell was a little surprised at not hearing from Jacko, but he had a much better track record than Carrie, so that wasn't as big a concern.

Just as her stomach announced that lunch would be a very good idea, Jacko came in.

"Hi," Nell said, glad to have another reporter to talk to about the arrest. "How extreme was Sheriff Hickson's dismay at the arrest?"

"Way extreme. Turns out Ronald Hebert is a cousin of a cousin of his. And you know how people are about family down here."

"Long night?" Nell asked him, noticing dark circles under Jacko's eyes.

"Uh … yeah, sort of. Look … I need to talk to you."

"Of course. Can we do it over lunch? I'm starving." Nell was betting that Jacko was going to bring up the general situation with Carrie—that she wasn't carrying her weight. Maybe it was time to stop the pretense of treating them as equals, she thought as they headed across the street to the sandwich shop. With enough direction and "encouragement" Carrie was an adequate reporter, but, without a severe attitude adjustment on her part, that was all she'd be.

The shop was crowded, so they decided on an impromptu picnic at the beach. It was about a five minute drive from the paper. Nell decided she could use the time to come to a decision about how she might respond if Jacko requested a promotion.

"How much of a story do you have on the sheriff?" Nell asked as she unwrapped her turkey-on-sourdough. They were sitting on the sea wall, which served as both table and bench, wrappers and napkins held down with their drinks.

"Not that much, really. I don't think it's a good or fair idea to play up the cousin-of-a-cousin angle."

"True. It's not really relevant and it would only make Sheriff Hickson mad."

"He told me I could quote him on the record as saying that he doubted a home-town boy like Ronald, someone we've know all our lives, could do such a thing."

"But the chief claims he has some pretty damning evidence."

"Yes, but..." Jacko trailed off.

"You're not convinced," Nell said, suddenly suspecting that this conversation had nothing to do with Carrie.

"I...I know Ronald," Jacko said, then was silent.

"Are you friends?" Nell probed. Pelican Bay was a small town and she knew little of Jacko's life outside the paper. It was quite possible he and the florist had met, although she was a little surprised.

"Not...really." Again he was silent.

"Do you not want to cover this story?" Nell asked. Jacko was struggling with something, and she was trying to think of a question that would get him to talk to her.

"I'm … afraid I'm part of the story," he said softly. He took a breath and hurried on, "I spent the night with him. The night that Joey Sayton was killed."

Nell found herself caught off guard by his confession. No, this was not a conversation she'd ever expected to be having with Jacko. She quickly silenced all the first questions she wanted to ask—You're gay? He's gay? How did you hide it so well from me?—and tried to focus on the underlying purpose of Jacko telling her this.

"Did he go out during the night?"

"No. No, he didn't."

"Could you have been asleep and not noticed?" Nell asked gently. Others would ask this same question and they would not be gentle.

Jacko shook his head, but answered, "Maybe. I don't think so, though. I woke up several times during the night and he was always there. He went to the bathroom once and I woke up then."

"Are you sure that it was just going to the bathroom? Could you maybe have woken up only when he came back and assumed that that was where he'd been?"

"No, I woke when he rolled out of bed, heard him go about his business, and he came back to bed. And I was still awake when he fell asleep."

"Are you sure enough of his not going anywhere to swear to it in court?" Nell asked.

"Oh, God, I don't know. We met at a bar over in Biloxi, had a few drinks together, and went back to his place. Don't think my landlady would approve of me bringing men home to spend the night."

"What time was all this?"

"If I'd known … known all this would happen, I would have worn a watch," Jacko answered with a rueful smile. "I guess I left my

197

place around eight thirty, got to the bar at nine or so, came back to his place sometime after ten and before midnight. Could I even swear to any of these times? No. Sorry."

It was possible that Ronald Hebert had killed Joey Sayton, strung him up in the tree in the picnic area while the bikers were still in the woods, and then met Jacko later that evening in the bar, Nell thought. She had considered not even finding out the time of Joey's death, keeping open the possibility that he hadn't been dying and dead in the oak tree the whole time they were there. A heaviness settled over her as she saw the almost inevitable consequences for Jacko. He would have to tell his story to people who would view him as tainted just for sleeping with another man, let alone a man who was a cruel murderer. She would have to check, but even if Joey had been killed during the time Jacko and Ronald Hebert were together, that was no positive proof that Ronald *didn't* do it—any prosecutor would argue that he'd slipped out when Jacko was asleep. The laws had changed, but attitudes hadn't.

For a brief second Nell considered suggesting he not tell anyone, but that would be futile. If Ronald Hebert hadn't already named Jacko as an alibi, he probably soon would. It wouldn't look good for Jacko to try and hide what couldn't be hidden.

"You know this won't be easy," Nell said gently.

"Am I fired?" Jacko asked abruptly.

"No, of course not. You're the only decent reporter I have" was Nell's initial, fierce response. But then she wondered if every good intention on her part would be enough to make it possible for Jacko to keep working in Pelican Bay after this.

"Thanks," he said softly. "What do we do now?"

Nell thought for a moment. "We finish lunch. That's what we do." She took a bite of her sandwich, then added, "Maybe we should talk to Harold Reed, the assistant DA. It might be ... easier." Easier than talking to those macho boys Chief Shaun and Sheriff Hickson.

They finished their lunch silently. Jacko threw half of his sandwich to the seagulls.

Then he turned to face her, "I guess now is as good a time as any," he said.

"Delay won't help. Not if Ronald has already told them about you," Nell admitted.

Jacko looked at her. "Do you think he will ... admit to that?"

"He's facing a murder charge. This may still be Mississippi, and not many people around here cheer for gay marriage, but he's still better off being called queer than facing the death penalty."

Jacko just nodded. They got in Nell's car and she drove; Jacko hadn't really agreed to talk to Harold Reed, but that was where she took him. She knew she wouldn't win any points with Doug Shaun for going past him—in fact, he might never take her to lunch—but her main concern was Jacko.

He asked her to go in with him, and she agreed.

"You know I can't say much in the middle of an ongoing investigation" was the first thing that Harold said as they entered his office. Of course, he thought they were there as reporters.

Nell explained they weren't, and Jacko told his story.

Harold listened impassively, not even blinking as Jacko described picking up Ronald Hebert in a gay bar. Harold asked the same questions Nell had, but his were more probing, hinting at the harsher questionings that would come.

Unlike Harold, Jacko was far from impassive, the wavering steadiness he'd started out with deteriorating into breaks and hesitations that almost verged on tears.

When Harold at last finished asking what he had to ask, Jacko allowed himself the obvious gesture of wiping his sleeve across his eyes, then he quietly said, "I can't believe that Ronald murdered—"

"Someone did" was Harold's terse reply.

Jacko abruptly stood up, as if he couldn't bear to stay any longer in this place where he'd been forced to blurt out secrets he never intended to share. "I have to wash my face. I'll see you back at the paper," he said to Nell, not looking at her. Then he was gone, his footsteps almost running down the hallway.

"It won't make much of a difference, will it?" Nell said. "His honesty will take him through hell and it won't make a difference. Unless..." She trailed off, not sure she wanted to ask the question.

"Unless?" Harold prompted.

"Time of death. What if the time of death is when Ronald Hebert can find about ten or so witnesses to place him in the bar?"

"I don't want this in the paper," Harold said, leaning forward, as if the smaller distance could better keep a secret. "The victim died approximately between four and six a.m. But the killer was brutal and clever and had left him to die." Harold leaned back.

"How?" Nell asked.

"Do you really want to know?"

"I've got too much imagination to not know."

"Joey was hung up in such a way that he could take some of his weight on his arms, but once he got too tired and couldn't hold himself up ... So the killer didn't even need to be there, and we can only guess at how long Joey might have been able to keep himself alive and how long he was in the tree."

Maybe Harold had been right, Nell suddenly thought. Maybe she didn't want to know. "So he was in that tree the whole time we were there?"

"I'm sorry, it's possible," Harold confirmed.

"Oh, God, that's horrible!" Nell burst out. She couldn't be a reporter anymore, remembering Joey's parents sitting at that picnic table, their son alive and within thirty yards of them.

Harold just nodded. They sat in silence for what seemed like minutes. Finally, Harold broke it. "Do you think that Jack will leave town?"

"No, I can't see that," Nell answered. "Or if he was going to, he would have by now. Why stay around to confess to sleeping with a man accused of murdering children?"

Harold gave a tired sigh. "You know the politics around here. Doug Shaun is convinced he's got his man. Sheriff Hickson is running around questioning why Ronald Hebert, who has lived in this town all his life, been a good solid citizen, albeit"—Harold consulted some notes on his desk—"'a little light in the loafers,' suddenly turns into a killer."

"Not to mention he's a cousin of his," Nell added. "And you think that Jacko will be a pawn between the two of them?"

"I know he will." Harold's phone rang.

Nell got up to leave. There didn't seem to be much else to say.

But as Harold reached for the receiver, he added, "The only thing that could put a stop to all that is another dead child."

Nell found her way out of the office. It was still a perfect day outside, as if the sun couldn't pay attention to human misery.

When she got back to the Crier building, Jacko wasn't there. She wasn't really surprised. If she weren't the boss, she wouldn't have come back either. Nell wasn't so much worried about Jacko fleeing as she was about how he was handling this. Reporters are the observers, not the observed; add that to a forced coming out and being linked sexually with a possible murderer, and Jacko was in a hellish position. Nell decided to give him some time alone and call him around closing time—and through the evening if she didn't hear from him.

She did mindless tasks to pass the afternoon, including the filing that she hated. (Thom, although he hadn't enjoyed filing, had had a much lower tolerance for unfiled papers than she did, so he usually just took care it.) Only after she'd sharpened just about every pencil in the office did she decide it was time to give Jacko his first call, then go home and see if her children were there, or if she had to do something to get them there.

She brushed the pencil shavings off her hands and sat down at her desk, only to look up and see Douglas Shaun framed in her doorway.

"Chief Shaun." She announced the obvious, surprised at his sudden appearance.

"Hello, Nell." He came into her office and sat down, not waiting for an invitation. "Where's Jacko?"

"You've talked to Harold Reed," Nell stated.

"Yep. Shame that I had to," he said accusingly.

"What was I supposed to do, parade my reporter through the police station to you?" she suddenly flared. "Given what Harold told me about the time of death, I don't see that the alibi Jacko gave Ronald Hebert would matter a damn."

"Okay, fine, I can understand why you made the decision that you did. But please call me, at least. Believe it or not, we're on the same side."

"Believe it or not, we are, but that doesn't mean I have to call you every half an hour and report what I've been doing. I knew that Harold would contact you, so you can't accuse me of withholding information. All I can see here is your ego smarting because I didn't do the little woman thing and run to you first."

Doug Shaun said nothing, his face a blank slate. Then he abruptly burst into laughter. "You know, you're quite attractive when you're irate."

"Oh, please..." Nell started.

"No, I'm serious," he interrupted. "Brings out the blue in your eyes."

"And this hardly qualifies as irate. You might not find me so 'attractive' if I was really angry."

"Point noted. I would like to talk to Jacko."

"I sent him home," Nell prevaricated. "Thought he'd had enough for a day."

"Will he be in tomorrow?"

"He'll be around. Let me talk to him and we'll set up a time."

Doug Shaun nodded either in agreement with her offer or because he knew that it was as good as he was going to get from her. He suddenly asked, "Are you going to keep him on?"

Nell was taken aback at the question and realized it was probably one she was going to have to answer over and over again. "Of course. I've decided to make the Crier tabloid. What better way to start off than with 'My Night with A Murderer—The True Tale of Passion in a Killer's Lair.' Then Jacko can out all the fine citizens of Pelican Bay who frequent places they're not supposed to be at. We'll have everything from the blood alcohol level of yacht club members to who's at the stripper bars over in Biloxi."

"Guess that answers my question."

"Why did you focus in on Ronald Hebert?" Nell asked, taking the conversation in a direction that gave her control.

"A hunch." She let her silence pull him to continue. "I ran a search for sex crimes in residents of Pelican Bay."

"You must have had a field day with that. Want to work on a tabloid?"

"Ronald's name came up."

"For what?"

"He was arrested over in New Orleans. Crimes against nature statute."

"The sodomy law?" Nell wondered if the chief thought she wouldn't be familiar enough with the law to know what it really covered. "Or I should say, the former law. If it's no longer illegal, is it still in the records?"

"He solicited an undercover officer for oral sex. Got arrested. Yeah, the law's old, but still there."

"You targeted Ronald Hebert because he's gay?" It was barely a question.

"Look, I got the killer. What do you want?"

Nell sighed, then replied. "I want it to be some monster that doesn't feed into people's prejudices. That was it—just an oral sex charge?"

"His car was seen near one of the crime scenes. And he was at Rayburn Gautier's funeral."

"He's the local florist. He probably goes to a lot of funerals."

The jangle of an unfamiliar phone sounded. It was Chief Shaun's cell phone. "Sorry," he said as he answered it, getting up and stepping out of Nell's office to do so.

She finished packing up to leave. She really did need to check on her children, although nothing more traumatic than having to wait for her to come pick them up now threatened their lives.

Just as Nell got to her office door, Doug Shaun came back in. She stepped abruptly back to avoid running into him.

"I've got to go," he said. "Report of some teenage kids drinking and running through a neighborhood, trashing mailboxes and cars. Maybe instead of lunch we can do dinner some other night?"

Nell was surprised. "Some night when I'm able to make arrangements for the kids," she reminded him. "The kitchen isn't pretty if I let them fend for themselves."

She started to move through the door, as she thought he would, but he was still facing her. Nell suddenly wondered, am I so blind I didn't see this coming? He leaned in to kiss her and put an arm around her shoulders. It was an awkward embrace; Nell felt like she couldn't remember how to kiss a strange man.

His cell phone rang again, and they both used it as a signal to pull away.

Then Dolan came through the front door. "Nell, you still here?" he called.

"Just leaving," she said. She and the chief walked to the door; he was talking on the phone as they left. Evidently he was getting an update on how many mailboxes had become victims of the rowdy teenagers, and how many people were complaining that something needed to be done.

He continued talking and walking with her until they arrived at her car.

"Good night, Chief," she said.

"Doug," he mouthed at her. Then he leaned in to gently kiss her on the cheek, as if sensing that she wasn't ready for more. Or maybe it was just the talking on the phone that kept him at that chaste level.

Nell unlocked her car and got in. She quickly started it, worrying that he might end his conversation and she would lose this time to think about what had happened. But the chief was heading toward the police station, still talking.

Why can't it be easy, Nell thought. His touch had reawakened some physical urges in her; not so much sex, but the desire to be touched and held. Even if she wanted him to kiss her, was it only to stave off her loneliness or did she actually see something in the man? He was, well, he was attractive, although not in a way she'd expected. She found herself thinking that it might be nice to have someone in her life, even if—if what? Doug Shaun wasn't the perfect man of her dreams. Even if she could see a number of rough spots ahead? Could she see a lifetime with him? Then she chided herself—that's not the right question at this point. Could she see going out to eat with him and having a good time? Yes. And did she want a chance to return his kiss?

Maybe, she admitted, especially if she could do it in some alternate world where she didn't have to worry about what Lizzie and Josh would do. Or even about how she might feel driving by Thom's grave. The widow McGraw didn't waste any time before enjoying other men's kisses, she imagined the gossips of the town somehow knowing. How can I still miss Thom so much and yet think about other men? Is there a proper period of grieving before you can think about sex again? Why the hell can't I just stay numb and asexual? The familiar drive home gave her no clear answers.

"Maybe I need to push Carrie in his direction and solve the problem," she said aloud as she turned into her driveway. Time to be a mother and not worry about strange men and their kisses. Mothers didn't kiss strange men, after all.

Both Josh and Lizzie were home, and they'd made it there without resorting to the mom cab. Lizzie was even in the kitchen, with a chicken on the counter and a recipe book open.

It would have been easier to have done it herself, but Nell wasn't going to discourage a budding cook. Besides, it gave her one of those "good mother" moments when the chicken came out of the oven, all roasted to golden perfection. She and Lizzie gloried in the feast they were providing. Nell helped Josh with the dishes, as Lizzie had used a more than usual amount of them.

All in all it was a quiet, calm evening.

Until the phone rang at two in the morning.

"Hello?" Nell answered it groggily.

No one spoke, but she felt that someone was there. Someone who intended to destroy her rest.

Suddenly she said, "You're not in jail, are you?"

The line went dead.

Nell stared at the phone in her hand for several seconds before finally putting it back down. Is it really possible they have the wrong man? she wondered. Or am I letting the darkness and being jarred into this make me paranoid? No, you're the newspaper lady, she reminded herself. You piss people off if you can't read their illegible handwriting and misspell their name. Most likely the call was a wrong number again, at worse a petty harassment from someone who didn't like what came out in the paper.

She slept again, but only fitfully, caught between thoughts of men kissing her and strange, haunting phone calls.

TWENTY-FOUR

THE MORNING WAS BRIGHT and clear and Nell's fears of the night seemed out of place in the bright sunshine.

It was a wrong number, she told herself firmly as she poured milk over cereal. Normalcy had returned; she was staring at three brightly colored bowls with bananas and strawberries cut up on top.

Then breakfast was over, books hurriedly found, her children at school and herself at work.

Jacko was at his desk when she arrived, early even for him. He didn't have kids to cajole him into keeping school hours. They had talked briefly the night before, but all Nell had gotten from him was a mumbled "I'm okay."

He looked like he hadn't slept much, his eyes red-rimmed with dark circles under them.

"Good morning," Nell greeted him.

"I'm sorry, but it's not." The toneless-ness in Jacko's words worried her as much as what he'd said. "I've got pictures of the body bag. Good reporter to the end," he added with a harsh, sardonic grimace.

"Another murder?" Nell asked, her fear from the late-night phone call instantly returning.

"Suicide, they said. They said that … he hung himself."

"Ronald Hebert?" Nell asked quietly.

"I saw them taking the body out. Asked what was happening and they said that justice had arrived early."

"How did you manage to be there?" Nell put her hand gently on his shoulder.

"Couldn't sleep. Was driving around. Don't know why I went by the jail … maybe because Ronald was there, just so not everyone would forget him."

"That's when you saw them bringing him out?"

"Saw a hearse, thought I might be a reporter and find out what was going on." He suddenly looked at her. "Does it ever get to you? This job? Ever wish there were things you didn't see, details you didn't have to write down?"

"God, yes. Save me from the day I become so inhuman that some things don't become ghosts to haunt me. Jacko, I'm so sorry." Nell put her arms around him.

Jacko returned her hug, crying as he leaned against her. Minutes passed, and then he pulled away, wiped his eyes, and then said, "I need to wash my face." He stood up abruptly, as if embarrassed by his crying.

"Coffee?" Nell asked as Jacko headed to the bathroom. It was one of their common morning greetings. Usually either Dolan or Jacko felt an immediate need for a jolt of caffeine as they came through the door, so they offered to run get coffee for all who wanted some.

He gave her a wan smile. "Yeah, that'd be great."

Nell headed across the street. She got two coffees and two blueberry croissants, chanting to herself as she recrossed the street, "I will go bike riding with Josh this afternoon. And tomorrow and the next day." That might atone for the croissant.

Jacko was back at his desk, his face scrubbed but still showing the effects of too-little sleep and a good bout of crying. He nodded thanks as Nell handed him the coffee and croissant.

"Do you want me to resign?" he asked quietly.

"No. Like I said, of course not. I need one good reporter around here. Unless you want to?"

"Not really, but ... but the fact that I slept with a man accused of murder might be all that people ever see of me."

"It might be," Nell admitted. "But let's see how things go. I don't want you to go. The choice would be yours."

Jacko nodded, then took a sip of his coffee, but there was an expectant look on his face as if he had something more to say. "I'd like to stay on the story."

"As a reporter or as a vendetta?"

"I want it to be as a reporter. I want ... some account of the vigilante justice that Ronald got."

"You don't think he committed suicide?"

"No, I don't. He just wasn't the type."

"Maybe not in usual circumstances. But he was far beyond that."

"I don't think he would have given up so easily. If he didn't do it, why kill himself so quickly?"

"What if he did do it? Can you be sure he wasn't the murderer?"

Jacko took another sip of his coffee. "No, I can't be sure. I don't think he was the killer. I don't think he killed himself. But I can't be sure. I'd like to investigate. I'd like to find out what the truth really is."

"Even if it's not a truth that you want to hear? What if you never find it?"

"At least I'll have looked. I don't think that there's any truth I want to hear," he added softly.

"Okay, I'll let you dig. But it's a short leash," Nell told him.

"Thanks. It needs to be. I guess I don't … I want to be a reporter, not some wild-eyed crusader. I trust you to keep me there."

It was a compliment, but Nell merely acknowledged it with a nod. "I want a daily report of what you've done and what you're doing. We'll meet every day at the end of the day—Carrie should be gone by then. There may be times when I'll go with you. And times when I'll go without you. Understood?"

"You're the boss, Miz Nell," Jacko said. He even managed a bare smile.

"Are you willing to do the obit for Ronald? If not, I can …"

"I'll do it."

"Okay. Also do a background on the county jail. Any other instances of jailhouse justice? Is there a pattern? Let's do the archives first before we tackle the present."

Jacko made a few quick notes, then turned to his computer with a nod in Nell's direction.

She left him to begin his day, going back to her office and the guilty pleasures of a blueberry croissant. I'm going to miss him, Nell thought as she glanced at the intent look on Jacko's face as he worked online. The terrain they'd just negotiated wasn't gentle, yet they'd easily understood and agreed with each other. Much as she liked and respected Dolan and Ina Claire and Alessandra and the rest of her staff, she hadn't found the easy camaraderie with them that she had with Jacko. It was hard to admit, but it would take a miracle for him to remain an effective reporter in their small town.

TWENTY-FIVE

NELL MET MARION AT a local coffee shop. "A mid-afternoon break," her friend had called it. They had already twice rescheduled any discussion of the library book Marion was concerned about, once because Marion's mother was ill and once because Nell got a call about a sighting of the elusive alligator. She'd rushed to the harbor but only managed to get a picture of something that might have been an alligator tail. Or a floating log.

Marion opted for mint tea, while Nell went for an espresso. The late night phone calls had penetrated her sleep, making her restless even when nothing happened.

"I presume that you've heard the news," Marion said as they sat down.

"Probably, but which news are you referring to?"

"Ronald's murder."

"You don't think he killed himself?"

"I've know Ronald for a long time—we went to elementary school together—and if I had to pick a person least likely to hang himself, it would be him," Marion said.

"Even if he'd murdered children and knew what was facing him?"

"Maybe I'm one of those wide-eyed innocents," Marion said slowly. "Like the neighbor who thought the serial killer was a nice guy. But I just can't fathom Ronald as a killer of any kind, and particularly not of children."

"Did you know he was gay?"

"An unmarried man in his mid-thirties who's a florist? I never suspected."

Nell chastised herself for her misstep. It had sounded like she was conflating his being gay with killing children, but she'd really been probing to see how well Marion knew the man she claimed wasn't a murderer. "I was trying to find out how much you really know about him," she said, hearing how lame her excuse sounded as she said it.

"Right," was Marion's terse reply. When she'd first sat down, she'd put her elbows on the table, leaning over her tea. Now she sat up straight, her arms crossed.

"I don't think that being gay and murdering children have anything to do with each other," Nell said. Defensively, she noted.

"Then why bring it up?" Marion retorted.

"Reporter's habit. Ask provocative questions."

"A habit that must not make you many friends," Marion answered coolly.

Nell wondered if this was the time to finally confess that she knew about Marion and Kate, and that she knew why Marion was so offended by her comment. She decided against it. It could sound too much like she was belittling Marion's anger, insinuating that Marion was only upset because she was gay, too.

"You're right," Nell admitted slowly. "I'm not very good at making friends. It was something I relied on Thom to do, and now ... I'm trying to find my way. I know how to be a reporter, but not … not really how to be the life of a party."

"Always asking the questions and never answering them might not be the best way," Marion said. But her voice wasn't so cold and she now leaned slightly forward.

"What questions have I asked and not answered?" Nell asked.

"You asked me why I came back to Pelican Bay. About what it was like growing up here, about my family, the library. We joked about it really being Perdition Point. But you didn't really talk about yourself. You never said why you stayed."

"Where else would I go?" Nell answered quickly.

"Anywhere. You're intelligent, talented, clearly have major organizational and management skills. It shouldn't be hard to find a job—and a place more fulfilling than Perdition Point."

"I've got my kids … this isn't a bad place for them to grow up."

Marion didn't say anything, but she leaned forward onto the table, her eyes questioning Nell.

"Maybe," Nell continued, into the silence Marion left, "maybe I'd planned my future here with Thom and … now that he's gone, I've been too numb to think of a future for myself without him. Or maybe I can't let go of his dreams and plans … and the memories here."

"We can endure a lot with love, but without love …" Marion trailed off. Of course, Marion had love to help her endure; Nell did not.

"And maybe I don't really know," she said. "I only know that I'm here and there's no clear direction anywhere else right now. Except to try and make friends," she added with an unsure smile.

"The grand experiment. I'm game if you are." Marion returned her smile.

"You're not the first person to tell me they didn't think Ronald was a murderer, of children or himself," Nell said.

"Jacko?" Marion asked.

"A good reporter never reveals her sources."

"You're not a reporter now, you're a friend, remember?" Marion gently chided her.

Nell realized that she did want to talk to someone about Jacko—what might happen to him and the ways she could and couldn't protect him. "Yes, it was Jacko," she admitted.

"See, it wasn't so hard. And don't worry, I'm a librarian. Nobody comes to us for gossip."

"We don't have to talk about this if you don't want to," Nell said.

"Actually, I'd like to. It's the reason I wanted to see you this afternoon, you know. That returned book we talked about? It's disturbing, and I think I should give it to someone, but I don't really know who to tell about it."

"You said there were drawings?"

"It might be evidence," Marion said.

"Then maybe you should take it to the police and not involve me," Nell said, but her curiosity made her hope that Marion wouldn't take her advice.

"That's the problem. Here, let me show you." Marion reached down into her large canvas book bag and produced a children's book. She handed it to Nell.

It looked like one of the picture books Nell had seen Rayburn Gautier taking home with him from the library. She gave Marion a quizzical glance.

"Look inside," Marion instructed her.

Nell started by fanning through the pages. She realized that someone, presumably Rayburn, had added crayon drawings. She stopped her skimming and began looking at the pictures. They were crude figures added to the scenes in the book. Looking closer, Nell noticed there were also additions to some of the book's pictures. The added stick figure was smaller than the other pictures, as if the added figure was a child with an adult. And the adults had been altered and were now anatomically correct, or at least the ones she assumed were the adults.

Marion clearly read the look on Nell's face. "Dolly mentioned Rayburn coloring in some of the books. When I shelved them, I looked at the pictures. You were there the day she came in, remember?"

Nell nodded and said, "I'm still not sure why you didn't show it to Chief Shaun? Or Sheriff Hickson?"

"Look closer at the pictures."

Nell flipped to a few more and saw what had prompted Marion's reluctance. The book was a picture book about different jobs, and only the pictures of people in uniform had been altered. Most of the uniforms had crude guns and badges added to them. If Rayburn was depicting the man who'd molested and finally murdered him, then that man wore some kind of uniform. Even that was speculation, although it seemed certain that a male adult had been having sex with the boy. Nell didn't like the thought that one young boy could be molested by one man and murdered by another. It made the world too savage to think of these crimes being so common that a child in a small town fell victim twice.

The drawings were too crude and lacking in detail to guess more than that. In one picture the gun was blue, in another it was orange. The badge similarly changed colors. There was a hat drawn in, but it was just a floppy thing on the head that could be the cowboy hat of the sheriff's office or the peaked cap of the police force. Or even a Smoky Bear hat of the forest service.

"So, what do I do with this?" Marion asked softly.

"I'm not sure," Nell said slowly. "I guess it should be finger-printed, the usual stuff."

Marion gave her head a gentle shake. "A lot of people have touched that book, probably none of them the killer. I'm wondering if it would make any difference."

"Maybe you could go to Harold Reed, the assistant district attorney. Last I saw, his only uniform was a suit."

"I don't know him, but that's a thought. Or I could go to Buddy Guy, hand it over to him, and tell him I'll vote for him in the next two elections if he takes care of it."

"Which is probably the same as going to Harold Reed, except for the extorted votes," Nell pointed out. In a more sober tone, she continued, "It could be anyone in any uniform."

"Not quite anyone," Marion interjected. "Unskilled as the drawings are, nothing indicates it's a woman."

"No, and although it does narrow the suspects down a bit—"

"And Ronald is eliminated, too. He never was even a Cub Scout. I think the butchest thing he ever did was go as the tin man for one Halloween."

"—it still leaves it open to a lot of men in uniform," Nell finished.

"I know. But Sheriff Hickson pulled me out of the harbor when I was six and thinking that I could swim like the big kids. It's hard to suspect him. Yet he also … let Ronald be killed."

A cell phone nearby rang. It took Nell a moment before she realized it was hers. She smiled an apology to Marion and picked it up. "Nell McGraw," she said brusquely to the interrupter.

"Mom?" the voice on the other end said. "I'm sorry, but I forgot my key and now I'm locked out. Josh isn't going to be out of his stupid bike class for an hour and it looks like it's going to rain," Lizzie finished in a voice filled with teenage angst.

"Okay," Nell said. "I'll be there in a few minutes. Try not to melt before I arrive."

She ended the call and said to Marion, "There seems to be a hurricane that we don't know about headed this way and my teenage daughter has locked herself out of the house."

"Time to batten down the hatches—and unlock the doors. Thanks for meeting me."

"Let me know what you decide to do," Nell told Marion. "Or if I can be of any help."

"Thanks. It's helped to talk about it. I might think it over tonight and postpone any decision until tomorrow."

"Don't wait too much longer. They'll move on to the next thing," Nell said as she stood up.

"Tomorrow. I'll do it then," Marion said quietly.

On impulse, Nell gave her a hug. There was a sadness in her that seemed to need it. "Tomorrow, we'll talk, okay?" she said as she let go.

"I'll call you," Marion agreed.

A crack of thunder suggested Lizzie might not have been exaggerating as much as Nell thought. She headed out of the coffee shop and home to rescue her daughter.

The rain gods were not kind and fat drops were starting to fall as she pulled into the driveway.

"About time, I could get drowned out here," Lizzie greeted her.

"I would have been here sooner, but I got stopped three times for speeding," Nell answered as she unlocked the door.

"Funny, very funny," Lizzie replied, in a voice that made it clear this was not what she thought. She ducked through the door in front of Nell. "That creepy cop guy was back around the school today," she added from the safety of the kitchen.

"What the hell is he doing back in town?" Nell was too angry to even apologize for the curse.

"Sorry, I forgot to ask him that. But he wanted to know where Josh was."

"You didn't tell him, did you?" Alarm put a hint of demand into Nell's voice.

"My little brother's right over there, can I hand you this rope and knife?" Lizzie, Nell noted, was getting quite good at teenage sarcasm.

"Maybe I should call the bike shop and make sure Josh is okay," Nell mused.

"Mom." Lizzie made it a two syllable word. "Sometimes you are so overprotective. Josh's only at the bike shop with Kate, ten other kids, and at least four parents. Very dangerous."

Am I overprotective? Nell wondered. What's the perfect line between keeping children safe and not smothering them? She also noted the hint of jealousy in Lizzie's tone, implying that Nell had left her standing out in the rain but was worried about Josh at the bike shop. Worse, was she treating Josh as more valuable, spending more worry on him because the "creepy cop" had asked about him than she was on Lizzie, who'd actually been confronted with the man? Or maybe it was just that Lizzie was standing in front of her and okay, and Josh wasn't.

"I'm sorry. I'm just having a moment of mother panic, wondering if Josh really is at the bike shop," Nell apologized.

"Janet's dad gave us both a ride in the back of his truck, so unless someone kidnapped him in the ten feet from the curb to the door, he's probably okay."

Now I can worry about my kids bouncing around in the back of a pickup truck, Nell thought, but she decided discussing it could wait until another time; or maybe she would just talk to Janet's mother. "Okay, you have an advantage on me. You saw him go into the bike shop?"

"With my very own two eyes," Lizzie answered. Then seizing on Nell's guilt, asked, "Is it okay if I get on the computer until suppertime? Janet and I are working on our homework over email."

Nell managed half a nod yes before Lizzie was out of the kitchen and into the living room where the computer was. There's not only the danger of riding in trucks—I should also check what homework is actually being done, Nell thought. She suspected it was one tenth homework and nine tenths chatting about boys.

"I'm going to go back to the office," she said to her online daughter. She was granted a bare nod of acknowledgment. "Call me when Josh gets in." Again she got a half nod. Nell took the cell phone left in the pile of purse and books, put it beside Lizzie, and repeated, "Call me."

Lizzie gave a guilty start at seeing her mother within screen-reading distance. "I'll call," she hurriedly agreed, just as quickly minimizing the screen she was working on.

Nell had time enough to read "way cute," which she doubted had anything to do with assigned homework. She bent down to give Lizzie a quick kiss on the cheek, to let her know she'd been caught and that her mother didn't mind.

Leaving Lizzie in the bliss of a home to herself, Nell headed back to the office, being sure to carefully lock the house door. And still wondering if she was being overly protective or a reasonable parent.

When she arrived at the Crier, Jacko was there, as they had agreed he would be. Carrie, as usual, wasn't. Nell hadn't seen her all day.

Jacko looked up at her and in a flat, tired voice said, "The sheriff told me to get the hell out of his office."

"What?" Nell stopped in the middle of the room, then caught herself and crossed to Jacko's desk. "Tell me what happened."

"I guess … news travels fast."

"He threw you out because you're gay?"

"Yeah, more or less. The minute I walked in, I knew that something had changed. None of the 'Hey, Jacko, how's it goin'?' Just a few mumbled hellos. So I put on my polite boy-reporter face, including the 'yes, sirs' and 'no, sirs,' and talked about the weather for a bit. Then I asked if there'd been any progress in investigating Ronald's death. That got me silence, a stony stare, and finally 'Suicide, nothing to investigate.'"

"This was from the sheriff himself?"

"Yes, ma'am, it was. I followed up with asking if there was a note or anything like that, and the only answer to that question was that I needed to get out of there. One of the deputies managed to say loud enough for me to hear, 'The only good faggot is a dead faggot.'"

"Oh, Jacko, I'm sorry."

"I can't be a reporter in this town anymore. They probably would throw me out of the sewage and water board meetings."

"It's crazy. You're the best damn reporter I've had since I started working on this paper," Nell said, feeling her anger start to build. And her sadness. She knew too well it was true.

"Thanks. So can I count on you as a reference?" Jacko attempted a wan smile.

"Good Lord, of course. But I don't want to lose you. Would you be willing to hang tough for a while and see if it dies down?"

"Yeah, well, it's not like I have another job waiting for me. But …" He trailed off.

But small towns have long memories, Nell finished silently. However, all she said was "Give it time. It might blow over. And I think I'm going to ask the sheriff a few follow-up questions." With that she went into her office, leaving the door open so that Jacko would be privy to her conversation.

"Sheriff Hickson, please," she said when the phone was answered. "Nell McGraw of the Crier." She was left on hold, but she finally heard the labored breathing of Sheriff Hickson as he picked up the phone.

"Miz McGraw. What a pleasure," he drawled.

"What evidence do you have that Ronald Hebert's death was a suicide?" Nell plunged in.

"You ain't gonna let that question go, are you?"

"First rule of reporting: when someone in power doesn't want to answer a question, you ask it over and over again."

"Look, I don't want that nelly boy reporter over here questioning me."

"You don't want him? Okay, then you'll get me." Nell hung up and angrily got to her feet. She also noticed that the sheriff had again ducked her question. She went into the main room and rummaged in the storage closet for a small tape recorder and notepad.

"I'm going to visit Sheriff Hickson," she told Jacko. As an afterthought, she added, "Follow me. Park discreetly out front. If I get thrown out, take some pictures for the front page."

"Yes, ma'am," Jacko answered, throwing her a mock salute as he got up to head to his assigned post.

The sheriff's office was near the jail and the county courthouse, on the outskirts of Pelican Bay. It was about a fifteen-minute drive from the paper, and Nell needed those minutes to calm herself down enough to be a reporter. Albeit an angry reporter.

Sheriff Hickson clearly intended not to be there when Nell arrived, but he only made it as far as the front door. They met on the top step of the building.

"Sheriff Hickson. What a pleasure," Nell greeted him.

He merely sighed.

"Just a few questions," she hurried on.

"A few quick ones. I got other places to be."

"Ray opened his bar again?" That's the only one you get, Nell admonished herself.

"Ma'am?" Sheriff Hickson gave her a confused stare, clearly not quite catching what she said.

"What have you learned from questioning the assailant who raped Ronald Hebert?"

That cleared the confusion from his face. "Who the hell let that out? And don't give me that 'sources' crap," he thundered at her.

Nell calmly replied, "You just did."

"Goddamn you, Nell McGraw! Where do you get off tricking someone like that?"

"I have to admit, Sheriff, you're the first one who ever fell for it," Nell again answered calmly.

"I don't want to see that in the paper!" he bellowed.

"What evidence do you have that Ronald Hebert committed suicide?"

"He was a faggot and he was in jail for killing kids. Any man with half a brain'd kill himself."

"Seems to me those very facts, that he was branded as being gay and accused of molesting and murdering children, would be likely to lead to him being attacked by other inmates. If he hanged himself, how do you explain the marks on his body?" Nell was again guessing, but how the sheriff reacted would tell her the story.

"He tripped and fell in the shower. How the fuck do I know? Happens all the time that people get bruised up in jail."

"Even bruises that would be described as classic defense wounds?"

"Maybe he had to defend himself in the showers, you know. And what sonofabitch leaked things from the coroner's office?"

"So you're admitting that within twenty-four hours of being taken into your custody, Ronald Hebert was sexually assaulted and had bruises all over his body that would be hard to self-inflict, yet you claim that he committed suicide? Before even seeing a lawyer or hearing the evidence against him?"

Nell hadn't expected this to calm the sheriff down, and she was right.

"Where the fuck do you get off, lady? Pardon my French. No, don't pardon it—you want to be a feminist, you can hear any language just like the men. What the fuck are you accusing me of? You want your own little private Watergate right here in Pelican Bay?"

"What evidence do you have that Ronald actually killed himself instead of being killed?"

"I got evidence, but I don't want it blazoned 'cross the front page. Seems you got enough stuff that you shouldn't know already."

"Can you explain why the public shouldn't know how their tax dollars are being spent? Who could you possibly be protecting by withholding evidence that Ronald committed suicide? Other than yourself?"

"What the hell are you accusing me of?" he demanded again.

Nell took a moment to calm herself and pretended to glance at her notepad. At least if the sheriff took a swing at her, Jacko would get a picture of it, she consoled herself. "I'm not accusing you of anything, but I am questioning you about letting a prisoner in your custody be sexually assaulted and possibly murdered. I'm questioning why you insist that he killed himself but seem to have no concrete evidence to that effect."

"Just him hanging in his cell. Not likely that anyone else put that sheet around his neck."

"I'm questioning why you won't answer my questions, and why you threw Jacko out of your office using his sexual orientation as a pretext to avoid answering those same questions from him."

"Thom wouldn't of caught me here on the steps going home, peppering me with questions like this," Sheriff Hickson retorted.

"Thom's not here anymore, Sheriff. That's something we both will have to deal with," Nell replied, fixing him with a cool stare. Don't you dare use my dead husband against me, she silently accused.

Perhaps Sheriff Hickson got the message, or perhaps he just decided that getting to that beer waiting from him at Ray's Bar was more important. He changed tack and said, "Well, Miz McGraw, we're in the middle of looking into all this, and I'm gonna answer the taxpayers' questions, but in due time. Just give us time to do an investigation before you run all this speculation on the front page. You got any last questions?"

A last question ... she could only think of one. "What if Ronald Hebert was innocent?"

"You really think that?" the sheriff demanded.

"I don't know. But I know that the law of the land gave him the presumption of it."

Sheriff Hickson just looked at her for a moment, then down at the steps, a sudden weariness crossing his face. "I hope to hell he did do it ... to hell. If he didn't, this would cut so deep it'd never heal." With that, he stepped around her and down the steps.

Nell let him go. She could think of no more questions.

She met Jacko at his car and told him it was time to go home. He nodded but didn't start the car, looking off into the distance. Nell started to say something but no words came. Maybe there were none. She left him to go home to her children.

She had a moment of guilt at realizing her cell phone was sitting on the seat on the car. That changed into concern when she realized that either Lizzie had forgotten to call as arranged, or Josh hadn't come home yet. The worry carried her almost all the way home, until her headlights revealed a boy on a bicycle. She followed Josh into the driveway, glad to be there and that her children were safe.

After taking care of mother things, like fixing something to eat that contained a few elements of something vaguely healthy and making sure that Lizzie really had done her homework (although she did forbear going over it with her editing pencil), Nell finally had a moment to assess her day. She decided to call Doug Shaun.

She wanted to see what he knew about the death of Ronald Hebert. She was still uncertain about what she wanted out of a relationship with the chief—and realized that calling him in the evening sent a signal she wasn't sure she wanted to send—but she felt she owed it to Jacko to see if she could find out anything.

First she called his home number; it rang three times and then the answering machine came on the line. Nell hung up. She wanted to talk to him, but not enough to leave herself in the position of waiting for him to call her back. Instead she tried his cell phone, but she got an "out of service area" message. She called again fifteen minutes later and got the same message. Nell decided to leave it at that. She would call again tomorrow—both Doug Shaun and Sheriff Hickson, she decided. She wanted to make sure the sheriff's investigation into what happened in his jail cells was progressing satisfactorily. Or even progressing.

Then Nell made the phone call she really wanted to make, to Marion Nash, partly to find out what she'd decided to do about the defaced book, but also to have someone to talk to. Again, she was met with only an answering machine. I must be the only one at home tonight, Nell thought to herself.

TWENTY-SIX

"NELL, YOU HAVE TO find out what really happened" was one of the last things Nell expected to hear from Mrs. Thomas McGraw, Sr., and certainly not during breakfast. She hadn't hesitated to pick up the phone—the morning presaged nothing more than a call about school events or who would pick up whom and where.

"What's going on?" Nell asked.

"Are the children there?"

"Yes."

"Call me the minute that they leave." Adding nothing further, Mrs. Thomas hung up.

Annoyed, Nell put the phone down, wondering what it was that Lizzie had done now. She was aware that her mother-in-law didn't much approve of the way she was raising Josh, either—bikes instead of football or little league—but didn't meddle as much because she didn't think any single woman, even herself, should be raising a son.

The children in question were involved in their usual school-morning chaos, locating books and the all-important purse that Lizzie never seemed to ever put in the same place. Josh was biking to school, so he was out the door first, and then Lizzie followed him. She was being picked up by her friend Janet and wanted to be on the curb waiting, as she considered that more adult than hanging out in the kitchen. Nell also wondered if Lizzie was operating on the belief that if her mother didn't see her using her cell phone to chat with the friend almost at her door, then it was okay. But the world of bills would catch up with her.

Nell took a moment to gather her own things, then called Mrs. Thomas, Sr. back.

"Nell?" She answered on the first ring.

"Yes," was all Nell got out before the woman continued.

"I'm on my way to Erma Nash's right now. They think she may have another stroke . . . and maybe she should. Maybe she should just go."

"Why? What's happening?" Nell asked with a glance at her watch. She wanted to be at work early.

"The sheriff was just at her place. I was the next person he called. He knew that Erma needed someone to be with her."

"To be with her? Where's Marion?"

"No mother should outlive a child," Mrs. Thomas, Sr. said softly.

"Mother, what's going on?" Nell demanded, but the chill was already in her bones, as if a part of her could hear the echo of metal screaming into metal, the death of her husband.

"Marion," Mrs. Thomas, Sr. answered. "It's Marion. They say she was murdered."

"What!?" Nell exclaimed, the chill slamming into ice that numbed her. "No, oh, no! Not . . . not murdered. How?"

"I don't know. Only what little the sheriff told me. I've got to get over there. You will find out what happened, won't you?"

"Yes, of course." Nell mumbled agreement, too numb to take umbrage to the preemptory note in Mrs. Thomas's request.

"Good. Call me later, I've got to go." The line went dead before Nell was able to reply.

She stood, frozen, her mind screaming that this was a bizarre mistake. The women she'd hugged yesterday in the coffee shop couldn't be dead. But Nell also knew that Thom's mother wouldn't be spreading rumors or racing ahead of the facts. And she had no sense of humor, certainly none as bizarre as this.

"Goddamn it!" Nell said to the empty kitchen as she slammed the phone down. "I'm just supposed to fucking investigate my friend's death because you fucking want me to." The curse was unlike her, but it felt good to flout her mother-in-law's rules and the task she had dumped on her, even if Nell was the only one to hear it.

"Marion can't be dead," she added, as if words could chip away at the stark reality.

But she could be.

Slowly the numbness lifted and Nell felt her thoughts begin to churn. The word that burned across her consciousness was "murdered." How? And why? She quickly gathered her things to head to the office, but she couldn't still her mind enough to avoid wondering what had happened. Could Marion and Kate have had the kind of fight that can escalate into violence brutal enough to leave one of them dead? That seemed impossible; that was not the people she knew. Or was it just some random horror, a burglary gone wrong or a drunken brawl that had spilled over on the wrong person?

As Nell got into her car, another dread came to her. The book Marion had shown to her—could she have been murdered because of that? And if so, did it tie into the murders of Rayburn Gautier and Joey Sayton? The dread coalesced into a wavering certainty. Improbable coincidences did happen, and that was why they made the papers—because they were so unlikely. Two and possibly three children were murdered, Marion Nash had evidence that seemed to indicate someone in a uniform had had a hand in those murders, and Marion Nash was killed. They have to be related, Nell thought. Nothing else made sense.

Be a reporter, she admonished herself. This is all speculation and no matter how likely it seems, I can't let it blind me to other possibilities.

The people and the traffic seemed to go at their normal morning pace, as if no one understood that the world had been pushed further askew.

As she pulled into the lot near the Crier, Nell wondered how people go on. When it isn't something you can walk past, but a death in the heart of your life, how do you get up every day? Suddenly she remembered her mother-in-law's words—*no mother should outlive a child*—and her even-more-haunting suggestion that it might be better for Mrs. Nash to fall into oblivion than live with the knowledge of her daughter's death. As much as Mrs. Thomas, Sr. rankled Nell, the woman had lost a child. And although Nell loved Thom and missed him, she'd always lived with the knowledge that one of them would leave the other behind, that death was unlikely to be kind and wait until they were old and take them together. But Thom's mother had always thought she would outlive her son.

As Nell entered the office, Dolan called out a cheery hello.

Nell couldn't return his greeting, instead said, "I just heard Marion Nash was murdered."

"What?" Dolan said, all cheer gone from his face.

"That's all I know. I'm on my way to see if I can find out more."

"Oh, God, Nell, that's too much. This town can't take so many murders."

Nell merely nodded and went to her office. She paused there only long enough to see if she had any phone messages, but there were none.

"I'm going over to the police station. Tell Carrie and Jacko we're doing a story conference at ten and I want them here," she instructed Dolan. Then she added, "If you see them, that is."

"Poor Mrs. Nash," Dolan said. "Who's going to take care of her now?"

Nell didn't answer; instead she headed out the door and across the green to talk to Doug Shaun. She briefly wondered if that was where he was last night when she couldn't reach him—investigating another murder. But the timing didn't make sense, if she thought about it. They wouldn't wait overnight to tell Marion's mother. Or maybe they would. She sighed. Maybe they thought Mrs. Nash could handle it better in the light.

She felt an irrational stab of anger at the "boys in uniform" and their way of arranging the world. Not so irrational; she reminded herself of Lizzie seeing that "creepy cop" again when Boyce Jenkins was supposed to be anywhere but here.

"Is the chief in?" Nell asked at the front desk.

"Hi, Nell, I'm here," Chief Shaun called, sticking his head out of his office as if waiting for her to come by. "Come in."

As Nell seated herself across from him, he said, "I gather you've heard the news."

"About Marion Nash? Yes, I have, although only that she was murdered. No details."

"How did you find out?" he asked, but it wasn't in the accusing tone that the sheriff might have used. It seemed more a question about what had happened to Nell.

"My mother-in-law, Mrs. Thomas McGraw, Sr., is very close to the Nashes. She called me this morning as she was on her way to sit with Mrs. Nash." Nell didn't add the part about being told to find out what had happened.

"Bad news moves quickly," Doug said. "This is ... well, I came here to resolve teenage boys joy riding in cars, not murders like this."

There seemed to be a genuine sorrow in his eyes. Nell wondered if he'd known Marion. He probably knew her at least by sight—the library wasn't far from the police station. Nell also realized that Doug Shaun had beautiful eyes for a man.

"Can you tell me what happened?" she asked, to get her focus away from wondering about the man and if there was something between them or if she was just needy and his shoulder was available.

"I don't know much. As usual, the sheriff and I are jockeying over jurisdiction. I think we owe it to Marion's family—and the people of Pelican Bay—to do the best investigation we can."

"So was she killed outside of town?" Nell asked. She felt the comfortable mask of her reporter identity slip into place.

"Yes. You know that motel out on Highway 90? The one about a mile beyond the city limits?"

Nell shook her head.

"No real reason for you to notice it. I don't think it's a place you'd recommend to your friends. It's the kind of joint truckers crash at for a few hours, or some of the guys on the oil rigs stay when they're between jobs. And the place where the good folk of Pelican Bay meet to ensure that they're not seen by their neighbors."

"You mean it's a prostitute hotel?"

"More of an affair hotel. Most of the working girls are over in Biloxi around the casinos, but I'm willing to bet the late-night desk clerk knows the right phone numbers."

"What the hell would someone like Marion be doing in a place like that?" Nell asked. It wasn't quite the proper reporter's question, but Doug didn't seem to notice.

"It's only a guess, but she was probably there for the same reasons most folks go there. Except for her, things somehow got out of hand."

"Got out of hand how?"

"She ended up dead."

"You're saying this was some sexual escapade that took a horribly wrong turn?"

"Maybe. It's possible they were playing on the rough edges. We don't know who the guy was, but if the sheriff's crew doesn't bumble it up, there should be semen and blood samples."

"From the … person who killed Marion?" Nell asked. She'd been wondering if Marion and Kate had decided on a hotel tryst, but any semen would rule that out. While she'd been surprised to discover that Marion and Kate were a couple, that had been nothing more than having her complacent assumptions proven wrong; now, she was genuinely shocked at the idea of Marion engaging in tawdry affairs that took place in cheap, out-of-the-way motels.

"I suppose it's possible that she had sex with some guy and then, after he left, someone else came in and killed her," the chief replied. "There could be the sickos who get off on spying on these kinds of hotels and after seeing the man sneak out, go after the woman. But I don't think that's likely."

"Why are you so sure it was a sexual encounter? Could it have been a rape/murder?" Nell asked. It was hard for her to accept that

Marion was dead, and harder still to accept that she'd been killed in such a manner.

"Anything's possible. But how did she end up at that motel? If she was abducted, would she have quietly sat in the car while the guy checked in and then not yelled her head off at those flimsy walls? I know it would be easier to still think she's the person you thought you knew, but I'd be surprised if it played that way."

"What should I print in the paper?" Nell asked the question more of herself than of him.

"I don't know. Depends on what you want her family to read."

"Not that their daughter was a tawdry…" Nell couldn't say the words used to describe such a woman. She couldn't even think it. Not Marion.

"Even if it's true."

His phone beeped, then a voice said, "Chief, Harold Reed is here to see you."

"Send him in."

"Doug," Harold Reed said by way of greeting. Then he noticed Nell. "Nell, hello. I can guess why you're here," he added grimly.

"I'm trying to find out what happened," she said.

"So are we," Harold replied, "so are we. I need to talk to the chief."

"Without a reporter listening in?" Nell said. She stood up to indicate she would leave and give them their privacy. She wondered how much of his desire for her to leave was based in not wanting a reporter there and how much in not wanting a woman to hear the details of Marion's murder.

"Thanks, Nell," Doug said. "I'll keep you updated."

"I'll keep you updated, too," Harold said. "Just as soon as I run it by Buddy Guy and his focus group." Then added, "Unless you promise not to quote me directly."

"Thanks, gentlemen," Nell said with a nod to Harold indicating he was safe from being quoted. "I'd appreciate anything you could get me before our deadline today." She left the office, closing the door behind her.

Nell slowly walked back across the town square. She hadn't found out much, and what she had was disturbing. She had held back from mentioning what she knew about Marion's sexual orientation—Jacko's honesty had accomplished nothing, and she wasn't sure that exposing Kate to the same kind of scrutiny would have a different result. Marion had clearly wanted their relationship to be secret when she was alive; was there any compelling reason to violate that secret now that she was dead? If the police knew that Marion was in a lesbian relationship, it might give weight to the theory that she had not just casually picked up some strange man and been killed by him. But Nell realized that that was only the way she saw it. Others might be more likely to assume that if Marion stepped outside one sexual boundary, she could easily cross others.

When she entered the Crier building, both Jacko and Carrie were there. Carrie was saying, "It's clear, Jacko, that you can't cover this story anymore, so you might as well give it to me."

"I thought I was the one who assigned stories here," Nell interjected.

Clearly surprised at her appearance, Carrie mumbled out, "Nell, I didn't see you come in. Jacko and I were just talking about things."

"Things?" Nell queried.

Carrie took a breath and decided to plunge ahead. "Look, we both know Jacko can't waltz into the cop shop and have them treat him like one of the boys anymore. Who else do you have besides me?"

Nell took a long look at her, rankled at how clearly Carrie had read the situation and how she was using it as leverage. "I still know how to report a story."

"Well, even so, you need me to take over some of Jacko's stories. You can't do it all."

Nell gave her the barest of nods, then said, "Jacko, I want you to keep researching the jail, like we discussed. I was just talking to Doug Shaun, so I'll continue to cover the police story. And you," she said to Carrie, "need to head over to the sheriff's office. Find out what you can—" Abruptly, Nell stopped. She'd been about to say "about the murder of Marion Nash," but if Jacko didn't already know, it would be a cruel way to break it to him. "Find out what they've been up to since Ronald Hebert died," she amended. She was reluctant to trust Carrie to ask the right questions, but after her encounter with Sheriff Hickson last night, Nell figured she'd probably get less from him than even her green girl reporter would. Of course, Carrie would find out about the murder of Marion, but by the time she got back, Nell would have talked to Jacko.

Carrie didn't do a good job of hiding her disappointment that she was assigned the corpulent Sheriff once again while Nell kept Doug Shaun for herself. Having already gotten part of her way, though, Carrie pushed for it all. "Why can't I cover the police chief as well? That way I can compare their approaches and keep track of what they're both doing."

"I'm friends with Doug and I have an established relationship with him" was what Nell said, but the thought under her words was, it was me he kissed and not you.

This flash of petty arrogance surprised her. She certainly didn't need to compete with Carrie, and even if they did fight over Doug Shaun and he chose Carrie, it would just prove that the chief wasn't someone Nell wanted to do more with than briefly kiss. But that quick intellectual overlay didn't disguise the fact that a part of herself wanted someone to want her—to look at her that way. Nell didn't know where this person would fit into the life of the widow and mother she was, so she turned away from it and back to her work.

Carrie looked like she might say something more, so Nell cut her off.

"Remember, we have a deadline looming. I need you to get as much as you can by five if not before. Otherwise, it'll be in next week's paper."

With that strong hint, Carrie grabbed her reporter's tools and the purse large enough to carry them all and headed out the door, her only triumph a quick call of, "Hold the fort while I'm gone."

"So, do you want to take over the sewage and water board meetings?" Nell sardonically asked Jacko.

"I might. Now that I've been outed, I can openly flirt with the chair. It might work as well for me as for Carrie."

"That's all we need. A sex scandal." Nell invented the headline: "Father of Five Caught in Sewer with Blond Hunk."

"Career Down the Drain," Jacko punned.

Nell shook her head, then remembered the somber news of the morning. "Come into my office, Jacko. I need to talk to you."

Once they'd sat down, Jacko opened the conversation. "If this is about Marion, I already know."

"It is. I didn't know if you knew."

"You were going to tell Carrie to look into Marion's death, then you stopped. You were trying to spare me. Otherwise, you'd have been reading her chapter and verse about what she needed to ask the sheriff."

"How did you find out?"

"We have … friends in common. Someone called me."

Nell wanted to ask if it was Kate, but Jacko was clearly reluctant to mention names. Instead, she tried from a different angle. "How well did you know Marion?"

"Mostly through the library. Some mutual friends."

"Are you aware of how she died?" Someone was going to tell him, Nell rationalized. It might as well be her. She wanted to see his reaction to the idea of Marion picking up a strange man and going with him to a cheap motel.

"Only that she was murdered. It seems so strange, so impossible. Do you think all the deaths can be related?" Jacko suddenly asked.

"Why do you think that?" Nell returned his question.

"I don't know … it just seems odd that this quiet town abruptly has two or more killers running around."

"Like evil should all come from only one source? And when you find that source and extinguish it, then the evil disappears?"

"I guess so. I know it doesn't really make sense. People get murdered all the time for all sorts of different reasons."

"Like you, I don't have anything to pin it to, but there do seem to be too many killings here lately. Believing in bizarre coincidences makes the world seem just too random and chaotic. If you should stumble across anything …" Nell trailed off.

"I'll let you know," Jacko finished for her. Then he quietly asked, "How did Marion die?"

"I haven't got much yet, but Doug Shaun said that it appeared she'd been murdered by a man she picked up. Mr. Wrong. Her body was found in that motel on 90 on the edge of town."

Nell watched Jacko's reaction. He was clearly taken aback by that news, but she couldn't tell if it was from the details of the murder or shock at Marion's having casual sex with a man.

"Marion out in some cheap motel …?" Jacko slowly said. "It just … doesn't square with … what I knew of her."

"What did you know of her?" Nell asked.

"Not … well, just that she didn't seem the type to pick up men and go to hotels. More … well, a librarian. When we met we usually talked about books."

Nell remained silent, hoping that Jacko would continue. He didn't.

Finally, she asked, "Are you up to writing the obituary?"

He briefly looked away, not so much avoiding her as holding some part of himself back. "Yes, I'd like to be the one to do it," he finally answered.

"Okay. Make it as long as you want."

Jacko nodded and turned back to his desk. Whatever Nell was going to find out about Marion's life, she wasn't going to find it out from him.

She shut her door to do some work. It only took a few minutes for her to realize she wasn't getting any editing done. Ina Claire's fans might have to wait a week before they got a look at her stuffed flounder recipe.

Instead, Nell picked up her phone, rummaging through her Rolodex for names she rarely called. Her first choice was John at the New Orleans *Times-Picayune*. If Jacko got a job there, he would still be close enough to occasionally do a feature story for the Crier. But that wasn't the only phone call she made. She also called colleagues in New York, San Francisco, Detroit, Boston, and San Antonio, anyone she thought might appreciate someone with Jacko's talent and hunger. I will miss him, Nell thought as she put down the phone. But taking care of a chore she had no choice but to do helped quell her nervous energy enough for her to settle in for a good bout of editing.

Sometime in the middle of it, Dolan entered her office and put a tuna salad sandwich on her desk and had her sign a few checks, but his was the only interruption until Jacko came in and silently handed her the copy for Marion's obit.

He didn't stay to watch her read it.

Marion Allingham Nash

Marion Nash, a librarian at the Tchula County Library main branch in Pelican Bay, was found dead Wednesday night. Police are investigating the circumstances surrounding her death. Ms. Nash was valedictorian of the Pelican Bay High School Class of 1995. She attended college at Vanderbilt University and received her MLS from the University of Washington in Seattle, Washington. After graduating, she lived in Seattle from 2001 until returning to Pelican Bay in 2007. While living in the Pacific Northwest, Ms. Nash was active in a variety of causes, including serving as vice-president of the local chapter of the Sierra Club, on the board of a social service organization, and as a volunteer for the Seattle AIDS Project. Upon returning to Pelican Bay, Ms. Nash was a member of the Unitarian Church and created a library outreach program to bring books into places where children and young adults gathered. A passionate outdoors women, she could often be found hiking or biking in local parks.

Ms. Nash is survived by her mother, Mrs. Erma Nash, and two brothers, Mr. Robert Nash of Torrance, California, and Mr. Ervin Nash of Knoxville, Tennessee.

The obituary went on to list the details of the service, to be held in Erma Nash's Episcopal Church, Nell noted. She also noticed what was left out. The secrets of Marion's life would be kept in death. The oblique reference to her volunteering for an AIDS organization and serving on the board of an unspecified social services organization were the only hints.

Nell read through the copy again, several times, before she finally had enough distance to look at it with an editor's eye. Two more reads only found one typo. She changed nothing that Jacko had written.

"Mom?"

Nell looked up. Josh was standing in her doorway.

"Mom?" he repeated. "I'm sorry to bother you here, but the bike shop is closed and I forgot the house key." Nell must have had a puzzled look on her face because he explained the relation between the two. "I'd planned to just hang out at the shop until I knew that either you or Lizzie were home and it wouldn't matter if I had a key or not."

Suddenly, Nell felt very protective of her son. Another mother had lost a child today; life seemed too fragile for her not to be grateful that Josh was standing in front of her explaining mundane things like misplaced keys.

"It's okay. I'm glad that you came here," Nell reassured him.

"I hope that Kate's not sick or anything," Josh said. "The bike shop is always open."

"She's young and strong," Nell answered. "Whatever it is, I'm sure she'll survive it." She'll just never be the same, she thought. She'll just always carry an almost unbearable burden of grief. But Nell could think of no way to gently convey what she knew to her son. Better a soft lie than a hard truth, she told herself.

But her gentle approach was quickly rendered useless. Carrie strode through the front door, and she had news to tell. "You won't believe what's happened! We've got a major sex and murder scandal. I just got the goods straight from the sheriff. Marion Nash, our quiet little librarian, was found strangled and naked—"

Nell leapt from her chair, trying to silence her before Josh got all the gristly details.

"Carrie!" she called from her office door.

The young woman looked at her, but clearly was still too caught up in her supposed scoop to notice that no one else shared her enthusiasm. "Nell, this is front page. Give me half an hour to write the story and—"

"Jacko's writing it," Nell brusquely told her.

"Mom? Miss Marion from the library is dead?" Josh softly asked her, a waver in his voice she'd never heard until Joey was killed.

"Jacko's writing it?" Carrie questioned. "How? I just found out a few hours ago. I've been with the sheriff all day. This is my story. I even went to that hotel room and saw all the blood—"

"Mom?" Josh asked.

"Carrie!" Nell almost shouted. "My son's here."

"It's not fair. It's my story."

"Write it then. Write it now. Just stop talking about it."

"But—"

"Write it!" Nell ordered her.

"But I get front page," Carrie retorted.

"Just write the story and we'll see," Nell answered, a hard edge to her voice. Only her son's presence stopped her from telling Carrie to write the fucking story and shut the fuck up.

"Mom? Mom, what happened?" Josh asked, standing beside her.

"Come into my office, honey," she told him, ushering him in with her arm around her shoulder and closing the door to anything that might be said in the other room.

He looked at her, waiting for an answer. Nell could see the hope in his eyes that it would somehow all turn out okay after all.

"I'm not sure quite what happened, but … but yes, Marion is … dead. I'm sorry," Nell added uselessly.

"But she was in the bike shop and she was okay."

"You saw her?"

"Yeah, and she was fine. How can she be dead now?"

"I don't know, honey, I don't know yet." Nell almost questioned Josh about what time Marion was there, where she went afterward, did she and Kate seem friendly or cool? But this was her son and the questions could wait, if she asked them at all.

"Will you find out?" Josh asked.

"I'll do what I can," Nell promised him, hearing the echo of her mother-in-law's request. She suddenly wished that she could turn away from this—not learn the haunting details, not be the one to have to decide how much of Marion's life to expose for public scrutiny. And she should get Josh away from the news room and the world of writing obituaries and discussing murder. "Why don't I take you home?"

Josh just nodded, his emotions clearly veering from shocked numbness to fear and grief.

"I'll be back," Nell said as she ushered her son through the main office. She was relieved to see Carrie actually bent over a computer keyboard and silent.

As she got in the car, she hoped that Lizzie was home. She didn't think it a good idea to leave Josh alone, but she knew that she would have to come back to work.

Letting themselves into the house, Nell was relieved to hear the sounds of Lizzie at the computer. The door was barely closed before the phone rang. Lizzie started to grab it, but Nell was closer. She was too afraid it might be work—and today work included the murder of a family friend—to let her children answer it.

"Oh, good, Nell," Mrs. Thomas, Sr. said. "I was worried that the children were home alone. I know you're likely to leave Lizzie and Josh alone when you're at work."

Which, of course, was exactly what Nell was about to do.

Mrs. Thomas continued. "And given what has happened lately, I think it's something you should take particular care to avoid.

Nell bit back her first reply: Thom didn't leave me well enough off to afford a round the clock governess. Instead, she asked, "How is Mrs. Nash?"

"Too hardy for her own good. She shouldn't have to live through this, particularly given the smut that's being said" was Mrs. Thomas's succinct opinion.

"What's being said?" Nell asked.

"Bizarre rumors about strange men in motel rooms. Not Marion at all. Her mother won't hear such talk. The police had the nerve to ask her and then act as if a mother wouldn't know her daughter well enough to know that couldn't be true."

"The police came and questioned Mrs. Nash?" Nell asked.

"Yes. That new police chief had the audacity to ask Erma about her daughter's sex life. As if all unmarried women these days have one."

And tell their mothers, Nell silently added. Doug Shaun might be a good policeman, but he hadn't won any Southern gentleman contests in this town. There might be ways to find the information he was searching for, but directly asking Mrs. Nash wasn't one of them.

"We finally had to shoo him away. You will tell him, won't you, Nell, how far wrong he is?"

"It wouldn't be appropriate for me to interfere in a police investigation," Nell stiffly replied.

"Someone has to do something to quash these bizarre rumors. The police asking questions about such things won't help matters."

"Mother," Nell said, some of her exasperation finally coming out. "I don't have the power to tell the police what questions to ask or not ask. They do their job. I only report on what they're doing."

"Yes, of course, but still someone has to tell the truth about Marion."

And just what is that truth, Nell wondered. Was Marion the person her mother knew, the woman Kate Ryan kissed, or the woman the police claimed her to be?

"I'll do my best" was Nell's answer.

"You're going to stay home with the children, aren't you?" Her mother-in-law returned to the original topic.

Nell saw no point in arguing this one. Instead, it was time for a flanking attack. "Of course. But I have to get the paper out. I need to make sure that whatever appears in print is appropriate. Can I bring Josh and Lizzie over to stay with you? As you said, it's not a good idea to leave them alone." Nell knew that Josh and Lizzie wouldn't much like the idea, but she was also hoping that an evening with real live children might make Mrs. Thomas less likely to interfere, lest she risk more exposure to the increasing frequency of their adolescent squabbles.

"You have to go back to work?"

"The paper has to go to press," Nell reminded her.

There was a moment's hesitation before Mrs. Thomas said, "Well, of course you can bring them by. It'll be nice to spend some

246

time with Elizabeth and Joshua. I'll tell Bernice that we'll have two more for dinner. Or do you think you'll be done before then?"

"I'm not sure how long it will take," Nell replied truthfully. She did consider calling Bernice on the kitchen phone and warning her that ordering pizza for her kids might be the way to go for dinner.

"Fine. I'll expect you to be by shortly." That was the end of their conversation.

As expected, Josh and Lizzie groaned about spending the evening with their grandmother and away from computers and a TV where they had some say over what was watched. Nell resorted to bribery and offered pepperoni pizza tomorrow for cooperation, or at least not outright rebelliousness, today.

After dropping her kids off, she headed back to the paper. The day had turned dark, clouds bringing an early sunset.

Jacko, Carrie, and Dolan were there. There was a tension in the room and Nell knew she was going to have to settle some disputes. She hoped they were merely editorial.

"Welcome to the Pelican Bay Inquirer," Dolan greeted her, holding up the story Carrie had written.

"It's the facts. We report the facts, remember?" Carrie huffed.

"I'm going to my office, taking off my jacket, and then I'll read it," Nell said as she walked past them, taking the story from Dolan as she went by.

She shut the door to give herself enough quiet to think, and to obscure from observation what she suspected would likely be liberal use of the red pencil.

A dank motel room on the outskirts of town was the last place that Marion Nash saw alive, was the first sentence of Carrie's article. *Her nude body, legs splayed open, was discovered early this morning by a shocked young maid.*

Nell settled for brutal efficiency and rewrote the entire story, not even bothering to see if she could save anything that Carrie had written. Any adult would guess that the murder of an attractive young woman in a sleazy hotel had sexual overtones; Nell saw no reason to spell it out to those too young to understand or those who preferred not to know. She was, she reminded herself, certainly capable of angering her mother-in-law, but she also saw no reason to rub the tawdry details of her daughter's death in Mrs. Nash's face. Nell also had to admit that she had significant questions about how and why Marion died, and she wasn't going to simply write the young woman's murder off as some debased and bizarre sexual killing.

When Nell opened her office door, Dolan, Jacko, and Carrie glanced up at her, different looks of expectation on their faces.

"What did you think of my story?" Carrie asked, the fool rushing in.

"I totally rewrote it," Nell answered in a calm tone that she hoped would influence Carrie's response. "The style that you used was inappropriate for this paper. Junior high kids read us for the sports and band sections. I'm not going to have them read about nude bodies with their legs splayed open."

"Well, it's true!" Carrie blustered.

"Is it? Or is it just what the authorities told you?" Nell answered back. "Did you actually see the nude body with her legs spread?"

"Well, no, but Doug told me—"

Nell cut her off. "He wasn't first on the scene, the sheriff's department was. Learn to be skeptical of everyone, Carrie, even handsome men."

"Why would they mislead us?" Carrie argued.

"What if they're not misleading us, but misleading themselves? They see what they want to see. Should we just follow blindly along?"

"This doesn't have anything to do with the two of you being friends?" Carrie shot back.

"Maybe. Maybe I have a very hard time seeing the Marion I knew doing that. Maybe since all her friends and family deny that she was the type of woman who would go to a sleazy motel with a strange man, I want to have a little more proof that the scene the police constructed is true before I put it on the front page."

"That won't help sell papers," Carrie rejoined.

"Some things are more important than selling papers," Nell answered. Then said, "Come on, Dolan, we've got a paper to lay out."

Carrie took her clear dismissal as a cue to leave the building. The day was far from over, but Nell doubted that Carrie would do much more work.

Most of the paper had been set up, so there were only the few last minute things they needed to add. Jacko didn't need to stay, but he did. To Nell it felt like a show of loyalty, a thank you that she hadn't quickly branded his friend as a sexual wanton. Nell wished she could find a way to ask Jacko a few more questions, even just to find out for sure if he really was telling her all he knew about Marion.

Dolan, as usual, offered to take it to the printer's. From that point on it would be more or less out of Nell's hands, save for writing the checks to pay for the process, looking over invoices, and listening to complaints from readers when the paper didn't show up where it was supposed to.

As they parted at their cars, Nell glanced at her watch. Another hour in each other's company would ensure that her mother-in-law and her kids wouldn't be eager to share an evening together again. Nell suddenly felt a pang of loss. It hadn't been this way when Thom was alive. He'd helped bridge the gap between his wife and his mother, knowing them both well enough to cajole them into getting along. But with him gone, their disagreements flared instead of simmered. And then Nell felt an even sharper, rawer pain. Marion was gone. Her death suddenly wasn't a puzzle to be solved, or a story to write, but the loss of the woman, the friend, the smiling face Nell hoped to see in the coffee shop.

If it hurts me this much, what the hell must Kate Ryan be feeling? Nell thought.

That thought told her where to go next. At least my mother-in-law's extended babysitting will serve some purpose, Nell reflected as she started her car. She swung by the bike shop, but, as expected, it was dark and closed. She headed to the house where she and Thom used to visit Toby Beck, where Kate now lived. It, too, was dark, but there was a light on in one back room. It's easier to cry in the dark, Nell remembered.

If I were a true Southern woman, I would be bringing a casserole or ham or something like that, Nell thought as she climbed the steps. She noticed the subtle changes that indicated a new person living in an old house. Toby's spartan porch had turned into a profusion of plants. There was a car parked in the garage, but not one Nell recognized as usually being by the bike shop. Kate did most of her commuting by bike.

For a moment, she wondered if she should be here, accidental witness as she was to their intimacy. An even more sobering thought occurred to her … what if Kate had killed Marion? Nell dismissed it quickly, first as just a feeling, but then she remembered that Josh had mentioned Marion being in the bike shop before she was killed. Was it likely or even possible for them to have fallen into that kind of hatred in so short a time? Neither woman seemed to be the type to have public fights, so Nell guessed that if Marion was at Kate's shop, it was because she wanted to be with Kate and Kate wanted her there.

Nell rang the doorbell.

A minute passed; then she heard footsteps from inside. Another minute passed before a muffled voice asked, "Who is it?"

"Nell. Nell McGraw. Kate, are you okay?"

Another moment went by before the door slowly opened. Nell looked into a face that could have been hers a few months ago, grief etched in raw lines and dark eyes.

"I'm okay," Kate answered. "Just have some passing bug."

"May I come in?"

For an answer, Kate slowly moved out of the doorway, making an entrance for Nell.

"I'm really okay," Kate repeated. "Just the flu or something. Tell Josh I'm sorry about the bike class."

"I'm very sorry," Nell said. The classic words.

Kate didn't reply. She just looked at her, understanding she wasn't just talking about the bike class.

"About Marion," Nell added, to make it explicit.

"I didn't think...she'd told you." And not told me she'd told you, was the clear but unspoken follow-up.

"She didn't." Nell explained her early morning walk and seeing the two of them in the park.

"So, you've known...for weeks now?" Kate asked.

"Yes. But I wasn't supposed to know, so I didn't know how to tell you."

Kate nodded slowly, and then the guarded look came back. "Are you here as a reporter or a friend?"

The question stung, although Nell admitted she should have expected it. "As a friend. And as someone who went through what

251

you're going through, just last year." To the question in Kate's eyes, she continued, "Thom. You don't even get the harsh mercy of a doctor's office and a few months to say goodbye. Just here and … then utterly gone."

Kate glanced away from Nell, as if she couldn't bear to directly stare at "gone."

"I am very sorry," Nell repeated. "I know that … there may not be a lot of people who know about the two of you …"

"That was Marion's choice," Kate said softly. "Until her mother either got better … or passed on." Then, in an even softer voice, she added, "I can't imagine that it ever stops cutting like the sharpest of knives. Does it?"

Does it really stop hurting or does it just turn numb? Nell wondered. "The knife gets dull as time goes by, but it seems to always remain in your heart. Maybe if enough time passes it becomes a scar and not an open wound. I'm not there yet."

"How long?" Kate asked. "How long for you?"

"Thom's been gone almost six months now. Not a day goes by that I don't miss him in some way." Nell knew it was the truth, but she didn't know whether it would help Kate or only make the grief ahead seem like too heavy a burden.

"And you're still here," Kate said in a bare whisper. "I don't want to wake up tomorrow, to think for a moment that she'll be here and then be slammed again with knowing that she never will be."

"Please don't think that. Don't think of doing that to yourself."

"No, I have neither … the courage nor the cowardice. It just … hurts so damn much." Kate broke down. She turned from Nell, as if that could hide the racking sobs that shook her body.

Nell remembered holding it in, being strong for Josh and Lizzie, all through that first sleepless night and the following glaring day.

But the second night, when she confronted the empty bed and the stark knowledge that Thom would never be there again, she'd sobbed just as Kate was now.

And she did what no one had been there to do for her. Nell put her arms around Kate. At first Kate was stiff, but the grief bent her until her head was on Nell's shoulder, the tears soaking through her sweater.

Minutes passed before Kate's shuddering sobs quieted. More minutes passed with her crying softly on Nell's shoulder.

"It's not true, you know," Kate said as she finally lifted her head.

"What's not true?" Nell asked.

Kate pulled away from her, as if suddenly embarrassed at crying in the arms of a woman she didn't know very well. "How she died. It can't ... be true."

Nell wondered if there was another version of Marion. "It's shocking to consider, and very hard to think of someone we love having a side we don't know about," she said carefully.

"I know Marion!" Kate said, the loss too raw to be past tense. "I know what she might do and what would be impossible for her to do."

"What do you think happened?" Nell questioned softly.

"I don't know. It makes no sense. No goddamn sense." Nell didn't immediately reply, and Kate took her silence as skepticism. "What if they told you your husband was killed by a male hustler in a sleazy hotel? Would you believe it?"

"No," Nell said honestly. "There were ways Thom could surprise me, but his sexuality wasn't one of them."

"The same with Marion," Kate retorted. "She'd never had sex with men."

"Never? Can you be sure?" Nell asked, then regretted voicing her disbelief.

"No, never. Not even once. She knew by the time she was fifteen that she preferred women."

"How did she know..." Nell trailed off, again realizing she was asking a stupid question.

Kate gave her the answer she deserved. "Did you have to have sex with women to prove you're straight?"

"No, of course not. But... there's so much pressure on everyone to be straight, it's hard to imagine someone—particularly someone from this small southern town—knowing they were gay in the same way we know we're straight."

"Marion did. She was like that. She was very good at seeing exactly what was there. I don't know what happened to her, but I know she didn't go off with some strange man to a cheap hotel room." Beneath the grief was the rage. Kate's words carried a burning edge.

Do I talk to Kate about what Marion showed me, Nell wondered, mention my suspicions and force them into her sorrow? She started to hold back, thinking her questions were too tentative to share with anyone else, but then realized that if Thom had been killed this way, and she were standing where Kate was now, she'd want to know. Anything that could bring back to her the man she loved, not let him die as some unknown stranger, would be a mercy she would reach for.

"Did Marion mention a children's book to you?" Nell asked.

"A book? Why?" Kate's question told Nell that she did know something.

"Marion showed it to me. Did you see it?"

"I saw a book," Kate said, still not directly answering Nell's question. Clearly still weighing how far she should trust her.

"The first boy killed, Rayburn Gautier, returned that book to the library," Nell stated.

"I knew it was one of the murdered children," Kate said softly. "I didn't know which one.

"Did she show you the pictures Rayburn scribbled in the book?"

"She mentioned them—what they were of—but I didn't look at them. I didn't feel I needed to."

"Do you know who she talked to about that book?"

"You," Kate answered bluntly, a tinge of suspicion still lingering.

"Anyone else?"

"Yes, she did talk to someone. But I don't know who."

"She didn't tell you?" Nell asked. She knew that she was pushing, and that too harsh a question could get her shown the door.

"She didn't get a chance," Kate retorted. "We talked about it that evening, but she still was undecided. She left a message at the shop yesterday that she was going to have a talk with someone who could help. We've learned to be discreet in the messages we leave each other. But . . . she never got a chance to tell me who . . ."

"You realize the implications of this?" Nell asked.

"I'm beginning to . . . but it still doesn't make sense. Why? Why kill . . . someone over some crayon drawings?"

"What if whoever killed Rayburn Gautier and Joey Sayton found out Rayburn left those pictures depicting what was happening? He might be worried enough to kill for it."

"But those pictures were little more than stick figures, Marion said. She had no clue to who the adult might be; she said you didn't either. Who would kill her over something like that?"

"Why kill children in the brutal fashion he did? Maybe he felt he couldn't risk there being something in that book."

"I keep thinking that none of this makes sense . . . but someone killed her." Kate's voice cracked but didn't break.

Nell knew the woman would spend most of the night crying, but for the moment they could focus on justice, not loss. "Who do you think Marion would have talked to?"

Kate didn't answer immediately, just thought for a moment. "My guess would be Sheriff Hickson, which sounds bizarre given what a good old boy bigot he is. But Marion had known him for a long time, since she was a kid. She might not like him but at least she *knew* him."

"You know that the pictures were of a man in uniform?" Nell asked.

"Marion mentioned that, but she said there was nothing she could recognize other than a badge and a gun."

"I wish I could take another look at that book," Nell said. "I'm guessing the killer took it from her."

"No, I have it," Kate said.

Nell stared at her. "Where is it?"

"Not here. So if you're the murderer, it won't do you any good to kill me now."

Just as Nell had wondered if Kate had killed Marion, clearly Kate had wondered about Nell's motives for coming over, since she'd been one of the few people Marion had told about the book.

"Don't worry," Nell told her quickly. She hoped she sounded reassuring. "The only person I might kill is my teenage daughter after the third time I tell her to do the dishes."

"I'm sorry," Kate said. "This is all too raw, and I don't know who to trust or even talk to. I'll show you the book, but I'd prefer not to tell you where it is. Are you going to investigate this?"

"There are questions I'd like to ask and see where they lead," Nell answered.

Kate slowly nodded her head. "I don't want Marion's death just written off as what they're saying. I want her killer caught … but I don't want to see anyone else hurt."

"I agree with all of that. I don't want to get hurt, and I have limits in how far I'll go."

"I'll help if you want. If there's anything you think risky, you can let me do it."

"No, I can't," Nell said. "I don't work that way."

"God, Nell, please understand." For the first time, Kate looked directly at her. "Right now nothing matters to me. I'm not going to wake from this nightmare, and it's making me crazy and stupid. I'd rather take a risk trying to find justice for Marion than be in a stupid bike wreck because I blindly rode through a stop sign."

"I'm not looking to do anything dangerous for anyone, either for you or me, okay? If it gets to that, we go to …"

"Who? Who do you trust?"

"I'm not sure. I hope I never get close enough to that river to worry about crossing that bridge," Nell answered.

"Okay. But I want to help."

Nell was startled by a knock on the door.

"Don't worry," Kate said. "I'm expecting people." She crossed the room and opened the door.

Nell recognized one of the women who entered as the new minister of the Universalist Church. A few months ago there had been an article about her in the Crier. Jane … Benning? Nell searched for the name. Two women from New Orleans also arrived, planning to stay a few days with Kate. Nell had to admit she'd pictured Kate as isolated in her secrecy. But of course, there are always connections and communities. Nell knew that given how little she and Kate really knew each other, there was limited comfort she could offer.

257

Nell exchanged greetings with the new arrivals. She was relieved to learn that the minister's name was indeed Jane Benning. The New Orleans women were introduced as Joanne and Alex, and then there was little to say. Nell took her leave. She and Kate exchanged a quick hug goodbye.

The hardest part of the evening loomed ahead, facing what were probably three unhappy people, and all of them unhappy with her: her mother-in-law at the extended evening of babysitting, and Josh and Lizzie for the extended visit with their grandmother.

However, Nell was nonplused to learn that Mrs. Thomas, Sr., was not above the kinds of bribes that she offered her kids, as Josh told her that there was leftover pizza if she was hungry. Pepperoni, of course. To make it worse, it appeared that her children and her mother-in-law had found common ground, with Mrs. Thomas falling into her habit of telling them stories about Thom when he was growing up, and Josh and Lizzie wanting to know ever more about the father who was gone.

Nell settled for some reheated pizza, preserving her dignity (and her right to nag her kids about a healthier diet) by removing most of the pepperoni as she waited for them to finish looking at Thom's high school pictures.

Although Nell didn't think she'd ever be close friends with her mother-in-law, for the first time she wondered if they'd both been so numb with grief that they'd built walls that weren't needed.

With promises that they could come again soon and see Thom's college pictures, Lizzie, Josh, and their chauffeur mom left.

TWENTY-SEVEN

IT HAD BEEN A later-than-usual night, as Josh and Lizzie had to tell Nell the new things they'd learned about their father. Most of the stories she knew, but still she listened as if it were the first time she'd ever heard about Thom going with his father to report on the sighting of a water moccasin on the steps of City Hall, and Thom, Sr.'s oft-repeated quote, "Most honest politician I ever saw—the fangs in plain sight."

As a consequence, the next morning was hurried, with both Josh and Lizzie perilously close to being late for school, and Nell actually late in getting to the offices of the Crier. As she was the boss, no one noticed. But the stack of things on her desk had only grown while she was away.

The newspaper should be on most doorsteps by now, Nell thought as she sat down at her piled-high desk. There would be the usual complaints about lost or missing papers. There would also be a number of phone calls asking about Marion's murder, Ron's arrest and supposed suicide, and all the rest of the usual topics—from a paper thrown in the bushes to the rumor that space aliens had landed on the beach. Nell had come to expect that. When news like a murder or hurricane, anything that directly affected people's lives, was on the front page, the calls came in asking to know more, to hear what had been left out of the stories, to learn what was new since the paper went to press ... almost as if wielding a pen gave her some godlike knowledge. The callers were always disappointed when Nell told them she knew no more than what was printed in the paper.

And she was right; there were already two messages asking if the police had caught Marion's murderer. Clearly, the number of recent violent deaths had rattled the populace of Pelican Bay. Nell reminded herself it was time to write about the young girl who'd been found floating in the harbor and remind people that she, too, needed justice.

She would return the calls later in the day. Maybe the police would have captured a suspect by then and she could maintain the illusion that she had extra powers by giving the people something that the morning's paper hadn't.

Nell set to the task of sorting through all the press releases that required some editorial decision. It was the usual stack of charity bake sales, retirements, golden anniversaries, any and everything that someone felt the local paper should pay attention to.

But two of the notices caught her attention. The first was accompanied by a picture of Philip Yorst, the commodore of the yacht club. The story was about last weekend's regatta and who had won it, and the picture was of Yorst handing out one of the trophies. What caught Nell's attention was that, as usual, Yorst was in his commodore's uniform, with its heavy braided epaulettes and multiple bands of gold at the sleeves.

The other press release that caught Nell's attention was of Sheriff Hickson swearing in several "volunteer" deputies—very important campaign contributors, Nell suspected. There were five men besides the sheriff in the photo, all in their volunteer deputy uniforms. One of the men was Wendell Jenkins. In the far background was a blurred face that looked like his son Boyce, supposedly run out of town.

Why are so many men in uniform? Nell wondered. Or maybe I'm just noticing it, she thought. Could she trust any of them? Yes, she could, she reminded herself. Even if Rayburn's messy drawings did mean someone in a uniform was involved—and that was a big leap—it was only one man. The rest were innocent. The only problem was knowing who that one man was. The voice on the phone had been no help; it reminded Nell of no one. She'd hoped the cadence of speech, or word choice, might have gotten past the disguise. The person had to know the area, she told herself. Had to know where the hidden well was, in the woods by the houses. But maybe he'd learned about it from reading the story she'd put in the paper. So that doesn't help, Nell told herself. But how had the killer gotten to Joey? He had to have known about the bayou, the one Josh had guided Doug Shaun to across the harbor. Who would be likely to know that? And was there any way she could find out?

Suddenly, she didn't want to be sitting in an office staring at pieces of paper. Where would an intrepid girl reporter go, Nell wondered. To the scene of the latest crime. She grabbed a camera, told Dolan she'd be back in about an hour or two, and headed out the door.

Nell vaguely knew where the motel was, but had never paid it much attention. "Vague" was a good word for it; nothing seemed distinct or memorable, even in a tacky way. The name, on a small, barely noticeable sign, was Motel 90, for the bypassed highway it was on. It was constructed of a yellow brick that had turned beige as it aged, and shaped like a short, thick U. The inner rooms faced into the center and the outer ones looked at the scrub pine forest on one side of the motel and a much newer self-storage warehouse on the other side.

Nell slowly drove around the parking lot. There were few cars here at this time of day—or maybe it was just that the adulterous couples had found another place for their trysts. One of the outer, far-back corner rooms was sealed with crime scene tape.

Okay, intrepid girl reporter, you're here; now what? What a sad, banal place to die, Nell thought, looking at the scarred, faded wooden door in the beige brick. She left her camera lying on the seat.

Suddenly she wondered if they'd established time of death yet. What Carrie had reported (and Nell had edited out) was that, according to Mrs. Nash, Marion was working late, and then would stop briefly by a friend's but still be home by ten to help her mother take her medications on schedule. But she'd never returned. Nell scribbled a few notes. Did Carrie actually talk to Mrs. Nash, or had she gotten the information secondhand, such as via Doug Shaun? Was the "friend" Kate, and what time had she stopped by? Since having a cell phone meant she could ask questions whenever they occurred to her, she dialed Doug Shaun's number. But modern technology failed her—her phone just gave her a hissing silence to indicate it had no intention of working in this location.

Just to make the trip good for something more than satisfying morbid curiosity, Nell went into the motel office. The elderly clerk at the desk hadn't been there the night Marion was murdered and had little to say, other than that it was a terrible thing to have happened. After hearing what a terrible thing it was for the third time, Nell thanked him for answering her questions. He then asked her if they'd caught anyone yet and she had to admit to knowing no more than what he'd already read in the paper.

Nell left the sad motel and headed back to the office. On the way, she swung by the police station to see if she could catch Doug, but he wasn't there.

Only Dolan was at the office when Nell got there, and he was on the phone telling someone that no, they had no new information. Nell waved at him as she headed for her desk.

There were three messages about lost papers. The Crier did have a distributor who was supposed to take care of that, but some people felt their lost papers needed the attention of the editor-in-chief. Mr. Creedmoor had left his weekly message about aliens landing on Ship Island, which they'd use as their headquarters when stealing all the shrimp in the Gulf for their alien dining. The final call was from Amy at the *New Orleans Advocate* about a possible job for Jacko.

Nell returned that call first. After a brief commiseration about the woes of journalism, Amy said that a friend of hers was starting a new paper in Austin, Texas, aimed at the Silicon Prairie crowd, and he needed to hire several people. Nell took down the information and thanked her. For a selfish moment she considered throwing it in the trash can. Some cock-eyed optimist part of her was hoping that with enough time, things would settle down and she wouldn't have to lose Jacko. But that would be an experiment with his life. Nell rewrote her scribbled notes legibly and left the piece of paper on Jacko's desk. He could follow it up or not.

The next phone call she made was to Kate. First she called her home number and got no answer, but decided not to leave a message. We're all being discreet, Nell thought. Then she called the bike shop, and was surprised when Kate picked up the phone.

"Kate, this is Nell McGraw."

"Nell. Hi." There was a tiredness in her voice.

"I didn't really expect to find you there."

"Better here than at home. At least there are things to do and that helps for a little."

Of course, Nell realized, Kate would have no part in arranging Marion's funeral or any of the attendant duties of a family after a death. After Thom died, Nell had stayed away from the paper for over a week. A lot of the time was spent with the details of death: going through his papers, the will, all the formalities, the stream of people with their casseroles and hams—to the point of prompting Lizzie to comment, "You have to live to be eighty, Mom, because I don't think I can eat any more ham until then." Maybe we have all these rituals to keep grief at bay, she thought; to prove to the bereaved that they can make it through the first day and the next and maybe all the other days. But she'd also kept away from the paper because there were so many memories of Thom there.

For Kate, the bike shop was the only routine available to her.

"I have a few questions," Nell said. "Do you mind? You don't have to answer, you know. I'd understand if you told me to disappear."

"No, ask your questions. I want to do this."

"According to Mrs. Nash, on the night she was murdered Marion was working late, then visiting a friend, but was supposed to be home by ten. Were you the friend she was visiting?"

"Yes, I was. And she wasn't working late. That was just an excuse so her mother wouldn't notice how much time Marion was spending with people who were just friends instead of her mother."

"So she was with you for most of the evening?"

"She came over for dinner—after going home to make sure her mother got something to eat. And ... stayed until just before ten."

"About what time did she get to your place?"

Kate didn't immediately answer. Then her voice was away from the phone as she said, "The helmets are on the back wall. Let me know if you need any help in sizing them." To Nell she said, "I can't really talk right now. Can we do this at a later time?"

"Of course. When would be a good time for you?"

"How about … early afternoon? I guess I'd rather talk to you than …" She trailed off.

Than go home with the memories and the grief, Nell completed silently for her. "I might have to bring Josh. I'm not sure what his schedule is today." She did know that Lizzie had band practice.

"Okay, that's fine. See you then."

Nell agreed and left Kate to the bike helmets.

She tried to plow through the multiple tasks on her desk, but couldn't stop herself from wondering what had really happened to Marion. She finally gave up and started making notes, trying to sort out who, what, where, how, and why.

If Marion was killed by the same man who'd killed the children, then Ronald Hebert had to be innocent, since he'd died the night before Marion did. Yet Doug Shaun claimed they had strong evidence that Ronald was guilty. Could the real killer have planted this evidence? But how could the killer know that Ronald Hebert's name would show up on a list of ancient sex crimes?

Nell realized it wouldn't be that hard to set up. If the killer was a man in uniform, then it was likely he had access to information on criminal records. If the uniform indicated an actual policeman or sheriff's deputy, that is. All he had to do was find someone on that list who suited his purpose and find out what kind of car he drove— someone in law enforcement could easily do that, or perhaps just sit in the coffee shop down the street from the flower shop and see what Ronald drove up in. Then the killer would anonymously call in seeing that car near one of the murder locations. As far as planting evidence of the crime in his house, Pelican Bay was still the kind of place where people didn't routinely lock their doors. Ronald Hebert grew up in town; maybe his door was unlocked. Or maybe Jacko wasn't the only person he'd taken home from the bar.

Once Nell thought it through, it seemed frighteningly easy to set up Ronald Hebert. Given a chance to talk, he might have been able to prove his innocence, or at least raise some awkward questions the killer might not want anyone thinking about. But had the murderer counted on the odds of a gay man accused of murdering and molesting children meeting the fate that Ronald had? Or was the killer someone in the sheriff's department who had also killed Ronald in jail? The latter would narrow her list of suspects, but Nell couldn't be sure.

She made a list of all the men in uniform she could think of.

Sheriff Hickson and his men. Jacko could give her a rundown on the deputies.

Philip Yorst, with his commodore's regalia. He was an outside suspect, but Nell didn't like him, so she put him on the list. Wait—he was one of Sheriff Hickson's volunteer deputies, along with Wendell Jenkins. What if Wendell and Boyce were in it together? Then it occurred to her that if the yacht club wanted to close down Ray's bar, killing Ray's young son would be an effective and brutal way to do that. She'd have to find out if any of the other yacht club members were also uniform addicts like their leader, and what connections they had with law enforcement.

Wendell had probably sold Ronald Hebert his car. And, as an honorary deputy, Wendell had no real duties that would keep him in a specific place, but also an excuse to be wherever he wanted to be without question. Like in the county jail. Nell suddenly remembered his "army" of salesmen in uniform.

Boyce Jenkins, supposedly out of town, was someone Lizzie claimed to have seen just a few days ago. No, she'd seen someone she'd labeled a creepy policeman. Nell needed to show her a picture to confirm it, but who else could it be? Boyce was clearly a man of violent temper. Yet she wondered if he had the intelligence to be the killer. Chilling as they were, the murders were well thought-out and executed. Boyce was a man of rage; could he manage the necessary patience and cunning? His father probably could.

Chief Doug Shaun. Nell almost scratched his name out. He would have been noticed in the county jail, either if he'd gone there to kill Ronald Hebert or just to whisper some encouragement to the right people. And I let Josh go in the boat with him the night Joey was killed, Nell reminded herself. Could I be derelict enough as a mother to send my son into the arms of a killer? She left his name on the list, but added a question mark to look into other police officers.

Nell couldn't explain why, but she felt sure that she knew the killer. There had to be any number of men in uniform in Pelican Bay, but the killer had called her in the night—for some reason he had chosen *her* to taunt. She could think of no reason other than it being someone who knew her and could picture the terror he was inspiring in her. Then again, since she was the editor of the paper, there were certainly people who knew her—or felt they knew her—who she didn't know. Or knew only in some minor, passing way, via a brief story that was only a few lines of type for her but significant to them. Perhaps one of the many daily callers who thought they had a great idea for an article, only to have her pass it by—or not even call back. Yes, the killer was connected to her. But she had so many connections, it would be impossible to narrow them down to the right one.

Her children weren't safe anymore. And she had some questions for the police chief.

Nell dialed his cell phone, not wanting to bother with the layers of secretaries she would run into if she called the police station.

"Doug Shaun," he answered on the third ring.

"Doug, this is Nell McGraw."

"Nell, I was just thinking about you." There was a hint of flirting in his voice.

"Good." Nell returned his flirtatious tone. "I was just thinking about you. And the arrest of Ronald Hebert."

"Isn't that over?" The flirting disappeared.

"Over?"

"With him being dead. There won't be a trial or anything."

"What if he didn't do it? Would it still be 'over' in your mind?" Nell asked.

"You're going to be a reporter, aren't you?"

"Yes, I'm afraid I am. What if Ronald was innocent?" she pushed.

"You've been listening to the sheriff, haven't you?" Doug's voice was easy, but Nell caught the gibe underneath it.

"What corners did you cut? Off the record," she added, because she knew he would never say it on the record and she didn't want to waste time negotiating it.

The chief was silent. Nell heard the sounds of traffic and realized he was in his car. Finally he said, "The obvious ones. Ronald Hebert was arrested over in New Orleans for being a little too frisky one Mardi Gras—with another man in a public place. Someone called in the license plate number of his car out in the park when Joey Sayton was killed. That's not really enough for a warrant, but I got one anyway."

"Why? Just his car and being gay?"

"Really, just the car. Some hunch—his car being out of place enough for someone to notice it at a murder scene." He quickly added, "But the hunch paid off, remember. We found enough to put him on death row."

"You found the evidence at his house? What did you find?"

"We're examining it. Don't want to reveal it just yet. And yes, in his back bedroom, in a closet. Not very well hidden at all."

"Easy to find, in other words. Or easy for someone to plant there?"

"What are you hinting at, Nell?"

"How hard was it for the police to force their way into Ronald Hebert's house?"

"This isn't a town that needs fifty padlocks on the door. I don't really remember. It took a few minutes."

"Have you found any forensic evidence to actually link Hebert to the crime scenes?"

"You're really going to push this, aren't you, Nell? The guy's dead and the murders have stopped."

"Marion Nash was murdered after Hebert's supposed suicide."

"But there's no link there. Hers was one of the stupid sex crimes that happens more often than they should."

Nell hesitated. Someone needed to know about the evidence linking Marion's death to that of the children. Douglas Shaun was new here, less likely to know about the bayou and the well in the woods. She would have to trust some man in uniform. He seemed the safest candidate.

"Rayburn Gautier turned in a library book with some rather provocative crayon drawings in it," she began. "Ones that might be linked to his murder. Marion Nash told someone about it, probably someone at the sheriff's department. The next day, she was murdered.

I have my hunches, too, Doug. And my hunch says that coincidences like that aren't likely."

"But they do happen," he countered.

"And how hard would it have been for the murderer to set up Hebert? What if he's in law enforcement? Who tipped you off about his car?"

"I can't really say…"

Nell cut in. "Can't say because you don't want to or because it was an anonymous call?"

"Okay, it was anonymous. But this seems so farfetched. Why would someone go to all this trouble?"

"If the crime is considered solved, the real killer gets away."

"You really think that's possible?"

"I do," Nell replied. "And you don't have to agree with me, but at least keep an open enough mind to consider the possibility."

"I'll consider it." Doug Shaun paused and added, "But only if you consider having dinner with me."

"I was hoping my theory was so compelling you wouldn't need bribes. But yes, I'll consider having dinner with you. I can't tonight, though."

The chief didn't ask why she couldn't, which Nell liked. He didn't assume he had any special access to her life.

"How about Saturday?" he suggested. "That give you enough time to make arrangements for your kids?"

"Saturday sounds good. But let me make sure I can set things up before I commit."

"Okay," he said. But then, as if he couldn't quite let it go, he softly added, "Nell, what if Marion really did just have a lonely night, picked some guy up, and things took a wrong turn?"

Nell thought a moment before answering, then decided that the chief of police needed this information. "Marion was a lesbian and not very likely to pick up any man."

He was silent. Then said, "Are you sure?"

"As sure as I can be short of actually sleeping with her."

"How did you find that out?"

Now it was Nell's turn to hesitate. Finally she said, "I'd rather not say. I will if I have to, but I saw what happened to Jacko and I don't want it to happen again without some compelling reason." She glanced at the clock. It was time to collect Josh and go talk to Kate. She felt protective of the woman and wasn't yet willing to turn her over to the questioning of the police. Or do I just want to be the one to ask her the questions? she wondered. She concluded that whatever her reasons were, she did need to talk to Kate first before revealing anything more.

"Nell, this is a murder case," Doug Shaun reminded her. "Don't withhold evidence."

"The only evidence that'll be withheld is the evidence you miss because you were looking in the wrong direction. If you're going to insist that Marion's murder was a random sex crime, what good will it do to drag even more of her sex life into public view?" Nell countered.

There was silence on the chief's end for a long moment before he finally answered. "If you've got proof of this, I'm going to need it sooner than later. Understood?"

"What I have may not stand up as 'proof' in a court. Keep that in mind," Nell hedged. If Kate decided not to cooperate and keep Marion's secret, Nell doubted there was much she could do. For a moment she wondered if she should have even told Doug Shaun, but decided that if it got him to re-examine Marion's murder, it would be worth it. "I have to go pick up Josh. I'll talk to you later."

"Later then. Don't forget about Saturday." His line went dead.

Doug Shaun wasn't a man to let her get in the last word. Which wasn't a point in his favor. Or maybe I'm reading too much into it, Nell thought. Maybe he has other phone calls or noticed someone going over the speed limit. She suddenly thought, oh please, tell me that I don't have to go through this adolescent craziness just to date a man. And then she thought, it's not fair. I did go through it. I found Thom, someone to love and hold and grow old with. And now I'm a not-so-young woman worrying about the meaning of how quickly a man hangs up the phone.

Hell, time to be a mother. Nell straightened her desk hastily and headed for the door. While she'd been talking to Doug, Josh had texted her to pick him up early since it was a half-day at school. He was down at the harbor doing a field trip ecology thing. Nell felt guilty for not knowing exactly what she was picking him up from; I only have two children, I should be able to keep track of their lives. How did someone like Velma Gautier manage, with her eight kids? But Rayburn was dead and she only had seven. Nell suddenly had a fierce moment when she could see briefly into another life—the child that was lost would weigh more than the others that were still there and okay. What would her life be if she lost Josh or Lizzie? Nell sat in her car, the key almost in the ignition. Grief shuddered through her. Thom was gone, and Velma Gautier had lost a son who read the same kinds of picture books that Josh read at that age.

Nell started the car and vowed that she would be a better mother; she wouldn't wonder what it was her children were involved in, but would know. Great, she thought as she headed out of the parking lot; I'll turn into the Mother Inquisitor, questioning my children relentlessly about their lives. Maybe Josh didn't tell me much about this harbor project because it's time for him to separate from me and find his independence. Maybe there is no perfect way to be a perfect mother. Mrs. Thomas, Sr. had her son return to the town he'd grown up in, a small town on the Gulf of Mexico, and still she couldn't keep him safe from the weavings of a drunken driver.

Nell found no answers to her mothering dilemma, but she did find her son. An odd relief washed over her as she spied Josh standing among the other members of the class. She pulled to the side of the road but didn't immediately get out—Josh knew she was here, he didn't really need his mother coming down to retrieve him. The group seemed to be enjoying the camaraderie of the project and the place, and Nell wanted them to have their moment. But then other parents arrived and the mood was broken. The children trailed off, some in tow of mothers, others called to waiting cars. Josh lingered a moment, helping one of the sponsoring teachers ... Mrs. Harvey? He put some nets and buckets in the trunk of her car.

"How many dead catfish did you find?" Nell asked as he got in.

"Only three, probably from the shrimp boats," Josh answered seriously, not expecting his mother as ask the joking questions his father would have.

"Should we do a story on illegal catfish dumping?" Nell asked, mirroring his serious tone.

"Or they could have washed up. I don't think it's front page news," Josh replied. "Maybe just the metro section."

That was something Thom used to say. Nell turned away to start the car, but also to cover the mist that came into her eyes at the way Josh had caught his father's cadences of speech. And for a moment, they'd kidded the way he and Thom used to kid, with that mock seriousness. It's been months since I've heard my son say something like this, Nell thought.

"The bad news is that we have to go by the bike shop on our way home," Nell said.

"But isn't it closed still?" Josh answered, although he clearly didn't think this was bad news.

"Probably, but I wanted to talk to Kate about something and she agreed to meet me there. I did warn her that I'd have you with me."

"Like I'm some big burden," Josh groused. "What do you need to talk to Kate about?"

It was a casual question, an acknowledgment that Nell stopping by the bike shop was not the norm, but only mildly curious about why she wanted to see Kate. "Some ad stuff she wanted in the paper," Nell threw off. It wasn't a complete lie; the bike shop did advertise in the Crier. "Tell me more about what it is the biology club is doing at the harbor."

Nell spent the drive to the bike shop listening to Josh explain how they were sampling water from different parts of the harbor and what they were looking for in those samples and how they were going to use the school lab to measure things.

The bike shop did have a closed sign on the door, but lights were on. When she tried it, the door was still open. Kate was behind the counter, finishing up paperwork. She glanced up as Josh and Nell entered.

"Hey, Josh. Just the person I need to see." Kate's smile was in place and her tone cheery, but Nell noted the dark circles under her eyes. "I've got a bike that I just assembled and it needs a test ride."

"Oh, boy, which one?" Josh answered excitedly.

In reply, Kate wheeled a shiny red and gold bike from the workshop. She and Josh launched into a discussion of components and other arcane bike lore that meant little to Nell. She gave Josh one of the helmets that were kept around for people to use when trying out bikes and sent him on his way.

"Don't have a wreck," Nell called as he was maneuvering out the door.

"Oh, Mom, I don't have wrecks," he said, taking her more seriously than she'd meant. "Don't worry. I'll be gone long enough for you to talk all you want about ads."

Neither Kate or Nell said anything until Josh was out of sight.

Nell finally turned to her and said, "Think he'll be back anytime soon?"

Kate shrugged. "He's welcome to come back later this afternoon and help me out if he'd like. Now, we're supposed to talk about ads?"

"He wanted to know why I would come by the shop," Nell explained.

Kate just nodded and then said with a bitter smile, "Does the Crier give discounts to widows?"

Nell remembered the brittle anger she still felt from Thom's death, how it came out as if it had a will of its own.

"I'm sorry," Kate said. "There aren't many people that know, that I can even say things . . . like that to." She gave Nell no time to respond to her apology and continued, "So, Nell McGraw. You said you have questions for me?

"You know you don't have to answer. I don't really have a right to pry into your life," Nell told her.

"No, you don't have a right," Kate coolly agreed. Then she softly added, "But your prying . . . is better than silence."

Nell nodded understanding, then asked her first question. "Where did you and Marion meet?"

"Did Josh tell you I used to be a forest ranger?" Kate asked. Then she continued without waiting for an answer. "Marion liked the outdoors, hiking or camping most every weekend. We ran into each other a couple of times. Shared nothing more than a questioning glance when I handed her a trail map, until one day she asked me when the next nature hike was. I told her one was about to start and she asked if I was leading it. I told her no, that I'd be doing a later one. She looked at me and simply said, 'I'll wait.' After the hike, she remained behind and asked me if I'd like to get some coffee after work."

"Where was this?"

"She was finishing her master's at the University of Washington. I was working at Cascades Park. And … that coffee led to dinner … and dinner led to … falling in love." Kate spoke slowly, caught in the memories.

"How long were you together?"

"I guess … about eight years."

"And you've been living here for, what, about … two years?" Nell had to do a quick mental calculation. Kate had cared for Toby for at least six months before his death.

"One year and eight months," Kate answered. She was silent for a moment, then said, "At first it was odd, our Gulf Coast connection. That she grew up over in Ocean Springs and her parents retired here, and Uncle Toby lived about twenty blocks away from them. But … then I started getting the letters from him. I guess he thought that since I was queer, I could be the one he told, and I got to tell the rest of the family."

"That he had AIDS?" Nell ventured.

"First just HIV. He either knew or suspected that it had progressed to AIDS, and I think he just said it to see how we'd react."

"And how did you react?"

"I'd had friends with HIV. But closer to my age, doing well on the meds. Toby was resistant to most of them. It was … different to find that my southern uncle was one of them. That he was gay was the open family secret, but when he got sick, we had to talk about the secret that no one wanted to talk about. My dad, Toby's brother, just went silent. He'd leave the room if I mentioned I'd gotten another letter and Toby was going to try another combination of drugs because the ones he was on weren't working."

"That must have been hard for you."

"My mother kept saying that blood was thicker than water and Dad would come through ... but he never did. The most involved he got was insisting that Uncle Toby's death was from cancer, that he didn't want AIDS in the paper. We compromised on pneumonia. He tried to bully Dr. Wilcox into not putting it on the death certificate."

"Why did you stay here after his death?" Nell gently asked.

"To piss off my dad," Kate answered, her anger still present. "Not really. Although it did, and I enjoyed doing it. Guess I'm not exactly the dutiful daughter. I'd brought us here—Marion wasn't sure she wanted to come back, but I knew that if I didn't take care of Toby, it would only be strangers. When we were thinking about it, I was just going to live here long enough to see him through. Marion had tried to come out to her mother a few years earlier, but it was like she'd never said anything. So, since we were planning on maybe being here six months, Marion decided she wasn't going to be an out lesbian in her mother's hometown. Right before Uncle Toby died, Mrs. Nash had her stroke. And Marion got caught in the dutiful daughter role."

"So Marion didn't tell her mother about you?"

"And risk giving her another stoke?" Kate answered sardonically. "Marion told her that she was a lesbian and the next day her mother asked her if she might meet a nice man and settle down in Pelican Bay. Don't talk about it, it doesn't exist."

"Who did know?"

"Here? In Seattle, we were out, so everyone knew there. But only a few select friends here. We … weren't planning to stay in town, so we didn't go out of our way to find a circle. It was just supposed to be a detour—we would spend a year here and then go back to the Northwest. One of those side trips that life requires from you, but we'd be able to go on with all our plans…" Kate was silent.

Nell waited for her to continue, but she didn't. Finally Nell prompted her with a question. "What time did Marion come over that night?"

"I guess around 6:30. I'd promised her I'd cook dinner if she could spend the evening with me."

"Was that hard for her to do?"

"Her mother … made it a point to need Marion whenever she tried to spend time with friends who were women … and she didn't want to claim she was going out with a male friend or her mother would be planning the wedding. So, she had to tell that lie for us to be together."

"Did she 'work late' a lot or was this an occasional thing?"

"We'd lived together in Washington," Kate said, as if trying to explain something to Nell that she wasn't sure Nell would understand. "So we definitely tried to see each other every day, but … not always. And just about every other day, we'd look at each other and think this is crazy—we're grown adults, sneaking around like teenagers."

Nell started to ask another question, but Kate cut in. "Marion had decided it was time to talk to her mother again. Her mother didn't have to like it, but she wasn't going to pretend any longer." Kate again fell into silence.

"So Marion came over and you had dinner," Nell said. "Did you talk about the book or the murders? Any details you can add?"

"We only talked a little bit—that she'd talked to you about it, and what you suggested, but she still wasn't sure where to go with it."

"Did she talk about who she might go to? Weigh the options?"

"She started to, but … we got sidetracked."

"Sidetracked how?"

Kate didn't answer, just looked at Nell.

Finally Nell understood. "You had sex?"

"We made love," Kate corrected, a harshness at the edge of her voice.

Nell hadn't meant to imply that she relegated their relationship to little beyond sex; she'd just used the words that came to her. But Kate, Kate who'd had to hide her love, couldn't bear to hide it any more. How do I say it, Nell wondered. Tell her I understand that she loved Marion fully and passionately, as much as I loved Thom.

"When I saw you meet that early morning in the park," she said, "you kissed and it … made me ache with the memory of having that kind of love in my life." It was the best apology she could manage. "You made love. But before, how much did Marion manage to say about her choices?"

"She only recounted her meeting with you—and you don't need me to tell you about that. I asked what she was considering. She did mention maybe going to Sheriff Hickson, but she wasn't sure. But she said 'we can talk about that later on the phone, but … we can't do *this* by phone.'" Kate stopped speaking, tears starting to slide down her cheeks. Behind anger was grief.

Nell could think of no further questions. She glanced around the bike shop for a tissue to hand to Kate, but saw none.

Suddenly Kate burst out, "I almost grabbed her and said don't go, just stay the night. I'd spent so many nights without her beside me. I didn't think I could stand another one." She pounded her fist

279

into the glass counter top with such force that Nell worried she would break it. The tears streamed down her face. She started to hit the counter again, but Nell grabbed her fists, holding them.

She's a strong woman, Nell thought, feeling the tension and surge of emotions coursing through Kate's arms. Her hands were literally trembling. Nell wasn't sure if she was doing the right thing, wasn't sure she should touch this woman she didn't know very well. In the end, she wasn't even sure that Kate wouldn't turn on her, the only target nearby, with her rage and loss.

For a moment the two women just stood, Nell with her hands wrapped about Kate's wrists. Then suddenly Kate pulled away. But it wasn't a violet break; instead, a pulling away and back into herself. Clumsily, she wiped the tears off her face.

"I know I'm intruding on your grief…" Nell said.

"Better than being left alone in it," Kate replied in a harsh whisper, her voice raw from crying. She reached out and touched Nell on the wrist, just where Nell had held her.

They were startled by the sound of the door opening. It was Josh returning from his bike ride.

"Better wash my face," Kate mumbled as she turned away. She headed hastily for the bathroom before Josh could see her.

Nell went to the door to help Josh keep it open and get the bike through it.

"Any wrecks?" she asked, in what she hoped was a light tone.

"Ten cars, two garbage trucks, and an eighteen-wheeler full of chickens," Josh replied. Nell suspected he'd been practicing that line the whole time.

"How was the bike ride?"

"Pretty good. But the lower speeds were kind of rough shifting. Needs to be adjusted." Josh looked around for Kate as he spoke. Clearly his mother was clueless in the arcane world of bikes.

"She'll be here in a minute," Nell said.

Josh used the time to put the bike back in the repair part of the shop, take off the borrowed helmet, and wipe the sweat out of it. He even allowed Nell to ruffle his hair out of its helmet-induced shape.

Even a few long minutes in the bathroom couldn't hide that Kate had been crying. But she brushed it off by saying, "My allergies have been bothering me all day."

Josh saw no need to probe beyond that and he and Kate spent several minutes discussing the merits and demerits of the bike. Nell let them talk, wandering around the shop so she wouldn't be the hovering mother. Why would a woman in a committed relationship with another woman go searching for sex with a man, after she and her partner had just made love? The more she found out, the more disturbed Nell was by Marion's death.

Then Josh and Kate were finished talking. Nell could see the tiredness etched in Kate's face, the cost of pretending she had no worries beyond adjusting bike parts. Nell thanked her, and wanted to just touch her hand for a moment, but Josh was between them and she could think of no easy way to maneuver around him or to explain why it was important she reach out to Kate.

But she did ask one last question as they were at the door. "The book? Where is it?"

"Hidden in a safe place. I'll call you later." That was all Kate said, turning away to hide the hand that was wiping the seeping tears off her face.

Nell closed the door and herded Josh back to the car.

TWENTY-EIGHT

NELL GAVE JOSH THE choice of staying home after lunch—with doors securely locked—or going back to the bike shop. He chose the shop. Nell dropped him off and then made a quick run to the office just to listen to the most recent phone messages; only about missing papers, as it turned out. Normally she would politely call everyone back, but today she didn't bother. In the phone listings for the Crier there was a clearly marked number for distribution problems, and she currently wasn't feeling charitable enough to call that number for people. There were no other messages and she still had questions she wanted to ask.

Her first stop was the DA's office. She ducked Buddy Guy as he was coming around a corner, knowing she'd have to make polite political chat, with Buddy suggesting stories, all of which were designed to give him good PR. Thom could do that kind of thing, be the perfect good ole boy without really promising anything. Even if she weren't haunted with Marion's death, Nell wasn't very good at it; she was more likely to say brusque things like "I really can't see much of a news angle to that."

Instead, she went in search of Harold Reed. Although it was a gamble to try to find him here—unlike Buddy, Harold actually did things like go to court—she still didn't want to call, didn't want to give any advance warning.

But luck was with her. Harold was in his office and willing to see her.

"Nell, I doubt this is just a social visit," he said after they'd seated themselves. "What questions can I safely answer?"

"Did Marion Nash come to you about a book Rayburn Gautier took out from the library?" Nell bluntly asked.

Harold sat forward, and his eyes only showed interest, not any of the emotions Nell suspected would be there if the question was one he didn't want to be asked.

"No," he answered. "Tell me about this book."

Nell thought for a moment, then countered with a question of her own. "Were you ever in uniform?"

Harold gave her a slightly quizzical look, but he answered her question. "Yes, it's how I got my law degree. Had to spend a few years in the Army JAG to pay for it."

"Did you ... enjoy it?"

"I discovered I liked the law, but didn't like the military. I did my time and got out. Had one kid and another on the way, so my wife wasn't too thrilled at me leaving a steady paycheck, but we made it." He gave a bare nod, as if saying, I've answered your question, now you can answer mine.

Nell realized that another reason she'd decided to tackle these men in broad daylight in their places of work was to protect herself. It wasn't likely the murderer could do much to her in these times and places. But whatever she was looking for, she hadn't found it in Harold. That decision made, she answered his question. "Marion

Nash told me about a book Rayburn Gautier checked out of the library, which was returned after his death. In that book, he'd drawn in some crude pictures of an adult sexually molesting a boy."

"How could you tell it was sexual molestation?"

"A phallic symbol is an easy thing to draw," Nell answered.

"All seven-year-old boys have phallic symbols."

"But they usually don't draw them on men with little boys kneeling in front of them," Nell retorted, sharper than she intended.

"Devil's advocate, Nell," Harold said quietly. "I have to ask the hard questions. You've seen this book?"

"Yes, Marion showed it to me. The day before she was murdered. I told her she needed to show it to the authorities. I suggested you."

"Why not Chief Shaun? Or even Sheriff Hickson, although I know you don't like him."

"As crude as they were, the pictures indicated a man in uniform," Nell replied. "Hat, gun, badge. But Rayburn wasn't prescient enough to write a name or a good-enough artist to tell us more than that."

"So that's why you asked about the uniform," Harold said softly. "But I'm afraid Marion didn't come to me. Are you sure she showed someone else the book?"

"I'm not sure, but she told me she was going to."

"Do you have it?"

"No, I don't," Nell answered. "But if need be, I might be able to get it." She trusted Harold, but not quite enough to hand him that.

He nodded, then said, "I'm guessing you're here because you think there's a link between Marion Nash's death and the deaths of the two boys?"

"You're guessing right."

"Do you have anything other than the coincidence of the book?" Harold asked.

Nell thought for a moment before answering. "Yes. Marion Nash was a lesbian. She spent the evening with her partner, making love. I don't think that makes her a likely candidate for picking up strange men for random sex."

Harold sat up straight. "Good Lord. It's all circumstantial, but I don't like the icy feeling I just got down my spine. You realize the implications of this?"

Nell nodded. "Ronald Hebert was innocent…"

"And the real killer is still out there," Harold finished for her. "And possibly wearing a uniform."

"You know these men, Harold. Who do you suggest? Who do we go to?"

"Let me think for a bit. We might want to call in the FBI. This is going to be a hell of a mess." He rubbed his face with his hands, then looked sharply at Nell. "And what are you going to do?"

"Keep asking questions," Nell replied. "Go to Sheriff Hickson and Doug Shaun and ask them the hard questions."

"Do you think that's wise? I can't imagine it's either of them, but if it's one of their men, those places are sieves. The front desk knows what was said before you're out the door."

"It'll be in their offices, not in some dark alley," Nell responded. "I don't think the killer is so brazen as to attack me in the police station or the sheriff's office. And I'm not the one the killer needs to worry about. I wasn't Marion's partner, and I don't have the book."

"And you're not going to tell me who the killer should worry about?" Harold asked, but he seemed to already know the answer.

"No," Nell admitted, "not yet. And … not alone. I trust you as much as anyone in this, Harold, but I'd rather be too cautious than not enough. Bring in three FBI agents and I'll tell you and them everything I know."

"I know myself well enough to know I'm a good guy, but I can't expect you to," Harold said, then made a decision, "I'm going to make the phone call. This afternoon, if I can set it up. If not, then tomorrow if at all possible."

Harold's phone rang. He started to pick it up, but added, "Don't do anything foolish."

Nell stood to go. "I've got two kids. Foolish dropped out of my vocabulary years ago."

Harold started talking and Nell let herself out. She wasn't going to do anything foolish, but that wasn't the same thing as not asking questions.

But as she got into her car, she questioned herself. Am I being the girl reporter going after glory? What am I going to stir up by continuing to push this? Isn't it better to wait until the FBI cavalry come riding up? As she tried to convince herself to leave it alone, she found herself still driving to the sheriff's office.

She sat in the parking lot, still trying to come to a decision. I know these men, she reminded herself, in a way that the FBI agents can't. I've heard the killer's voice. Even though it was disguised, there can still be clues of cadence and vocabulary. And then Nell realized that the real reason she wanted to keep asking questions was an irrational one: I'm the witness. That's why the killer called me in the middle of the night. He doesn't want to kill me, but to have me watch as he kills others.

It was that irrational thought that finally won the struggle. Nell got out of her car and went into the sheriff's office.

The person at the desk was her usual polite but ineffective self. Nell didn't understand how someone with fingernails the length of talons could dial a phone, let alone type. She recognized Nell but didn't seem to have been told not to let reporters, particularly intrepid girl reporters from the *Pelican Bay Crier*, through the door. It did, however, take the woman close to half an hour to track down exactly where Sheriff Hickson was. She didn't bat an eye when she told Nell that he was down at the harbor for the reopening of Ray's Bar. Or bother with an explanation that he was doing security, or something that would appear less damning on the front page of the paper.

Again sitting in her car, Nell contemplated whether she wanted to confront the sheriff on his home turf. She didn't quite answer that question, but she did decide the Crier could do a story on the reopening of the bar, with perhaps an exposé of how the sheriff spent his work day.

With that, Nell stopped by the office long enough to get a camera and glance at the blinking lights of her phone messages. Probably all missing papers, she decided. If enough papers didn't arrive at their proper destination, she could at least rely on the disgruntled subscribers to hunt her down should the killer decide to kidnap her.

When she arrived at Ray's Bar, a sheriff's patrol car was parked prominently in front. There were a few balloons out by the door and a hand-lettered sign saying "Ray's Bar is Back." Nell got out and snapped a few pictures of the patrol car.

"Afternoon, Miz McGraw."

Nell looked up to see Velma Gautier bringing out a few more balloons to make the other ones look less forlorn.

Velma clearly saw the camera in Nell's hand. "You not going to make trouble for Clureman, are you?" she asked in an almost pleading voice.

This is when I really need Thom, Nell thought. He could talk his way out of this. But she merely said, "You have to admit, it seems a bit improper for the sheriff to be spending time in a bar while on duty." God, I do sound like a prig, she thought as she heard herself.

"He's not here for the bar, but for Ray. Trying to get him to have a life again."

Nell nodded as if understanding, but she wanted to ask, who is going to help you get a life again?

Velma continued. "Ray didn't really want to do it, open the bar again. Hit him too hard to lose little Rayburn. But Clureman talked him into doing the right thing. He needed to be away from his sadness and … well, we need the money. Still got mouths to feed." Velma held Nell's gaze through this speech, then looked down at the ground when she was finished, as if asking for mercy and afraid that she wouldn't get it—or would somehow be blamed for what Nell's camera caught.

Nell slung the camera over her shoulder. The sheriff could continue his good ole boy ways. She could catch him another time.

"Let me help you with these," she said as she took some of the balloons from Velma's hands. "I'll run a photo of the reopening of Ray's Bar."

"Thank you, ma'am. That would be very kind."

Nell started to say that the Crier ran photos of yacht club do's all the time, so it seemed only fair that Ray's Bar got its share of notice, but instead she just tied balloons to the shutter hinges. The salt air had made them rusty and it was hard to move the shutters to get the string around tied. Both women worked in silence for several minutes. Thom would be bantering, not letting the silence build, Nell thought. What do you say to a women whose son has been murdered?

Finally they finished and Nell merely said, "I'm so sorry for your loss." Maybe it was another in the string of wrong things she'd said, but she also knew how hard it was for her when people didn't speak of Thom, as if she wasn't living with it every day.

Velma looked up at her, then down again as if she wasn't used to the powerful people of Pelican Bay noticing her. "Miss him," she said, still looking at the ground, "Miss him hard."

"I think my heart would be ripped out and scattered in pieces if something happened to one of my children," Nell said.

Velma looked up at her, then slowly nodded. "Ripped out and scattered, that's what it is. But I got to pull the pieces back for the rest of the kids and Ray."

"We do go on, don't we?" Nell said with a sad, ironic smile, then wanted to pull it back. She'd gone on after Thom's death, but it wasn't the same thing as going on after the death of your child. She wondered if Velma Gautier would think her some emotional parasite for equating the two.

"Thom was a good man," Velma said, then echoed Nell. "We do go on." She returned her small smile.

Nothing would make Ray's Bar into an architectural gem, but the balloons did take away some of the desolate look.

Nell's cell phone rang. She grimaced an apology to Velma and fished the phone out of her purse. She stepped away as she clicked on the screen, so as to not hold the conversation right in front of Velma.

It was Harold Reed. "The FBI men weren't as impressed with our circumstantial evidence as we were. They'll meet us Monday morning."

"I suppose we should be thankful it's Monday morning and not next month." Nell sighed.

"I'm not thankful," Harold replied. "This is murder, and I got the impression they're busy on the trail of some casino corruption. I'm making a few more phone calls. Keep your cell phone with you," he instructed.

"With me and battery charged," Nell agreed.

"Where are you?" Harold asked, clearly realizing that Nell on the cell phone meant Nell not in the safe office of the Crier.

"I'm covering the reopening of Ray's Bar."

"I suppose Sheriff Hickson is there," Harold commented dryly.

"There is a sheriff's car out front, but I don't really know who it belongs to," Nell said innocently.

That question was quickly settled with the opening of the door of the bar. Hickson walked out with Ray. Perhaps it was to take a look at Velma's handiwork or perhaps they just wanted a word together.

"Miz McGraw," the sheriff said upon spying her. "What a pleasant surprise to see you here."

Somehow Nell doubted that. "Now I do," she said to Harold. "Catch you later." She hurriedly hung up and put the phone away, trying not to look like she'd just been talking about the sheriff.

"Since the yacht club parties get more than their share of coverage, I thought it was only fair that Ray's get some notice," she said to him in as breezy a tone as she could muster.

"Said she might run pictures in the paper," Velma added.

Sheriff Hickson's glance from Nell's camera to his car wasn't subtle. He hooked his fingers in his belt and said, "Well, let me get that car out of the way. Give you a better shot."

"Thank you, that would be kind," Nell said. "But I've already got some shots of the outside of the bar. Why don't I get some of you and Mr. and Mrs. Gautier standing out front.

"No sense having me in it," the sheriff demurred. "It's Ray and Velma's place. Get their picture."

"Naw, Clureman, we wouldn't be open without your help," Ray cajoled. "C'mon over here." He threw an arm around the sheriff's neck, then belatedly remembered to put the other arm, the one that ended at the elbow, around his wife.

Nell dutifully snapped several photos, taking care to make it obvious the sheriff's car wasn't in her view.

"Didn't think I'd get much of an opening crowd," Ray said as Nell snapped the last picture. "Not the press and all," he went on genially, as if surprised Nell had bothered but happy for the notice nonetheless.

"I suspect Miz McGraw was huntin' for me," Sheriff Hickson said.

"Not really," Nell hedged. "Velma and I run into each other every once in a while at the library, and I wanted to come out in support of her." It was just on the border of a lie, Nell knew, but it was also something that she wanted to be true.

Ray gave his wife a pleased smile and Sheriff Hickson gave Nell a disbelieving frown.

Nell continued. "But as long as we're both here, can I ask you a few questions, Sheriff Hickson?"

"You do know how to hunt a man down, don't you?" he answered resignedly.

"Not at all. I just take advantage of opportunities when they present themselves."

"Why don't y'all come in and have a drink? On the house," Ray said.

"C'mon, Miz McGraw, y'all need to see the inside," the sheriff said as he took her arm to lead her into the bar.

Nell was aware of what he was doing—changing the balance in his favor. Out here, it was neutral territory; they were visible to anyone driving around the harbor and Nell had a clear path to her car. But the bar was the sheriff's territory, with his friends. Ray and

Velma were friendly now, but Nell knew their welcome would disappear if the sheriff made it clear that she wasn't wanted there.

But his hand on her arm and Ray's welcoming smile gave her no choice but to enter the bar.

It's just a bar, Nell reminded herself. Although its owners might not be pleased if she angered the sheriff, she doubted they would do more than ask her to leave. At least she hoped that she wasn't headed for cement overshoes and a long swim.

At first the only thing she could see was the hot pink neon beer sign over the bar, but then her eyes slowly adjusted and she could make out the interior. All the usual things were there: the bar itself, with a stuffed marlin hanging behind it; a pool table; a juke box; and an assortment of chairs and stools.

One of the older daughters—over twenty-one, Nell hoped—was behind the bar. She declined the beer that was offered to her and instead asked for a club soda, closing the few feet between herself and the sheriff. She leaned against the bar next to him.

"Non-alcoholic," the sheriff said as he hoisted something that looked very much like beer. He took a sip, then said, "That a gin and tonic you got there, Miz McGraw?"

"No, club soda," Nell retorted. "I'm still working, and after work I have my children to take care of." Of course he knows it's club soda, she reminded herself. He's just baiting me—and trying to get me to react like a huffy prig. And succeeding, she admitted. Trying to recover, she said, "So now that we're enjoying our non-alcoholic, approved-for-working-men-and-women drinks, how about those questions?"

"Guess you picked up some of those big city reporter tricks—ask questions where ever and whenever you can."

"I did look for you at your office, but you weren't there," Nell answered. "I guess I think that people who are paid by the taxpayers should be held accountable."

"Accountable for what?" he returned.

"Insuring that the prisoners in their jails are kept safe."

"Just like a bleeding heart liberal, standing up for the rights of a faggot child molester," he shot back at her.

Nell was relieved to note that Ray and Velma were on the other side of the bar, chatting with some new customers who had just entered. She also noticed that she, Velma, and the daughter behind the bar were the only women in a room of about ten men.

"I'm sorry, I must have missed the trial in which Ronald Hebert was proven guilty," Nell coolly replied.

"And I suppose I should be held 'accountable' for saving the taxpayers the cost of housing him and trying him until the lawyers finally ran out of excuses to keep his sorry ass off death row."

"What if Ronald Hebert was innocent? What if someone framed him to get away with the murders? Or do you think Doug Shaun is such a perfect cop that he could never be wrong?"

The sheriff was nonchalantly downing his beer, but he stopped in mid-guzzle at the mention of his rival's name. "Doug Shaun can be wrong five times 'fore getting out of bed."

"So you admit it's possible that Doug overlooked evidence that Hebert was framed?"

The sheriff took a hard swallow of his supposed non-beer before replying. "It's possible, but even Doug Shaun couldn't of messed this one up," he finally said.

"But what if he did?" Nell probed. "Who'd ever know? Except the real killer?"

The sheriff gave her a hard look. "You think the killer's still out there?" He chugged the rest of his beer, then said, "You been watching too much TV."

"It just seems a little too much luck has come Doug Shaun's way. We have a killer who cleverly plots his murders, seems to have an obsession with detail, but suddenly one anonymous phone call and he's caught. Then the suspect dies before he even got a chance to tell his side."

The sheriff didn't answer, instead moved down the bar to beckon the bar tender for a refill. Unless the kegs were mixed up, the tap his beer came out of wasn't the non-alcoholic one. After taking his time, he rejoined Nell.

"So maybe Doug Shaun planted that stuff, to get the glory of catching the killer," he answered.

"But where would Doug get it?"

"Simple. Doug's the killer." The sheriff chortled. "Want me to go arrest him? Tell him Nell McGraw sent me?" This time he let out a belly laugh.

"What about the murder of Marion Nash? Are you going to let him solve that one, too?"

That cut the sheriff's enjoyment short. "You sayin' we ain't doin' all we can?" he shot at her.

"Do you believe the theory that she picked up some strange man and was murdered in a brutal sexual crime?"

"I guess it's what makes sense … but hard to think that Erma Nash's daughter grew into something like that."

"I don't think Mrs. Nash believes it," Nell said gently.

"You been talkin' to her?" he asked sharply. "Mr. High and Mighty Police Chief went out and questioned her. Askin' those kinds of questions. Don't know why being treated like that didn't give her a final stroke."

"No, I haven't talked to Mrs. Nash. My mother-in-law did."

"I got all the respect in the world for Miz Thomas. You'd do well to follow her."

"She asked me to look into Marion's death—to prove that Marion wasn't the tramp she's being painted to be. Still think I should follow Mrs. Thomas?" Nell needled him.

"You find out anything about Marion's death, you come to me, you hear?" Sheriff Hickson looked directly at Nell to give his words weight. "Not that boyfriend of yours. You come to me."

"Doug Shaun is not my boyfriend," Nell retorted. "And he seems to be doing a better job of solving murders in this town. So why should I come to you?"

"Because I care about Marion Nash. To him she's just some stupid girl that picked up the wrong man." Under his breath he muttered, "Didn't think I'd live to see the children of this town dying 'fore me." He took a long swallow of his beer, then shot at her, "But it's just another story to you, ain't it?"

"No, it's not just another—"

He cut her off. "Sell a few more papers, right? I've been here all my life, grew up here. Seen a lot of changes. Just didn't think I'd see the day Mr. Thomas's paper was nothing but a junk paper."

"Junk paper?" Nell flared. "Ronald Hebert was a child of this town, too. But maybe because he was gay he doesn't count. Or maybe it's not nice to think your neglect and bigotry might have killed him."

"You put that in the paper and you'll regret it," he retorted.

"If I can ever prove it, it'll be in the paper, you can count on that," Nell shot back.

They glared at each other, a contest of wills. Nell started to bring up the book in Marion's possession, partly to see the sheriff's reaction and partly to prove she had reasons beyond mere speculation for believing that Ronald Hebert was innocent and the real killer was still free. But she hesitated. Sheriff Hickson knew the woods and the bayous here; he could easily have engineered the deaths of Rayburn and Joey. He certainly had access to the boys—what if he'd been the one molesting Rayburn and it had escalated into the boy's death? Smiling faces can hide a lot, and so can drunken ones.

"The day you got more than just women's intuition, Miz Mc-Graw, you put it on my desk. Now, y'all have to excuse me, got other folks to talk to here."

Nell finished what was left in her club soda, found Velma and said goodbye, and then was back out in the sunshine.

What have I learned, she thought. That the sheriff is an asshole—but I already knew that. Was he a jolly little kiddie diddler who'd finally progressed to murder? The man had the ego for it. And Nell suspected that beneath that good ole boy exterior was a cunning man. Asking him about the book would have served no purpose—if he knew about it, he'd deny it, and it would tip him off that Nell knew about it. Even if Marion hadn't gone to him, it wasn't likely he would have let Nell know that.

Harold had denied that Marion had brought the book to him, and Nell believed him. For what that was worth. And Doug had seemed genuinely surprised when she'd told him about Marion, so that seemed to rule him out. It narrowed things down nicely, Nell thought; either Marion went to the sheriff or she didn't. She may have talked to Sheriff Hickson himself or to any of his deputies. But still, the killer could be any of the rest of the uniformed men in town: father and son Jenkins, Philip Yorst and his yacht club henchmen, the entire Air Force base over in Biloxi, and a few that she probably wasn't aware of.

Nell started her car. Time to get back to the safety of her office. At least there the only danger awaiting her there was irate subscribers.

As Nell entered, Jacko approached her, "Can I talk to you?"

"Yes, sure, come into my office," Nell said, and he followed her back. "So, what's up?" She slung her purse onto the desk and turned to face him.

"You remember that possible job in Austin? They called me today. We did a phone interview."

Nell sighed, softly, she hoped. "I guess you'll be leaving beautiful Pelican Bay for the scorching plains of Texas." She tried for a light tone to cover her disappointment.

"The thing is, they want me to start Monday."

"Monday?" Nell echoed. "As in Saturday, Sunday, and Monday?"

"Yes, or at least as quick as possible. I don't want to leave you hanging … but I'm not doing much real reporting now anyway. Even the sewer and water board doesn't want me."

"I will miss you, but I'm not going to ask you to stay just to be rejected by the bigots on the sewer board."

"I'll finish up everything I've been working on, file all those things I've meant to file, so that … whoever replaces me will have a chance."

"You don't need to do that. Just tell me where you are on things—"

"No, I need to finish up," Jacko interrupted. "You taught me a lot of things, Nell, about reporting and … about integrity. I at least owe you a clean desk."

"But will you have time to get packed and out of here?"

"Don't worry. I'm young, don't have much. It can all be thrown in the back of my car in an hour. My landlady's happy to see me leave, particularly as I've already paid to the end of the month."

"And I'll pay you to the end of the month," Nell said.

"You don't need to do that."

"Yes, I do." He started to shake his head, but Nell continued. "I'd pay Carrie to the end of the month, and you've probably already done more work than she has."

"Thanks. I admit it would make my life easier. I'm staying with the owner in Austin. He said he's got a spare bedroom and he needs me as soon as possible, but I'd like to have my own place sooner than later."

"Good. All I ask in return is that some day after you've won the Pulitzer, you come back and visit and write a story or two."

Jacko blushed at the compliment. "I might like to do a few stories for you before that. It might not be easy to do it long-distance, but I ... don't just want to walk away from Ronald's death."

"I think his death and Marion's are linked," Nell said. "I don't want to walk away from either of them. I'll take all the help I can get, even long-distance."

"Marion is another ghost I don't want to just leave behind," Jacko said softly. "Another reason I can't quite leave. Her funeral is tomorrow."

"I talked to Kate Ryan," Nell said. "Sort of widow to ... widow."

Jacko nodded, then said, "I like Kate, I like Kate a lot. She and Marion ... were what I wanted to be when I grew up." His jaw clenched briefly. Then he said, "Kate is probably the main reason I can get packed in an hour—she offered to help, and she takes no prisoners when it comes to efficiency."

"Let me know if I can help in any way," Nell offered. "Josh has a major crush on Kate. He'll probably be glad to help, too."

"Thanks," Jacko said with a slight nod, an acknowledgment that they handled parting the same way—a quiet, understated goodbye. "Let me get back to work. I have some research I want to complete." With that, he left Nell to the less-than-pleasant task of calling the people who would accept nothing less than a personal conversation with the editor-in-chief about their missing papers.

In the late afternoon, her phone rang. Since she'd already taken care of the first, second, and third level of irate patrons, Nell felt it safe to answer. Mentally she also noted that Josh was at the bike shop and Lizzie had texted that she was studying with Jennifer. The ringing phone shouldn't harbor any immediate crises.

"Nell, hi, this is Doug. I'm calling about two things. First and most important, to see if we're still on for tomorrow night."

"Uh … yes, we are," Nell answered, although she'd made no progress on the child-minding front. But she didn't want to admit she'd been too consumed by the day's events to remember tomorrow's.

"And, secondly, on a more business-related note. I've been thinking about what you said about Marion's death. You're right; it does seem an odd coincidence to have so many murders in such a short time here. I'd like to take a look at that library book, if you can arrange it."

That was another thing she'd been putting off. "Thanks for not blowing me off, Doug," Nell said. "I'll have to get back to you on that."

"Soon. Please do it soon. I'd like to get this over with."

"Tomorrow, sometime, if I can arrange it," Nell answered.

"Good, I'd like that. But before dinner. I don't want to be doing business when I intend on pleasure."

They agreed to seven for dinner and that Nell would call him earlier in the day about the book.

After putting the phone down, Nell glanced at her watch. She needed to talk to Kate Ryan again. She straightened her desk, then turned out the light.

Jacko was still at his computer, staring intently at the screen. He didn't notice Nell until she spoke.

"You can go home, too," she said. "You've got a busy weekend."

"Got a few more things to do. That I want to do. I may have some interesting background on our suspects."

"Anything you care to share?"

"Not just yet. Let me get the whole picture and then I'll fill you in. Are you going to be around tomorrow?" he asked, then softly added, as if suddenly remembering, "Maybe after the funeral?"

"One way or another, I'll be around tomorrow. Call me on my cell phone if we don't connect otherwise."

"Yes, ma'am."

"And, Jacko, don't work too late," Nell said as she went out the door.

The days were getting longer, darkness receding to let the light linger. Right now it was a golden afternoon, with the low sun visible in the sky.

Nell headed to the bike shop. She could ask Kate if she would be willing to talk to Doug sometime tomorrow.

"Mom, what are you doing here?" was how her son greeted her as Nell entered. "I promised Kate I'd finish putting together this bike and then clean up the workshop."

Nell tried not to take it personally that her son preferred the company of another woman. It will only get worse, she reminded herself, so I'd better get used to it. Kate, given both age and sexuality, would be merely amused by Josh's crush. She also decided that a discussion about her son leaving in a timely fashion could wait until Kate wasn't listening in.

"You can finish the bike and clean to your heart's content," Nell assured him. "I might even leave you here overnight, just to get that much cleaning out of you."

"Ah, Mom." Josh didn't want to be teased by his mother, of all people.

"I'll leave you be," Nell told him. "I'm here to talk to Kate."

"Oh, yes, about the ads," Kate said, a sad, ironic quirk of a smile on her face. "Come into the back office. I have something to show you. If you need any help, Josh, just holler."

Kate led Nell into a room behind the counter. As many times as Nell had been in the bike shop, she'd never been in the inner sanctum. Some things that had clearly belonged to Toby still remained: the plaques and awards for his community service; pictures of him, some with people Nell didn't know, one group shot with her and Thom in it, and one with a much-younger Kate. Nell was initially chagrined to notice that Kate had a desk neater than hers, but then she noticed the stacks of catalogues and other paper effluvia of a small business stacked less neatly on a book case in the corner of the office.

"Guess it's time to start thinking about end-of-school ads," Kate said, but her tone was sardonic and the smile even smaller than her first small one.

"Not yet, please," Nell said. "I'm of the old school. Let's get through Easter first."

"I guess you're here about this," Kate said. She went to the back of the office and unlocked an old file cabinet, one that seemed little used. From that she took out a locked cash box, also old and battered, and then took out the book Nell recognized as the one Marion had shown her.

"I guess I am," Nell admitted, adjusting to Kate's abrupt change of subject. "I'm just conjecturing, but I think Marion went to someone in the Sheriff's Department."

"Other than me mentioning she was considering it, is there any other reason why you think that?"

"That's just it—I can't really name a good solid reason. Maybe because I don't like Sheriff Hickson. I think he allowed Ronald Herbert to be killed. Drove him to suicide. Plus, they cover Tchula County, not just the city of Pelican Bay. Makes it more likely they'd know the bayou route into the park."

"Ronald didn't kill himself," Kate said fiercely.

"He might have technically killed himself," Nell replied, "but if he did, I'd bet it was because he knew he wouldn't survive for twenty-four hours in jail."

"And hanging in his cell was better than ..." Kate didn't finish the sentence. Better than being tortured and raped; neither of them needed to say those words.

"But I have no proof of that, and no way of knowing whether Sheriff Hickson just turned a blind eye to what he thought was justice or whether he had a direct hand in killing Ronald."

"And no proof that Marion was killed for this," Kate said, throwing the book down on her desk.

"May I look at it?"

"Help yourself," Kate said. "I'll go check on Josh. He's probably about ready for me to look at the brakes anyway." She added softly, "Please find something I missed, find something that will ..." She was silent, then left the office.

Nell sat at the desk and opened the book. She'd only glanced at it when Marion had shown it to her. Now she took a long look at each page. But the pictures were maddeningly inexact. A child with crayons crying for help, but without the words or skill to do more than indicate something that shouldn't happen to any child was happening to him.

Nell moved the chair next to the window to look again. The gun and badge were always there, but sometimes they changed sides, always facing out whether the figure was in left or right profile. She was hoping for something like an indication that the figure was left-handed. There was no crude drawing of the kind of stomach that Sheriff Hickson had, although that may have just been beyond Rayburn's ability to figure out how to draw. The penis was quite evident, but it was just a long blob, no indication of any special characteristics or, for that matter, even pubic hair or testicles. Maybe that was a clue, but again, Nell couldn't be sure it wasn't just something Rayburn couldn't draw.

One thing she did notice in the daylight that she hadn't caught in the desk lamp was that a yellow crayon had been used to outline around the shoulder. Maybe to indicate a shirt? The tan of the sheriff's office? Sometimes the child stick figure was close in size to the book drawing; other times there was a difference. But again, that could be due to Rayburn's artistic skill more than any real size difference.

Nell looked through the book a third time, but she couldn't see anything more than what she already had seen.

What do I have, she thought as she closed the book. The person who molested Rayburn might be short, might be wearing a tan or yellowish uniform, and might have light pubic hair or none all together, and might have no testicles or small ones.

Nell had a brief vision of walking over to the sheriff's office and telling them "drop your pants, boys, I want to see them all." But she could summon no mirth at the thought. I'm tired, and I want this over, I want my children safe again, and I want … what do I want for Ronald and Marion? she wondered. Justice? It didn't seem enough.

"Any interesting reading?" Kate appeared in the doorway.

"I wish I could say I cracked the case," Nell answered with a sigh. "I noticed a few things, but whether they're clues or bad art, I can't be sure." She ran down the list for Kate.

"Not much, really." Kate agreed with Nell's assessment of her meager findings.

"It might be better to bring in someone who knows what they're doing," Nell said. "Neither you nor I are forensic experts. Would you be willing to talk to Chief Shaun about what you know?"

Kate didn't immediately answer. When she did, it was with a question. "Why him? What makes you think he's safe?"

"I guess the same things that make me think the sheriff is guilty. Instinct. Nothing I can put my hand on as a sensible reason. Josh had to tell him about the bayou leading into the park. That had to be the way the killer snuck in and out. At least Doug seems interested in doing his job. I've also talked to Harold Reed in the DA's office, and he's arranged for the FBI to come in, but nothing is going to happen there until Monday."

"How do we know that the FBI is safe?" Kate asked, but she clearly didn't expect an answer as she quickly added, "Let me think about it, okay?"

"Okay, but call me as soon as you can," Nell said.

"Tomorrow," was Kate's answer. "I'll call by then."

For a moment they were silent, in the office with the fading afternoon light, and then Kate said, "Thanks for your ... for helping, for being here."

"Of course," was the only reply Nell made before Josh interrupted with a question about where a certain tool was.

"Time to go home, Josh my boy," Kate answered. "We can finish the bike tomorrow."

"Can we?" he asked, his question mostly directed at Nell.

"We'll see," she answered, not wanting to burden Kate with watching her son.

"It's fine if he comes by," Kate said, understanding Nell's hedge. "I'll be closed in the morning for ... the funeral, but he can come by around 2 or 3." Very softly she added, "Josh's a ... good distraction. I like his company."

And you'll need distractions after going to Marion's funeral, Nell thought. But she didn't mention that, just made the necessary arrangements, including that Josh could stay as late as Kate wanted him and then that she could take him over to Mrs. Thomas, Sr.'s, while Nell went out to dinner.

Josh down, Lizzie to go, Nell thought as they left the bike shop.

Lizzie, miraculously enough, offered her own solution by asking to go to a slumber party, one that would start in the afternoon and stretch until sometime Sunday-ish. Nell managed to extract from Lizzie a promise that she would do all her homework that night, plus do all the dishes in exchange for Nell's letting her be gone for so long.

She didn't exactly tell her children she was going out to eat with a man; she wasn't sure how they would take it. As a betrayal, Nell suspected, although they might not call it that. One dinner wasn't enough to venture onto that treacherous ground. So Nell only mentioned some vague plans and for once was thankful for the self-absorption of youth, as they asked no questions.

Lizzie did do the dishes and even stayed on the computer long enough to do several weeks worth of homework. Nell caught a glimpse of an email to Janet, so she knew her daughter wasn't as studious as she was making out to be. But as long as her rebellion was confined to illicit emails masquerading as homework and not porn sites, Nell was content to let it pass.

TWENTY-NINE

THE PHONE RANG. NELL struggled out of sleep to answer it. The foreboding came back; a few nights with no calls and she'd hoped it might be over, her nights no longer disturbed by the jar of the phone.

"Hello," she said.

Silence answered her.

"Who is this?" she demanded sharply, to keep her fear at bay.

The silence stretched and then a voice answered, "Who do you think this is?"

Nell sat bolt upright. It was the voice that had woken her the other times. "What do you want?"

"What do I always want? The pleasure of your company."

"You sick bastard…" But Nell caught herself. He wants me angry and off guard.

"Most reporters would die for a story like this, Nell. I'm doing you a favor."

"Where do I find the body this time, you sick piece of shit?"

"There is no body. I've decided to mend my ways, Nell, dear."

Nell fumbled with her cell phone; maybe she could call Doug and when he heard her end of the conversation, he would know to trace the line.

"And turn yourself over to the police?" she asked.

"I'm not that mended. But I do want to give you one piece of advice. Stay away from Doug Shaun. I don't like him, and I don't like you with him."

The line went dead.

Nell sat for a moment, holding both phones in her hands, then put the bedside phone down but still held the cell phone, debating whether or not to call Doug.

Exhaustion made the decision. The caller was gone; he had undoubtedly called from an untraceable cell phone and that's where they'd track the call to. She could stay up all night waiting while they went through that process, or she could do it in the morning. What difference will it make, she thought as she lay back down.

But before she could try to sleep, Nell got up and glanced into Josh's room and Lizzie's room. They were both asleep, snuggled under the covers. She also checked the locks on the front and kitchen doors before going back to bed. It was a long while before sleep returned.

THIRTY

HE PUT THE PHONE down. Sleep would come easily tonight. His decision was made. He liked Nell, hoped that she'd heed his warning, but he doubted it. People made their choices and she would have to live with hers.

It was, he had to admit, a challenge, different from the others. They had seemed so straightforward and simple compared to what he would have to accomplish here. The timing would be difficult, but he could manage that. He was almost relishing the task.

He would have to get that book, of course. He'd told the boy not to tell anyone, but he hadn't thought to admonish him not to take crayon to paper. Too bad he hadn't paid attention to what the child was drawing. At the time, he'd just thought it cute, defacing library books. It was part of the game. Let the kid get away with the forbidden, from candy bars to defacing books. That was how he got what he wanted—giving them something they wanted. But he should have taken the book. It would have been simple; the boy brought it sometimes to the woods. In the future he'd have to warn them not only not to tell, but also not to draw pictures.

Now on to the problem of Nell McGraw. She was wrong, of course, but she'd come closer than anyone else. He liked that about her. Given time, she might even put the pieces together. But time was one thing she didn't have.

He had no more use for Nell McGraw as a witness. It was time for her to become a victim.

THIRTY-ONE

THE SERVICE WAS AT eleven. Lizzie and Josh seemed shy about going, so Nell left it at that. The last funeral they'd been at had been Thom's. They hadn't known Marion well—she was just the woman at the library—and she saw no reason to reawaken memories.

She left them squabbling about who needed the computer more. Nell thought of suggesting they work together, but knew it would only be seen as an un-understanding mother interfering. She did tell them she'd be back in about two hours, and she expected Josh to fold the clothes and Lizzie to prune the holly bush in the back yard. They would probably trade chores, but as least it wouldn't be Mom assigning tasks along traditional boy/girl lines. And it would assure that neither of them could hog the computer the whole time.

As she drove to the church, Nell wondered whether Marion's killer would be there. Would he dare? She answered her question—of course he would. Calling her in the night was a demand for attention. He would be there to view his handiwork.

With that uneasy thought, she pulled into the parking lot. It was already full. Marion was young, her death sudden and brutal; it was an emotional jolt that brought people out in a way that the lingering illness of the end of life didn't. None of us should be going to this funeral, Nell thought. And that's why we're all here.

She nodded and murmured greetings to the people she knew. She saw Mrs. Thomas, Sr. up at the front of the church, next to Erma Nash, who was in a wheelchair and bundled up as if against both cold and grief. The family resemblance told her that the two men standing with them were Erma's sons, come into town for the funeral.

Sheriff Hickson was also with them, old Pelican Bay families that seemed to know one another. Would he dare, Nell wondered, kill the daughter and console the mother? For the first time she found herself wavering in her belief that he was the murderer. Even at this distance, the sorrow on his face seemed genuine.

She would talk to her mother-in-law after the funeral, Nell decided. Plus, she preferred to find a seat in the back, not only because she didn't feel she was a longtime family friend of the Nashes'—not the way Thom would have been—but also she wanted to observe people. Glancing around, Nell was relieved to see Jacko in one of the back pews. He was in the far corner, as if trying to make himself unobtrusive. One group of people started to enter that pew, but then noticed him and moved on.

Christian charity, Nell thought, might mask some of the greatest sins of all. She nodded a greeting at Jacko, then slid in beside him.

"Careful," Jacko whispered to her. "You might get a reputation sitting next to me."

"Not one I'm worried about."

Then Jacko half stood and said, "Kate, over here."

Nell turned to look at Kate. She was barely recognizable as the woman from the bike shop, instead dressed in a sober dark blue dress, her only jewelry a strand of black pearls. With her was the woman that Nell recognized as the Unitarian minister, and during their introductions, Nell learned that the man with the minister was her husband.

She and Kate managed the idle talk that seemed necessary, about the weather, her church, Nell's paper. Since Thom's death, Nell had learned the importance of these moments of no consequence—they kept you going, they passed the time, made small connections, offered a sort of padding that allowed you to move through the shocks and losses. Kate answered a few questions when asked, but otherwise was silent.

If I'd brought Josh, she'd have been forced to put on a mask, pretend it was just a friend who'd died, Nell thought, but then realized that was exactly what Kate was doing. Josh being here might have added another layer onto that mask.

Doug Shaun entered. He caught Nell's attention, but there were no seats near her and he disappeared somewhere into the middle of the church. Like Sheriff Hickson, he was in dress uniform, but that was the only similarity; the sheriff's was a little tight around his stomach and although it had been ironed in the recent past, the pull of the sheriff's corpulent body was already bringing the wrinkles out. In contrast, Doug's uniform was crisp and handsome, the deep blue set off by the gold braid at his shoulder and the gleaming brass on his hat, tucked appropriately under his arm.

The service began with the drone of somber words and somber hymns. Nell fought off the memories of other funerals, but images from each caught at her. Thom's, her father's from his sudden heart attack, and a few bare years later her mother's, from the slow cancer. The familiar words echoed in the church and in her memory: "Ashes to ashes, dust to dust."

She heard a soft catch of breath and noticed that Jacko was silently crying. Nell reached over and took his hand. He returned her clasp, holding her hand as if it were a lifeline.

From the front of the church, a strangled sob and then the words "my daughter" echoed. Nell glanced over at Kate. She, too, had tears sliding down her cheeks. Nell took her hand as she had Jacko's. Kate's grasp wasn't as fierce as his was, but she didn't let go and after a few minutes twined her fingers through Nell's.

The service ended, and Marion's casket was brought down the aisle. She felt Kate shudder as it went by, but she made no sound. Nell watched the mourners leave, looking for the one face that had triumph hidden behind the grief. The sheriff had red-rimmed eyes, his face haggard. Wendell Jenkins was there; he, too, looked downcast. With him was his supposedly banished son Boyce, in a black suit that looked like his father's. Nell felt a flash of anger, then wondered if Boyce had come back just for the funeral or if the "boys" had decided the ban was over. Or if he'd ever even left. But Boyce actually looked somber, following his father's lead. Philip Yorst had had the good taste to leave his yacht club uniform at home. Buddy Guy was there, shaking hands even as he was making his way down the aisle, but doing so in hushed tones. Nell saw Harold Reed and his wife; he nodded at her. Behind him was Doug Shaun. Intermixed in the crowd were several other members of both the police force and the sheriff's office.

Nell saw what she wanted to see, finding a hint of malice in Wendell's furrowed brow, guilt in the sheriff's crying eyes, a sly look from one of the deputies. But she knew she saw these things only because she wanted to ascribe the blame to these men. If the murderer was here, he was hiding his guilt well.

Finally, their row stood. Kate let go of Nell's hand, as if she didn't want anyone to see her weakness or their connection, but Jacko held on as they made their way out of the church. Only at the door did he let go, softly saying, "Thanks."

They made their way down the church steps, and then Kate abruptly said, "I've got to leave." With that she strode across the parking lot, leaving them behind. Jacko hurriedly followed her.

Nell started to go with them, but Doug Shaun took her arm.

"Nell, I should have called and offered to escort you," he said.

Nell was looking beyond him at Jacko and Kate. Jacko had taken the keys from Kate and was leading her to the passenger side of her truck. She can cry with him, Nell thought.

"That's kind of you, but there's no need," she said to Doug. "I don't require a police escort everywhere I go." But maybe I do, she suddenly thought. Another glance at Jacko and Kate showed Jane, the Unitarian minister, taking what Nell guessed were the keys to Jacko's car. He would drive Kate home, take care of her; they would drive his car either there or to his place. There was little she could do at the moment.

"And I know it's probably inappropriate to say this," Doug said, pulling her attention back to him, "but that dress really shows what an attractive woman you are."

Nell shook her head to fend off his compliment. It *was* inappropriate. This was the dress she'd worn to Thom's funeral, and having another man tell her it made her attractive seemed almost blasphemous. But, of course, Doug couldn't know the history and the memory of the dress.

She pulled him to the side and said, "I got another phone call last night. The same voice."

This did manage to get his attention off her attire. "Are you sure?"

"As much as I can be. The voice is disguised. I suppose that anyone using the same technology would sound about the same. But he spoke to me the same way. The creepy pretense of intimacy."

"What did he want?"

"To jar me out of my sleep. He said he hadn't killed anyone—and left no clues that we'd find a body, in any case. But he did warn me to stay away from you."

"Really? Did he say why?"

"No, just that he didn't like you and he didn't like me with you."

"Are you going to take his advice?"

"He's not my version of Ann Landers. But now we know it's someone who doesn't like you."

"And someone who seems to have some sexual attachment to you—or likes to imagine he has."

Nell didn't like that thought. She wasn't even sure she wanted Doug Shaun to have a sexual interest in her, let alone a perverted murderer. "He called around 2:30 in the morning. I guess you might as well try to trace the number. Maybe he was stupid enough to call from a phone that can be linked to him."

"Maybe. But I'll bet it's a throw-away cell. Perhaps we'll get lucky. Maybe we can track it to the store he bought it from and someone will remember something. I'll do … just a second." Doug turned slightly away from her and took his cell phone out of his jacket. He may not have turned it off for the funeral, but at least he'd turned it to vibrate.

"So should I get one of those?" someone behind Nell asked.

"Makes sense," someone else answered. "What if your car breaks down? I've got some good deals going right now."

Even at funerals, life—and commerce—went on.

The crowd parted enough to give Nell a clear view of Mrs. Thomas. And Mrs. Thomas a view of Nell.

"Be back," Nell mouthed to Doug. She had to talk to her mother-in-law, even if it was only to hear her question why Josh and Lizzie weren't there and who was watching them with Nell gone. She edged her way through to where Mrs. Thomas was talking to Marion's brothers.

There was a round of polite introductions. An awkward silence followed but was cut short by the need to begin the funeral procession. The brothers left to help Mrs. Nash into the car that would follow the hearse bearing her daughter's body.

"Where are Joshua and Elizabeth?" Mrs. Thomas asked.

"I left them at home," Nell said, then added, "Funerals bring back memories of other funerals. I didn't think they needed that."

"God, yes, they do," Mrs. Thomas replied, and a sudden wash of grief crossed her face.

We're both remembering Thom's funeral, Nell thought. And her mother-in-law was watching another mother go through the loss of a child. Nell stood awkwardly, watching the imperious woman struggle to not cry.

Then Mrs. Thomas swayed, as if she might lose her balance, and Nell reached out to her. Their embrace was stiff, almost clumsy.

"Mother," was all Nell said.

"Poor Erma. She doesn't yet know how lonely she will be." Then Mrs. Thomas pulled away and said, "I need to go with them." She leaned in to give Nell an awkward kiss on the cheek and then turned to go. One of Mrs. Nash's sons appeared and took her arm. She would follow with them.

Nell turned from the hearse and found herself face to face with Wendell Jenkins. And Boyce.

"Sad thing, isn't it, Miz McGraw," Wendell drawled at her.

"More than sad. Brutal and senseless. Evil."

"When you go to a place like that … bad things happen," he added sanctimoniously.

"Oh? And what bad things happened to you there, Mr. Jenkins?" Nell shot back.

"What are you accusing him of?" Boyce stepped in. He still had the coiled feeling of anger and violence about him.

"Your father alluded to personal knowledge of the kinds of events that happen in 'places like that.' I was curious to learn what he meant," Nell said. "I thought you had … moved on."

"Boyce and Marion went to school together. Boy wanted to come pay his respects. Didn't think you'd get riled about someone coming to a funeral," Wendell said.

"If you think Marion deserved her death, then I doubt your 'respects' are worth much," Nell retorted.

"Look, lady, you think you're so much better than us 'cause you write the paper," Boyce said in a low, threatening voice. "You might want to think again."

"Wendell, you get that boy out of here right now," Sheriff Hickson said in a voice that matched Boyce's threat. He was standing just behind Nell. "You act up at Marion Nash's funeral and I'll personally put you in jail," he said directly to Boyce. He stepped around Nell to put himself between her and Boyce.

"This woman is making accusations against Dad," Boyce said defensively.

"Oh, please, like I haven't seen the pictures of the casino girls," Nell said. She hadn't, of course, but she'd heard enough to believe that some photos existed. Alessandra might even be able to get a few. "But I won't listen to you talk about Marion like she was trash who deserved what happened."

"Miz McGraw, you need to go home to your children," the sheriff told her. "Boyce, you got half an hour to say hi to your Maw and then you got to be on your way."

Nell decided that although she had no intention of doing what the sheriff told her, save on her own time, it was also time to leave the Jenkins boys alone.

She headed back across the churchyard to where she'd left Doug, only glancing over her shoulder once. She was gratified to see that Sheriff Hickson was actually making them leave.

Boyce Jenkins moved up even higher on her list of suspects. He did seem to have some sexual hatred for her. And he had good reason to include Doug Shaun in that hatred.

"Hi, sorry about the phone call," Doug said as she rejoined him. He was just putting his phone back into his jacket. "Do you think I can look at that book?"

Nell had hoped to ask Kate about it but hadn't had a chance. And just now didn't seem like a good time—it had to be a horrible day for Kate, and Nell was reluctant to push.

"I haven't been able to arrange it yet," she said. "It may take a little more time. Possibly later this afternoon, but I'm not sure."

"Okay, but I'd like to follow up."

"I would like you to follow up," Nell agreed. "I'll do what I can."

"Fair enough. We're still on for tonight, right?"

"Still are."

"Nell, Chief Shaun." Buddy Guy joined them, hand already out for shaking. Nell listened to a few of his "starring Buddy Guy" ideas for newspaper stories before Philip Yorst also joined them and chimed in with ideas for yacht club stories, including one about how the number of beer cans clogging the harbor had increased since the reopening of Ray's Bar.

After the minimum amount of polite time had passed, Nell made noises about having to get back to her children. She didn't out-and-out lie and say there was a babysitter who had to leave, but Lizzie had a limit to how long she would look out for Josh before regressing to whining adolescent angst. Nell guessed this was about Lizzie's limit, and it was certainly hers.

When she got home, she was more or less right. Improbably enough, Lizzie was out in torn shorts trimming the shrubs and Josh was ensconced in front of the computer. The clothes were yet to be folded.

Children—and life—are full of surprises, Nell thought.

THIRTY-TWO

Of course, the minute Josh realized that Nell had returned, he jumped up from the computer and hurried to the laundry room. Nell took a few seconds to glance at what he'd been doing online, including checking the websites he'd been to. She did this openly most of the time, as she wanted her children to know she cared what they did and also that there were limits to what they could do. So far, no XXX hot girls sites had come up, although she was already working on the "mom" speech, a separate version for Josh and Lizzie, for when it did happen. Curiosity being what it was, she knew it was when, not if.

But today wasn't the day. Josh had been engrossed in nature sites, and it was the literal birds and bees that had kept him from the laundry. Or actually the snakes and sharks.

Mid-afternoon, after a long shower, Lizzie left for her marathon slumber party. A little while later, the phone rang. It was Kate.

"Nell, hello. I just wanted to let you know I'm at the bike shop if Josh wants to come over. That is, if it's still okay with you."

"Of course it's okay with me. But . . . how are you? Are you up to it?"

"I need to keep ... keep myself going. Josh helps me pull out."

"If you're sure. I know he'll be happy to come by."

"I'm sure. Send him along whenever. A new shipment of bikes arrived yesterday, so maybe between the two of us we'll get them put together tonight."

"Consider him sent." Nell continued before Kate could hang up. "Have you thought about showing the police the book? Chief Shaun asked about it today. Will you talk to him?"

"I guess. I ... yes, I'll talk to him. Maybe I should have a friend with me. Or a lawyer."

"I don't think you need a lawyer," Nell answered. "If you're comfortable with me, I'd be willing to be there."

Kate hesitated, then said, "Depends. Which side are you on?"

Trust takes time, Nell realized. Kate had reasons to be slow in granting hers—her partner had been killed for this book.

"Truth and justice," she replied. "The side we all should be on."

"Who's truth and who's justice?" Kate asked, a bitter edge coming into her voice.

Nell surprised even herself as she suddenly burst out, "It's not justice that you had to sit in the back of the church. It's not justice that Ronald Hebert was convicted and executed because he was gay. It's not justice that I had to find another job for one of the best reporters I've ever had because he slept with another man. It's not fair and it's not right ... and it's not just."

Kate was silent for a long time, then she said, "Thanks. I ... needed you to be angry. I needed ..." She was again silent and Nell realized that Kate was either crying or trying not to cry. Finally, Kate broke the silence again. "Tell Josh to get over here. I've got bikes to put together. And I'll talk to your cop friend whenever." With that, she gently put the phone down.

Nell went back to the living room to give Josh the good news. He was out the door in less than ten minutes. Nell felt a stab of envy as she watched him go; it was a beautiful clear day, perfect for biking, perfect for being out behind a shop putting together bikes. It seemed like such a carefree and easy existence. Should I call the bike shop to make sure he gets there, she suddenly worried. Can I lose a son in eight blocks of brightly lit street? Nell quickly picked up the phone again. "Josh's on his way. He should be there in a few minutes," she told Kate.

Kate understood her undercurrent of worry. "I'll call if he's not here—wait—I see him turning onto the block now."

Nell thanked her and hung up.

The phone rang again and this time it was Jacko.

"Any chance you can swing by the office? I've got a few things for you."

"Ready to swing," Nell answered. It wasn't as pure and free as flying in the wind on a bike, but she was ready for an excuse to get out of the house, ready to be the intrepid girl reporter once again.

It took her fifteen minutes to get ready to leave, not bad for a forty-something-year-old woman, she decided as she drove to the office of the Crier.

Jacko was there waiting for her. No one else was about, but it was Saturday. Only the intrepid reporters show up on weekends, Nell thought as she entered the main room. And the ones decent enough to tie everything up before they leave for their new job.

"What's up?" she asked.

"It's all in this stack," he said, indicating a pile of paper on his desk. "But to summarize: the county jail seems pretty clean, much as we want to hate Sheriff Hickson. The only other prisoner death was a heart attack and that was five years ago. But I did run into something interesting. Seems your good friend Wendell Jenkins has a blot on his record."

Jacko paused to take the top sheet off the stack. He handed it to Nell and said, "Back in his college days, he was a drinking man and allegedly brought an underage girl back to the frat house, poured alcohol down her throat, had sex with her when she was unconscious, and never bothered to notice when she didn't wake up."

"She died?"

"Yes, she was sixteen years old. Not only that, but Wendell got his frat brothers to help him get rid of the body. Only thing that got him caught was that one of them felt guilty about it and went to the campus cops."

"But I gather Wendell got off?"

"More or less. Even back then the Jenkins had money. He claimed she lied about her age, that she was loose, had sex with all the boys—she wasn't around to contradict him. He got slapped on the wrist. Remember this was almost forty years ago."

"Not a time when rich white boys took a fall for girls who put out," Nell said disgustedly.

"But here's the real interesting part. Wendell hadn't wanted anyone to find her around campus, so they drove all the way back to Pelican Bay. And dumped her body in the old well in the woods."

"Where Rayburn Gautier was found."

"Exactly," Jacko confirmed.

"That's very interesting. Think maybe the son heard about dear old dad's ways and got ideas?"

"You think it's Boyce?"

"I'd like to think it's Boyce and Wendell. I wouldn't mind seeing them both in jail. How solid is this story?"

"Enough to put on the front page," Jacko replied, answering her question. "Most of this came up at the inquest, so it's public record, although buried public record."

"Maybe it won't get him arrested. The statue of limitations may have passed. But it might make people buy their cars somewhere else," Nell said.

"Wendell got his money early, his father died shortly after this incident, and his only brother was killed in an accident when they were teenagers. He seemed to have gone through most of the money by his late twenties, because that's when he started the car dealership and had to actually work to earn his way."

"What kind of accident?" Nell asked. "Could it have been not so accidental?"

"I couldn't find out. It was brought out in what seemed to be a ploy to gain sympathy for Wendell. You know, 'family tragedy, the only surviving son,' that sort of thing."

"That's great work, Jacko. Ace research. What else is in that stack? Or is it all about Wendell?"

"I researched Sheriff Hickson but found nothing you wouldn't expect. The usual campaign stories. Married his high school sweetheart. A few stories where he comes off as not the most enlightened being, but since you wrote most of those, they can't be news to you."

"No, they can't. Too bad you didn't find anything as interesting on him as you did on Mr. Jenkins."

"In contrast, it seems that Chief Shaun is a remarkable hero. He solved a couple other baffling murders during his career. He was an only child and his parents died young."

"That's an interesting contrast. Maybe on next week's front page we'll do stories comparing the two of them."

"Wish I could be here to see it," Jacko said wistfully.

"Damn it, Jacko. I wish you could be, too."

"This stack is my parting gift to you," he said as he stood up. "It's 'hit the road, Jack' time."

"You're leaving now?" Of course, he's leaving now, Nell answered her question.

"I'm packed and ready to go. I want this to be one of the last things I do. Say goodbye to the Crier office."

"I wish …" Nell started, but Jacko cut her off.

"Me, too." Then he wrapped his arms around her and gave her a tight hug.

Nell returned it, not wanting to let him go. Then she did.

Jacko grabbed the bag that contained his person effects and turned to go. "Look out for Kate" were his parting words. Then he was out the door, leaving Nell alone with his empty desk and the final pile of reporting he'd left for her.

She resolutely picked up the stack of paper and took it to her office. She trusted Jacko, but she wanted to read it for herself. Besides, she'd have to write the story on Wendell Jenkins, and it seemed a fitting way to spend the remains of the day.

THIRTY-THREE

WHAT A DIFFERENCE FEMINISM makes, Nell thought as she finally looked up from the pages in front of her. Seen through that prism, what Wendell Jenkins had gotten away with became an ugly crime. But back in the sixties, when it had taken place, a privileged upper-class white boy wouldn't go to jail for what would be considered a girl's bad judgment.

Nell glanced out the window, surprised at how late it was. The sun had almost set; only a lingering evening light remained.

Time for me to get ready for my date, she reminded herself. But instead she glanced at the information that Jacko had gathered on Doug Shaun. In the last town where he'd worked, he'd solved the brutal murders of three members of the high school cheerleading team. It was some place in New Mexico; Nell didn't recognize the name of the town.

Let's hope he can solve Marion's murder, she thought.

When she looked up from the sheet in front of her, Doug Shaun was standing in her doorway. She tried not to appear startled, but his quietness had once again taken her by surprise.

"Nell, I saw your car out back. Should you be here alone?"

"Why not? The Crier is in the middle of town. And most people can't manage to be as quiet as you are."

"Any word on the book? Is your friend willing to talk?"

"Yes, to both. She said anytime."

"How about now? We get business over with and then have dinner."

He was still in his dress uniform. Nell, now wearing a comfortable pair of jeans and a cotton sweater that used to be Thom's, had intended to go home again to change for dinner.

"You've caught me in old jeans."

"You look fine. I was thinking about a seafood place across the bay. It's homey, but the food is great."

"Okay. Let me close up shop here."

Nell scooped up the pile Jacko had given her and put it in her briefcase. She could continue reading it tomorrow. Tonight she was going to be an adolescent girl struggling through her first official date in almost two decades instead of the intrepid girl reporter.

Doug waited patiently as Nell closed and locked up the office.

"I should drive my car home," she suddenly said.

"We'll get it later. Why don't we take care of the book now and swing back by?"

Nell nodded and followed him to his car, a late-model red sports car.

"Where are we going?" Doug asked as they got in.

"To the bike shop. Kate Ryan and Marion were partners. Kate has the book," Nell told him.

His cell phone jangled, and he started the car and answered it at the same time. "I'm in the area, I'll run by and sign them now" was his end of the conversation. He put the phone away and said to her, "A detour. I have to run by the station for a few minutes."

"I'm not starving yet," Nell said.

They were there in another half minute. Doug left Nell in the car to take care of his business. She sat still for several minutes, then pulled the pile of papers out of her briefcase. If I'm dating the man, I might as well read about him, she thought.

Doug had also worked somewhere in Iowa. While he was there he'd solved another brutal murder—a farmer, his wife, and their four kids had been stripped and tied up in the snow to freeze to death. The killer had died in jail.

Nell quickly glanced at the next story. Doug Shaun had solved the serial murder of young children in the next town he'd worked in, in North Carolina. The first victim was a girl, the child of a poor single mother whose occupation was listed as waitress. The last one was the son of the mayor.

In that case, Doug Shaun had killed the murderer in self-defense. Pieces of the victim's clothes were found in the killer's house. He'd been a loner no one liked or trusted.

Nell was jerked away from her reading by the opening of the car door.

She watched Doug get in, the braid encircling his arm turning orange in the ginger-hued sodium lights.

A yellow circle around his arm.

What if it hadn't been a shirt but braid that Rayburn was trying to draw?

The night of Marion's murder, she'd tried to call Doug on his cell phone.

He started the car.

But she hadn't been able to reach him. He'd been "out of service area"—just as she hadn't been able to get a signal when trying to call from the motel where it had happened.

"What are you reading?" he asked as he pulled out of the parking lot.

I'm leading him to Kate. And my son.

"Some research that Jacko was doing for me," Nell answered.

"Research on what?"

If Doug Shaun killed Marion in an attempt to get the book, then he'll kill Kate to get it, and to keep her from testifying about Marion. And if he kills Kate, he'll have to kill me. And if Josh is there . . . no.

"Doug, I'm not feeling very well. I'm sorry. Maybe you'd better just take me home."

"I'm sorry to hear that. I was looking forward to this. Okay, I will, after we go by the bike shop."

Nell sat silently for a moment. But he was driving towards Kate and Josh and she had to do something.

"If I've figured it out, others will," she said in what she hoped was a calm voice.

"Figured what out?"

"You've had quite a string of successes, always being there to solve brutal murders. Always in small towns, where murder is . . . uncommon. I'm not a genius, Doug, but I've caught the pattern."

He was silent, but the air had changed, as if his anger and hate was coming for Nell, a slimy cold that made her want to rub her palm on her pants to get it away. She held still, pretending she was in control of herself.

"No, you're not a genius. If you were, you might have caught it in time." His voice had changed, the monster no longer hidden in human form. "But you are very intelligent, more so than most people. I'm going to solve another hideous murder after tonight."

"You're insane," Nell spat out, fighting the fear that was reaching into the bone.

For an answer, he grabbed her by the hair and shoved her face down into the console between the seats. "No, not insane. Just powerful. Very, very powerful." He jammed her hair under his thigh to pin her down. Nell heard the soft snap of leather. His holster.

She struggled to sit up but felt the cold metal of his gun against her temple.

"Admit it, Nell, you like power. You like your editorial pen. I'm going to be very nice to you and give you a little of my power. You know Kate Ryan is going to die—there's no way around that. And I know your son is with her. I saw him when I drove through that part of town. Bad timing. But he might be better off dead than an orphan."

"Goddamn you!" Nell yelled, hoping someone might hear. But Doug Shaun shoved the barrel of the gun harder against her head, forcing her face against the stick shift.

"You get to choose, Nell. It can be quick. Or it can be slow. I'm going to give you that much power."

The car stopped. They were at the bike shop. He'd blown through every stop sign.

"People will know we went out tonight," Nell said. "Right now it's my word against yours, but if you kill us—"

He overrode her. "I'll call in a missing person report, that you and I were to meet but you never showed up. Don't bother, Nell. I've thought of all the angles."

Nell burst into motion, twisting away from his gun. Someone will see, will hear, out here on the street. If he fires the gun, they'll hear. Even if I'm killed, it might save Josh and Kate.

But he was strong enough to not really need the gun. He grabbed her hair again and twisted it, pulling her head back.

"Remember, it's your choice, Nell. Slowly or easily. Right now I'd say you're making the wrong choice."

Then he whispered to her the things he'd done to Rayburn Gautier, and to Joey Sayton and Tasha Jackson. The way he'd put duct tape over their mouths, their muffled screams as he'd watched the fear each moment brought.

"I'll do that to Josh. Remember, it's your choice" was how he ended his litany of horrors. Then he grabbed her by the shoulders and backed out of the car, dragging her out the driver's door. His hand clamped over her mouth and he roughly pulled her to the shop entrance.

Daylight was gone, and the bike store, with its closed sign, invited no more business. Nell couldn't turn her head to look around. It happened so quickly, this brief second when they could be seen from the street. But there was no one there to see them, and then he was shoving the door open and taking Nell behind the walls of the store.

"What's going on?" Kate called out as she emerged from the back of the shop.

Nell twisted away, getting his hand off her mouth. "Run!" she shouted. "Get out!"

"Don't move!" Doug Shaun countered. He threw Nell to the floor but kept a booted foot on her shoulder. "If you want your mother to live, Josh, you'd better come out."

"Mom?"

Nell couldn't see Josh, but she heard his questioning voice. Then he yelled "Let her alone" as he saw her on the floor.

"I said don't move. Your mother will be okay if you just cooperate. I need to see that book, Kate."

"Stay in the back, Josh," Kate said.

"No, come out here where I can see you," Doug countered. "Just get the book, Kate, and everything will be okay."

"Let her get up. I'll give you the book if you let Nell get up."

332

He didn't reply, but Nell felt the pressure of his boot lift. She rolled away from him and slowly stood.

He had the gun trained on Josh. He didn't need to say anything; the threat was so heavy in the air.

"I'm getting the book," Kate said. "It's in my office." Keeping her hands up to show that she wasn't going for any weapon, she walked toward the desk in her office. Doug shifted so he could keep her in sight.

"Are women and children your specialty, Doug?" Nell asked. She hated the man, she realized—hated how much brutal power he had over them. Her fear twined the anger into a rage. If it was just her life at risk, she would throw herself at him, scratching and clawing, going for the eyes, the genitals, turn into a screaming virago. She wanted him bloody, bruised—dead.

"I vary my routine, but I've found that women and children get the most attention."

"And that's what you want? Attention? Like some little adolescent boy?"

He jerked his head to look at her, then caught himself and turned back to watching Kate. "Don't push it, Nell. Remember our bargain."

"You're too insane for me to have any hope you'll keep your end."

"Not insane, Nell. Powerful. Don't forget that. Hurry up, Kate," he yelled. He kept his gun aimed at Josh as a reminder.

Nell didn't dare look at her son; she couldn't bear to see the terror on his face. I can't let Shaun do this, she thought desperately. But all his other victims probably thought the same thing. As slowly as she could, Nell put her hand in her pocket, remembering the cell phone there. If she could punch in 911, maybe they would have a chance. Or maybe it would upset the chief's plans enough that this time he wouldn't be able to execute the perfect crime. She ran her fingers over the buttons.

Kate came back out of the office, holding the children's book. It looked so out of place in a room with a man holding a gun on them. She slowly walked over to Doug, holding out the book.

He reached for it.

Kate only gave the barest of nods as warning. She suddenly lunged, putting herself between the gun and Josh, shoving the pointed edge of the book into his face.

The gun went off. Kate had to know he would kill her. She stumbled back, blood flowing from the wound.

Nell threw herself at him, screaming "Josh! Run! Get help!" She grabbed the gun hand, forcing the second shot meant for Kate to blast through the glass counter.

I hate you, you fucking bastard—will do anything I can to hurt you. Trying to control the gun with one hand, Nell used her other fist to pummel his face in the same place Kate had hit with the book. Nothing mattered except hurting this man as much as she could and saving her son.

For a moment Doug Shaun was off balance, but then he recovered and grabbed her hair, jerking her head around. Nell kept fighting, telling herself that no pain could stop her. She brought her foot down as hard as she could on his instep. He grunted in pain and loosened his hold for a second, but then jerked her head back again.

"You can't win, you bitch," he hissed at her.

"Let her go," Josh yelled, grabbing the arm that was tearing her hair out. Nell saw Josh sink his teeth into Doug's wrist.

It became a macabre dance, Nell holding on to one arm, Josh the other, Doug twisting and turning to fling them off. Nell kicked again at his instep, knowing it wouldn't stop him but wanting to do anything that she could to hurt him.

She'd tried to punch in 911 on her phone, but she had no idea if it had gotten through or, even if it had, if it would help. Cell phones didn't give one's exact location.

Then in her peripheral vision, Nell saw Kate trying to stand up. She wrenched Doug's arm toward her to keep him from seeing her.

He twisted again and managed to shake Josh off. But Kate was standing now, with a big wrench in her hand. She swung at Doug, landing a blow on the back of his neck.

He cursed at her and the gun went off again. Nell had still managed to keep him from aiming at anyone, and the shot skittered across the floor.

Kate swung again, this time hitting him in the shoulder. He used his free arm to knock her down.

She was bleeding heavily and went down roughly to her knees. But she swung the wrench one last time, this time bringing it hard against the soft back of Doug's knees. He lost his balance.

Nell used her leverage on his arm to help pull him down on his stomach. Then she fell on his arm, letting her knee crash into his wrist and pin his hand and the gun in it down. Something inside her let go—the hatred and fury. With her other leg she kicked at him, not caring what she hit just as long as her foot landed. She put one knee on his back, grabbing his hair as he'd done with her and slamming his face into the floor. She found the blood-slicked wrench and smashed it repeatedly onto his hand.

When the chief struggled to get up, she landed a kick to his face. Then shoved his head into the floor again.

Josh had found a roll of duct tape and was attempting to bind Doug Shaun's feet.

"Careful!" Nell gasped. "Don't let him kick you." But Thom had taught Josh some of the self-defense moves he'd insisted Nell learn. Flopped across the man, Josh rolled down his legs, using his weight to pin them down.

Nell drove the wrench again into Doug's hand, finally causing him to release his grip on the gun.

Kate crawled across the floor to help Josh. Her face was white. She was in pain. The two of them managed to get his feet taped together.

Doug tried to heave himself up, as if realizing he really might lose to two women and a boy. He managed to throw Josh off and pull away from Kate.

Nell again grabbed his hair and slammed his face into the floor. Then again. She felt no remorse at the blood that welled up out of his nose. Then Josh was back with the duct tape, and he and Nell were able to pull the chief's arms behind his back and lash them together.

Kate was no longer moving.

Nell could finally loosen her grip on him. She grabbed her cell phone and this time dialed 911.

"The bike shop on Grove Street. Get an ambulance here. Someone's been shot," she said immediately, not even waiting for someone to answer. "And get … the sheriff's department here."

Nell took the gun and kept it with her. She would shoot the man if she had to. But she wanted Police Chief Doug Shaun to go to jail.

Josh found a first aid kit, and he and Nell used it to try to stop Kate's bleeding.

An eerie silence fell over the shop, broken only by the raspy breathing from Doug's broken nose and Kate's faint, shallow panting.

Nell and Josh talked only briefly, and then only about what to do for Kate. By some unspoken agreement, they knew they needed to listen—to hear Kate still breathing, and for any sounds that Doug was escaping his bonds.

In the distance, a siren wailed. It came closer and Nell realized it was coming for them. For the first time, she felt a faint trickle of relief.

THIRTY-FOUR

IT WAS JUST BEFORE midnight when Josh and Nell finally arrived home. Harold Reed had dragged the FBI to the scene to hear what was going on. For once the sheriff didn't argue about jurisdiction. He hadn't even seemed to get a little joy from arresting his rival, instead just looked shocked and upset at what he saw on arrival at the bike shop: a bloody and unconscious Kate Ryan being worked over by paramedics, and Nell and Josh huddled together, her blood on them.

They'd spent hours talking to both Harold Reed and the FBI, and then several more hours at the hospital waiting for word on Kate. All Nell learned was that she'd made it out of surgery but was still in critical condition.

As they pulled up to the house, Nell saw that all the lights were on.

It seemed strange, until the door slammed open and she saw Lizzie there.

"Where were you?" her daughter demanded as Nell and Josh came up to her.

"It's a long story," Nell said. Then she remembered. "I thought that you were at a slumber party."

Josh, exhausted, silently pushed past his sister into the house.

"Susie got sick, so it was canceled. Janet's mom dropped me off hours ago."

Nell and Lizzie followed Josh inside. In the light of the kitchen, Lizzie saw the state that they were in, with Kate's dried blood still on their clothes.

"Mom! What happened? I've been here for hours not knowing…"

Nell realized her daughter was terrified. It was not long ago that her children had waited for her and Thom to come home on another long night. I'm the same fragile flesh and blood that he was and he didn't return, Nell thought.

"It's okay, honey. Josh and I are okay," Nell reassured her.

Lizzie burst into tears. "But I've been worried for hours."

Nell simply wrapped her arms around her daughter. Lizzie hugged her tightly in return and even grabbed Josh tightly when he joined them.

As Nell held her children, she felt both the relief and the horror. They'd come so close to not coming home, to leaving Lizzie alone with a fear that would inexorably change into a reality.

Nell kept murmuring "It's okay," just to say something and try to make it okay.

Despite the late hour, the three of them stayed up talking for another hour. Nell was honest with her daughter about what happened that night; she knew Lizzie would hear about it from numerous sources and she didn't want her to learn anything from other people first. But she didn't tell either of her children how much she'd worried about them. Nor did she share the whispered horrors Doug Shaun had told her.

Finally, they were all beyond exhaustion and went off to bed. Yet Nell still had to check all the locks. Even with the real killer finally caught, the fear was still too close to allow her to let her vigilance down.

No one got out of bed much before noon the next day, but despite that, they tried to maintain as normal a Sunday as possible. At least, as normal as could be with Lizzie being kind and considerate to both Josh and Nell.

The phone rang and kept ringing, but Nell let most of the calls go to the answering machine. She may have been a reporter, but that didn't mean she wanted to talk to other reporters.

Improbably enough, Sheriff Hickson came by to see how she and Josh were doing. He didn't stay long, and Nell doubted that they would ever be close friends, but the man could be kind and he was certainly honest; she would give him that.

The good news of the day was that Kate was doing better. She was still considered to be in serious condition. But, as the doctor said, she was also young and strong.

THIRTY-FIVE

TODAY I'M GOING TO be a reporter, Nell told herself. She would be a witness soon enough, but now she was here only to be a journalist, to do what she knew how to do.

It was time for the perp walk—for Doug Shaun to be walked out of jail and into the waiting sheriff van to be taken to court. She did note that Sheriff Hickson had made sure the van was parked as far away from the building as was possible without being ridiculous. He clearly intended for the cameras to get as many shots as they wanted of Doug Shaun in prison orange. It was a gray day, with a hint of chill from the damp in the air.

There were cameras from all over. This story would go national—a rogue killer police chief who both murdered and framed people for the murders.

"Nell, good morning." Harold Reed approached her.

"It's a morning, Harold, and we're alive. I can't call it good," Nell replied.

He gave her a nod, bringing her away from the pack. "Buddy will do the official press conference, but I thought you deserved an update."

She nodded for him to continue.

"Doug Shaun was a clever man, but even he couldn't resist taking trophies from his crimes. We only found things from what he did here, but we have some leads from the other places and will probably find more things in storage. Every other town where he murdered wants a piece of him."

"I'll bet they do. Will Buddy let him go?"

"Not until he's tried here and put on death row. I'm sorry to say you were right about Tasha Jackson, the girl we found on the beach. Seems she was his first victim here."

"How good is the case against him?"

"Pretty tight. We'll see how strong the forensic evidence is. We do have his DNA from Rayburn, Joey, and Marion. We can test that."

"Pretty arrogant of him to leave his DNA at the scene."

"Yes, but he thought his would never be tested."

"Has he confessed?"

"No, and I doubt he ever will. I guess you should know he's claiming that Ronald Hebert was the killer of the kids, and that Kate Ryan killed Marion in a lovers' quarrel over her having an affair with you."

"Kate having an affair with me, or Marion?" Nell asked ironically.

"You and Marion, I think."

"I have my children as witnesses that I haven't been doing anything other than nagging them to do their homework and get to bed on time in the evenings," Nell answered with a wry smile.

"No one, not even the sheriff who opposes all things feminist, believes that one."

They were pulled from their conversation by a commotion at the jail entrance. It was time for Doug Shaun to have his moment of infamy.

"Thanks for the update, Harold," Nell said.

"Just don't quote me until I check with Buddy." He slipped back through the crowd in search of his boss.

Nell turned her attention to the jail. A path was cleared, with deputies stationed every ten or fifteen feet. There was a large crowd, although the length of the walk thinned out the people. The media was out in droves, but also a number of the curious were there. Nell was startled to see Velma Gautier.

If it were my son, I'd probably be here, Nell realized. I'd want to see the evil that had shattered my life. Velma was in a shapeless coat, one that showed how much weight she'd lost over the last few weeks. She was across from Nell. I'll talk to her afterward, after he's walked past, Nell decided.

Several sheriff's deputies came out, followed by men in suits who Nell thought might be FBI. Next was Sheriff Hickson, and following him were two burly deputies escorting Doug Shaun.

Nell felt a tinge of triumph as she noted the bruises on his face and his smashed-up nose. He looked straight ahead, as if this had nothing to do with him.

They brought him down the steps, the cameramen and women whirring to attention. Nell listened to the familiar click of shutters. She lifted the camera she'd brought, again reminding herself that she was a reporter today.

As Doug Shaun came closer, she willed herself not to step back. The fear was still there, and she had to tell herself that he was handcuffed between two deputies and there was nothing he could do to her. She brought the camera up to her face as he came near. She wanted some protection if he looked her way.

It was through the lens of the camera that she saw what happened next.

Velma Gautier stepped in front of him. From under her shapeless coat, she pulled out a shotgun and placed the barrel at his chest.

Nell didn't hear what Velma said, but she caught that one moment with her camera, that second when Doug Shaun finally felt the fear he had given to so many others.

Velma pulled the trigger.

Nell stopped taking pictures.

She later learned that Velma had aimed just below his heart, whether by design or by fate. The blast hadn't killed him instantly, but did cause too much damage for him to survive. It took several minutes for him to bleed to death.

Nell left the scene knowing she was no longer a reporter but once again a witness. She would write this story in first person.

From the jail, she went to the Crier office. Jacko's empty desk was the first thing she saw. Dolan wasn't there, but he had left a note saying he'd be back in an hour. She would talk to him then. As a friend.

She left the Crier and headed into town. Ron's Flower Shoppe had reopened, run by a cousin.

"What do you have that would cheer up a friend who ... is in the hospital?" Nell asked the woman behind the counter.

"Some irises and sunflowers?" she suggested. "Nice color combination." Nell could see a resemblance in her to Ronald.

"That'd be great."

The woman added softly, "You're the first customer in here all day. Like the flowers are guilty."

"No, the flowers aren't guilty," Nell said. She started to say neither was Ronald, but his cousin would know that soon enough. Right now Nell needed the common, simple things that could get her through the day. Like flowers for a friend.

EPILOGUE

"OF COURSE, BUDDY ISN'T going to prosecute Velma," Harold Reed told Nell. He'd taken to dropping by the paper about once a week, usually on the day they went to press. That was also usually the day that Ina Claire brought in samples of her recipes for the staff to try. Sometimes Harold's wife and Dolan's wife would join them and they'd all go out to dinner.

But today wasn't press day, which meant that Harold had something to pass on to Nell. Sometimes it was a story, other times something she couldn't run, like political in-fighting at the court-house, but it was always something Harold understood Nell would be interested in.

Velma Gautier had not spent much time in jail, instead going through a number of psychiatric interviews. It seemed that Buddy's strategy was to delay and defer until the people of Pelican Bay only remembered what an evil man Doug Shaun was, not how his life had ended. They'd also reopened the investigation into the death of Tasha Jackson. She had not, as Ella Jackson so fiercely asserted, just wandered off. Nell suspected that Buddy saw this mostly as a way to heap more damnation onto Doug Shaun, but it would also win him points in a community where he hadn't polled very well in the last election. Tasha Jackson's family was, after all, still alive and voting. But no matter the reason, it had removed the taint of responsibility from her family, and now they were left with only the heavy burden of grief.

"Buddy wouldn't get any votes if he prosecuted her," Nell answered. "So is that decision official enough for me to report it? Oh, was it a poll or a focus group?" Then she added, "Am I really so cynical?"

"More likely it's Buddy's astute political instincts. And no, you're just getting to know Buddy. It's as official as it's going to be. But is reporting this decision going to do anything other than drag poor Velma back into the spotlight?"

Nell thought for a moment. "I report the news. A small story on a back page." Then she asked, "How do you feel about no prosecution?"

"I don't like it, but I don't lose sleep over it, either," Harold answered. "With that man, I would have pulled the switch myself. Although only after he'd been ground through the wheels of justice. Still, how can we let any citizen, no matter how wronged, get away with vengeance?"

"Sometimes I think I should have just killed him then," Nell said. Harold knew what she meant by "then," as he'd questioned her in minute detail about what had happened; if Doug Shaun had made it to trial, Nell would have been a major witness. "That way, Velma would have gotten her vengeance with no blood on her hands."

"So why didn't you?" Harold asked. "Self-defense. It would have been easy. Even I wouldn't have prosecuted you."

Nell struggled for a moment to find the words. What had happened was almost beyond language, veering into a land of primal

346

emotion. She'd had dreams, almost nightmares, where she did kill him—a brutal physical death, pounding his head against the floor or sinking her fingers into his neck and feeling the breath slow and stop. Part of her was disturbed at how thin her veneer of civilization was; threaten her cubs and she became a mother lion. But another part of her reveled in the strength she'd found within herself. She had defeated the monster.

"I thought the best justice for him was to be brought before the system he'd so used and abused. I wanted to see him in a courtroom in chains, being led to prison. He was addicted to power. I wanted to see him lose it. That would be as close... as we could get to justice."

Josh politely knocked on the open office door. "Mom, sorry to interrupt," he said, and then his words rushed out. "Tomorrow is supposed to good weather and the bike club is going to go out, but I need you to sign my permission slip."

"Kate's well enough to bike again?" Harold asked.

"Yeah, she started last week," Josh answered as he handed Nell the much-folded piece of paper.

"Good for her," Harold said. "Speaking of which, since summer is on the way, my wife and I are thinking of taking up biking. Think I might swing by the bike shop on the way home." He stood to go.

"Sounds like a good idea, Harold," Nell said. "Maybe we should get Kate to start a biking group for those of us over forty but under death." She signed Josh's permission slip.

"I'll make mention of it to Ms. Ryan," Harold said as he left. Josh was right behind him, clutching the precious paper.

There had been enough forensic evidence to link Shaun to Marion Nash's murder, and with no trial, her relationship with Kate Ryan was known to only a few people. Nell had called it a "close friendship" in the story in the Crier. She'd gone with Mrs. Thomas, Sr.

to see Erma Nash and tell her what had really happened to her daughter. Nell thought that Mrs. Nash might find some comfort in knowing her daughter had experienced a strong and enduring love. But Mrs. Nash had cut Nell off, turning to Mrs. Thomas and saying, "It didn't happen that way. Marion picked the wrong man to go out with, that's all." On the way out of the Nash house, Nell had stopped by Marion's room to get the ring Kate had given to her and return it to Kate.

Kate had said nothing when Nell handed it to her, not even to ask Nell how she'd gotten it. She simply slipped it on her finger so that it nestled against the matching one she still wore.

Nell had wondered if Kate would stay in Pelican Bay, expecting any day to see the *Closed* sign hung permanently on the bike shop's door. When Nell visited, Kate seemed noncommittal, as if the future wasn't a place she could bear to look at yet. Maybe starting up the bike club again meant that Kate would remain, at least for a while.

Nell glanced out the window at the gray sky. It had rained most of the morning, but now the clouds were changing from dark to fluffy white. She felt another stab of missing Thom, wanting him there so she could tell him about Velma, or maybe that Josh would be biking for a while. And she wanted Thom to hold her and say he was so glad they were all okay.

One small strand of sunlight crept through the clouds. She stared for a moment longer, then went back to rewriting Ina Claire's latest recipe.

THE END